The Lonely Path

Genesis

By: Ryan Pagnutti

Originally, I felt like I was going to dedicate this book to half the world; my family, friends, everything that inspires us.
But December 14th, 2013 changed all that. Thanks for teaching me how to be a man, a real man.
This one's for you Dad. Rest in Peace.

This work is a culmination of all things imaginative throughout my life. I want to send my appreciation to every inspiration we find in our lives. May our limits know no bounds.

I also want to thank all my friends and family that I bounced ideas off of occasionally talking them to sleep. All your input was incredibly helpful and always considered. My editor Lottie, my beta-readers Chris, Mike and Ranji and first fans Bree and Mel.

Finally, this is a special acknowledgement to my brother Chris, whose help was unparalleled during the entire writing process and should be considered more a co-author at this point. If the words on these pages were ore from my mind, you refined them into the precious jewels that now exist. Talking with you always renewed my excitement to push forward. Thank you for that.
I love you brother.

"Let your imagination spill out across these pages and forge them into something great"

Chris Pagnutti

All maps created on inkarnate.com

Copyright © 2019 Ryan Pagnutti
All rights reserved.

Table of Contents

Prologue 5
Chapter 1 9
Chapter 2 26
Chapter 3 47
Chapter 4 60
Chapter 5 75
Chapter 6 87
Chapter 7 102
Chapter 8 109
Chapter 9 128
Chapter 10 144
Chapter 11 157
Chapter 12 167
Chapter 13 177
Chapter 14 187
Chapter 15 213
Chapter 16 230
Chapter 17 242
Chapter 18 257
Chapter 19 273
Chapter 20 284
Chapter 21 293
Chapter 22 299
Chapter 23 315

Chapter 24 331
Chapter 25 345
Chapter 26 353
Chapter 27 362
Chapter 28 376
Chapter 29 390
Chapter 30 398
Chapter 31 418
Chapter 32 429
Glossary of Characters 433

Prologue

As the thunder rebounded off the rolling plains, it sounded like the sky was splitting apart overhead. Pandemonium was everywhere. The Apocalypse. The Genesis, an ancient evil, was upon them. The genesis of genocide, these world-born men called it, the beginning of their end...

The sky was black. Everything was black around him save the firelight held by some of the surviving fighters. Cold rain pelted down in heavy sheets, chilling him until his breath puffed out in little clouds before his face. He was panting, his mouth was dry, as though he had just taken a long run without water. Above him thunder exploded again, rippling out visible waves of energy through the clouds, ground rumbling beneath the force.

All around him minions of the Genesis army fought with the men of Tehbirr. Hundreds of thousands of them. Flaming arrows volleyed through the air. Streams and balls and domes of magical incandescent lights arced and flashed and burst in colourful brilliance. Calvary was made useless after the storm had turned the ground into a heavy mud. But they fought resiliently alongside their brothers and sisters nevertheless.

Minions of the enemy were endless. Having all been created from the same unearthly matter, there was an everlasting sea of them in the shadows. Every minion, no matter how pitiful or grand, was inherently made up of a smoky, scale-covered epidermis, though each was terrifying in its own right. A few stood out among the countless hordes of Basrak swarming over the land. Winged monsters dotted and streamed through the sky, diving down into the fray, like an eagle hunting a mouse, only to drop fully armoured men, screaming, from a fatal height.

Coming over the near hillock, their silent war screams sounded like a million whispers all at once. The Genesis pushed forward with its onslaught, its consumption.

He couldn't give up, but he was so tired. How long had this battle gone on for? He looked up at the rushing scaly shadows, blinked a magical set of eyes, and released another breath of energy. Light beamed out around him in a perfect dome and pulsed outward, disintegrating any of the minions it contacted instantly, replacing thick black smoke with white steam.

That was it. His threa was drained. His reservoir of magic empty. Diyo fell to his knees. There was nothing else he could do, he looked up, disheartened.

He was so tired of this war.

Still the Genesis swarmed all around him. Men fought, and men died. The fallen ones were soon hidden beneath the black smoke that seemed to brew out from the Basrak's feet. Another tower in the distance toppled over and a silent cheer went up through all the ranks at once before they continued their assault.

Diyo dropped his head in the shame of defeat. *You were supposed to be here by now. How long have you been gone? A century? A millennium? An eon? We can't wait anymore. I can't...*

Hushed, angry whispers grew louder and more intense around him as men fell back, demoralized. He sank to his knees. Other magickers had fought bravely since the outset of the battle, but none wielded the power of Diyo. He *was* magic. His vanguard were the only ones to stand their ground and keep the enemy at bay for the most part, but even they were fleeing in retreat now.

He slumped onto his heels and sunk deeper into the muddy ground. Diyo began to weep, hitching his head rhythmically until he was almost laughing through his delirium. He screamed out to the ominous clouds above him. "Why! Why did you leave!"

A bolt of lightning tore through the air in sharp, angular lines and struck the earth right before him. Another explosion in the sky took the army away for a blinding moment. *Is this your response? Are you saying, "I am here!"?* Diyo questioned in his confusion. *Is this for me? A delivery of energy. Yes, it must be from Him. He was always generous...*

Diyo regained focus and glimpsed the men again. Already on his knees, he placed his hands onto the energized earth around him. He stared ahead with cold focus, drew a deep inward breath, and when his lungs reached their capacity, his threa opened like a valve to his purest soul. Diyo's fingertips grew an almighty polarity that soon began attracting the residual, dissipating energy from the light. There was untold power in lightning, and it fed him with renewed strength as more Basrak came rushing toward him.

Diyo began to rise, tiny streams of energy sparked from his fingertips as they separated. Throwing his hands out, coursing fluorescent pink incandescence through their ranks. It enveloped them like an instant, electric spider-web, making the shadows violently clutch or spasm in pain before spilling into steam. He threw up a translucent shield around his men, dissipating black projectiles in mid-flight. Fleeing men saw this and surged around their leader as Diyo pushed forward with his repulsion of the Genesis, releasing another dome-shaped pulse of golden brilliance, evaporating minions in circular stamps across the battlefield.

Near the centre of an empty circle stood one surviving minion, a bolwa'ar. The Genesis equivalent to Tehbirr's trolls, only the smallest bolwa'ar were the size of the largest trolls. The hulking beast brushed Diyo's magic off like a cold breeze and roared defiance in its silent voice.

Diyo watched, before he charged alone and tackled the monster. The bolwa'ar absorbed the small man's contact and tried to throw him off, but Diyo held on with glowing magical hands that had locked into position.

Together he and the bolwa'ar twirled and danced for a few heartbeats. During each revolution, the bolwa'ar's discomfort became more apparent as Diyo filled the unholy monster with unearthly power. Finally, the bolwa'ar let out a grunt and stopped before a blinding light as bright as the sun exploded the beast from within.

Men cheered before Diyo as he spun to face the Genesis once more and again began swaying the battle with his all-powerful magic.

That was when something happened and he lost all control. As if the earth recalled its stolen energy through his feet, demanding Diyo's threa drain itself unwillingly fast. He looked up and saw on the horizon a massive cyclone of darkness approaching through the sky. It's top, spanning half the horizon, gathered and swirled the clouds, only adding to its size, as it loomed closer. His magical warding shattered, and the movements of his spells became a ridiculous-looking dance.

His magic was stolen from him.

This was what the Genesis did. Consumed.

Files of silently crying Basrak quickly plugged the holes in the battlefield, and soon he was once again amongst the fray. His escort were the first to fall, men screaming and wailing in the pain of death. Frozen, twisted faces spattered in blood lay all around him. Some stared into the sky, or outward to the horizon, others were pressed down into the mud until eventually everything was drowned beneath the black smoke Basrak.

The relentless whispers and scale-covered shadows closed in and slowly began overwhelming him. Consuming him.

As his body rushed upward, Diyo's eyes shot open. He was alone in his cavern, drenched in sweat from brow to belly. He licked his lips; his mouth was dry. Suddenly, unconsciously, he remembered.

The storm had been much like that in his dream of the Apocalypse. Balls of rain instead of drops, gales of wind created from breaths, thunder that tore open the sky and lightning that punished the eyes for witnessing. The world was still young then, untouched by the Genesis, untouched even by man.

There was only Him. Diyo remembered feeling like a child in his presence now, he had expected a new beginning, but he never anticipated that meant His leaving. Not until Diyo bore witness and watched Him give life to the world through incredible sacrifice, promising one day to return.

"You'll know what to do, old friend." He remembered a voice telling him once. "I'll come back when the time's right."

Words spoken with such confidence in their certainty couldn't be dismissed as anything but truth.

Soon after He left, the world's first storm had begun and Diyo huddled under the only tree on the planet as a bulwark of lightning came straight toward him. That was when he blacked out.

Diyo poured a horn of water, gulped down a drink and cursed that he couldn't remember more, before huddling back into his bearskin blanket. Suddenly, his everlasting sense of duty rekindled, and he felt ill at ease. Nightmares of the Apocalypse had been recurring with varying details, but always with the underlying threat of Genesis. Diyo understood that could only portend one thing.

"He needs to come back..." he voiced aloud.

Or we're all going to die.

Chapter 1

Three horses stopped calmly on the muddy path, their coats damp with morning dew. The early sunrise on fresh rain had left a slight fog in the air throughout the dense, green forest. On the lead horse, sat a hooded man with an athletic build. The other two carried one boy each, both of whom appeared to be no older than seven or eight years but had already seemed to grasp riding like running. One of the boys wore a cape of the purest white, the other wore one so black that it was like a fluttering absence in the space surrounding him.

The hooded man swung his foot over his steed's neck and dismounted, both feet sinking into the ground at the same time. He was dressed in elegant clothing. The crimson cotton shirt he wore hung loosely to his wrists and was captured at his torso by a black leather vest. Over his right breast was a golden brooch, an eagle that looked as if it were perched upon the pin, stalking for prey.

He raised his hand, motioning for the boys to stay, and took a few steps ahead before putting his hand to the ground. His first two fingers studied the depression sunken a quarter-inch into the mud. Lifting them, he rubbed his thumb gently over his fingers and looked west into the woods, then east.

The man stood up slowly to his full six-foot height, taking off his hood with care. On his head sat a golden crown of humble design – white and canary-yellow twin bands intertwined. Short black curls danced around it, hiding part of his ears. He was a handsome enough man, with smooth skin – almost flawless, save for a pinky finger length scar just under his right eye – a perfectly tamed beard, and a sharp brow that complemented his well-proportioned nose.

"Tell me what you see here, boys? Show me what you learned in your time away," the king asked, waiting with anticipation.

The two children dismounted quietly. They approached the markings and knelt to study them, whispering between each other about breed, direction, size.

They were on their return from an ancient royal tradition, a culture walk. When a child of noble birth came of age, they travelled to other lands to spend a year living among different places and expand their knowledge, learning about the various customs, religions, and traditions. For centuries, this had helped the future leaders to gain worldly experience and greater understanding of their subjects. It had been a long year for the king and queen, although there had been excitement and joy, there was always a part of them that yearned for their children.

Once in agreement a moment later, the boys stood and approached their father. Keeping their voices low, they began to share.

"There was a boar that passed through here eastwards, not long ago," the boy in black said.

"He's big too. Maybe two hundred pounds," his brother added with a confidence that belied his age.

"That's impressive, Raphael. Two hundred pounds is what I'd say too," the king said in honest surprise. "And it's impressive you know the animal and direction, Kael." He was careful never to forget either of his twin sons. The two were not identical, though they were undeniably kin, Kael had inherited his father's black hair and Raphael his mother's blonde.

"Can we go after it?" Kael asked excitedly.

"No, we have to get home."

"Why?" Raphael countered.

"I can't tell you that. There's no fun in ruining a surprise," the king responded as he climbed back up into his saddle.

The boys simultaneously came out with, "Surprise?" before they shared a look of excitement and raced back to their own horses. They were about to move when the king suddenly stopped and leaned over his mount's neck as if he were listening to the forest. Turning to his children, he signalled them to stay close to him, then turned back, gripped his dirk in one hand, and gently snapped his horse's reins with the other. Kael and Raphael noted their father's cautious movements and followed expertly as the three began a trot down the muddy forest trail.

Around the first corner, the boys saw their father's tension ease and his grip release as a welcome figure approached on horseback. They recognized the Knight-Commander from the palace. Halder was a decade older than their father, with tufts of silver hair poking out from under his rider's cap. The man was constantly attached to a hawk, and one followed him now, perching on his shoulder as he slowed his mount.

As the two parties joined, Halder rode next to King Hectore and began a hushed conversation next to his ear. The hawk leapt from one shoulder to the other to avoid the king's presence. Kael and Raphael couldn't make out any words, but they could see their father's earnest look toward Halder as they pulled away.

The conversation ended, and the expression lingered on the king's face for a second, as if he were studying the Knight-Commander, his eyes contacting Halder's soul, searching for some greater truth. Then his face broke into a grin, stretching from ear to ear. He even allowed himself to laugh a little.

"Boys, I'm sorry, I didn't think your mother would be..." he caught himself, "finished with your surprise this early. I have to go, stay close to Halder. He'll see you back safely."

"Like you needed to say it, my king. Come along, little princes. It's been a whole year since you left us for your culture walk. Tell me what those Northmen showed you..." Hectore heard Halder say as he snapped his reins and began racing down the forest path as fast as he could. He knew the boys would be safe and capable of following the old scout home.

His horse's hooves showered clumps of mud as they exploded into their next stride, and the passing trees became a blur of green to his left and right. Hectore rode as hard as he could around the bend out into the fields where a lonely tower stood sentry, and he could see the first pastures where smallfolk were already beginning their day. His city was atop a long, steep slope that naturally slowed his horse, but he pushed forward toward the four layers of great walls that bordered his city like rings on a target, vast distances between each wall left enough room for a battleground between each one. Over a thousand years ago when Anemir Rai, the First King of Saintos, claimed this land after discovering the palace, he erected these great walls and added a ring of sentry towers beyond its outskirts. He'd built a foundation that would last an eternity.

When Hectore arrived at the city gates, he was met by an escort of ten mounted soldiers. He made his way toward the Royal Palace as the escorts around him kept announcing his arrival with "Make way for the king!" to clear the path onward. Hectore assumed that word of their news had made its way through the city by the smiles he received, or perhaps it was because he was smiling so radiantly himself. Either way, passing through his people warmed his very soul.

He strode through the immensely heavy doors to the entrance of the Royal Palace. The ostentatious architecture was unlike anything else in Tehbirr, a perfect orchestra of peaks and valleys, angels and gargoyles, tumultuous war and harmonic peace. Thick, heavy walls were inlaid with pristine white and black marble swirled together in a medley of contrast. Picturesque frames housing a collection of windows: circular, square, pointed-arched, and arched, all somehow arranged in an interplay of harmonious geometries. Some windows, like the kitchen's, were simple and plain, while others, like those of the royal temple, were picturesque and spectacular. Throughout the palace, balconies overlooked the city with hundreds of miniature men carved from stone as bannisters, holding their thick railings above their heads in triumph. There were courtyards and beautiful gardens filled with streaming fountains and hedge sculptures decorated with blooming flowers to bring them to life. Even the training ground bailey had a punishing organization to it that was oddly inviting, as if to say, "you're always welcome to join, but here we pay with blood."

Paying no mind to the grandeur around him, Hectore sped through the grand foyer. Torches anchored to the marble pillars illuminated this path until the morning light crept in, but he could have walked it in the dead of night with complete darkness. This place was his home and had been for most of his life now. The king raced up the grand staircase that opened to two different parts of the castle. His queen, the love of his life and soulmate, his *amiro*, Annabella, would be in their bedchamber, so he headed to their suite in the west wing. Down the hall, he heard a great cry he recognized as hers. Panicked, Hectore started running toward the room, arriving with his chest heaving and his brow beaded with sweat.

Annabella was lying on the bed with her legs facing away from the door. The realm's most gifted magicker, Hennah Asa, was between them, looking far too matter-of-factly for the situation. The king's wife even then, wincing in pain, covered in sweat, was still beautiful in her own way. She was wearing a white gown, pulled up to her knees with her top half unlaced for air. A drop of sweat trickled along her shining forehead, beading on the tip of her pointed nose. Her dark auburn eyes met the kings. "Hectore! You're here, good..." A smile erupted on her face, then a tear of both pain and joy dripped from the side of her eye as her smile turned into another agonizing cry. "AAAAAAAAAaaaaaaaaaaaahhhh now I actually can kill you!"

"Okay my queen, de baby's crownin'." Hennah said through her thick accent, disregarding the king's arrival, her voice inflected with encouragement. "One more gude poosh!"

Queen Annabella squeezed all her strength into one push, blowing the bead of sweat from her nose. Her face, having turned seven shades of red, was plagued with perspiration and then relief. Hennah came up with a babe in her arms, wailing and pink-faced. She scanned the crying baby with her free hand. Her magic would clean airways and strengthen the baby, assuring his health and immunity. The charm would last a few months and wear with no lasting effects. As she finished, her body jerked away, almost violently, and Hennah hurriedly handed the now clean infant to the queen.

At the baby's touch, the queen sank back into her pillows as if her heart had melted. "Aw, it's a boy!" she cried out happily. Overwhelmed with both love and relief, she cuddled him close and kissed his forehead.

Hectore noticed that Hennah was restless, constantly fidgeting in the corner, glancing back and forth at the newborn with contempt. "Hennah, is something wrong?" he asked, concerned.

Hennah raised her eyes and matched his; a malevolent look lurked in them. "Dis baby will bring doom," she told him, the last word exaggerated by her curt, foreign accent.

"Hennah, perhaps you should leave!" Hectore said sternly, "We thank you for your time and help," he forced out, withholding true words and actions he knew he would regret.

Without hesitation Hennah was on her feet, "I know de way," she said and out the door she was.

As she left, the door swung shut behind her and the queen looked up from her baby to her husband. "She can be a real bitch."

"With a capital 'W' unfortunately," the king added to lighten his queen's mood. "But a talented witch, the most gifted magicker in our lands. I wouldn't trust another to deliver our baby safely. She's strange, and she's awkward, but she's never lost a baby or mother as a wet nurse." It worked. Annabella looked at him as if he were a silly, little boy.

"What should we name him?" he asked her, welcoming a new topic.

"Well, we named the twins after the brothers from Melonia. But I... I want to name him Arlahn," Annabella said with delicate enthusiasm. She knew this would catch Hectore off-guard, and he fell back a step, shuddering in remembrance of his own father, a tear welling in his eye. But when he blinked and looked back at his wife, it was gone.

"Arlahn is a good, strong name," he said, agreeing and forcing a smile. "I'll go and wait for the boys and let you rest."

Annabella wanted to stop him, but she saw the anguish in his face and she felt guilty for causing it. She had mentioned his father, who had been taken from him when he was just a boy. Annabella had only ever known Arlahn Rai by name, but Hectore spoke of him like he was a god. It struck her as a child's proud exaggeration, but his feelings about him seemed to be resolute.

Hectore left the room and closed the door softly behind him. Sitting down on the top stair, he pulled a long, curved pipe from his belt. From his trouser pocket, he produced an herb that he crushed into his pipe and lit with a match. He had just blown his first smoke ring when the scout Halder and his sons came into the foyer and up the stairs. Hectore stood to meet them, concealing his pipe in his hand and leaning over to place the other hand on Kael's shoulder. His boys had already made him proud at such a young age, and now he had another.

"Kael, Raphael, your surprise is in my bedroom. Go and have a look," he spoke tenderly.

They raced past him and fought to open the door, Kael smashing Raphael along the wall before he could push it open.

"Eh! Be gentle around your mother," Hectore scolded them.

He was right behind as they ran into the room to see what their mother was hiding. Their eyes widened as they peered into the cloth.

"Raphael, Kael, meet your new brother, Arlahn." Annabella smiled as she looked lovingly at the newborn. "Sounds like a stable cleaner's name," Raphael japed.

Kael abruptly added, "He can shovel my horse's shit."

"Hey!" the parents cut in together, and Kael immediately knew his mistake before Annabella had told him. "Language, Kael, you don't get to speak like that yet. I certainly hope that's not all you learned abroad."

"He is your brother," Hectore told them, walking toward the baby. A year away from home let the boys forget, he thought. "And now it's your duty to look out for him the way you do one another. He'll be just like you in some ways and completely different in others." The king sat on the bed and accepted the fragile, blanket-wrapped package from his wife. "But our blood runs through his veins the same as yours, and for that, he'll have a good family to love and protect him always." He looked at the baby who had calmed into a slumber and claimed, "His name will be Arlahn, after my father long passed, may his light shine brightest."

"May his light shine brightest," Annabella echoed softly, placing a tender hand on the King's.

At that reminder, Kael made a face to Raphael. "Arlahn is a good name, I guess."

*****

"Arlahn!" The familiar voice jolted him awake.

"Ma-awmh, why'd you wake me up?" Arlahn rasped out in a croaky morning voice. He was four years old, already at an age to be annoyed by his mother's waking him up, unlike the excitement he had shown as a toddler. Arlahn raised himself up onto his elbow and rubbed the morning crust out of the corner of his eye. Shafts of pale light slanted in through diamond-painted windows. Slowly, his eyes fluttered open again, soaking in the morning sun, chestnut irises circling his constricting pupils. Sitting up completely, a little smirk assured his mother that, even though his eyes were barely half open, he was awake for good. "Hurry, time to get up!" She stood enthusiastically from his bed, throwing his covers off of him in an attempt to coax him. The ocean blue dress that rippled loosely about her figure swayed with the quickness of her movements. "You're going to be late for Elder Rufus' lecture. That old man can be grumpy sometimes for no reason at all. You don't want to give him any more excuse to chew your ear off."

Arlahn looked quizzically at his mother, not understanding the expression. "I swear, he can talk so much you'd think he was a disgruntled, drunken bard." Annabella caught herself beginning to digress as she sorted through a pile of different clothes. Finally, she walked over to Arlahn with a cream coloured cotton shirt, holding it up to his neck as she examined how it would look. "Wear this one." She pulled the shirt away and hung it in his right hand.

"Why do I have to go see Elder Rufus? I wanna stay home with you and Father. I wanna learn more from you. Like what's jisqwuntle dungken mean?" Arlahn stared at Annabella expectantly.

"It's what happens when you drink too much." Her tone was wise but soft, which was probably the reason why Arlahn was easily distracted by two sparrows mating outside his window. "As for staying home," she continued, catching his attention again, "I'm sorry, son, but you have to go to see Rufus. It's the will of your king and father to meet the other children and learn. Many heads are better than just one."

"Father says Jofus was old even when he was my age."

Annabella smiled. "He may be an old man, but he is wise beyond his years. Remember what he teaches you," she told him.

Arlahn spun quickly on his left hand to the edge of his oversized bed. Shivers shot up his legs and tickled his spine as his feet touched the cool stone floor. Standing in his undergarments, he pulled the cream cotton shirt over his head before his mother helped him with a pair of blue silk pants. They were so loose that Arlahn's feet shot through them with ease, but a thin band around the waist kept them well-fitting and comfortable.

Arlahn's bedchamber was spacious, but not unnecessarily large. It contained few furnishings, perfectly suited to the every need of a four-year-old and his imagination. His bed sat adjacent to a rack of wooden swords and shields and toy knights on little horses that stood in the corner opposite the door. A massive oak armoire sat alone on the fourth wall, and an otherwise empty floor left plenty of space for Arlahn's marvellous games.

As they left the room, he took his mother by the hand, and together they walked down the wide halls of the palace, receiving bows and good mornings from the servers passing by, busy with their work. Arlahn looked at the carved murals in the stone panels along the way. Some were of animals and creatures, exceptional views of the life after death, the gods and kings and men all sharing the Graceland. Others depicted monsters and demons and fiery wastelands, or ancient battles from a great war long forgotten. He listened as his mother explained how the building itself was a mystery. As a bedtime story, his father had also once told him that legend said that the palace had been built at the beginning of Time, and that it was much older than any written record in Pellence. This surprised Arlahn, as the founding of Pellence, when King Anemir claimed it for his people and named the land after his beautiful late wife, was well-documented.

"Your father searched through as many archives as he could find," Annabella said as they made their way down the great stairs to the foyer. "He read about battles and campaigns, powerful alliances broken, and fragile truces lasting through an age, but found nothing about any architect or stonemasons who held any credit for building the structure. However, if there is only one thing that this palace is noted for throughout history, it's its inimitable beauty."

At that, the large palace doors in front of them opened, and Annabella led Arlahn outside by his hand. The little boy squinted up at the orb of burning light high in the sky; he could see how perfect of a circle the sun was within the blinding blaze that surrounded it. There wasn't a cloud above, and the heat of it clung to him. Arlahn wondered about the sun — why was it that every day this ball of light would rise and fall, in exactly the same way, while everything else in the world constantly changed. Perhaps he pondered a little more deeply about such mundane things than other children his age, as his two older brothers were constantly testing and challenging him. But deep down, Arlahn was just as naïve and innocent as any of his peers.

On the horizon, he could see another orb creeping over the hills as if it were a sunset. Only this one was not bright and white, but rather orange and desolate.

Mother and son continued on the winding path that led down into the city. Once they reached the threshold of the palace grounds, Arlahn took up his mother's hand again, despite being flanked by the small escort with which they met. He was not a shy person, but even as young as he was, Arlahn knew of dangers lurking in the dark corners of the world. The stories about the wilderness that his father told him each night often spoke of evils and creatures that reeled and excited the boy's imagination but frightened him in reality.

In truth, the upper city, where almost all of Arlahn's out-of-palace activities took place, was completely safe, even if the young prince were to wander about on his own. Nevertheless, Hectore's legend helped to instil an air of caution around everything his heirs would do, a trait vital to the survival and success of any monarch in the lands of Tehbirr.

Arlahn and Annabella walked past food stands and jewellery stores, tailors and blacksmith shops. Everywhere they went, they were met with respectful bowing of heads, good mornings, and gentle smiles. One baker came out with two dumplings and insisted the queen and her son have them as a gift. A guardsman had begun to shoo him away before he reached them, but Annabella stopped him and accepted the man's gesture. "Thank you, I bet they are nothing but delicious."

The buildings in the upper part of the city were well-kept and clean. Made mostly from stone, they were all covered with the same coral-coloured clay roof. The two carried on walking for a few minutes after they had finished their dumplings until finally Annabella came to stop in front of a weather-beaten door.

Arlahn looked up and saw a wooden sign dangling from iron loops, swaying in the wind ever so slightly, hanging just above the door. He couldn't decipher the letters yet, but he guessed their meaning.

"We're here, aren't we Mother?" He turned his gaze from the sign to his mother and suddenly grew sad, falling into her and tugging at her dress in retreat, crunching and crinkling the fabric further.

"Raph told me he's half deaf, so he screams at everyone all the time!" Arlahn sniffled. "And... and Kael said... that... that one time... he scared a kid so bad... he *peed* himself right in his seat, then Elder Rufus beat him with his stick for dirtying the floor."

His mother threw her head back with a healthy laugh and promised him they were only teasing. "They've learned a lot from him. Arlahn, don't let them fool you," she assured him, hoping that her son would be able to see Jofus' wisdom through his sternness and tedium. She knocked on the door and when it opened, a stooped, ancient, grey-haired man stood behind it.

"My queen." He quickly bowed his head, not in the same fashion as everyone else, but curt and grim. Even for his seemingly old age, he was still spry. "I was expecting you, but only half expecting you on time." His leathered cheeks wrinkled as his toothless grin reached from ear to ear. Jofus Rufus had been a royal mentor since before even King Hectore's childhood, which afforded him certain informalities with the Rai family, as well as their unconditional respect. There was likely no one in all of Tehbirr with as broad a knowledge of all scholarly disciplines.

Annabella chuckled. "Good morning to you too, Jofus."

"Well, what are you waiting for, my prince?" he said with a mask of discontent falling over his face. "Come on now, you can't educate yourself standing outside," Elder Rufus spoke as if the boy was completely oblivious to everything. "In you go."

Arlahn reluctantly let go of his mother and began to wobble his way through the door when Rufus' cane clapped him on the rump, and he jumped into a faster strut.

"Ow!" he complained, turning back to give his mother one last, longing glance and rubbing his rear.

"Well, next time hurry when you're late, little prince," the old grump said.

Rufus turned back to the queen and gave her a sly wink before following the Prince in.

Hearing the door close behind him, Arlahn took note of his surroundings. Hushed clamour began as several groups of children began speaking amongst themselves. He could tell by their clothes that these were not deprived children, for they were all clean and properly dressed in elegant attire for their first day.

Each child was already seated in a chair, aligned in rows, all facing him. He gulped and felt a lump squeeze its way down his throat. Unsure about what to do, Arlahn walked to the closest open seat and sat down. The walls were decorated with maps of Tehbirr and the Sainti realms, and there were the banners of the Wardens of the Realm, two on either side of the royal sigil. On the mantle below those maps, were all manner of unusual things; jars full of that preserving, hazy-yellow liquid, their contents strange and unknown. For that, Arlahn was grateful, for there was only one jar which he could recognize the contents of, and the sight of a fetal pig was disturbing enough. There were also bundles of dried roots, pots with fresh herbs sprouting out from the soil, and piles of rolled up parchments beside a wall of leather-bound books. In one corner, Arlahn saw several easels supporting pages of geometric diagrams, arcs and arrows, and cryptic-looking symbols that he instantly recognized as being similar to those that his brother Raphael often had strewn about his bedroom.

"Alright, class!" a voice projected over all the noise. It was Elder Rufus. The power of some men's speech would elude them over time, turning their voices into soft, wise sounds. Such was not the case with Jofus Rufus, the man spoke with a depth in his tone that commanded authority. "Today, we have much to learn. Since this is the first day for many of you, I expect you don't know who I am. I doubt you ever truly will, but you may call me Elder Rufus."

He paced back and forth at the front of the class with a slow limp, going over their schedule and what they should expect to learn while they were with him: reading, writing, basic mathematics, and histories of the realms of Saintos. "In a few years you'll learn economics, sciences, navigation, anatomy, and all the rest." At the end of his speech, having seen he'd lost the interest of some children already, Jofus feigned a state of confusion, standing still at the front of the class. Only then, while Elder Rufus stood trying to remember something of great importance, only to have it lost again, had Arlahn's focus started to drift away. Suddenly, the old man spun and slammed his cane into the long desk of the first row of children. The end snapped up violently with a crack and settled pointed straight at Arlahn. The entire room jumped at the slam and then fell into an eerie silence.

"You! Tell me where we are?" Jofus demanded.

Startled, Arlahn looked at all the other children in the room who were now staring at him in complete silence. He awkwardly shifted his weight over in his seat and said, in a mouse-like voice, "Umm... we're in your school in the upper city?"

Jofus softened slightly and briefly at the honesty and innocence of his reply. "No, boy. I mean, what do you call this place where we all live?"

"Pellence?" Arlahn answered in the same mousey voice.

"Speak up, boy!" Jofus half shouted. "At my age, I can't hear every squeak that comes from a mouse!" It seemed as if he was getting more and more irritated.

Arlahn cleared his throat and repeated himself loudly and clearly this time. "We're in Pellence, Elder Rufus."

"Very good," Jofus seemed to flavour each syllable with a condescending spice. "Now, who can tell me where Pellence is?" He gestured to a map on the adjacent wall.

The silence fell over the children once again. Each child was afraid to speak. As simple as it was, none of them had ever considered this question.

To them, Pellence was just *here*. What if they got the answer wrong? What would this old grump do? Would he hit them with his stick or shame them as he had just done to Prince Arlahn? After a short while, Jofus grew tired of waiting.

"Well!" he said. "I don't have all day to sit here watching you watch me, so if you children aren't going to talk, then I will. Pellence is what we call a capital. It's the greatest city in all of Saintos. Now, Saintos is the kingdom ruling over the world on the west side of the Skyrim Tower. Everything on the east side is Damonos. Both continents together make up the world we call Tehbirr, our planet."

"What's the Skyrim Tower?" a young, brown-haired boy squeaked out.

"The Skyrim Tower is part of Tehbirr's Spine, a massive mountain range that almost cuts our world in two, north to south. The tower itself is near the middle and reaches higher than birds fly, higher than the clouds, some say, but I think that goes without saying. Listen to the name, boy. There's a light at the top, it shines a different colour at each new moon and can be seen from hundreds of miles away. Over time travellers have grown to use its visibility as a sort of guide for direction when the True Star is hidden at night. But other than that lad, nobody knows much else about it, except that there's no entrance. Few men have ever attempted to climb it, and even fewer have ever returned," Jofus answered the boy.

"Well who put it there?" the little blonde-haired girl beside Arlahn asked intelligently.

"Ah! That, Luzy, is a question that can be asked for many things in this world. I mean, really, who put *us* here?" Jofus looked at each child in turn, seemingly revelling in their ignorance. "Heh, your brains look more wrinkled than my face, little ones, let me remedy that. Which brings me to my lesson for today. Since we've used up half our time already, we'll settle for a brief history on Tehbirr."

The children settled into their seats to hear the old man's story. "Once, long ago, perhaps with the beginning of Time, two lovers came to this world. Some people call them Jidban and Tunique, but the fact is that their real names are unknown. These lovers possessed powers that people nowadays wouldn't even be able to comprehend. Together they created this world, if you believe the story. These two beings of magnificent power worked together and crafted the very earth upon which we live. They shaped the lands, covered it with trees, filled it with life. They raised mountains to the sky and flooded lakes for the world to drink." Jofus was strolling casually back and forth through the rows of the classroom as he continued his lesson, intentionally crowding any child whose attention may have been drifting.

"They worked hard to create harmless creatures and ferocious beasts. Everything they made held intricate purpose, from the gentle animals, like dogs, cats, and horses, to the hostile beasts, like the huge buffaboar of the plains, or the great kahki wolves, who prowl thick forests, and even medak bears that are so tall they couldn't stand up straight in this room." He pointed to the ten-foot ceiling with his cane and a few children gasped in shock.

"All the insects, flowers, well you see where I'm going with all this, *everything* that's natural in our world. Some believe they even created the First People. Eventually, when they had finished what they set out to do, a clash between them became inevitable. You know how lovers can be..." A few silent children exchanged confused looks. "No, I suppose not actually. Some say that they disagreed on what they wanted to do next with the world they created. Others think creating was their only intention, that they were simply artful souls. Either way, they raised the Skyrim Tower and divided the land in two, one part each for them to do with as they pleased. This is how the world of Tehbirr was created, and how it was split into Saintos and Damonos."

Jofus stopped as if in thought for a moment, and then began his lecture once more.

"The world of Tehbirr is a very interesting place indeed. Saintos is now divided into five realms. The Freefolk of the South live spread out across the Neddhiwan Mountains and the Cooperith Forest. These mountain men are always tinkering and are extremely dexterous – that means they're good with their hands – they've proven to be quite crafty and inventive. Living off the land, their culture is ceremonial, devoted to the Wild. Due to the abundant supply of rich ore in their mountains, mostly anything metal in Saintos was originally crafted by the people of Neddihw. Their banner is the one furthest right on the wall; a yellow sunburst behind a green tree on a stone-grey mountain peak." The children spun in their seats to look behind them at Jofus' display. "Directly north of the Neddhiwan mountains is the heart of our land, where we live, Pellence. You all know what Pellence is like, or at least you think you do. And of course, you all know our Royal sigil, the snarling beast before outstretched eagle's wings. Northwest of Pellence is Esselle, a vast and enlightened land, rich in tradition and arts. Scholars and great minds travel from all over to learn their advanced knowledge. And for that, they earned the banner of the quill and scroll with a compass below it. I spent a lot of time in Esselle when I was a youngster, which is why I know everything, twice. To the east, between Tehbirr's Spine and the Sprit Sea, you'll find Corduran, which is more of a city than a realm, but it's still a famous port filled with sailors, soldiers, and swindlers, many are all three. Not the most wholesome of places. The folk there are sometimes as unpredictable as the sea itself, but order is maintained through strong leadership. If you hadn't guessed, theirs is the banner of the three-mast ship on the open, blue sea. And Melonia, our final realm of Saintos, is due north from Pellence. The Melonian people come from a robust and proud heritage. Before the Damonai HolyWar, they were more of an isolated and autonomous land. And although they were the first to fall before the GodKing Tumbero, they were also the first to rally behind our HighKing Hectore. Unlike Esselle, Melonia keeps little record of their history, but its land gave birth to one of the greatest heroes of the past, Juliessa FirstBorn."

The children all perked up at the sound of the name, for each one had heard several of the heroes' legends in the form of bedtime stories.

"The Melonians are a well-rounded people with much pride in their battle prowess. Their tapestry displays a white shield with a sword and axe crossing. Before we were united as a continent. What little contact people did have usually resulted in pointless skirmishes arising from nothing more than petty differences. But over a thousand years ago, one great king had a vision. He bargained and fought to unite the five regions and settle their differences. Working together, under the leadership of that great king, the people of these lands built roads from city to city, with magnificent bridges and mountain passes – sometimes tunnelling straight through the mountains, which had never been done before. They established a trading system and converted currencies and standards of measurement. From vast pools in Tehbirr's Spine and other nearby mountains, this incredible king routed great aqueducts to the cities. You think that running water in your kitchen appears from magic? Over the centuries, Pellence, like all of Saintos, became a wonderful place to live. And it can all be accredited to one man." Jofus continued his pacing, studying his students' faces to determine their level of interest. His assessment was a little more promising than he would usually expect from a group of five-year-olds. Then, Elder Rufus looked right at Arlahn and asked, "Can anyone tell me what the name of this great king was?"

Arlahn did know the answer to this question, he sat up proudly and proclaimed, "His name was King Anemir, Elder Rufus. He was the first Rai king, my father's great, great, great, great, great, great, great, great, great grandfather." He beamed as the class chuckled behind him. Even Jofus rewarded him with a wry smile.

"And I'm sure you missed a few greats there, little prince."

He tapped the desk with his cane for silence.

"But right you are indeed, Arlahn. It was King Anemir Rai, who named the lands Pellence after his *amiro*, his soul's dance partner."

"What about the countries of Damonos?" little Luzy asked curiously.

Although it was a logical question to ask, Jofus was caught slightly off-guard. He began to explain how, like the lovers Jidban and Tunique, the lands of Saintos and Damonos have quarrelled for centuries, and because of it, there has been little information documented about their lands and way of life.

"We know them as soldiers and warmongers, occasionally even conquerors. But they've been defeated and forced back to their lands before, most recently by our King Hectore and his Brotherhood."

Arlahn swelled with pride hearing his father's name.

"How did he beat them?" he asked eagerly. His father never spoke of the past.

"With his mind," Jofus answered Arlahn, with as much profundity as he could muster, yet still to the class' dismay.

"That's boring," a pudgy boy in the back called out.

"Is it boring to swing from chain to chain along the outside of a castle, fighting your way through an endless army of soldiers to rescue a beautiful princess?" Jofus asked.

"No. But how do you do that with your mind?"

"Keep coming to my lessons and pay attention, maybe you'll learn how to use yours and find out," he told them. "Ask your king yourself, if you ever get the chance. Ask him what his greatest weapon is. Remember, a mind can be sharper than any blade."

"Tell us more about rescuing the Princess!" a freckle-faced girl shouted from the end of Arlahn's table.

Jofus opened his mouth as if to answer when a series of loud midday bells began to chime and echo through the city. He paused, then sighed.

"Well class, that's a discussion for another day. I want you to remember all I've told you, and I'll see you in two days for another lesson. Until then, practice paying attention. Listen to your parents at the dinner table tonight." Jofus limped over to the door and slowly opened it, gently swinging his cane to help usher the class out.

The children filed out of the building and lost themselves in the crowd of people shopping in the city. Some went to waiting parents or servants, a small group of girls ran off, chasing a beautiful butterfly, while a few boys snuck away to play in the public pools.

It was hot and stuffy in the bustling streets, and Arlahn wanted to join the other boys headed for the pools but his stomach protested, and he found his escort close by. His eye drawn first to the crest on the veteran scout's iron-banded buckler, with its gilded outstretched eagle wings. In the centre, atop the wings, the shield bore the white-gold head of a snarling beast, revealing pointy fangs. Arlahn had heard Kael call it a lion before, but he thought it looked more like a wolf.

After greeting one another, together, Halder and Arlahn leisurely walked back up to the palace. One day, not long ago, Halder had taught Arlahn to check over his shoulder, he had created a memory game for the youth. Asking him to frequently check and note the articles of clothing that each person wore, then reciting any that repeated. Despite the relative safety of this part of the city. He had learned about abductors from his father and knew the value of his life. After the third look with no repetition, Arlahn grew tired of the game. "What do you think my family crest stands for, Halder?" he asked.

"That's funny," the old man said, though he didn't so much as smile. "I asked your father that same question long ago. He told me it was knowledge behind strength, thought behind power. It was a good answer, I reckoned. Why do you ask, little prince?"

"Well... Kael says it's the strength of a lion in front of the kingship of an eagle."

"Eagles are kingly birds, indeed. But a little snobbier than your father," Halder agreed. No one knew animals better than Halder, Arlahn had learned. The old man once confessed that he could converse with them, just like they were speaking now. But Arlahn wasn't sure if he believed it. He would often introduce himself to animals as if they were people and a creature had never responded yet.

"I think it looks like a wolf's head though, the will of the wolf."

"Aye, I could see that too." His escort nodded as he rechecked the buckler strapped to his left arm. "Never met a man with more willpower than your father."

They arrived back at the palace and were greeted by Annabella near one of the gardens that flanked the various walkways in the main courtyard. She was standing in an impossibly white gown that wrapped around her neck and crisscrossed over her chest. The robe flowed freely from the waist down, held together with pins and embroidered stitches to keep the uniform shape. She looked at her son with unconditional affection, her head tilted as it always did when she smiled at him.

As Arlahn approached, Annabella turned to keep in stride with him. Her caring hand reached out and found the boy's light brown hair, played with it, then brushed it smooth again. "How was your day?" she asked with her fingers still entangled.

"It was okay... Mother, did Father really rescue you?"

"Who told you that?"

"Elder Rufus today... he said that Father fought an endless army to save you."

She smiled and pulled her son close as they strode inside, and the massive palace doors closed behind them.

"He did."

Chapter 2

The thick, burly general of Esselle's TrueBlades walked into the armoury with his massive war hammer propped on his shoulder. One end was a huge square-faced block, while the other came to a menacingly sharp point, meant for smashing shields and skulls with the same relative ease.

He walked to an empty stand, leaned his weapon against the near wall, and removed the helm from his head. Silver had infested his thick dark beard and short-cropped hair. The general licked his thumb and wiped at a blemish on the right cheek guard of his helmet before sitting it atop the stand. Firelight danced from sconces on the wall. He unbuckled his large steel breastplate, the three-sword crest of the Essellian TrueBlades square on the chest, and wrapped it around the pegged arms of the stand, re-buckling it. Behind him, he heard the door close. The general turned, saw that no one was with him, and turned back. "Damned wind," he began to mutter to himself, but before he could finish, a spear from the rack against the far wall toppled to the ground. This time, the general took up his weapon and spun around, set to attack. His breathing slowed, eyes scanning the shadows of the room.

"Come at me!" he shouted. "Are you a whoreson or just a coward?"

Hidden in the shadows beside a pillar stood a tall silhouette; a man dressed in black from head to toe. Slowly, he detached from the shadow and revealed his presence, an oversized hood kept his face concealed.

The general tightened his grip on the hammer as the man stepped further into the light. He now began to see the sharp features of his face. This man's expression spoke of one thing: death.

"Coward? Whoreson? I would put DeathShadow before these creatures of flesh. There is no point in fighting, General, lay down your weapon, drop to your knees, and I'll give you a soldier's parting," the man said in a calm voice. "One of honour."

The general re-evaluated his opponent and noticed that this was no regular soldier or bandit. This man was an assassin. He looked again at the man's black clothes. He had a scimitar in a scabbard on his back, two daggers on either side of his hip, three throwing knives on each forearm, and two spikes protruding out of his elbows. "Who be you, filth?" he shouted with frustration, "to stalk in the shadows then speak of honour?"

In the silence that followed, the general thought of how this man's existence in Esselle was an impressive feat in itself. Over ten years ago, Warden Nakoli Rali had grown disturbingly paranoid that he was going to be assassinated for repainting his shield when he denounced his Damonai heritage. Despite the Warden's paranoia, a malevolent, bloodthirsty viceroy, bent on revenge, hired an assassin. But the viceroy was too cheap to get a man of the calibre that the general now faced. Once the attempt failed, Warden Rali grew furious when he learned of his viceroy's betrayal and tortured both men to horrible deaths, after which he offered a hefty sum to all who gave information on the whereabouts of any assassin. It was his obsession; he founded the Essellian TrueBlades, a unit of elite soldiers, whose sole purpose was to hunt them down relentlessly.

"Who be you?!" the general repeated with chagrin in his voice.

The man was stone, his stare ice.

I am Mordo Lobo, the man about to end your life. Mordo was always this way when he confronted his *deadees*, as he called them. In control. He enjoyed ending lives. It was the only way he found his own inner peace. Finally, Mordo nodded, narrowing his eyes.

"I told you... I'm Death."

The general swung his war hammer from right to left, but Mordo easily jumped clear of the powerful yet slow attack. Having hit nothing but air, the general came back at him with a lunging reverse thrust. Mordo was impressed by the strength the man displayed, making a fifty-pound hammer appear almost weightless. But this just increased his excitement for the kill. He swiftly drew the sword on his back and, moving to the side, parried the general's attack, deflecting it away at a harmless angle. Mordo countered by snapping a left-handed jab to the general's jaw, but the large man's head absorbed the blow like a cliff absorbs a wave.

The general swung left to right this time, and again Mordo leapt clear. He circled around the man, holding his sword out to keep the brute at bay.

"Well coward, I haven't got all day," the general finally said.

Mordo darted in and swung a feint attack that the general easily deflected. With a quickness that Mordo hadn't anticipated, the general tried a sideways counter slash, leading with the menacing point of his war hammer, but just missed the assassin's retreating jaw, instead smashing out chunks of a support pillar. Mordo recoiled and rolled around the pillar to the other side. Although his face was still void of expression, a small jolt of the reality of death touched him. He was uneasy on the inside. That was a rare feeling for Mordo, one he appreciated deeply when it came. He began circling again.

"This folly has gone on too long, assassin. If you've come to claim my life, then try and claim it!" the general roared thunderously.

"Careful what you wish for, General," the assassin warned. He switched his posture and lunged into a series of attacks.

The general noted the change and deflected most attempts until the tip of Mordo's blade scratched through the leather jerkin and into his flesh. Unaffected, he came forward with an impressive riposte, only he was too slow. Mordo stylishly dodged and parried all of the attacks. Anticipating the end of the general's flurry, he stepped forward, past the general, slicing his arm in the passing. The general grunted and grabbed the thick cut on his left bicep, as Mordo sheathed his sword and stood confidently, looking at the older man.

"Perhaps had you been in your prime..." he began.

Suddenly the war hammer shot up into the air toward his jaw, looking to shatter it the way a rock breaks a window. Mordo ducked under the attack and drove his right elbow spike into the general's midsection. Spinning as he came up, he sent the other spike into the general's back.

The massive figure fell to his knees, then slumped onto his ass. He sat there for a moment, wincing and blinking hard. Mordo waited for him to tumble over. But he didn't. Reluctantly, the man shook his head, fought through the weariness that was clear on his face, and came to stand once again. As Mordo Lobo watched, a glimmer of admiration passed across his expression – a very rare show of respect for one of his deadees. They don't make 'em like they used to, he thought.

"That's my boy!" Mordo chortled as he allowed the general to stand. "I would have killed you ten times by now if you were any of your men. You should be proud to have delayed me this long."

The two clashed once again, and this time it was the general, fuelled by adrenaline and pride, who landed a heavy forward boot on Mordo's exposed chest. The assassin was knocked clear off his feet and landed on the flat of his back, grinding several inches across the rough stone floor. He kip-upped into a defensive position, embarrassment written all over him after realizing his hubris, embarrassment that he quickly transformed into focus and vehemence. When the general came at him for another attack, Mordo pulled a dagger from his hip and lunged forward to meet him.

Just as the war hammer went up in a massive cleave toward the assassin, for which there would be no defence, Mordo vanished.

The general swung through the air, withdrew his attack, and looked around frantically. "What kind of wytchery is this?!" he exclaimed, studying the room in a sense of panic.

Mordo Lobo appeared before him, as if an invisible cloak had dropped from around him, and plunged his dagger into the general's heart, severing the right atrium. The general's eyes were bewildered. His mouth opened, spitting out a trickle of blood, gasping in intermittent breaths. Then he fell to his knees, looking down at the blade that stuck into his chest and saw the red seeping out onto his clothes. As he glanced up at his killer, the general spoke only one word.

"Why?"

Mordo, who was still close, holding onto his dagger, looked the man in the eyes.

"You called me coward. But I told you, I'm Death. Or at least, I walk in His shadow. Doing His bidding in this world. Extending His touch." The assassin closed his eyes, took a breath of relief, and then returned his cold, blank gaze onto the general. "I killed you, General, because I needed to."

The general could see now that this man was telling him true, he was hollow behind that costume of flesh.

"You're a... soulless... bastard."

Mordo Lobo said nothing more but pulled out his blade. The general, who gasped one final breath, slouched over and fell sideways to the floor. Mordo stood and watched the life fade from the general's eyes before he leaned over and cleaned his blade off on the dead man's jerkin.

"Perhaps," he retorted as he stood up over the corpse, sheathing his blade. "You were a worthy opponent, General, I won't forget our duel here."

The general didn't reply.

Mordo looked down at the man and thought to himself, would that man have beaten me if I hadn't used the *nsuli*? The thought was short-lived.

I walk alongside Death himself. His ego quickly clouding any doubt.

He turned and stepped toward the door, pressing his ear against the wood with his eyes closed to listen closely for noises on the other side. Convinced that he was still alone, Mordo swung the door open and walked down the long hall. At the end, he squatted in the corner near another door. He couldn't open it himself because he could hear the conversation of at least two sentries stationed on the other side. He would have to wait for someone to open the door, then sneak out shrouded in his *nsuli*.

Several minutes passed before anything happened. The instant the door handle clicked, Mordo willed himself invisible. The door swung ajar, and he watched as two six-foot-tall guards, garbed in identical plate armour, came out discussing women. Silently, Mordo slid through the door, right under the arm of the guard who was closing it. He easily walked past the guards stationed on the other side and out toward the castle gates. He had just made it through the barrack's walls when he heard cries and pandemonium begin. For some reason, creating chaos in the outside world gave Mordo a sense of inner quiet, he felt in control of those moments too. And Mordo loved control.

He walked into a vacant public latrine and released his invisibility. Throwing back his hood and concealing his weapons, he then ground any of the general's wet blood into his dark clothes so that it could no longer be seen. Now safe from discovery, Mordo went back outside to meet the turmoil of the marketplace.

Mordo Lobo could will himself invisible whenever he pleased. It was his *Power*. But on a few occasions, he sustained the *nsuli* for too long and lost it against his will. Using his Power was like the soul's equivalent to tensing a muscle – he couldn't do it forever. The few times Mordo had abused his *nsuli*, he was punished with paralyzing migraines.

Slipping out of the crowd, he walked past a few more makeshift stands that had been erected along the road. Finally, he arrived at a wooden door with a sign above it that read "Hennah Asa - The Good Wytch".

Mordo opened the door and walked into the empty foyer. It was a rare sight. He had been here many times in the past and had almost always seen at least one, if not four or five patients, waiting for her services. Hennah was an extremely talented magicker, especially in the rare healing disciplines. Mordo could only think of one other magicker with a prowess that surpassed that of Hennah.

Catalina, before she went mad over a hundred years ago, was the most requested magicker in all of Tehbirr. Her Power was her curse. As the legend goes, with a whisper of her spell and the touch of her soft hand, she could revive you from a mangled and lifeless state, breathing renewed life into dead bodies. Word was, she could even change a man's appearance. Her virtue was known throughout the land, but Catalina slowly became more and more reclusive, often turning away those who sought her help. Her story claims that one day she walked into a forest and was never seen again. Since that day, all who enter those woods have shared her fate. Catalina's Forest, or as the Sainti people referred to it, the Passage of the Dead. Some say she went mad or became possessed by a demon. Others claim that she fell victim to an evil trick all those years ago and was trapped there. As if someone could trick her. These were stories that fathers told their children to frighten them into obedience. The truth, perhaps, no one knew. Mordo was jealous of this notoriety. One day, people will tell their children of DeathShadow, he promised himself.

Staring at the empty room, Mordo couldn't help but wonder if Hennah was following this same pattern. Although he didn't care much for human interaction – others meant nothing to him – he didn't dislike the time he spent with her. She gave him purpose, and he was very good at doing whatever she proposed.

Mordo walked through the curtain separating the foyer from a hallway with four painted doors: red, blue, yellow, and green. Each door led to its own patient room, all neatly organized. As he made his way down the hall, Mordo studied the artwork hanging on the wall beside each door. The closest to his right was remarkably detailed. It depicted a snow-covered mountain in the distance. The snowy path between the trees hid the earth, save a few protruding shrubs and boulders, and there was a trademark scribbled in the bottom corner in red paint. Mordo glided past it and looked to the next painting ahead. This particular canvas was his favourite. He stopped to admire it. Inside the golden frame, it was a ball of pandemonium, black dominating red swirls and dots. It almost seemed to him as though the sun had grown dark and angry with the world and was beginning its fury in the sky.

Mordo knew Hennah would be in her private room at the end of the hall through a fifth door, a black door. Opening it, he ambled into the room. Hennah was standing at her desk to the left of the entryway, covering a spherical object with a black cloth. Ignoring this, he told her blankly, "No witnesses."

He hadn't made a sound until that point. Yet Hennah turned to face him, unfazed. He could never startle the old wytch, never sneak up on her or catch her off-guard. It was as if she felt his presence before he was there and had a keen ability of knowing when his task was complete. Those were his words, she knew, spoken only when he had lengthened Death's Shadow.

"Well done, DeathShadow," the ageing mage replied in her thick, clipped accent. She smiled a toothless grin. "In riturn, I 'ave some eckstra application poisons anda few medicines, dere on de desk. I made dem myself, don't mix dem up. And of course, your paymint."

She threw a fist-sized purse in the air toward him. Mordo snatched it and peered inside. It was only half full, but he was still more than content with the amount for killing just one man. He tucked it away into a pouch behind his wide belt. Money meant something different to Mordo than it did to the rest of the world. When Mordo wanted some *thing*, typically, he merely took it. But money could buy him *service*, someone's time to do something he couldn't be bothered with, or didn't know how to do himself.

"May I go, or do you need me, Caliph?" He asked the magicker.

"No, you may go. Dank you for your work again, it is Godly work you are doing 'ere, DeathShadow." With that, she smiled reassuringly at the deader.

Mordo turned and began to take his leave.

"Wait," Hennah called out, stopping him at the door. "I wasn't going to bother you with dis just yet, but I feel that it would be proodent to begin sooner rather dan later. It is not urgent, but you may still begin if you wish. Dough, you will not be killing."

"What would you ask of me if not my blades?" Mordo answered openly, somewhat confused.

"I need you to make arrangements."

"Arrangements for what?"

"Mordo, add dese items to your safehouses." Going to her desk, Hennah plucked the top of a few loose pages and handed him a list scribbled in pen. "As I said, it is not urgent. Aldough, dere is one item on dat list which may take some time to acquire."

Mordo could barely make out the writing, but he studied the list silently. "Extra blankets, additional whetstones, extra clothing, wooden practice swords, daggers, staves." The list went on, but the last scribble made Mordo squint. He had to make sure he was reading the crunched words correctly. "This says, 'go to *his* tomb and retrieve *his* swords.'"

"You know of whom I speak," she retorted.

"Even if I can find the so-called mythical way into *his* tomb, find and retrieve *his* cursed swords, it's the blades themselves that choose who wield them in combat," Mordo said intelligently. "Everyone knows this. Why would I want cursed swords?"

"Not you. Dat is who de arrangements are for, my DeathShadow, de one who can wield dem is rising up again. Dere presence has been felt. Da GodKing's Guardian has been born anew! Not anoder one of deese impostas dat sit upon da trone. But as I said, dere's no need to rush, my friend, it will be a long time coming. As you know, purrfection has no sense of time. I do not need to tell you dat a new Guardian means a new GodKing."

Mordo fell silent, pondering what Hennah was planning to do, how informed he actually was, and how informed she actually was. But she had called him DeathShadow... he liked that. She had also taken to the names deader and deadee in place of killer and his mark. She knows how to play people like a child plays with his toys, he realized then. He wondered how a woman could act so tender and loving to the sick and suffering one hour and order the death of noted generals secretly the next. It made him think that maybe someday he could learn to feign compassion too. Maybe... Someday...

"I'm to have an apprentice?" Mordo sounded disappointed. "I work better alone."

"And you will for a while yet, DeathShadow. But who better to train a spirited young fighder destined to take up de Guardian's Blades?"

She knew he wouldn't, couldn't, protest any further, and he didn't. He only stood there for a second longer, clenching his jaw.

"I should be off if you expect me to accomplish all this," Mordo said. He knew that Hennah enjoyed her own companionship once she had retreated into her personal study. With that, he awaited Hennah's nod, then opened the door and walked through, letting it close behind him

Outside in the city streets, Mordo dwelled on the idea of taking on an apprentice. He had no doubt in his own ability to kill, but could he teach another his level of greatness? Bring someone else to the plateau of control he had when he was with his deadees? It would take time he knew, "Perfection has no sense of time," Hennah's voice echoed in his head. If he had an apprentice, it would be one that was second to only him. They would be perfect killers. Like *Death* Himself. Already, Mordo was starting to change his mind.

Esselle was a sparsely laid-out city and the wide block roads of the main streets were almost never congested because of it. However, his recent kill had drawn a crowd that was only now starting to wane. Mordo turned left, going back the way he had come, and found himself once again observing the merchant stands along the way. The first exuded an overpowering smell of fish, and a small pile of the day's fresh catch covered the table as the vendor was cleaning them. Mordo sped past, walking over to another stand across the street which was more his style. The display held ornate daggers and sheaths of different sizes and origins. They were nothing like the weapons Mordo would equip himself with. The decoration did nothing but add useless weight, and their design was too conventional, but he enjoyed browsing such things nonetheless. Glancing down at the table, he noticed a nice whetstone, next to a pile of arrowheads. This is actually quite convenient, he thought. Mordo picked up the whetstone and felt as if he had found another piece of his inner puzzle. This was probably the only item on the table that someone like him would use.

"Are you interested in anything, master?" the portly merchant asked him.

"How much for the stone?" Mordo asked.

"For you, two silver," said the merchant, showing a smile.

It was a ridiculous price for a whetstone, but Mordo pulled his new purse from his belt and placed two silver coins where the whetstone had been.

Without a word, he put the stone behind his belt and walked off. The merchant collected the coins, and when he looked up to thank his costumer, Mordo had already lost himself among the crowded street.

*****

The morning light tiptoed through the open double doors that lead out to the balcony and covered the marble floor. A thin silhouette stood in the doorway as Hectore's eyes slowly opened and soaked in the brightness of morning. It was Annabella. She was standing in her sleeping gown – a loosely draped white silk dress with invisible seams, perfected by a Gifted tailor. Dannisera Moren was the only Gifted tailor King Hectore knew of. She was also one of the most renowned and accomplished artisans in all of Saintos. Her Gift allowed her to magnify her vision exponentially, which gave her the ability to create incredibly intricate art. She could carve sculptures with detail so lifelike that it was almost maddening, and her paintings possessed a clarity that made them seem alive. She also perfected a method of threading fabrics without seams, making ornate gowns and suits to look as though they had been cut from a single piece of fabric. Among her other wonders of the loom and needle, rare that they were, were fabrics that were waterproof and fireproof, yet breathable, and another that was thinner than sheepskin, yet virtually impervious to the wind and cold. Hectore recalled meeting the old artisan once in his youth. He had been appalled to see that her legs were horribly disfigured and rendered useless. Though she had a chair with wheels and a table for her crafts, and that was all she had claimed she needed.

The beauty of Annabella's gown meant little to Hectore and paled in comparison to her own, visibly naked beneath the thin, translucent fabric. Her curves had never left her, and even after childbirth, her hips still seemed to beckon him. She was the most beautiful woman Hectore had ever seen back when they first met, she still was. Her sun-bleached blonde hair hung down, reaching below her shoulder blades as she leaned in the balcony doorway with her back to Hectore, watching the sunrise bathe the ground further west.

Hectore rose and sauntered over to those beckoning hips. Softly, he wrapped his arms around her and slid his fingers between hers. He gently kissed her soft, pale cheek and propped his chin on her shoulder. The little curls in his hair tickled her ears.

"What are you thinking, my love?" Annabella whispered.

Hectore lifted his head and he soaked in the beauty of the world around him. Snow-peaked mountains to the north-west reflected the sunlight like a million diamonds. Large pines looked like lush moss growing in cracks of the mountain from that far away. The land below was covered in an abundance of thick forests, flowing toward Pellence. Directly underneath their castle was the western half of his city. From this vantage, it was a labyrinth of rooftops, some with gardens, some had clotheslines crossing one another, but most were slanted shingles made of red clay. Hectore saw skinny plumes of grey and black smoke from the chimneys of the early rising blacksmiths and bakers. He could hear the morning clamour as the city awoke, with vendors setting up their shops, farmhands preparing for the day's labour, and priests chanting their morning hymns. These people were his family as well, large or small, noble or base-born. They cared for him, because he cared for them.

"This place, this life, our children, you. It makes every horror from my past worth it."

Annabella pulled her head away so that her deep auburn eyes could meet Hectore's. She kissed his lips and spoke with a giggle, "Rufus told Arlahn the story about you and me." Then she added tenderly, "I love you for what you did. I always will." Annabella smiled. "But today is special for someone else."

Together, hand in hand, Hectore and Annabella returned into their bedchamber.

"Ah yes, of course. It's amazing how fast they've all grown. I can't believe it's already been five years since the boy was born. I'll take him down to the market today when he gets back from his lesson," Hectore said as he loosened his grip on his wife. He wouldn't soon forget his son's birthing day either, the way the magicker Hennah Asa had recoiled from his son as if he were plagued, and how she had claimed he was Doom. Wise as she was, Hectore had known Hennah to embellish certain things without any apparent reason. Thus far, she couldn't have been more wrong, Arlahn was by far the most gentle and innocent of his three children, interested more in tales of gallantry than monsters. Unlike Kael and Raphael, whose favourite game was Shadows in the Dark, and who used each other to fuel a level of competition that was almost unhealthy.

Annabella released Hectore's hand and retreated behind a dressing screen that was adorned with the image of a man and woman, one in black, the other in white, both wrapped in abstract, convoluted designs made of gold thread and jewels.

"Oh, he shouldn't have to go on his birthing day!" Annabella complained. Seconds later, the white silk gown had been flung over the top of the screen and hung there.

"For most others it's just another day," Hectore replied ominously. Despite the joy of celebrating his son's birth, Hectore's mind was somewhere else right now. The palace had received a bird earlier in the week that told Hectore of how his friend Raphael, an Essellian general, was killed. His son's namesake had been found in the castle's barracks. No one knew what happened, except that there had been a great struggle. The world had a way of suddenly growing darker around him when he was reminded of his past, and it again became marked by torture, betrayal, and death. A brooding sense of despair had always lingered in the King, as if through all of his mentionable accomplishments, there was one deed that always haunted him.

"Don't sound so grim." Annabella tried to snap him out of it, so she reminded him, "We're not most others, we're his parents."

The HighKing stayed quiet a second longer than she liked. "Alright," he finally agreed and smiled, "you're right."

"Can you take him this morning too? I have old Wender coming into town with his Ritual Gift," she asked, pushing her luck further.

"Of course."

"Did I tell you I love you?" Annabella poked her head out from behind the screen and winked.

"Only twice so far today," Hectore replied warmly. "Tell Arlahn I'll be in the yard when he wakes."

Hectore went over to his armoire and pulled a cream-colored top loosely over his head. He wasn't going anywhere this morning that required him to look kingly, and he was thankful for that. He was the HighKing of five realms in Saintos, but whenever he was not expecting to make a formal public appearance, he preferred to dress in the casual clothes you might find on a middle-class nobleman. "They're more comfortable," he would always protest, pointing out slack and mobility in the right places.

Annabella came out from behind the screen and gave her husband a kiss. She was glad to see that she had returned him to Hectore *the father* before he left. When he bore the face of Hectore *the HighKing*, he was that same man who won his throne back all those years ago. And although she loved him completely, Annabella always feared that cold, hard, unrelenting side of her husband, willing to do whatever needed to be done so that *good* – or at least the lesser of two evils – would always prevail.

She looked at herself in the full-length mirror, spinning from side to side to check her reflection from all angles. Since she too had no formal engagements today, Annabella had chosen a simple green dress and pinned her hair back in several places with small golden butterfly pins. She walked out of the door and continued down the hall toward her son's bedchamber, pulling the door handle down carefully to open the door. She snuck up to his bed, quiet as a cat, and sat down gently, making sure not to wake him.

"Arla-aaahnnn…" she whispered in her soft, rhythmic voice.

Slowly, the boy's hand rubbed his eyes and he raised his head. Annabella burst into a smile as sudden excitement shot out from Arlahn's eyes. He knew what waking meant.

"Happy birthing day, Arlahn!" She leaned over and gave him a big kiss, hugging him close and tight. "Once you've gotten dressed, find your father downstairs. You don't have to go see Elder Rufus. You'll spend time with him this morning."

Arlahn's mouth opened as his expression grew into one of overwhelming joy. Unable to contain his happiness, he rocked excitedly back and forth, shaking his hands in the enthusiastic way that only a child of five could.

"Thank you, Mother!" he hugged her again and squeezed her as hard as he could, grinding his teeth together in his effort. This forced a funny expression on his face that the queen laughed at when she saw it.

Annabella took Arlahn's cheek in the palm of her hand and a flurry of emotions shot through her. The mixture of infinite love that a mother has for her child, the determination to protect her baby, no matter the cost, and the ever-present fear that any harm should come to him one day. These were feelings that only a mother could truly understand and never rid herself of. More to herself than to her son, she whispered, "I love you, Arlahn. I would never let anything bad happen to you."

A tear formed in her eye, and Annabella edged closer to him on the bed. "I remember your birthing day," she began, "when you finally came into my arms, I knew you were perfect." Regardless of what that crone wytch had claimed, he was perfect to her from the moment she saw him. "Do you need any help getting dressed?"

"Mother, I'm five years old now, I'm grown up enough to dress myself I think," Arlahn replied, shaking his head.

"Alright then." Annabella smiled. "Have a wonderful day, my son." She kissed and bid him good morning one last time, then stood up and walked gracefully out of the room.

Arlahn hurried to his feet and started shuffling through his armoire, flinging clothes thoughtlessly behind him on the floor to find anything suitable he could pull on. In a few moments, he managed to put his trousers on backward and his shirt inside out. He looked in the mirror, laughed a little at his reflection, then redressed himself properly and dashed out of his room, making sure to close the door behind him.

Arlahn came running into the courtyard where his father was standing with one foot forward, back arched, and his hands extended, pointing up to the clouds. The pose stretched Hectore's torso and elongated his figure. Noticing Arlahn coming toward him, Hectore released his stretch and stood upright. He wore matching bottoms to his loose-fitting cream top, but they were stained with the browns and greens of the earth as the material reached his bare ankles. Clearing the curls from his forehead, he smiled at Arlahn like a proud father. Arlahn began to speak as his running slowed to a stop. "Mother said that because it's *my* birthing day, I don't have to spend time with Elder Rufus today. She said that you and I could spend the morning together." His tone made it clear that he was trying to justify his every word by the will of his mother.

Hectore stood a moment, contemplating, then leaned over and placed his hand on his son's shoulder. "Alright, Arlahn. Since you and I get to spend the morning together, we'll do something *you* would like to do, and something *I* would like to do. Sound fair?" The king had a way of making his ideas sound like yours.

"Yeah I like that," the boy agreed

Hectore and Arlahn discussed what they wanted to accomplish during their morning. Arlahn was content enough just to be with his father. Business often pulled Hectore from his family, but no one blamed him. He couldn't have done a better job as a father considering he was the HighKing of five nations. Arlahn and Hectore decided to finish the stretches Hectore had started.

After that, Hectore snatched some wooden play swords and asked Arlahn if he could help him with clearing the courtyard of the imaginary evil military. Together, they slew many vile monsters, a troll, and even the legendary giant Lukza, from Arlahn's favourite of his father's night tales, Isla the GiantSlayer. Normally Arlahn preferred when his heroes were not heroines, but Isla had accomplished the impossible. She had vanquished the Giant King Lukza.

His father fought with a fluid grace even in play, stepping and shuffling, jumping and swirling in the air, his wooden play swords arcing and slicing toward the imaginary Lukza. He pretended that the blow was countered and fell to the ground, clutching at his chest as he tried to resist the giant crushing palm that wasn't there, calling for Arlahn's help. Arlahn attempted to imitate his father's moves, jumping and spinning. He stumbled on the landing but recovered, delivering the fatal blow to their pretend foe. The battle was over. Hectore got up chuckling and tousled his boy's hair, "We've done it, son."

Arlahn looked at the wooden sword in his hand. "I'm not as good as you though. How did you learn all of that?"

"My childhood wasn't the same as yours. When I was just a few years older than you are now, my life changed. And I had to change with it. I learned things then that you will discover when you're much older still. But you *will* learn them, son, in your own time, I promise."

"What do you mean?" Arlahn pouted, throwing his arms up. "How come you never talk about your past? I only hear about the things you did from Elder Rufus, or Mother, or Halder."

"They have better memories from those times, son. Before you can rescue and free someone, first they have to be conquered, enslaved," Hectore tried to explain.

"But you *did* stop the bad guys. Why does it make you sad?"

"Because of what it cost me to stop them," he told his son. Wanting to change the subject, Hectore interjected, "Now come, it must be time for our midday meal. I'm half-starved."

Arlahn looked up at the sun high in the sky and felt a rumble in his stomach.

He and his father met Kael, Raphael, and Queen Annabella in the Great Hall to eat a delicious lunch of noodle hairs in tomato sauce, with aged cheese and round loaves of fresh bread, and discuss their day's events. Even though they barely took up half of one of the many tables in the Great Hall, which was designed for hundreds of guests, the air was full of conversation over the sounds of cutlery on platters. They all finished up with smiles on their faces.

Afterwards, Kael and Raphael returned to their weapons training with Zeth Venetos, the master-at-arms. They were six years Arlahn's elder and already training with weighted wooden swords, having impressed Zeth so much that he was upgrading them to full steel in the new year. On their way out, Kael challenged Raphael to a race there, and they took off in a dash. Annabella smiled at them and placed a hand on Hectore's.

"I'm done with my meetings for the morning, so I'm going to take care of what we spoke of earlier." She stood, going over to Arlahn, and knelt to bid him a good afternoon. Then she brushed his hair back and kissed his forehead before she left.

Once the servants had cleared the tables, the King asked to be alone with his son, and the few remaining kitchen staff took leave.

"Now we get to do what I want," Hectore told him. "We're going to the market to get you a gift, but first I have something I want to show you. Something special, something secret."

Arlahn glowed with excitement and immediately hopped from his chair. "What is it? I want to see," he urged, taking his father's hand and dragging him up.

"Ha, alright, alright!" Hectore chuckled. "Are you showing me, or am I showing you?"

"Which way?" Arlahn asked, shrugging his shoulders up and flapping his arms in childlike confusion.

"We're already here."

The little prince's head went crooked as if falling off a hinge and his eyes squinted. "What?"

"When I was a boy," Hectore began, "on my fifth birthing day, my father showed me this same secret, and I've shown it to your brothers as well. One day, you'll bring your own children here and show them too. But this is something that must remain a secret to our family only, do you understand?"

Arlahn was curious, so he told his father, "I understand."

"Alright, follow me."

Before lunch, the King had changed into a brown leather doublet, trimmed with scarlet and dark grey leggings, ready for their afternoon in the city. He walked over to a mantle between the hearth and the display plaque of Anemir Rai's sword and shield, gestured toward it with a hand. "This is the sword and shield of our great ancestor, Anemir. The real sword was said to have been stolen during one of the raids hundreds of years ago. This one is a replica forged by a smith at the time. Petyr Rai, the king then, paid the smith handsomely for duplicating it so well. See how well the scrollwork is etched along the blade."

Arlahn studied the sword, it was a one-and-a-half hand double-edged blade, the etched scrollwork along the back was foreign to the boy, but it looked elegant and meaningful.

"But the shield is the *actual* buckler Anemir carried with him centuries ago."

Arlahn cast his eyes toward the iron-banded wooden buckler. It was a perfect circle, and in its beaten and time-worn centre was the ancient sigil of the Rai family: a pair of outstretched, wings behind the snarling white-gold face of a beast, with chunks of onyx for eyes and alabaster for teeth.

"That's nice, Father," Arlahn said, somewhat disappointed. The walls of the Great Hall were adorned with all kinds of battle prizes: axes and spears, shields and swords, tapestries and banners, horns of great heroes and helms of fallen kings. This wasn't much of a secret. An old shield and a fake sword, both of which he had seen almost every day of his life.

"That's not your surprise," Hectore said, reading his dismay. "This is."

Then he reached over to the mantle and grabbed a small wooden horse, rearing on his hind legs, its hooves stopping a book pile from slanting. Hectore gave the horse a quick jerk and spun it right around. Then he cranked the horse down, so its hooves were on the mantle, and pulled it along the length of the mantle toward the display. After the first few inches, the horse's front legs began to *magically* gallop on their own for another two feet along the mantle. There was no sound from the horse, and if there had been any noise in the room, Arlahn might not have heard the faint "click" over his shoulder. He looked around, inspecting the display, but the sound seemed to have come from nowhere. Hectore gently took up the buckler on the display with both hands, he moved it a quarter-turn clockwise until another tiny "click'" sounded, and with those two little clicks, the entire display plaque swung inwards... A hidden entrance.

Taking the torch from a sconce beside him, Hectore walked through the entrance, turned, and said, "Come in and close the door behind you. There's nothing to fear, your brothers loved it!"

Arlahn followed his father into the stone hallway. Grabbing the handle of the door behind him, he closed the secret entrance with the least bit of effort. Perfectly weightless and without a sound, the door eased automatically into the seal, leaving only stone walls around them. It was when the darkness closed in around him, and Arlahn knew the horse had run back to his books to trap them inside, that a cold finger ran up his spine.

The only source of light was his father's torch, and the flames danced their orange and yellow light back and forth on the walls, unveiling crude old carvings in the stone beside Arlahn wherever there was the glow of the torch.

"It is the tale of the Great Beginning," Hectore said, showing Arlahn a series of pictures of what seemed to be falling stars, crashing into the world. "Starting with the First Fall, the arrival of Jidban and Tunique..."

"You think they came from the stars?" Arlahn asked.

"I think we don't really know anything that we think we know about them," Hectore replied. "I think they came here for reasons of their own and settled with this planet. I think this palace could have belonged to them at one point. But then why doesn't it belong to the gods still?" Hectore had led Arlahn deeper into the darkness until it swallowed them. The uncirculated air was dank and hard to breathe in, leaving a funny smell in his nose. He was scared. He wanted to stop his father and turn around, but he knew he must be brave. Kael and Raph must have been brave. They loved it, he said. And Arlahn was a Rai. There was the blood of kings inside him. He decided he would push on, he *had* to push on. They came to the first fork in the path that broke off in five different directions like an outstretched hand. Turning to the left, they took the path beside the one they had come from.

"There's also a sense of duality here," his father continued, "angels and demons, peace and war, black and white are in the very granite of the walls. There is no doubt that this is an old place of struggle... But, over the centuries, we have made it our home. A Rai place." Taking a right at the next fork, Hectore reached for Arlahn and took his hand. "Stay close now."

"These paths will seem a maze at first, son, but once you get to know them, they become more like the streets of the city and you can get to almost anywhere on the palace grounds. Each path has more carvings, or scriptures, from the Great Beginning than the last. These tunnels have more history than a library."

Beside them, the carvings depicted were primitively drawn, battling in a great war, until two were left standing atop a mountain, ready to challenge one another with the sun before them. Hectore stopped at the end of the tunnel, the torch in his hand flickering light across the walls. He knelt down on his knees. "Speaking of which, this is the only place where the passage shrinks. It leads to our library," he said, pointing the flame down the tunnel. "Come on, we're almost done." Arlahn crawled smoothly through the tunnel behind his father, although it was no longer than ten feet long. At its mouth, it opened behind a great steel heat shield that Arlahn recognized because of its holes and black gouges. They were behind the hearth.

"How do we get out?" Arlahn whispered.

"First, you look through the holes to make sure no one's there, then you press this little button here."

Hectore touched a finger-long protrusion in the wall beside the steel shield. Then father and son peered through the tiny holes in the hearth and saw that there was no one in the room behind.

"Can I?"

"Of course."

Arlahn pressed the finger in until it was flush with the stone wall and the steel shield "clicked" ever so slightly, the same as the plaque had before.

Hectore placed two fingers inside a gouge in the metal and slid the whole piece open wide enough to slip through. They emerged behind the soot of the hearth. There were purple couches and red cushioned chairs around the fireplace in a semicircle, all were still empty. "Make sure to step over the soot when you're all alone," Hectore said, lifting his son over the black coals. "You don't want to drag dirt out from behind a wall."

That made sense to Arlahn. "That is amazing, Father." He had been wary to enter the tunnel and legitimately scared inside with all that darkness around him. But now that he was outside the walls again, with the daylight filling the air, he felt reassured and proud to have made it through. It already seemed like a dream to him. Hectore noticed the clear relief on Arlahn's face. "Did you not like it?" he asked.

"It was scary at first," he admitted. "But you said Kael and Raph went through no problem."

"If you thought it was scary, then you were brave for walking the way with me," his father told him.

"Kael and Raph must have been brave. You said they loved it."

"They were excited. But you faced your fear going into the dark. That's when a person is brave, Arlahn. That's something to be proud of."

"Will you show me the rest later?" he asked with renewed confidence, trying to sound heroic and willing.

"I will, another time," Hectore answered, placing the torch in a sconce bracket beside the fireplace. "Now go change your boots and meet me at the front door."

Arlahn raced up to his room, tugged on a pair of calf-high, leather boots in place of his doeskin slippers and donned a rich leaf-green tunic. Meeting his father in the entrance, he smiled at his approach. "Are you ready?" he asked before they left.

Together, they went down to the market of Upper Pellence. Whenever the Rai family went about in public like this, they always had a cohort of elite guardsmen in commoner's clothes to discreetly watch over them from a distance. These were Hectore's Kalendare. Instead of the traditional heavily armed formal escort, his means of protection made it even more difficult for assassins to plan an attack, without making a big spectacle of his casual outings into the city. Knowing this, the people were especially respectful of his presence and only approached with their hands in clear sight.

The market district was made up of many tall buildings. Well-established merchants had shops located on the ground floor of apartment complexes or royal administration buildings. Other merchants operated more makeshift stands that they would pack up each night and set up each morning, often moving about like a fisherman in his boat.

Arlahn was searching for a gift as he walked through the wide, crowded path with his father, gawking at the colourful jingling trinkets hanging from merchants' stands, when he accidentally collided with someone.

He looked at the young girl he had clumsily walked into. She had light freckles on her nose and thick, glossy hair that shone the black of obsidian. On her wrists, she wore heavy manacles that had begun to chafe her skin and was being dragged by a length of hempen rope. Her innocent sky-blue eyes looked deeply into Arlahn's, connecting with his very soul, it seemed, and he could feel her fear of the man who led her. Stevano Grent was his name. Arlahn recognized him from the quarterly State of Pellence meetings that were held in the castle a week before each solstice and equinox.

Arlahn wished he could help her, but he didn't know how to intervene with the pretentious nobleman. He had no doubt purchased the girl to be a maid in his home; it wasn't uncommon to purchase servants when they were young because there was much less resistance against the masters' rules than there was with older servants. On the other hand, older servants were better workers off the hop, so it was a trade-off that masters weighed carefully. Hectore had told Arlahn that he wished he could outlaw slavery, or at least implement a code of conduct for it, but too many nobles, like Grent, would oppose him. "Men will always be greedy," the King explained. Without the nobles' support, the risk of a revolt or coup could ruin him, as it did for his own father, Arlahn the First.

The girl looked to be close to the same age as Arlahn. Her frame was a little smaller than his, but she was still a healthy young thing.

"Apologies, Your Grace, the rat didn't look where she was walking," Grent said.

"That's alright. It was an honest mistake," the King told him.

The young slave held her stare a moment longer until she looked up at the HighKing then back to Arlahn and bowed down low, grabbing his hands in hers, her chains clinking gently as she did. "Apologies, Prince. I didn't look where I was walking."

The sound of her voice was beautiful music to Arlahn's ears and the need to help her swirled around him once more. He opened his mouth to say something just as Stevano pulled her away with a yank on the rope attached to her manacles. They disappeared into the crowd and Arlahn stood searching a moment until his father broke his focus. "Arlahn, what if we get you a wristlet? Something like your brothers have."

The piece his father was talking about was made from several bands of cured leather weaving through one another. Although Arlahn liked the idea of finally getting a wristlet like his brothers, he could still see that girl's sadness in his mind's eye. But he smiled up at his father and nodded agreement with forced enthusiasm.

They entered an expensive, well-lit shop at the corner of a main intersection, and the owner came over to welcome in the King and his son with a big smile. "Come, come, let me show you my wares, King Hectore."

"Actually, Jersay, your wares are for the eyes of my son, Arlahn. He's turned five years old today," Hectore told the merchant, placing a hand on his son's shoulder.

"Well, happy birthing day, little prince. What can I show you?" The man leaned over and rested his hands on his knees to look Arlahn in the eye, an everlasting smile on his face.

"A wristlet, sir," Arlahn answered.

"Please?" Hectore humbled.

"Please," the young prince repeated in a quiet voice.

"Excellent choice. You know, the man who sells me these wristlets bases all the variations on his own. He swears it's the source of all his good luck," Jersay said retreating behind a counter in the corner of the building. "Have to agree, he's the luckiest man I've ever known to step on a ship. Tell me, which one do you like?"

All over the table were necklaces, rings, earrings, marriage bands, and all manner of trinkets, most of their purposes Arlahn could only guess.

Jersay returned, producing an entire stand of leather wristlets, and Arlahn stepped closer to better look at the patterns in the leather. The band that caught his attention was made up of three strips of flat leather, braided and bordered with white and canary threads, like the colours of his family sigil.

Arlahn pointed at the band and the merchant lifted it off the hook. "Wonderful choice," Jersay crooned. He wrapped it around Arlahn's wrist and joined the clasp to secure it. "Perfect fit as well, little prince." Hectore tried to pay the merchant, but Jersay politely refused, claiming it an honour to give a gift to the Prince on his birthing day, and bade them farewell. Arlahn felt an extra bit of confidence in his stride on their way home.

The palace had just come into sight when Zeth appeared, garbed in complete mail, approaching with one hand rested on his sword hilt.

"My King, my Prince, happy birthing day to you on this glorious fall afternoon," he greeted them, having not forgotten the occasion. But as he joined them in stride, Zeth's expression became more morose and he looked over at Hectore. "My King, I was just coming to find you. There's a matter that you've wished to personally oversee whenever this complaint has been brought forth. I apologize, Your Grace, but Judgement has been asked for."

Arlahn had never seen his father pass on Judgement before. His brothers were old enough to have attended a few hearings, but he had always been whisked away to his room. However, the way Zeth was speaking hinted toward something of a different nature. Something unfamiliar to him altogether, it gave him a sense of the funereal.

"I see," Hectore answered, his expression suddenly darker. "So be it. If a plaintiff and a defendant have come forward, I'll be there. Arlahn, go back to your room and wait for me there. Bathe and get dressed for your supper."

"But Father!" Arlahn started.

"Now!" Hectore demanded in a tone that beckoned no argument. Arlahn was shocked at his father's sudden change of emotion. He squeezed his lips tight and obeyed, dragging his feet through the palace entrance. As they reached the top of the great stairs, Arlahn reluctantly detached from the group and began toward his room.

Chapter 3

Hectore was a fair man. At least, he had always believed as much. When he began his reign, it was not something he had particularly wanted – at first, it seemed more of a duty or a chore to be king. But the fey man that Hectore had named Harbinger had been correct about finding his *amiro*. Whenever they'd met throughout his life, the short man in green had always been correct, seldom as that was. He had told Hectore that Annabella would be his key and she was. She humbled him and showed him how to rule a kingdom of five realms properly. It all began in the form of mere suggestions and harmless advances at first. "Encourage the wealthy to donate their surplus food to those less fortunate. Pass on our garments rather than tearing them up for rags. Keep a seat at our table for a guest each supper so you can hear their stories and learn from them." Hectore eventually realized that it was precisely this kind of compassion that she had taught him that was ultimately responsible for almost every improvement in the social reform attributed to his rule. Without her, he would have never predicted the ripple effect that such kindness could propagate throughout a society.

Their relationship had now evolved to a point where Annabella was comfortable speaking freely, occasionally even challenging Hectore, and he would always consider her words with great consideration. She was mindful enough to remain a proper queen in court, though, never questioning the King's final decision in open. She would stand by his side while the rages of all the elements stormed down on them. She really was his *amiro*, his other half, his true completion that transcended this ethereal life they were currently living.

Hectore no longer saw the realms of Saintos as his sole dominion but rather theirs. Annabella had shown him that love could rule as well as fear, but to rule well was to be loved and feared all at once. To be respected.

He never enjoyed governing punishment. But it was a necessary thing. Hectore had lived much of his life in a world without order and saw the destruction it could cause. Others from that world still remembered and so they welcomed his Judgement in place of the Damonai alternatives from the past, where steel and blood had been the only resolutions.

Hectore was escorted into the throne room by Zeth and was greeted by a servant named Tod, an orphan boy that had been caught stealing his food. The boy had accepted his pledge of servitude after the King convinced the baker out of his original proffered punishment: cutting off a finger, the usual penalty for such an offence. Tod was holding a pillow with the King's humble crown in its centre. He didn't speak but merely lifted and offered the crown to its owner.

The king snatched it almost viciously from the pillow and slammed it on his head. He noticed how its meagre weight always seemed doubled when dealing Judgement. The room had a score of witnesses and another of guards, both fanned out to either side of the Queen, who stood next to the throne, waiting. A few servants and a few Kalendare worked around them without disturbance, moving about the others as naturally as their shadows.

Among the plaintiffs were a father and his daughter, a tall young woman with pretty auburn hair, huddling into her father with her hands tucked into her chest, clutching him, trembling. She would have been a beauty, but her eyes were red-rimmed and swollen from sobbing.

The defendant, a man of near thirty years, was wearing brown farmhand clothes that were soiled and soaked at the knees. With manacled wrists, he held a bloodied rag to his head that covered the better half of his face.

Hectore cursed the circumstances of his presence as he marched past the witnesses and climbed the three small steps up to his throne. The throne room was usually his favourite place in the palace with the Golden Throne in the center of its floor that had been made to look like the sun's orb, six feet in diameter, littered with rubies, almandine, and amber. Encapsulating himself in it gave Hectore a warm feeling that began on the inside and swelled to his skin. With the mirrored dome ceiling above, he could use the concave reflection to see behind him by merely raising an eye. But the floor below was by far his favourite feature of the ostentatious room. Covered with rich shades of pink, and blue, and orange, and purple made to resemble far off galaxies and nebulae in the granite, while innumerable specks and chunks of white emulated stars, near and distant, scattered erratically among them.

None of this beauty pleased Hectore in this moment. He was not there for his floors, but for the people standing on them.

"I'm told I'm here to acknowledge the crime and pass judgement. Is there any denial to the claim brought forward?"

The farmhand defendant bowed his head, unable to look the King in his cold, hard eyes. He appeared frightened and ashamed.

He should be, Hectore thought.

"You realize that without a response. I have to acknowledge your guilt."

"There's noffin' for me to say, Your Grace," the farmhand said.

"Nothing for you to say!" the Queen raged. "How about sorry to the girl?! Would that you could take back what you've done to the poor thing." She quieted. "Men always either talk or beg."

"Beg, my Queen?" the farmhand said like it was foreign to him.

"For forgiveness," the Queen told him.

"For their lives," the King added. "Now, tell me what happened."

Zeth stepped forward and began speaking. "Bregan was out on a patrol when he heard the screams, Your Grace."

Hectore raised a hand for silence. Even though Zeth's relationship with the King pre-dated his rule and he had always been a loyal man and a friend, the King dismissed him coldly. When Hectore was passing his Judgement, he was not a friend. He was no longer a man, nor a king. Trials brought something else out of him. He became a cool, hard weight, set on balancing the scales.

"If it was Bregan who found him, let him speak."

A young man with brown curly hair stepped forward, one hand on his sword-hilt. "Your Grace, it's true. I was out riding with my troop when I thought I heard a screech. As I got closer, the screeches turned to screams and grew worse, Your Grace."

"That's coz he was raping my daughter!" the father blurted out in a fit of anger.

Again, the king raised his hand with an icy glare that snuffed the father's fire. "Finish, Bregan."

"Yes, right, well. When I got close enough to realize it wasn't fun but foul play, I gave a holler. That was when the bastard got up and tried to run, Your Grace. For all the good it did him with his pants down. The fool tripped and smashed his head on a rock. I swear I didn't harm him myself, only apprehended him and brought him here at once."

"As you should have. Well done," the king said. "Now, about this rape..." he continued, turning his attention to the young woman. "How did it happen?"

The young woman began to cry again then, and her father spoke instead, claiming his daughter's maidenhood. But the king quickly silenced him with his hand and a look that conveyed the annoyance that was building within him. After a moment, the swell of emotion faded, and Hectore waited patiently for the girl to start talking. He had never really been a patient man, he had become a man of action during the war and the practical side of him always worried about maximum efficiency, no matter the task. Time was too valuable to waste in his eyes. It was Annabella who'd had to teach him to be more empathetic when it came to matters of emotion. That sometimes waiting wasn't wasting time but exercising patience. Because of her, he would sit and wait for as long as it took until the girl spoke.

"I... I was bringing in... my family's clothes, Your Grace... That's when... the man, he grabbed me by my arms... he said I was teasing him, Your Grace... He threw me to the ground and said he would make a woman out of me." The girl said, her speech breaking to sniffle back tears.

"You said nothing to him beforehand?"

"No, Your Grace, I've only seen him a few times in the fields. I was out to hang some of my small clothes."

The king leaned back a moment in his throne then lurched forward, resting his elbows on his knees. He sat, looking at the farmhand, studying the man. "And your story?"

The man glanced up from under the rag at his forehead and remained silent a moment. "I won't deny it, Your Grace. I ain't no fool. I know what I did."

"Do you know that rape is a most heinous crime, one that has never been tolerated in my reign?"

"Yours or the queen's reign?" the fool snapped in a moment of arrogance, unaware that he had just sealed his own fate.

Annabella stepped out from beside Hectore. She had her hands clasped together and a stern hatred in her face. She descended the three steps and slapped the farmhand full in the face. The man knew better than to retaliate and the queen stood dominantly over him after looking the man up and down. "You've obviously never met my husband before." Turning back to the king, she gathered herself and politely stated, "Your Grace, I see my mercy is not wanted here. I suppose I'll see you in the Blood Garden." Before she took her leave, she gave the farmhand one last lingering stare of disgust.

Although a part of Hectore wanted to take the man's head then and there, he didn't betray any such emotion in his face. Instead, he sat back and said in a stern voice, "It's true, the queen has aided in my ruling. She taught me to listen to you, and even allow you final words to make peace with your gods. Rest assured she could have been your only saviour at this point. You may have ruined this young girl's life far worse than you've ruined your own."

"I doubt that," the farmhand whispered.

"One more quip from you and I won't leave a choice for punishment!" Hectore warned the man who lowered his eyes once more.

He turned back to the victim and asked her, "What is your name, young lady?"

"Hellen, Your Grace."

"Hellen. I'm so sorry that a citizen of my kingdom has wronged you in such an unforgettable way. I accept your testimony as truth and ask that you request a punishment for the accused."

The woman shared a look with her father, who gave her a quick nod. "Your Grace, we would give the man a choice. Lose one head, or the other."

Hectore's expression hinted at his pleasure. "The Crown sees the punishment befits the crime." He shot the man a look. "Your choice?"

"Sir, please, no..." the farmhand started.

"Is that what she told you before you pinned her down?" the king cut him off in a seething, icicle of a voice. "No, I told you. The queen and her mercy have left this room. Your time for leniency has passed. Choose."

The farmhand contemplated for a long minute. "I've met a few eunuchs in my day. Never quite seemed right after and I don't want to live as half a man."

"Then you won't live at all," Hectore proclaimed. "Zeth, take him to the Blood Garden."

Zeth seized the farmhand by the arm and hauled him away, the man's manacles clinking and rattling with the forceful shoves.

Hectore rose and began to approach the young girl. "Hellen, you may choose to be present for the punishment, but I would advise you spare yourself from any more horrors on this man's account."

When he arrived in the garden, the colour of the blooming flowers foreboded what was coming. It was all around them. As the clutch of winter began with fall, the red of the roses had wilted and withered into a deeper, more sinister shade.

In attendance was the queen, a small group of soldiers, and Hellen's father. Having taken the king's advice, Hellen herself was not present and he was grateful for it.

The farmhand was waiting at the chopping block, bare-chested with his bound hands beneath him. Beside him, Zeth was at hand with a handful of other soldiers, holding Hectore's greatsword Justice. The weapon was a terrible thing that promised its name. It stood in its sheath, the crossguard at Zeth's belly. He lifted the scabbard up and let Hectore slide the four-inch-wide blade from its home. The sound of metal singing as it scraped against wood and leather made the farmhand shiver, and he squirmed on the stump.

"Do you have any last words to make peace with your gods?" the king offered the rapist, both hands tensing tighter around the greatsword's hilt while the tip stabbed deeper into the earth before him.

The man readjusted himself, swallowed a lump and bit down on his tongue. He'd seen this before, the king realized then. Most men struggle and beg for their lives but that just makes a messier end. Acceptance was the best way.

"Then, in the power entrusted to me by the Realms of Saintos, as HighKing and Protector of its People, for the crime of rape, I, Hectore Rai, sentence you to die."

Hectore took up Justice and in one smooth motion brought the shaft of steel around and clove the farmhand's head clean off, right above the neck. The head thumped on the ground and rolled forward. A gush of blood pumping from the man's severed jugular onto the grass, painting it red too.

Through the shrub of roses to his left, Hectore heard a screech, followed by a gasp and faint whimpering. The sounds made the king's heart stop in his chest. He knew those soft whimpers, recognized their innocence.

Turning, he saw his son's face through an opening in the shrubbery. Having forgotten the world, Annabella was already running over to console him. But there was nothing Hectore could do now. Once the deed is done, it can't be undone. Hectore looked at his son, who had stepped out from behind a bush crying. Arlahn gave him a terrified glance and recoiled back into his mother's embrace. "The boy should have been waiting in his room for me!" Hectore claimed, turning to Zeth. He hammered the blade back into its sheath and stormed through the garden, pausing beside his family for a moment. "I told you to bathe and get dressed. Will you do it now?"

Absolutely horrified by his father, Arlahn managed to incorporate a "YAAaaa" into his next wail before cowering into his mother's chest.

"Good." Hectore left with a stern look of displeasure on his face. He realized this was the first time Arlahn beat his brothers to an experience. And it was an execution, one of death.

*****

When it came time for supper, everyone in the family was already in the Great Hall, seated at the high table. This time, however, unlike their private lunch hours ago, the room was packed with people, old and young, wearing faces familiar and strange, all there for the same reason: to wish the Prince a happy birthing day. The noise grew insatiable at the sight of his arrival as men and women banged their cups on the tables and sons and daughters stamped their feet to the ground.

Arlahn smiled as he walked up to join his family at the high table, taking a seat beside his mother, while his brothers were at his father's side. The great Wardens of the realms sat flanking the Rai family like the banners in Elder Rufus' class. To Arlahn's left was the ancient Caldin Baile and his older wife Raella, up from the Southern Freefolk. And beside her, sitting alone, was the younger but still silver-haired Nakoli Rali, from the western realm of Esselle. Raphael sat next to Kael, with his uncle, Benson Wellcant, to his left. Benson had been named Warden of the East by Corduran after Hectore's Rebellion and shared his fair hair and features with his sister, Annabella. Alongside him, from Melonia, way up north, sat the dark-skinned Rodrik Rond, with his wife, Mandi, and son, Pietrey, a spry boy who was a full head taller than his Arlahn's brothers, with tight black curly hair. They each wished Arlahn a personal happy birthing day in turn going down the table and he thanked all of them courteously.

The servers began delivering trays upon trays of food. Some were platters of carved up pork, others had slabs of ribs lathered in a thick spicy sauce, and others still carried stuffed roasted ducks. They brought out trenchers overflowing with bread and big wooden bowls of fresh salad. And all the while, every cup was refilled with wine for the women, mead for the men, and milk for the children. King Hectore rose, greeting and thanking everyone for their attendance on his son's fifth birthing day. He made a point to specially thank each of his Wardens for making such arduous journeys.

"Now that the food has been served and our cups refilled, let us raise a glass to our prince and bless his health! May his light shine brightest!"

As Hectore finished, cheers erupted across the hall, followed with scattered chants of, "May his light shine brightest!" and cups colliding before they were raised to mouths.

Even with all the attention on him, Arlahn felt small surrounded by the cacophony of the hundreds that filled the Great Hall. He slunk back into his chair, took a bite of his roasted duck, and glanced at the armour plaque he'd disappeared through earlier as he chewed. He wished he could crank that horse and run him along the mantle to disappear again.

At the end of the high table, there was no empty seat, which was rare. It was customary for his father to keep an extra chair at his table while he ate. Each night, the Rais would dine with a new citizen, and his father would get to know them personally. But last night, it had been the master-at-arms, Zeth, and his son Zephoroth, who seemed a few years older than Kael and Raphael, but shared their passion for fighting and mischief. Arlahn learned that Zeth had known his father even before the Great Rebellion.

When dessert was served, all Arlahn's favourite fruit and pastries were arranged on his platter in the shape of a smiling face.

He snatched up a dumpling in one hand and bit into the fresh crust. The warm, saucy apple taste filled his mouth and tingled the taste buds up to his cheeks, and Arlahn sunk into his element. He could hear Raphael and Kael telling their father of how Zeth had let them begin dueling with the other older kids like Bregan and Zephoroth. Zeth trained the boys in the combat arts while Arlahn was in class with Jofus. Then, every other day, the children switched instructors, and Arlahn would get to learn how to hold and swing a sword properly. Kael and Raphael seemed much older than they really were, and their strength and cunning grew rapidly with each passing day. But it would be a few more years before their Gifts would manifest and they became something more than human. It was this way for each descendant of the Rai bloodline, true heirs to the throne.

"Only a handful of Gifted individuals lived in Tehbirr, but each Gift was something incomprehensibly uncanny. Having a Gift is unique and supernatural. It means you were Touched by Him," Arlahn's father had told him one night. Just like any child of five years old, Arlahn believed that his father was the source of all truth, but Hectore himself didn't fully understand what it meant to be Touched. It was like something he knew intrinsically but could never put into words.

Arlahn flaunted his new wristlet to his brothers. The act reminded Nakoli Rali, the Warden of the West, of his own birthing day present for the Prince. And so, it began.

Nakoli had brought with him a great leather-bound book. As he presented it, he read its title for the Prince. "'The Tales and Adventures of Juliessa Firstborn, the Warrior Queen, Hodsun the Pirati, Isla the GiantSlayer, and Boranius the Brave.' A marvellous read with attention to true details, my prince."

At mention of Juliessa, Hodsun and Isla, the little boy's eyes grew with excitement.

Caldin Baile had brought with him a hand-carved wooden knight. But this was no ordinary knight that stood still in its pose. The dextrous Freefolk of the South had somehow found a way to make moveable joints in the wood. Upon closer examination, Arlahn noticed a smoothed-out rivet between the wood in critical locations that allowed him to move the knight this way and that. He almost immediately started dreaming up imaginary adventures this tiny warrior would partake with its toy peers.

Rodrik encouraged his son to deliver their present. And so Pietrey handed the Prince a wooden box with black and white squares on its surface, opening the lid to show him the fragile glass contents. Little figurines made up to look like soldiers. "It's a game called Battlegrounds. We taught it to your brothers on their Culture Walk. They enjoyed playing with me."

"Lucky Arlahn!" Raphael shouted with an excited look of his own. "Tomorrow we can all teach you and play it together." Raph was so excited he leaned over to share the great news with his twin, Kael who could see clearly from beside him.

Arlahn's uncle Benson was the last to approach him. He was carrying something wide and thin under a blue cloth. "My nephew prince," he began unveiling its contents, "it's not a usual gift, but hopefully you'll grow to appreciate it. It is old and very delicate, so I pray that you keep it in a safe place. I present you with an original scripture of the ancient prophecy fulfilled by your king father."

"How?" Hectore asked his brother-by-marriage, talking as if they were the only ones there.

"Everyone needs a pastime. There are thousands of sailors who travel through our ports. I encountered a merchant last year with it. He said you two had met before and knew you would appreciate it. I was reluctant at first, but once I saw it, I knew I had to have it, and I was ready to give up a small fortune. The man chuckled when I asked a price. He told me I *had* to take it, so that I could bring it here today."

With delicate care, Benson placed a piece of bark before Arlahn, and the young prince climbed on his knees to better look at it in its entirety. The piece was over an inch thick and solid to knock on. It had rough edges, with an imperceptible bend that would have gone unnoticed if it hadn't been lying on a flat table. In neat lines along the surface, the writing was thick and elegant, each character in that special font that Arlahn had only seen at the top of certain pages in his books. As pretty as it was, between the strangely shaped letters and his lack of experience, Arlahn couldn't make out the words just yet.

"It is said that this piece of bark is from the mythic Tree of Life itself, Arlahn," his father told him. "It was peeled off by Jidban and Tunique and they burned their prophecy into it. There's only one in the world. The

Damonai stole it before I could find it myself. It's said that the words lead the Chosen One to Graceland and everlasting peace."

"And here's to our prophesied King!" Benson shouted, raising a glass. A loud ruckus of "TO THE KING!" took over the hall for a few seconds in another round of cheers.

Happiness washed over Arlahn's body like waves upon a shore. With all the entertainment around him, he hadn't noticed that his mother had stood and left. Upon her return, he glanced over and saw she was standing with her arms tucked behind her back, hiding something.

"Now Arlahn, you've been told the meaning of a Ritual Gift and you've seen your brothers'. But this was the Gift that was chosen for you." As she spoke, she produced a dagger, sheathed in white gold.

Arlahn's eyes shot wide open. It was marvellous. Custom dictated that nobility should receive a gift such as this on their fifth birthing day, a month before they left for their culture walk. Kael had received a full-length sword and Raphael a bow. The weapons were to be mounted to the wall of the sleep chambers and remain there untouched as the years passed and the boys grow. Only when Arlahn became tall enough to lift and replace the dagger on his own, would he be allowed to equip himself with it.

The Prince bound upon his mother, caressing her tight. Annabella unsheathed the dagger, displaying it to him, and he looked closely to better observe his new gift. Virtually everyone within a twenty-foot radius bent in to catch a glance of the stunning blade. "This is not one of your toys, my son," she told him cautiously as he made an attempt to grab it. "You get to touch it for tonight before it gets mounted," Annabella explained. "But please, be careful."

The white ivory handle was too large for his small hands, but this didn't phase him in the slightest. The dagger's quillon had a beautiful design with blue and green gems encrusted near the thumb, and the curved, pearly blade shone with a frosted finish that showed no sign of use. It was exquisite, crafted from the finest smith. Arlahn studied its every detail, burning each one into his memory.

The rest of the celebration passed with little disturbance from then on as music played and the dancing began. But it was his ritual gift, the dagger, which occupied the majority of Arlahn's attention.

Later in bed, when Hectore was tucking his son in for sleep, Arlahn asked him about the prophecy his uncle had given him. His father had convinced him earlier that the wooden plaque should be placed in the Great Hall, instead of his own bedchambers, to better preserve it.

"It's part of our history, and our future," he told him. "I've seen the tablet before but thought it was destroyed."

"What does it say on it? It's hard to read that writing," Arlahn said, excusing his own illiteracy.

"It's a very ancient tablet. Turned to stone from the ages," Hectore said, picturing the piece again in his mind. "The word at the top is a title. It says 'Generation.'" Then, without any reference except that from his mind, he recited the prophecy in an almost rhythmic voice.

> "Spawn from darkness, I will grow from revolution,
> Seeking retribution to fulfill my constitution.
> Withdrawn from my partner, I will find motivation,
> To fight the complacent over enslavement.
> Stopping those who prey like a ruthless demon,
> I'll provide the reason to incite your freedom."

After a commanding pause, seemingly entranced by the flow of words, the little prince asked from beneath his covers, "How do you know it all?"

"It's not something you forget easily when you spend half your life hearing that it's about you."

"What does it mean?" Arlahn asked.

His father shook his head, unsure. "*I believe it's about being all you can be. Our potential is our greatest waste, son. We can all* be *so much.*"

Together, they sat there alone in a comfortable silence until his father asked at last, "What were you doing in the Rose Garden, Arlahn?"

"I thought that because I'm five and we spent the whole day together, I was old enough to see what you were doing." He swallowed. "Why did you kill that man?"

Arlahn had been a wreck when he saw that horrible scene in the Rose Garden. Before he had wondered how the grass sometimes grew red, now he knew. For a half-hour, he could do nothing but sob and shake and wail in his mother's arms, but eventually she had worked him into a warm bath and washed the salt from his face. Now he had calmed and was ready to make an agreement to what he saw.

Hectore took his time finding the right words. "What that man did to a young woman was like killing her, on the inside." He touched the boy's heart. "Because he admitted to doing such a horrible thing, he was given a choice."

"He *chose* to die. Why?"

"Because he felt so bad for what he had done," Hectore lied to preserve his son's innocence one more night.

"Why did you have to kill him?"

His father understood what Arlahn was asking. "*I had to.*"

"But why you, though?"

"Arlahn, my boy, there are times in life where you mustn't ask things of others you wouldn't be willing to do yourself. I could not have asked Zeth or Halder to take the man's life. That would be casting a great burden off on them."

"Okay," Arlahn agreed, considering it a moment. "What about when you ask Kael and Raph and me to clean our bedchambers?"

Hectore smiled at the innocence of his son's thoughts. "I do that to teach you about responsibilities," he said. "But it's getting late. Time for sleep."

"Noo!" Arlahn pleaded, taking up his father's hand with both of his and pulling him down on the bed. "Can you tell me a story first?"

"Alright. One story. Which one do you want to hear?"

"Tell me one of the stories about the palace."

"The one about Anemir?"

"Yeah!" Arlahn nodded, his eyes wide with excitement.

"When our great ancestor Anemir first came to these lands, he had set out to explore from the east. He travelled with his best friend and second in command, a man named Xion. On their sixth day Anemir crested the Garrison's Hill and saw the palace but it was too far and too late to make it there before nightfall. But that evening, while everyone slept in view of its keep, Xion, along with a few greedy men, slipped away, entered the palace, and closed the great gates before the next sunrise. The following morning, when Anemir was refused entry, he gave Xion three days to open the doors.

"Two days passed, and Anemir, having tried everything to please his old friend, gave him one more chance to surrender. Xion claimed it was his right to own the castle, but he had sworn a Holy Blood Oath to Anemir. You remember that a Holy Blood Oath cannot be broken and must be upheld for life? Only Xion didn't care about oaths anymore. He had the palace. Anemir couldn't let the betrayal stand, nor let his friend keep what he had claimed. If he had, the next time Anemir told someone "No," he would have been defied once more. After that last sunset, with still no answer from Xion, Anemir knew what he had to do."

Hectore tucked the blankets tighter about his son's chest. "So that night, he snuck in past Xion's stationed guards..." Though the stories detailed Anemir's slaughter of these guards, Hectore chose to leave that detail out of this bedtime tale. "... He crept into Xion's bedchamber and woke him up with a palm over his mouth" – and a knife to his throat – "and told him that he was to give up this revolt, that he would be spared his life for their friendship's sake. Xion surrendered and the next morning the doors were open for Anemir's people. Soon after, Xion was banished from the land. The story was that Anemir and Xion were so much like brothers that Anemir couldn't punish him for what he had done. So he rode with him back east, to the Skyrim Tower. There they marked the very edge of our land, and he bid his old friend farewell till the end of their days."

By the end of his father's story, Arlahn had great trouble holding his eyes open any longer. His father tucked the furs around him tighter and kissed his forehead goodnight.

Just before he passed into sleep, his mind slipped back and found its way to the slave girl he'd met that afternoon in the market, with her big blue eyes. There was a great wistfulness hidden behind them. A touch of melancholy hidden in her rosy pink lips. Desperation behind the blood that rushed to her soft cheeks when she blushed after apologizing to him. But for all that, she was the prettiest girl he'd ever seen. Arlahn tried to push the thought from his mind, but her image stubbornly remained.

He tossed from one side of his bed to the other and pulled the sheets tight around his shoulders once again. Slowly, he felt his mind release its clutch on the girl. Arlahn let the black wall fall before his eyes and drifted asleep.

Chapter 4

Serah-Jayne rode her black horse into the clearing, a short distance off the path. The horse stopped and she swung her leg over the pommel and dropped lightly to the ground. She ran her slender, long fingers along the length of the horse's neck and grasped the reins in one hand. Slowly, she walked the horse around in circles, allowing it to cool down from the long ride. It was late evening, and she had been riding from Pellence since dawn. She led her horse to the shade of a nearby tree and removed the saddle, placing it on the ground. After inspecting the contents of her saddlebags, she pulled out a hemp sack full of oats and grains. She held the sack while the horse ate greedily so that she could carefully ration her supply, then she let the horse amble on down to the river where it began to drink deeply. Serah-Jayne placed the bag back in a pouch attached to the saddle before she walked into the middle of the clearing, scanning the treeline as if she were expecting to find something other than trees, grass, and rocks.

Slowly a short, handsome man emerged from a path leading in a different direction to that from which Serah-Jayne had come. His clothes almost offensively contrasted with the rugged fall surroundings. He was wearing a green velvet doublet that was trimmed with gold. On his waist, the trim swirled and turned to form a seemingly abstract and indistinct picture. Dark green leggings and doeskin moccasins completed the ensemble.

He walked up and kissed the young beauty on the cheek, his light stubble tickling her skin. "I see you're in a good mood today, Wildflower," he said, touching a white blonde lock of hair that hid in the bangs of her thick ebony mane.

"Yes. I'm so sorry for the last time we met, my dear. I didn't mean to act out. You know better than anyone that I don't mean the things I do when I..."

"Put the thoughts from your mind," the man interrupted, "I know that you sometimes lose control of your *amrak*, I always tell myself that it's not the real you. It can be easy to lose control." The last line he spoke to himself, breaking his gaze with hers. After a deep sigh, he looked up back into her eyes.

Serah-Jayne could see a look of weariness in his almond eyes. He was young and physically strong, yet something inside of him always made him seem tired and worn. She was starting to get a sense of what he was tired of. Diyo, as she called him, had found her a long time ago, when she was a young girl. Now she was in her thirties, and Diyo looked just as he did all those years ago. All that time, he had brooded with the weight of knowing what was forthcoming, at times seeing the world days, months, even years in advance.

Before the silence grew to an awkward standstill, the man spoke.

"Please, sit, we have much to discuss. There are tough decisions to make and I'll need your help. Will you help me?" The tone of his voice was almost hypnotic. Serah-Jayne felt warmth creep into her bloodstream. How could she say no?

"Of course I will help you, Diyo. I've just come from the great city of Pellence, to do as you asked. The boy has your dagger. I approached the merchant before his encounter with the queen and spoke the words just as you had said them to me. He took the dagger happily from me and promised to sell it only to the queen." She smiled affectionately at him. "I did what you asked. I'll always do what you ask." For he was her saviour.

As a young girl, Serah-Jayne witnessed the brutal murder of her parents. Two men had approached them while they were walking through the meagre streets of their eastern settlement. She remembered…

"Excuse me sir, but I cannot seem t'find the stables 'n this dark. I'm just a simple passerby. Not familiar with these parts." One of the men grumbled with an exaggerated cough after he spoke.

"Continue down this street and turn right at the—" Serah-Jayne's father turned to point the way when the passerby pulled his dagger and plunged it into her father's side. She leapt forward toward the man when his assistant swooped in and threw her aside. Slamming into the wall, she was dazed as she watched the killer turn and stab his dagger into her mother's chest. Blood dripped down between her breasts and crimson lines grew thicker as they stained her mother's blouse. The assailant stepped over to her father's body and stripped him of his rings and the coins in his purse. All Serah-Jayne could do was watch.

The killer and his partner, towering over her parents, turned their gaze to Serah-Jayne. She could see the look of murder in their eyes. These men were no passersby. These men were evil, genuinely, and now she was a witness to their crimes. They began to walk purposefully toward her when Diyo arrived, and just by thrusting his palm out at one of the killers, a ball of blue fire engulfed the man in flames where he stood. He swung his arms frantically and staggered on a few steps before flopping to the ground, his body screaming, rolling, writhing in pain until he lay still, charred black. The killer's partner, money in hand, dropped his prize to clutch at his chest with one hand and his throat with the other, his face turned orange to red to purple to blue as he struggled for breath. He was all but lifted from the ground and Serah-Jayne watched him until he fell limp and collapsed.

Diyo walked over to Serah-Jayne and crouched down to her. "Are you hurt, child?" he asked.

She stayed quiet and stared the man in the eyes. Slowly, she shook her head, grief pouring down her face.

"I'm very sorry about what happened here, but I want you to know," Diyo fell onto his left hamstring to sit more comfortably, "that I'm here now, and I will not let any of these, these scumbags hurt you. I'm here to help."

"I'm sure you'd be quick to sell me to the nobles when you get your chance," she mustered with a quivering voice.

"I would not do that. I am trying to be a friend to you." He stood once again, offering his hand to her with a three-quarter smile so as not to undermine the gravity of what had just happened to the little girl, but rather to reassure her that she was safe. "Otherwise I could have just left you here with them but that would not have ended well. I have seen your people. They are cruel and corruptible. You however, young girl, are not like the rest of them. You are special. *Touched*."

"Touched? What do you mean, by who?"

"*Him*," he replied as if she should know of whom he spoke.

Serah-Jayne remembered taking up his hand.

"I think I'll call you Wildflower," Diyo said coolly, never asking her true name. "What would you like to call me?"

"Diyo," she said confidently. She had never heard of any such name, but the sound of it suited the man somehow.

Serah-Jayne thought back to the rest of her youth, growing up in the town Cebel, north of Melonia. She was a beautiful and fierce girl, with a will stronger than most. Among the Northerners, she was well known for her hair like ebony that shone the darkest brown with a single blonde streak that drank in the sun. When Serah-Jayne had grown a little older, the men began being less and less courteous about her beauty and made more and more suggestive remarks about private nights together, unafraid to ask which colour hair grew where. For all their drunken talk, they had never tried anything though, these Northmen. She was content with the life she had been given.

But one day, Serah-Jayne returned from a casual nap during her walk in the fields to find the whole village utterly in ruins. She walked through the destruction, frantically looking for someone to explain to her what had happened. But the first man she saw was screaming curses in a blind rage, ripping and prying at the skin on his own face, like he was burning from the inside and the air around him could quench the flames. She turned to see others, friends and neighbours, fighting one another, and a poor soul running from a torched building with flame wings around him. When Serah-Jayne found her small wooden home, it had caught ablaze and was tattered with flames. Diyo had provided it for her, he told her it was an old abandoned hunt camp that predated the village. Rushing in to gather a few of her possessions, she caught a glimpse of her reflection in the dirty mirror that hung on the wall at the door. Serah-Jayne stared at her hair, face frozen in disbelief. Her whole head was blonde. As she looked, the blonde colour began slowly receding back, turning once again into the familiar contrasting darkness, until it settled into the lock of hair draped behind her ear.

    She left the house and searched among the fiery rubble and debris. Everyone in the settlement was dead or dying. How an entire battle could have occurred while Serah-Jayne slept in the fields a few minutes' walk east of the settlement, she could not surmise.

    Diyo had often visited Serah-Jayne while she lived in Cebel. Yet it seemed he had a sixth sense for when she needed him most. That same day, he showed up and found her wandering amongst the chaos. She ran to him and buried herself in the sanctuary of his chest, before planting a kiss on his lips in the rush of sheer gratitude at seeing a familiar face. They were still close together when a man stumbled from a broken shop with blood and smoke stained to his face. He looked toward her and then Diyo, and retreated back, screaming uncontrollably. The stranger ripped a hatchet from a nearby stump, where men had been splitting logs not hours ago, stared at them a moment, and then swung the hatchet right into his own stomach. That was when Diyo had covered her eyes. Keeping Serah-Jayne close, he'd led her from the city, stopping only once on their way.

    She had watched Diyo approach the town's chief in the centre of the town's square. The poor man was all but dead. He was hanging from spikes that had been driven through his palms and feet. Serah-Jayne came to learn that this was how the Damonai signalled their victory. She looked on as Diyo stopped a few feet short of the defeated man and cupped his hands together. He whispered inward and, as he began to raise his hands, the spikes pulled themselves from the wood. The dark-haired man levitated there a moment, as if held by a giant palm, the pain washed from his face.

He was lowered to the ground, where he slumped upon landing. Diyo approached him and knelt at his side like a father who finds a hurt son, telling him something that Serah-Jayne couldn't remember now. The rest of that day was a blur.

Today, however, it appeared that Diyo was the one who needed Serah-Jayne. The thought that she could repay his kindness lightened her mood and she smiled endearingly toward him. It had been more than twenty years since Diyo showed up at the village to save her for the second time, and for all those long years, she had held her feelings for him in a bottle. Diyo enjoyed being alone and he had a sense of duty that was much larger than his need for companionship. He would meet with her and visit for as long as she could hold her eyes open, but whenever she fell asleep, he was gone, and never once had he asked for her company in his travels. This reality was the one thing that always corked her emotions back into that bottle.

"Please, sit," Diyo beckoned her again.

He raised his open palm and directed it at a fallen tree. Slowly, he moved his hand over to the ground next to where Serah-Jayne was standing. The large tree rolled into place according to Diyo's will and stopped right behind her. All she had to do was sit, knowing her backside would find the log. "I still don't know if I'll ever get used to your courtesy, Diyo," she said with a mischievous smirk on her face.

"I am a dying breed," he replied as he sat down next to her with a serious look on his face.

"I have some things that I need you to do for me. Something... something is awakening in Tehbirr. The world is being disturbed from its slumber. I can feel it in the rains and winds... I feel it in the sun. There's going to be a change in this world, Wildflower, one that even I haven't been prepared for. I've seen it in my dreams. I don't know if I'm strong enough for what's to come," Diyo continued, "but your Gift, it's a power that even I can hardly fathom. It has been given to you so that you may do what is necessary of—"

"Necessary!" she snapped, interrupting him. It was as if a bolt of enraged lightning suddenly lanced into her heart. Her voice grew furious when she heard the word. But when Serah-Jayne spoke next, her voice was not hot with anger. Rather, it was so cold and forlorn that almost made her tremble. It was as if "necessary" had stolen the innocence that she'd treasured so dearly. "I hate that fucking word. Everything's always necessary, Diyo, the bad, the horrible, why can't I just live a peaceful life? Why am I burdened to witness what is necessary?" She looked at the surrounding trees, longing for their unbreakable tranquility. Serah-Jayne let out a deep breath and relaxed a bit, but only a bit. "I feel like I've seen enough for two lifetimes already. And all I know is that ever since this goddamn blonde streak appeared, so many strange things have happened to the people around me. Nothing in my life can be normal."

"Inexplicable and mysterious is the nature of your Gift, not meant for this world of men but for that of gods. I don't doubt that you have seen more in your life than most. But something bigger than both of us is happening. Whether the things you bore witness to good or bad, those were the events that came to pass for a reason, events that *needed* to pass. You cannot dwell on the past, Wildflower. Reflect on it, learn from it, but when you lay to rest at night, the past has already happened and you cannot change it, so leave it behind you. Our future, ah... now that is an imagination of the things to come, hopes and dreams, plans and ideas. A false promise we please ourselves with. It is the Now that is ultimately the only thing that matters. It's the decisions we make in the Now that allow us to lay down our past and create the portrait we'd like to paint of it." Diyo stood up and walked a few paces to stretch his legs. He turned to face her. "You have seen too much horror in your life. I won't ever deny that. But if I told you that it meant everyone else in the world would get to live as peacefully as you wish to, would you deny them?"

"No," Serah-Jayne relented.

"You have been given a Gift of unthinkable power. A burden, you called it, to bear witness to what has been necessary. But there have been good necessary moments as well. I would see you paint a healthy portrait for this world because your brush strokes indeed affect all of Tehbirr." He waited for her to surrender to the reality of his words. "Do you remember King Hectore? You've met him once before."

"The boy who became King, it's kind of hard to forget."

"Aye, that's true enough. But did you know the invasion that dethroned his father began in that northern Melonian settlement, the one I found you in?"

She didn't. He could see it clearly in her reaction.

"If your Gift hadn't turned against the people there, the Damonai would never have invaded the main city. There would have been no war."

"Are you saying I started the Damonai HolyWar?"

"I'm saying, Hectore became the true HighKing because he wasn't raised as a king. And a true HighKing is what Saintos needed."

"So what business do I have with the true HighKing of Saintos now?" Her eyebrow cocked up as her expression turned quizzical.

"Not the king. His sons. I don't want you to meet them just yet. I will need you to reach out to them with your *amrak* though, we must keep an eye on them, find their *amiros*. They are Touched, same as you. We'll need them at their finest. With this change in Tehbirr, I think it's finally time." Diyo returned to the fallen tree Serah-Jayne was sitting on, loomed above her as more of a presence than a man.

"Time for what?" It confused her when he spoke like this. During these times, she grew to understand that Diyo was not a normal human like others, he bore responsibility for the entire world and its actions. Serah-Jayne doubted if he wasn't just Touched like she was, but something more.

"*He* is coming. The Rais have always been vital to *His* plan. I don't know what's going to happen next, but the world and so much more literally depends on it. To be honest... I'm afraid."

"Who *is* He?" she asked Diyo. "You always talk about Him..."

"The swallower of planets and suns... The bringer of life and death... The Rahnolean. He must be coming soon. Only I don't know when."

Serah-Jayne didn't answer. She didn't know how to. Diyo was an everlasting well of knowledge. He knew everything about everything. To hear him speak of something with uncertainty for the first time made her think that perhaps, like he said, something monumental was happening. Had anyone else been spewing these claims, she would have humoured them and gone about her day. But coming from Diyo, it made her feel small.

"Will you stay with me tonight?" he asked in a rare display of dependency, sitting down on the ground to lean against the trunk.

"You know I will," she replied with a look of adoration in her eyes as she slipped down beside him.

Using his magic, Diyo gathered several rocks into a circle, as though they came alive under his will. He did this without so much as a few pivots of the wrist. Then he whirled his hand in a spiral motion and a fire roared up from the ground, as if chasing after its source.

Serah-Jayne always loved seeing him do that. She looked over at the man she adored so much. She regarded how his face had barely aged in all the years she'd known him. In the glitter of the firelight, she could see the whites of his eyes were scribbled with veins.

"Is there something else wrong?" she asked him, sensing a brooding weight on his shoulders.

"It's the Chosen Children. Their presence was never strong in Tehbirr, but neither was it ever this faint. Along with the Rais, there's always been a handful of others like you who are Touched. Normally I can feel them, it's how I know where you are from time to time. Lately though, the presence of those who are and will come to be is fading. I feel them leaving, but where are they going?"

"I don't know, but we'll find out together. Do what *needs* to be done, just like with the boy who became King."

"With you here helping me, I'm not so bad off," Diyo said, lying on his side.

Serah-Jayne sat in silence, staring into the fire for a moment, then she smiled and laid down next to him. As he wrapped his hand around her body, he held out his palm for a second and the fire dimmed but retained its warmth. She caressed his arm across her chest, holding his hand over her heart, and rested her head. Letting out a deep sigh and it felt like a massive weight had rolled off her body.

This was right.

The two stayed up all night laughing and reminiscing on times past. Diyo always made Serah-Jayne feel like he cherished their time together, limited as it was. That feeling comforted her in a way that could only come from him. It was as if they had known each other in another life.

She watched the flames, content to lay in peaceful silence.

"Why is it that you've been so good to me all this time?" she finally asked in her most passionate voice.

"There are many reasons why I've done the things I have. A long time ago, people believed that in each person's life, they had one other person in the world that they were sacredly bonded to, an *amiro*. Most people live their entire lives without meeting such a person. Instead, they settle for someone else," he told her poetically.

"And you think that you and I are *amiros*?" Serah-Jayne asked him, hoping he would hold her forever.

After a moment's contemplation he said, "Maybe... I think that you and I are bonded in a different way."

She pulled away, rolling onto her back to look Diyo in his eyes and asked, "You don't love me?"

He paused, staring back at her, his eyes shouting "I do love you, more than anything." But his mouth said, "Wildflower, I believe our connection is beyond deep. It has led us to great things, and we have greater things ahead, but I have no wish to start an argument. So I can leave now or..."

"No!" Serah-Jayne stopped him, snuggling back into his warm embrace. "I don't want you to ever leave," she childishly wished aloud. Diyo lifted himself on his shoulder, rolled her over, and kissed her full on the lips. At first, it caught her by surprise, but she accepted it gracefully along with his tongue. A single kiss and he retreated again, humming a sad song until their breathing fell into rhythm and Serah-Jayne's eyelids became lead. Finally, to the soft sound of his lullaby, she succumbed to sleep.

Her eyes opened to glowing embers. A light smoke trailed through the air. She realized she was alone; Diyo had probably left shortly after she fell asleep. Why couldn't she have stayed up a little longer? Serah-Jayne walked over to the shallow stream where her horse stood, ready, and leaned over to drink from the current. Coming up, she unhitched her horse, slipped her left foot expertly into the stirrup, and smoothly mounted, telling herself with forced enthusiasm, "Alright then. Let's go do what needs to be done."

She turned him toward a path in the trees and snapped the reins, clapping her heel on the Melonian horse's jet-black rear. He obediently began to trot down the trail, picking up speed as they rode deeper into the woods.

*****

Controlling the bridge that was the balance between independence and communion, forever compensating for the scales that are perpetually in motion to suit our desires and needs.

*****

They had been walking since the morning light was slowly creeping over the forest ridge, which lay to the east of the palace. It was now close to noon and Arlahn's legs felt like they were rubber. *How many hours?* he wondered. *How many hours have we been walking in near complete silence?*

Arlahn hadn't been included in many of the hunting trips his father and brothers had been taking for as long as he could remember, and now he watched how Raphael and Kael proceeded expertly across the forest floor.

Kael moved with a fluidity of a seasoned ranger, hardly ever making a sound, while Raphael left no sign of the Wild undiscovered as he passed by.

Raph was about to jump from one stone to another when the landing rock caught his attention. It wasn't a rock at all, but rather a pile of glossy brown nuggets. At first, his nose scrunched up at the thought of what he was seeing, but when he realized what his discovery meant, Raphael waved to get his father's attention. Bow in hand, Hectore sped silently to where Raphael stood and crouched down to the pile of droppings on the ground. He squinted at them, sniffed the air lightly, then his eyes immediately shot up and stared into the distance. Together, the four began to creep through the forest once again in silence until Hectore scurried over and stopped at a large beaten tree. He was wearing his black leather vest with the golden eagle pendant, which he wore each time he took his boys hunting.

He laid his hand on the maple and studied how the bark of the tree had been scratched and scraped. Motioning with his other hand, Hectore summoned the boys to advance to his position. Slowly, Raphael, Kael, and Arlahn moved across the forest floor, stepping only on rock, moss, or tree root, lest they made any sound.

Arlahn had been anxious to get out of class and away from Elder Rufus' endless lectures and condescending tone. He was hoping that if he could impress his father today, maybe the king would start including him in more of these hunting activities and he'd be rid of a few more of Elder Rufus' classes. So Arlahn was going to impress them all. He was going to be perfect. Kael and Raphael had already taken to the hunt. He was going to be like them.

Making sure he did his best not to step on any branches or dead leaves, Arlahn arrived at his father's position. Noise was an immediate giveaway, hunting was about surprise. "Hunting is about the stalker and its prey, surprise, and decisive action," their father would tell them after each sign they found.

Arlahn crouched down surreptitiously to better understand what his father was observing on the tree. Instantly, he noticed that it had been attacked by something in the forest, something hard that had been rubbing and grating against it. The epidermis on the tree had been scraped down until it appeared clean and new. Only after he finished noticing the bark, Arlahn realized his father was pointing out deeper into the woods. Slowly, the boys poked their heads out past the tree and peered into the distance.

Not twenty paces in, Arlahn saw a large four-legged, chestnut-coloured elk. Its head was bowed down and chewing on the leaves of a plant. Arlahn watched as the animal stripped leaves from the branch with its mouth and ate them casually, pointy antlers protruded from the sides of its great head. Arlahn sank down again carefully, and mouthed, "There's something there!" His finger pointing in the same direction that Hectore's had a moment before.

Hectore raised his index finger to his puckered lips to remind the boy the importance of silence, Kael shook his head, and the quiet resumed. Breathing through their noses, the silence was deafening, the suspense hurtful.

The king lifted his right hand cautiously above his shoulder and pulled out a thick arrow from the quiver that was strapped to his back. He began to rise inch by inch, with his bow held firmly in his left hand, then he notched the arrow between his fingers and pulled it tight into the bowstring.

At that moment, excitement rose in Arlahn. This was the climax to the gruelling and relentless morning. He had spent hours walking in complete silence with his brothers and father, and so he couldn't help himself, he was too curious to see what his father was capable of. Arlahn had only ever heard stories of how the king was a remarkable swordsman in battle and always wondered if his father knew how to fire a bow outside of the practice range.

He leaned out from around the tree, leaning further and further out for a better view until, like slipping on ice, Arlahn quickly realized he wasn't leaning anymore but rather falling. Frantically, he searched for something to counterbalance his weight, but out of instinct, he shot his hand out to brace himself for impact. The palm of his hand came crashing down on a dead branch, snapping it in half with a violent crack that might as well have been a thunderclap in the peaceful forest.

Hectore knew his time was up, he saw the head and the tail of the elk spring into the air, simultaneously staring in their direction. Raphael and Kael jumped up to see what was happening as the elk bounded into a full sprint in the opposite direction of the commotion. Hectore aimed his bow and his hand drew back the arrow to the corner of his mouth with blinding speed, his brows furrowing as his eyes concentrated on the elk. He followed the bouncing animal for half a heartbeat until a thick tree obscured his vision. He lowered his bow again and cursed under his breath with a loud grunt. Frustrated, Hectore exploded into a sprint after the elk, bow and arrow still firm in opposite hands.

There was no way Hectore would catch an elk on foot, he knew this. The other thing that Hectore knew was that, although the elk was faster, any animal of such a size would have to zig-zag through the trees or risk his antlers being entangled. Hectore would use this to his advantage.

He was running in perfect stride, hurdling over any branch, stub, or fallen over tree that leapt up before him. Leaves cracked and drops of moisture were flung from his boots as they pumped through the forest floor. He had almost caught up to the elk when he saw that it was starting to veer from its path. Hectore knew he couldn't stop and guarantee a kill through the trees so he followed the elk for as long as he could. In the blink of an eye, the creature changed directions and was separating itself from Hectore quickly. This was it, his last chance. The elk was getting away. Hectore cried out as his legs pumped with unnatural speed.

He closed such a large distance in so little time that he was soon running beside the elk, red-faced and puffing. If he had drawn a blade of some sort, he could have maybe stabbed its artery, but all of his blades were on his horse. Hectore did have an arrow in his hand, however, and was considering the right spot to aim for to not waste his attempt. That was when the elk became aware of Hectore's proximity. In another blink of an eye, it sprang almost perpendicular into a clearing of moss-covered ground where a large maple had recently toppled. Hectore quickly nocked the arrow to the bow before he leapt with his right foot onto the tree's broken stump then bound to a massive boulder with a flat rock face. His left foot absorbed the contact and he pushed off of it with all of his remaining strength. He was almost ten feet up now, spinning as he soared through the air to get the elk in his sights one last time. He pulled back the bowstring ever so smoothly to his cheek again, and this time without hesitation, he released his arrow. The snap from the string vibrated in a low tenor as the arrow took to the air with a high-pitched "whissss".

The thin razor tip of the arrowhead dug itself deep into the elk and it keeled over, face first, tumbling to the ground in a sad display. Hectore landed with his bow hand out for balance. As he approached the elk, the trees nearby began to rustle. Moments later, Kael, Raphael, and Arlahn emerged from a small cluster of shrubs. Arlahn stood wide-eyed in amazement that his father had slain such a monster with a single arrow.

"Way to go, Arlahn, you almost made father lose that one," Kael snapped in annoyance. "Why did he have to come with us anyway? We would'a been home by now if it wasn't for him always slowing us down and scaring away the one animal we see."

"Kael, he's the same age you were when I first brought you hunting. Remember? The first time we went out, you and your brother were excited too. We missed two hares that day," Hectore said, trying to turn the attention away from Arlahn.

"I don't remember missing any hares," Kael said surely.

"You don't remember because you didn't see them run off."

"I remember we were out hunting once and it had just got to the good part, and then we had to go back home because Arlahn was born. He managed to ruin that hunt too," Raphael complained.

"See! It is always his fault!" Kael bellowed in a tone that seemed unbearably fractious to Arlahn.

"IT IS NOT!" he cried out in a fit, eyes welling up. Arlahn crossed his arms and pouted, his face trying to resist crying in front of his brothers.

"Stop tormenting your brother. We weren't hunting then, Raph. That was only a test. We were coming home from your Culture Walk," Hectore reminded them.

Typical sibling rivalry, the king told himself. Hectore ordered Kael and Raphael to fetch the horses, explaining how to track their own steps along the forest floor. It would be easy enough, given the careless haste they made during the chase.

Arlahn walked closer to the animal that Hectore had felled. Its antlers looked to him like tree branches that had been broken off, sharpened, and melded to the animal's scalp. He studied the thicker fur that encompassed the elk's neck and head. It was a darker shade of brown than the rest of the chestnut-colored body.

"Don't get too close yet," his father warned sitting down to rest a good distance away. "It may still have a touch of life and could be dangerous. And it deserves its peace."

Arlahn looked at the arrow protruding from the elk's ribs. It was as thick as his finger, and almost half of its length was plunged into the beast. The tears that had previously welled up in his eyes fell as the young boy began weeping quietly for the creature.

Ah, the innocence of children. I hope you don't change, son, Hectore thought to himself. "It won't be long now," the King told him instead.

After several heartbeats, the silence was broken.

"Was it easy?" his son asked him.

"Killing should never be easy, son. Remember what I told you? It's a serious thing to take a life. Any life." Just then, the beast let out one last bellow of a sigh and rested its head down with its final breath.

"It's alright now," Hectore said, approaching. He knelt and placed a gloved hand on the elk's neck. "Be at peace. Your sacrifice is honoured," the king told the animal.

"It's a difficult spot to hit." He pointed at the arrow for better clarification. "Heavy bones like the head and shoulders are too strong for an arrow to kill an animal like this. But bigger animals have soft spots too, just like everything and everyone in this world, Arlahn. See this?"

With great effort, Hectore braced his feet against the fallen maple next to the elk, and pushing with all his strength, he rolled the elk on its back. Arlahn could see the razor tip of the arrowhead through the side of the elk's chest.

"My arrow went in here, between the ribs," his finger followed the arrow on the outside of the carcass, "through his lung and pierced into his heart. It's not what you call an easy death, but it's quick... Arlahn, everything in life has meaning and value. This animal didn't die for nothing. We put almost everything in this body to use. Its meat will feed us, which keeps us alive and healthy, and its fur will keep us warm in the cold. But that's not even the tiniest sliver of its true value. While it lived, it played a role in this world so subtle, yet so complex, that no one can even begin to *truly* understand it." Hectore knew this lesson was beyond the five-year-old's capacity, but he also knew that he would remember its essence, and he trusted that Arlahn would someday understand its implications. "Think back to the scratches it made on the tree. That tree will now heal those wounds and be stronger for it. And that tree, too, is playing its own role in the world, and it has intentions of its own. We're all here for a reason, son. I don't know how else I can explain it. That maple continuously battles in a silent war with all the nearby trees to be the closest to the sun. All the while, if you look close enough, you'll find that the tree is home to the countless lives of bugs and critters. We're all connected in ways that you wouldn't imagine. When we do certain things, there's a ripple that spreads further than you know."

Just then, Kael and Raphael returned with the horses. Together they gutted and quartered the elk and loaded the hide, meat, and other useful tissues and bones onto one of the mounts. While Arlahn rode with his father back to the castle, they continued to talk. "Father, how come you like to take us hunting so much? I mean, we're the royal family. We have enough food to feed our whole city," Arlahn asked justly.

"There's a reason why I teach all these things to you and your brothers," Hectore replied

"Yeah? And why is that?" Arlahn demanded

"Because I'm a king. Not only that, I'm the HighKing. I rule over five realms. In order to understand your people, you have to sometimes live like your people. Experience their struggle. So many influences will shape you. Everyone I met either did or tried to do something with me. Some were trying to help, while others tried to hurt. No matter what I was given though, Arlahn, I always had a choice. I chose to make the best with what I had. At one point, things weren't so great for the people of Saintos. There was a wicked ruler, bent on his belief of entitled power, covering the land in chaos. Then one day, I met a man. For some reason he found me, like fate. He told me I could save them all. But first I had to save myself. To find food and shelter. Then he told me to find my *amiro*, that your mother was the key." Hectore looked down to see if Arlahn was still paying attention. He was. "I took up my claim to the throne and stopped at nothing until I reunited the people of Saintos. Do you see where I'm going?"

"Nope! But keep talking, I like to hear." Arlahn wasn't ashamed to admit he didn't understand the underlying moral in his father's story. He was young and knew he still had much to learn.

"What I'm telling you Arlahn, is that you must be willing to rise up and meet challenges without the fear of failing. You must even be ready to challenge them back when you need to. But everything happens here for a reason and everything has a role to play. You must consider what will come of your actions. The length of their effect on others around you. If I can teach you boys all I know, you will become even better men than me." Hectore's smile was long and thin. He laughed inwardly at the blissful ignorance painted across Arlahn's face and tussled the boy's hair. Arlahn grinned back. His son had a knack for making him smile. "But I've already forgotten more than you'll ever know."

Chapter 5

Three horses slowed to a walk down the path, one in the lead, two trailing slightly. The riders were men, all wearing hooded cloaks the grey of dense smoke. The lead rider carried a deer behind him on his horse and a greatsword sheathed to its flank. One rear rider, with a bow slung over his shoulder, had a boar tied down behind him. The third man, who was unarmed, simply rode gracefully along with the party.

The cloaked hunters were blocked by a band of horsemen loitering across the path, playing games of knucklebones and jostling one another. Other men cooked and moved around casually as if they had made this path their home. Most of them were dressed in boiled leather that had been weather-beaten and torn. As the hunters drew to a halt, they waited. The lead rider looked around at the group blocking the way, none of whom paid him any mind, trying to identify their leader. Finally, he demanded, "Why is the path blocked?"

A man came forward. He had a seasoned look about him with silver beginning to dominate his hair. He wore brown leggings, torn at the knees, and a matching brown dust-beaten leather jerkin. "Because this is Grosmon's path now, young fella. And if you want to pass, I suggest you give us your mounts and wares. It's a one-sided deal, I'll admit, but at least you keep your lives." The man named Grosmon cocked his head and smiled an ugly, arrogant smile with crooked teeth that were stained all the shades of yellow and brown.

The swordsman on the lead horse looked slowly to the archer on his right, then over to the unarmed man on his left. Together, all three smoothly dismounted from their horses and stood firmly by their steeds. The unarmed man placed a hand on his gelding's neck, and the archer studied the group, while the swordsman rested a forearm on his greatsword's cross-guard. "Bandits then," he said. "And I assume that if we refuse your generous offer, you'll be forced to refrain from sparing our lives?"

"Sharp as a tack this one is, eh fellas?" Grosmon said before he gave them another hideous smile. The crowd behind him exploded in raucous laughter.

That was enough to make the swordsman draw his steel. It was a massive, menacing thing – a two-handed greatsword with a blade as long as his leg. It shone in the daylight as the sun, sitting high in the clear blue sky, broke through the treetops in skinny slants.

"Ah, ah, easy now. You can see there's seven o' us. We've got you two-to-one. Unless you mean to give up your steel, but such a pretty sword needs its scabbard, I think." The man kept his hideous smile but turned to his companions. Each of them had paced to their horse since the start of the conversation and now had their hands on sword hilts, axes, and a spear, waiting.

"Please, there's no need for bloodshed. Just let us pass and we'll part peacefully," pleaded a soft voice, coming from the unarmed man.

The lead rider stabbed his thick blade into the ground and raised his hand for silence, his sword dancing back and forth slightly in front of him. "These men don't bargain."

"Well that's not all true y'know." The leader of the bandits' voice was scabrous as he began walking slowly toward them, hands on his hips. "But the chances of you leaving here without doing what we say are—" His right arm was up in a flash, dagger in hand, its path directed at the swordsman's throat.

But a hand shot out from behind the man's cloak and caught Grosmon's wrist. With blistering speed, another hand shot out, grasping his forearm, and he began to cry out in pain. With movements like a lightning bolt, the swordsman reversed the direction of the blade, and Grosmon's cry transformed into a gasping breath. The pepper-haired bandit stumbled back and looked down to see that he was stabbing himself in the chest with his own broken arm. Red beads dripped from his mouth onto his hand before he toppled to the ground, dead.

The swordsman transferred his gaze to the other enemies. They had drawn their weapons and were beginning to descend on the three men. A black arrow shaft tore into the spear wielder's throat and he staggered backward, falling flat on his back with blood gurgling from both wound and mouth. The archer drew another arrow to his bow from the quiver on his mount's side, turning slightly to raise an eyebrow at his companion.

"Always have to initiate everything, don't you?" he said with a hint of sarcasm, nocking the arrow to his bowstring.

The swordsman ripped his own blade from the earth, taking up the weapon in both hands. "As if I had a choice?" He gestured to the man slumped on the ground with the knife buried in his chest up to the hilt. Lowering his sword, he lunged forward, stabbing the closest attacker on his left and disembowelling him, nearly six feet away.

One bandit raised his axe to hack the swordsman's flank when an arrow struck him in the ribs under his armpit. His flinch was enough of a pause for the swordsman to elbow him full in the face, snapping his head back, and the man fell to the ground, coughing up blood before the end of the greatsword punched into his chest.

Two more bandits turned to the swordsman, who was now clearly the greatest threat, and came down on him together pushing him back half a step. One of the men was over-anxious and came at the swordsman ruthlessly, only to have his scream cut off with the rest of his head. The other bandit wailed and swung overhead at their attacker's back, but without a moment's hesitation the unarmed man, who had so far been cautiously watching the situation, reached around his waistband and pulled out a pearl blade. An ornate dagger blocked the bandit's steel just inches before it struck an exposed shoulder. The previously unarmed man tightened his grip with both hands and held the bandit's blade in its place long enough for the swordsman to strafe to his side. Before he could deliver a punishing blow, a black arrow shaft drove itself into the man's chest, and he fell to his knees and slumped over. Six bandits now lay dead on the ground. The last, with disbelief and terror written clear across his face, fumbled and stumbled onto his horse and fled past the three warriors, flying between the archer and his ammunition.

The hooded riders stood a moment in complete silence, then replaced their weapons. Now that they were alone, they removed their hoods, and although all three men looked different in their own right, they all shared a set of common features. The dagger wielder had the same sharp, dark brow as the others but was clean-shaven, his shoulder-length hair clinging to his forehead. He knelt beside the dead man before him, his soft chestnut eyes looking at the dead ones staring back at him. He gently closed the lids and said, in a most pious tone, "Be at peace," then rose.

"Come, Arlahn, we've been gone all day, don't waste time now," the swordsman told him.

Arlahn took a step forward and looked around with penitent eyes. He turned to the swordsman, who had just replaced his weapon in its scabbard, and stormed over to him. "What's wrong with you Kael, we just killed these men? *That* was our only waste of time."

Kael sniffed. At six foot he was a few inches taller than his younger brother, with dark hair, like their father's, that he kept short to avoid the same curl. His chin was covered with a full black beard, which made the contrast of his ice-blue eyes stand out. Re-cinching his scabbard to his horse, Kael said, "They were cutthroat bandits. They got what they deserved. Besides, if they had been any good at it, if they were smart, I mean, they would have surrendered. Losing a finger is better than a head." He reached out and tapped a detached head with his boot.

Arlahn hammered his brother hard across his jaw. Before he could assess the ramifications, he felt the boulder that was Kael's fist slam his ribcage and was thrown to the ground with tremendous force. The breath leapt from his chest upon impact, and he gasped desperately to get it back.

"Why?!" Kael demanded, suddenly furious. He stared down at his winded brother for a moment then walked away, shaking his head. The archer, Raphael, said nothing but watched his twin stalk off. He recognized the frustration in Kael's mirroring features. Raphael replaced his bow and walked over to Arlahn, offering him a hand.

His brother winced in resonant pain and took up the offered hand to help his feet find solid ground again. "They didn't... have to die..." he managed through struggled breaths.

"Yes brother, they did," Kael told him, turning around.

"We could have just told them who we were."

"Did you not hear their leader?" Kael interrupted. "If we told them that we're the Princes, they probably would have just demanded a double toll, knowing we are good for it. If we hadn't paid them, they were going to attack us."

Raphael raised his hands as if displaying the path around them like a picture. "And if they had stopped someone else brother, would it not be the blood of the innocent spilled on the earth?"

Arlahn knew there was no use arguing – Raphael's logic was always sound. Still, something inside him believed that there could have been a peaceful alternative to what had transpired here. All he could think of now was that they would have to explain all this to the king and it would just further complicate their father's already complicated agenda. He hung his head in defeat and looked back at his brothers in his periphery. He couldn't bear to look them in the eye. These two men, who were only a few years ahead of him in age, were leaps and bounds ahead of him in *life*. His brothers never faltered. They were men of greatness. True Rai men, Arlahn thought. The kind all his childhood stories told of.

Kael and Raphael's Gifts manifested at a very young age and their power proliferated much more quickly than normal.

Raphael, Gifted with *mniman,* had an incredible perspective of situations and was a genius tactician. Although he could never quite articulate the effects of his Gift, even to himself, his usual description was that the *mniman* seemingly gave him a "third-person" perspective of his surroundings, almost a bird's eye view with complete objectivity. He didn't mean this literally, of course – he could no longer remember what it was like to not see through the *mniman* – but he knew he saw things differently than other men. Armed as such, many a bard's tale sang of his exploits during the Corduranese Invasion, where he defended the city to victory against a force many times larger than his own. The way his brothers told it, their uncle and Warden of the East, Benson Wellcant, was removed from the battle when a stray arrow caught him in the shoulder. With Benson being tended to, Kael took a reserve and led them thrashing into the fray, leaving Raphael behind in command. It was just like Kael to initiate and Raphael to observe. Raphael assumed control of the army and found himself playing their childhood game Battlegrounds but where the stakes were realistically grave. Being able to subconsciously calculate when and where to sacrifice, allocate, and reserve his military resources with inexplicable precision, Raphael controlled the battle better than any veteran general.

But it would not have been nearly so easy without his brother at the forefront. Kael had achieved more of a physical prowess, dominating that battlefield for his brother. Since then, he had never entered a combat tournament without taking home championship hardware. Kael maintained the stature of a tall, athletic soldier, however his frame was illusive, for it contained giant-like strength. The *kjut'tsir*, Kael's Gift, gave him a raw physical strength that was unmatched by any man that Kael had ever known. And the misdirection caused by his slight frame was almost as powerful as his unnatural strength.

They were seen as mere boys before the Corduranese Invasion but were known far and wide as great and fearless leaders thereafter. Arlahn, on the other hand, having entered his twenties now, still hadn't manifested his Gift. It shamed him to always be living in the shadows of his brothers, for not only were they masters of their Gifts, but they also wielded them with great reverence and never abused their power in the name of vanity or personal gain.

Arlahn looked up at Kael, seeing that his fury had only lasted the moment. He approached his brother and swung his arms around him in a gentle but firm embrace. Pulling himself away, he turned to Raphael, then back toward Kael. "You're right. I'm sorry, brothers. Forgive me." His head dipped in shame once again.

Kael punched his brother's shoulder, lightly this time and Arlahn looked up to meet the sapphire eyes. "There is nothing to forgive, brother. You've done nothing wrong. You saved my life today. I won't ever forget that. You just care deeply, Arlahn. It's something I've always admired you for. But sometimes you let yourself care too much."

"It isn't your fault," Raphael added, "it's just that sometimes you seem to live in one of your childhood bed tales, where the good always beats the evil."

"And why can't good win over evil? Why doesn't love conquer hate?" Arlahn countered defensively, trailing his last words, almost feeling like a child again.

"Because you can't trust that love will stop a man who's running at you with an axe. Some men are just genuinely evil. For some reason, they like it. It makes them feel powerful," Raphael explained. "Think of the men who attacked Marly's parents. Did they get what they deserved?"

"They did," Arlahn yielded. He knew the story of his sister-to-be, who had been attacked in their carriage from a group of leftover warriors after the Damonai were repelled out of the city. Raphael, Kael, and a cohort of men had arrived just before the bandits had raped Marlyonna but too late to save her mother and father. With her parents slain, Marlyonna had lived with the Rais since that fateful day, and soon after, she and Raphael discovered a passion that would bloom into an engagement.

"It's like Kael said, they could have chosen a punishment from father. A finger *is* better than a head."

"Speaking of Kael..." Arlahn trailed off as he looked around, noticing his brother had disappeared.

Just then, as if he'd heard his name, Kael emerged from a bush beside the trail and Arlahn gave him a confused look. "Where'd you go?"

"I cleared the bodies," Kael answered.

Arlahn looked and noticed only the blood on the ground. Even the bandits' excess gear was gone, only horses remained.

"Do we want to know where?" Raphael asked carefully.

"Probably not."

"You've always worked fast, I guess," Raph noted, dropping the matter. "Help me tie the reins to one another."

Raphael pulled a coil of hempen rope from a clamp on his saddle. The other two men did the same, and the brothers tied the bandit's horses together in a chain. With everything secure, Kael walked to his mount and climbed into the saddle, then tapped his steed's hide and began to trot away. The others followed suit, with Arlahn trailing as he pulled the train of horses gently behind the trio.

It was early evening and the sun had painted the distant snow-capped mountains red, orange, and purple when Kael, Raphael, and Arlahn strode through the great city's second wall. The crowd of people in the wide cobbled streets was thinning quickly as shopkeepers, blacksmiths, apothecaries, and a variety of stands were closing up for the night. Meanwhile, the pubs and inns were just beginning to arm up their hearths. Hooves clapped on the cobblestone as the Princes trotted through the streets. Their eyes met momentarily with several of their Kalendare, the elite under-cover protectors of royalty.

The townsfolk watched with admiring eyes as their young princes rode in. They were proud to live among such exceptional men and applauded their presence.

Entering through the gates of the third wall of Pellence, Arlahn turned a sharp right and returned the newly acquired horses to the stables. In front of the doorway stood a stout man with a heavy untamed beard, his burly arms crossed before his chest.

"Take these horses. Please find good men to ride them," Arlahn said graciously to the stable head, who looked perplexed. Six horses? He knew the man was wondering where they had come from. Avoiding any questions, Arlahn turned swiftly to leave.

"Hmm, oh yes, these do look like fine horses, my prince," the stout man noted just in time before the Prince left.

Arlahn ignored the remark and walked out.

Rejoining his brothers before the palace gate, they walked in and handed their horses off. Kael carried the boar over his shoulders like it weighed no more than a pillow. While Raphael and Arlahn struggled with the doe. They carried the animals through the main foyer, then down a hallway to their left into the kitchen area, where they relieved themselves of their loads. The in-house butchers immediately stopped what they were doing to begin cleaning and quartering the animals, lest the meat spoil and go to waste.

The brothers returned to the hall, where a short, colonnaded wall allowed for the overwhelming beauty of the atrium to be seen.

Arlahn left his brothers and walked into the open space. The shrubs had been trimmed into sculptures and painted with blooming flowers every year since he was a child. After each spring, sculptors would come from all over to clip the hedges in the palace atrium into something new and exotic. He walked between a rabbit made of white camelias and a jumping fish of delphiniums and mint, then made his way to the centre of the room. Next to a squirrel and his acorn, there was a large round basin, made entirely of stone, with water arcing from the mouths of exquisitely detailed angelic figures positioned around its perimeter. At the centre of the basin stood a beautiful marble sculpture of a naked woman with a flawless face. Water coursed from the tips of her hair, down her stone body, and into the pool below.

Arlahn loved being in the atrium. When he was a younger boy, he would run through the sculptures pretending they were real as he played with his brothers. During the winter months, some of the same sculptors would come back and carve statues from ice, but the stone woman remained eternal. He closed his eyes and drew a long breath, allowing the sounds of water to fill and wash his mind clear. He felt at peace listening to the serene sounds of the fountain, pouring, splashing, and swirling calmly. With his eyes closed, it became the only sound that filled the world. Meditating for those few moments helped cleanse the Prince from the frustration that lingered after his encounter with the bandits.

He was disturbed by a young servant girl, who presented him with a goblet of Illium wine. Illium grapes were the finest in all of Tehbirr, revered for their color and sweetness. "Your brothers are looking for you outside your King Father's study, my prince."

"Thank you," Arlahn said, taking a gulp and handing the goblet back to the young brunette. "Have the rest, if you like, it's very good."

He turned, giving the fountain one last look, then left.

Arlahn found his brothers outside the king's study. "Ah! You're here. Come on, we're going to tell Father about the bandits," Raphael told him.

They opened the double wooden doors to the study and found Hectore sitting behind an oversized oak desk. He was getting older now, Arlahn saw, but only on the surface. What had once been black curls were now highlighted by silver. His face was still kind and yet strong, but over the years it had become a little weathered. Despite the countless conflicts he had survived, his face still bore only a single scar, horizontally just below his right eye.

"Boys!" Hectore greeted them warmly. "Tell me a story of your hunt."

"Father, do we have a story for you!" Arlahn told him, taking a seat.

The three brothers took turns telling the story. First, there was the beautiful shot Raphael made that dropped the doe. The boar was brought down by two wounds, one arrow from Raphael, and a spear skewer from Kael. Then they told him of their run-in with the bandits on their return but none of them mentioned the following disagreement.

"I'm glad you boys stuck together. Sounds like you all saved each other. That is good to hear at least. Where did you say the last bandit fled?" Hectore asked.

"South, southeast, my King," Kael answered, more as a soldier than a son. "He'll probably just find another gang to run with, petty criminals. Should we prepare a search party to track him down?"

"No, he'll do his best to avoid the public now. But this is the third bandit encounter in the last three months."

"They're growing bolder?" Raphael suggested to his father.

"Perhaps, how was the game hunting?" he asked then.

"It was a bit sparse actually. Brought down the only two animals we saw all day. Nothing really small and common like grouse or rabbit though."

Hectore took that bit of information and chewed on it. "Either the bandits are growing bolder. Or it's something else. Something worse."

*****

The woman was gorgeous. She had jet-black hair that hung loosely curled about her shoulders. Her skin was as soft as satin, and her ocean - blue eyes beamed through the domino mask of intricate lace that noble Essellian women wore. Dressed in a long overcoat with three golden buttons, trimmed with fur about the wrists and hood. Her heels clip-clopped against the stone as she walked down the torchlit streets and turned into an underpass.

Instantly, she felt a hand grab her arm and pull her in. She was about to scream when another hand clamped down over her mouth. "Quiet, you little bitch!" the man hissed behind her, slamming her into the column of an arch.

He let go of the woman's arm and grabbed her handbag. Chances were it had few coins or anything of value, but little was better than none. The young woman ripped the bag back from the thief and stomped her pointed heel into his foot then drove an elbow into his stomach. The man winced in pain as she ran back into the streets.

At each intersection, she passed, more and more evil-looking men were stirring in the shadows of the Essellian streets. Of course, "evil-looking" is subjective, but each had a menacing look in his eyes and an obvious purpose – to bar any path of escape. As her desperation grew, the woman glanced around frantically then ran into the darkness of a narrow, unobstructed alley. Her attacker limped into the middle of the empty street.

He was furious. "Go get her! Bring her back to me, I'm gonna have fun with this one now."

Five of the rogues left their posts and followed the woman into the alleyway while the thief stood, waiting alone in the middle of the street. A series of strange noises echoed out of the darkness, followed by low grunts. Slightly confused, he took a step forward. "I said bring her to me. I'm going to break her!" He was contemplating walking into the alley himself when a man stumbled back into the light, a throwing knife plunged into his neck.

A slim figure emerged behind him, dressed in black from head to toe. Its loose-fitting clothes allowed free range of movement, in spite of the arsenal of weapons that were strapped all over the assassin.

Confounded only for the slightest moment, the thief drew a long dagger from his side. "Come at me assassin, and I'll see your head severed from your body," he threatened.

The dark figure paused a moment. "Your delusion is amusing. It's funny how your little *haiku* comes so close to the truth of what's about to happen, only you have the subjects reversed." The voice was somewhat muffled by the black garment covering the killer's face, but it sounded high-pitched and adolescent. "See, *assassins* have marks. Marks can be missed. You, thief, aren't so lucky to have an assassin standing before you. Our kind is fewer and farther between."

"*Deaders...*" the thief's voice was suddenly thin and weak, as if something from myth had become reality before his very eyes.

The deader unclipped from their waist a black circular cloth with a length of rope attached. "I liken it to the difference between a line cook and a chef. We both kill for a living, but assassins do it *à la carte*, we do it made-to-order. See, thief, there's an art to killing a leader such as you. Steps that have to be completed to ensure a clean kill. First, you make sure the deadee feels empowered, enter the young woman you thought was a victim. Second, you need to cut communication so that there's no support coming to help. Your men are already dead. Third, you isolate the deadee." The assassin stepped toward the leader who was now quivering in fear. "And I'm sure you've already figured out what happens next."

"DeathShadow." The man registered who he was talking to. He looked about to see that his remaining three men were already dead where they stood. He'd never believed the myth, but now, face to face, he knew what was about to happen. He only hoped the end was swift.

"Worse. His Wraith."

The black figure started walking toward the man, picking up speed. Silent as a ghost, footsteps turned into a full sprint. The thief lashed out with his dagger but the deader was incredibly fast. With movements utterly unresolvable in the darkness, the deader disarmed the thief, slapping the dagger from his hand, and swung a heavy kick into the side of the man's knee. He stumbled, but before his knees touched the ground, the deader had dropped the black cloth over his head. The thief saw fabric fall before his eyes, and nothing more.

The deader nimbly mounted the victim's shoulders and took up the length of rope, whose other end was woven around the fringes of the cloth and now wrapped around the thief's neck. As the deader heaved, he jumped off the man's shoulders, spun, and leapt back to the ground with the guillotine hood flying away at the end of the rope. The man on his knees sat headless. Two big gushes of blood pumped out from his neck, and he slumped over.

With several quick flicks of the wrist, the deader released the tension on the rope and the man's head rolled out to the ground. Wraith walked over to the corpse beside the alley from whence he came and recovered the throwing knife, cleaning it on the dead man's clothes. Then the Deader ran and high-stepped onto a barrel, leapt to a stand, and sprung up the building beside it, side-scaling the wall in seconds like a big black ant.

In just a few short minutes, Wraith had left the Essellian street littered with nine dead bodies. The apprentice had left no surviving witnesses. The master would be pleased.

Silence grew in the night.

Wraith hopped down from the walls of the city of Esselle, hood still shrouding his features, and made his way to a fallen tree in the nearby woods. The great fir had torn out of the ground at the roots and wiggling through them, Wraith slipped down into the safe house underneath. Mordo had safe houses all around Saintos where he could elude any pursuers. DeathShadow could walk as a ghost, invisible, but not forever. Wraith had seen the master bedridden once from sustaining his Power for too long. The young killer was thankful to not have a Power. Though the master did not share this attitude. The apprentice had to train for years before Mordo trusted him. His tutelage was strict. Together they trained in places like this, in the forests under the shadow of darkness. Wraith had only recently been granted permission to carry out the kill command alone.

He replaced the guillotine hat on a root knob and found a rolled-up parchment left on the lone table.

Mordo had left a note. It was written in a script that only Shadow and Wraith could understand. Wraith interpreted it:

"Gone to speak with Evris. Once the thief is killed in Esselle tell the merchant Pical he can continue his night trade with us. We're expecting a sensitive package. Watch him though. I think you're right, he's getting soft. Stay in the area and await my return Wraith. DS"

Chapter 6

A wooden blade was hefted at his neck. Kael ducked it, his own practice blade sliding across the man's belly. Six more men were in a semi-circle around Kael. He was holding a wooden replica of his broadsword, trimmed and studded in a tungsten alloy to simulate its weight, though everything felt like a needle to the Prince. It was almost midday now. Birds flew in the air high above and the clouds were a heavenly white. Their lazy drift across the sky contrasted the adrenaline-induced frenzy in Kael's heart.

The Prince stood balanced, both hands gripping the leather strapped around the wooden hilt. The six men started to engage. Kael side-stepped and parried into a riposte, stopping a decapitating blow at the first man's neck. The second trainer made his move, thrusting for the Prince's belly. But Kael flicked his wrist – not a normal feat for someone holding a claymore – and spun the spear up out of his attacker's hand. As the man reached in vain to maintain his grip, Kael jabbed his sword between the man's side and arm, purposely deflecting the tip off of his plate-mail to avoid injuring him too badly. One trainer managed to land a blow on Kael's flank then. The Prince spun round in an instant, switching blade hands to his left to drag the metal along the attacker's throat, and punched him in his chest. Using his momentum, he grabbed the man with his right hand, and Kael hurled him as gently as he could into two of the remaining men around him. Those three would be getting the next day off.

The next few seconds were swift. Kael dispatched the rest of the trainers, starting with the one standing, finishing with the ones on the ground, wrestling the man's body off them. He was testing himself. The encounter between his brothers and the bandits had fascinated Kael and he needed to know if he could have defeated them alone. He was the most prestigious fighter in Pellence, and perhaps all of Saintos or even Tehbirr, aside from his father, Hectore. He had never encountered a real opponent that could truly test him in a fight, and it was not for lack of trying. Since he was a boy, Kael had picked fights. He was always looking for a challenge, but Hectore was his only real superior when duelling. Only what Kael was to everyone else, Hectore was to Kael. Although the king was getting older now, the two would duel in private once a year, and Kael could never land anything but a glancing blow on his father, even after his father encouraged him to use his Gift.

Arlahn walked into the training ground, wooden sword in one hand and a practice dirk in the other, glaring at Kael. "Teach me!" he demanded. He had donned the sand-coloured training gear most men were wearing.

Kael looked at his baby brother. He bore a strong resemblance to how the king must have looked when he was the same age. Smaller than the average soldier, but still a strong core and stronger shoulders. His wavy brown hair was getting long.

"Alright," Kael agreed after a moment, "but you know I can only teach you form and technique. The strength that I have in me doesn't grow in you."

"I don't care about your strength, Father doesn't have it either. So long as I can move like you. My dagger's never lost its edge. I don't need your strength to protect myself. I need to be better. Like you and Raph."

"Alright then brother, show me what you know."

The two princes circled one another. Kael was moving slowly, observing every move Arlahn made, complimenting Arlahn's graceful movements as they reflected his own. Finally, they began. The sound of wood against wood clat-clat-clattering filled the training ground as other soldiers gathered around to watch this dance between brothers. Cheers and wagers started amongst the crowd of swarming men. Soon there were more of them than blackflies on dung.

Arlahn was not the worst of fighters by any means. He would challenge any veteran soldier but would also probably make the first clumsy mistake and die. He knew this and constantly tried to fix those mistakes. He would polish himself to shine so he could no longer be in the shadows of his brothers – Arlahn wanted nothing more than to revered at their level. Kael, on the other hand, had fought, killed, and survived through a great battle in Corduran. His Gift, the *kjut'tsir*, fuelled his muscles making him resolutely fearless, giving him an unquenchable thirst to experience. He was faster and considerably stronger than the average soldier. In short, he was abominable in single combat.

"Your footwork is sound brother, but your defence is too weak," Kael told him. "Are you planning on fighting without a shield all the time?"

"Father fights with two swords. Seems to me the best defence is offence."

At that moment, Arlahn lunged forward with an impressive riposte. Thrusting and cutting, making quick, short slashes left and right, stabbing high and low with his dirk at Kael, in a manner that would have perhaps left another man on the ground. But not Kael. Keeping pace, he back-stepped and parried until he could counter riposte with a move that would have decapitated Arlahn, the wooden sword resting on his brother's shoulder. Kael had no intention to demean him in front of the crowd that had gathered, so he withdrew quickly and circled again.

"Offence can be the best defence if you mind your spacing. Stay at blades length until you're ready. That dagger has to be your shield now, keep it up all the time. Trust your instincts."

Once more, the tick-tock sound of wood striking wood began. It was rare to see the brothers duel for this long, but then again, this was more than a mere training exercise, it was a lesson. Several times their swords clashed and each time the crowd would erupt. Often neither would gain on the other, but now and then Kael would land a quick blow on Arlahn, only to recover quickly and resume instruction. On the rare occasion Arlahn would barely touch one of his blades to his brother's skin, he had to be on his guard the most. Kael never spared a second giving better than he got after someone touched him in a fight.

Arlahn usually reacted by leaping backward frantically, trying to deflect every blow the best he could, but Kael's attacks were relentless and would always result in Arlahn being knocked down and winded with a new bruise. Arlahn had sparred with Kael enough times to know whether or not his brother's strikes were channelled through the *kjut'tsir*. It seemed more like a sixth sense to Kael, rather than something that he consciously controlled. Whenever he needed an extra bit of spring in his movements, the *kjut'tsir* was just there without needing to be asked.

Their bodies glistening with sweat from the hot sun and over an hour's exhaustion, the brothers retired to the armoury where several large barrels had been filled with water. Forming a cup with his hands, Arlahn drank several mouthfuls then splashed some on his face. He leaned against the barrel and took loud, deep breaths as one often does after quenching their thirst during strenuous exercise. The sound of a door closing came from behind him. Grabbing a fresh cream-coloured shirt from a stack on a bench and pulling it over his head, Arlahn looked to his brother. "I want to visit PJ's mountain" he said suddenly.

Kael, who had been replacing his practice sword, ceased all movement as if a bee had just landed on his nose. He raised only his eyes to glare at Arlahn out of the corners. But he could see nothing but earnestness in his brother's expression. "Arlahn, you can't just *go visit* PJ."

"Why not? I've seen you and Raphael leave for his camp a few times, and every time you come back you seem to be even more inexorable."

"Inexorable?" Kael chuckled. "I think you've spent too much time with Raph."

"It means impossible to stop."

"I know what it means. Sadly no one's spent more time with our brother than me. I was there when he learned half those fancy words in Esselle. I suffered all those tedious lessons."

"You didn't have to go. Raphael went 'cause he wanted to learn," Arlahn pointed out.

"I know, but it's not just the books in the city that'll teach you things, there's a night life there. I found it eventually, or created it maybe, now that I think about it..." His voice trailed as he remembered his time there, "either way. My point is suffering is always easier when you have someone you know to do it with. But it's not the same suffering that you do with PJ. In the mountains, you really are alone. And no man's impossible to stop, Arlahn. That's one thing you learn."

"You know what I mean. It changes your drive to train, the way you think."

"I'm a student of war, brother. That's what's in my nature. You're a student of beauty and love. And I know you think so, but there's no shame in that. Without people like you, people like me forget why we fight. Until eventually it becomes butchery."

A familiar voice joined the conversation from behind them. "Arlahn, some of the training that happens in his camp is treacherous... or maybe unorthodox is a better word. And you know that lately more and more bandits are taking to the pathways in the forests," Hectore spoke as he entered the armoury, dressed in a leather doublet with a deep red undershirt. He walked over to the water barrel.

"I'm not afraid of some bandits!" Arlahn interjected.

"No, I suppose you wouldn't be. I saw you two duelling just now."

Before Arlahn had a chance to justify his position, Hectore was already speaking.

"You were both impressive. I could feel the inspiration growing among the soldiers that were watching. That's a powerful thing. Bregan seems to be quite the riot-starter. He's so much like his father! He had betting going before you two even finished your first circle. They're going to be proud to serve under men like you." His smile broadened as he turned to Arlahn. "Pientero is a hard man. But I'm sure that after I tell him of what I saw here today he'll accept training you. Normally for the Rais, he waits until after your *Gift* has surfaced. But in truth, he's never denied me a reasonable request. Can I ask you though, why do you want to see him now?"

Kael gladly conceded that the issue was now in his father's hands. He splashed some water on his face and exited the armoury, leaving the king with his brother. That was when Hectore went to sit on a bench.

"The first thing you need to know is that my friend's camp is a Brotherhood, one large family. And like our family, once you're born into it, you're theirs. And once you get there, you can't leave until PJ says you can."

Arlahn waited the few seconds it took for Kael to close the door before he answered.

"I'm tired of being just their little brother, never living up to them. I want to find my way."

"Ever since you could walk you've followed your brothers. I could have sworn you wanted so badly to be their third twin. Maybe it is time you turn from their path and take your own."

"If only I knew how. I'm tired of all the praise they get for being Gifted," Arlahn said, unable to shade his jealousy.

"So that's what this is about? You're upset because your Gift hasn't awakened yet? PJ can't help you with that, son."

"That's not what I'm upset about, Father. It's just hard growing up surrounded by you and Kael and Raph."

"But not because we're Gifted?"

"I know to you it sounds foolish. But please, let me go see PJ in his camp. Maybe he can help me. He helped you."

"Alright, fine," Hectore gave in reluctantly to his son's wishes.

"Really?" Arlahn asked with similar degrees of excitement and shame, revealing the very youthfulness he had been trying to hide. He thought for a brief moment, trying to anticipate what a term with PJ would be like. He suddenly grew desperate to gain at least some of the ground that he felt separated his brothers' skills from his own. "Could you not train me a bit first, so that I could be prepared for him? I just think it would be better if I had a head start. I'd learn faster that way."

"Learning fast isn't Pientero's way, learning properly is more important, he'll teach you. Like I said, his methods are unorthodox, but if you think you're ready... I'll make arrangements to go see him," Hectore said, dipping a long ladle into the water and sipping from it. "Pientero was my mentor, if there's anyone who can find your potential, it's him. Do you know what they call him outside of the Brotherhood?"

"What?" Arlahn asked automatically.

"The Poet of Battle."

"Do you think I'm ready, Father?"

"If you're willing to be," the king said, remembering his first individual lesson with Pientero.

It was a black starry night and Pientero Jessonarioko's group of soldiers were settled around campfires. They were joking and feasting on dried meat and oatmeal. The day had been a fruitful one. They had ransacked a supply wagon that had been travelling to Pellence. The city had already fallen, but the supply wagon had been dispatched from an outlying settlement before the GodKing Tumbero heard the news. The loss of a supply wagon meant nothing to the evil GodKing. Tumbero was sending his generals throughout the land, mainly to take inventory and analyze how bad things really were. Hectore and Pientero saw to it that his generals were kept busy.

A tall man with a thick brow walked up to his younger companion who was seemingly in his early twenties with jet-black hair and an almost baby-faced complexion; unscarred and smooth. "Get up, Hectore!" the older man demanded. Without hesitation or inquiry, Hectore sprang to his feet.

Together they walked away from the camp and entered into a clearing in the forest. The clouds were bunched high in the night sky but gave sufficient light to see most of what was around. Pientero made his way to the middle of the clearing. Turning on his heel, he faced Hectore. "You were pivotal in today's battle young man." His voice was strong. "But there were times where you could have done better."

Drawing a long, curved blade from his scabbard, he flipped it up, offering the hilt to Hectore. "Come. Try to hit me. I want to show you something," Pientero told him, being so cavalier that Hectore briefly passed it off as a joke. When Pientero faced Hectore with a look of intent, Hectore's stomach almost knotted.

"I'm not going to attack you with a sharpened blade, let alone while you're unarmed!" he refused.

"I know," is all Pientero said, moving the hilt closer. "You are going to swing and swing and swing at me though, in a sad attempt to attack me."

Pientero's cocky demeanour somewhat disturbed Hectore. He searched every moral fibre to articulate how much he opposed this order, but he knew that despite himself, he was at Pientero's command. A flicker of rage grew in his heart. Hectore snatched the hilt. He did an "on-guard" and swung a few lazy slashes at Pientero, obviously and intentionally off-target. With a movement faster than the eye could see, especially not in the faint light of the moon, Pientero picked the blade between his thumb and fingers and disarmed Hectore so unexpectedly that he momentarily lost his footing.

"I'm fucking serious, you little shit. I guarantee you won't hit me," Pientero said, stabbing the blade right next to Hectore's head with a furrowed brow. Hectore lurched up, took up the blade again, and this time, without warning, he lunged into a furious flurry of attacks. With each slash, thrust, and cleave, Pientero simply dodged, ducked, and side-stepped every cut, critiquing as he moved with the ease of a leaf drifting in the breeze. "You think well but your body fails you. Telegraph your movements too much, young man, and you will fall." As he finished his speech, a backhanded forearm crashed into Hectore's chest and he dropped like a sack of grain.

Extending his hand, Pientero helped Hectore back to his feet and began instructing once more. Each time the teacher found a flaw in Hectore's technique or mind frame, he would offer advice to help the young man improve. The rage that Hectore was feeling moments before quickly turned to enthusiasm. He was learning and understanding things about combat that seemed so simple, yet they were things that he would have never come to terms with on his own. This one-on-one time with Pientero was sacred. Even though the other men were revelling in their own debauchery, Hectore relished being singled out by Pientero for this special lesson. Just as the thought struck him – Why me? – Pientero stopped in admiration and said, "There's something about the way you react in battle though lad, it's most uncanny, inspiring almost. I've never seen such a thing. And believe me, Hec. I've seen more battle than a stable boy's seen horseshit."

"All I know is one thing can't be argued: His training is truly without comparison, son," Hectore told the Prince. "I'll go see him. I can't send the ravens and I can't send riders because no one can find PJ unless he wants them to. That's the way it's always been with him; you don't find him, he finds you. It's only a couple of weeks. You and your brothers can mind things while I'm gone." Hectore rose and moved toward the door, Arlahn following him. "But when he agrees to train you, remember, in the mountains you are his son as if you are mine, his word is rule."

"Thank you for going to see him for me, Father," Arlahn said. Then, straightening his posture, he continued, "I guess I should go back to the palace and begin my studies."

"There is something you need to hear though, Arlahn," his father told him before he could move. "During my campaign to regain our throne, I learned one thing that no book or man has ever taught me. It took us seven months of planning before we sacked Pellence for a final time. All that time spent in battle fighting, all the hours spent hovering over maps planning. It all comes down to a single day, even a moment sometimes. And regardless of how much training you've had, when it finally does come time to launch the assault or make that tough decision, you'll find yourself doubting every choice you've ever made. Your stomach will tie itself in knots and you'll wonder if what you're doing is the right thing. All the planning and training in the world can only get you so far."

"What do you do then?" Arlahn asked.

"Take a leap of faith," his father replied.

Arlahn thought on that for a few heartbeats then opened the door for his father when Hectore made one final remark, with gravity in his voice. "Oh, and one last thing. Don't ask Pientero about his past. It's a bitter subject, you'd do best to avoid it."

Arlahn heeded the advice and left the armoury behind the king. As he walked across the training grounds, the sun had begun to hide and daylight was running over the horizon alongside it. He was three-quarters of the way across the yard when he saw a golden-haired archer in the corner of his eye. It was Raphael, no doubt. Arlahn stood at the entranceway and watched as his brother rifled shots into a target some distance away. The first two arrows hammered home into a well-worn red-painted bullseye. Then the next few began to spread more and more until finally they reached the white circle. Confused with the results, Arlahn looked over to his brother who was now implementing his new speed-shooting technique. Holding five arrows at once with his bow hand, he would take one up by the nock, pull it down to the string, aim, and release, all in one motion. The whole process took a short breath. By the time the bowstring snapped back into place, the next arrow was already in the archer's hand. Taking his time, Raphael would bullseye arrow after arrow, but efficiency was another character his brother worked to master. Sacrificing accuracy for speed at the moment, Arlahn and Raphael knew it was only a matter of time. Practice is the pursuit to perfection, their father had told them. Arlahn watched as the shorter time his brother took between shots, the less accurate the following shot was. Raphael looked at Arlahn, cursed in clear frustration, and shook his head at him. Arlahn decided not to approach, he should study rather than watch his brother shoot, he figured and walked clear of the training area. His stomach grumbled, arguing for food instead, so Arlahn began his search through the city.

*****

The buildings were mostly two or three stories high after the city's third perimeter wall. The entire city was surrounded by four concentric tiers of walls, the outermost of which stood as a protective border, lined with high towers. The distance between the first and second walls was just enough for a battleground. Buildings were scarce between those first two walls, as the land had been turned into crop fields and the ground itself was sloped just enough to slow a horse's pace. It was designed to be a trap for any army capable enough to breach the outer wall. In fact, there were just as many murder holes and arrow loops on the inner side of the towers as there were on the outer. Inside the second wall, there were housing units and other buildings mostly organized along dirt roads and a few cobblestone avenues. The deeper into Pellence a man travelled, the more walls he'd pass through and the bigger and denser the buildings stood.

The Prince walked down a cobbled street and stopped at a fruit stand. He picked up an orange-red apple and observed it. From his pocket, he pulled out a coin and placed it on the table in front of the merchant. The man said nothing, merely smiled and nodded, acknowledging that payment was received. Arlahn continued on, crunching into his apple.

Once he was back in the study chamber of the library, Arlahn walked past a young girl and two elderly men who were reading silently, apart from one of the old men, who was muttering to himself. Arlahn approached a shelf of books that covered the section of wall from ceiling to floor. He walked alongside it, dragging his finger against the spines of the books. Finally, he stopped and pulled one from the shelf.

Plopping it open on a table, Arlahn straddled his legs over a wooden bench and sighed. He hated studying. Words on paper bored him unbearably. What application did they have to the world? he wondered. He was not foolish. He understood that knowledge and information were contained in the pages he read, but he often wondered how frequently in his life he would need to know anything he had read off of a page.

Arlahn reluctantly cracked open the book and began to read. The weight of his head sat in his hand, and for several moments, only his eyes moved.

"Magics" read the title along the top of the page.

"There are many incantations that a magical being, known as a magicker, may call upon. Being a magicker is a rare honour that is given to some. There are four different kinds of magickers, depending on their skill and specialties. Wizards are the most common and basic of magickers, capable of casting illumination and preservation spells. Warlocks achieve a stronger, more elemental control of the world around them. Wytchs are rare and extremely powerful beings. Among their many talents, they can manipulate a being's health, and on occasion can achieve spiritual revelation. Enchanters belong to an extinct form of magic. There are no formal scriptures on enchantment, as the practice was only passed from master to apprentice. Consequently, it was forgotten long ago, though evidence of this magic exists in some objects. "Though there are different kinds of magic, each new form is more elaborate than its predecessor. An example of this would be an illumination spell opposed to creating combustion. A magicker may see in the dark for quite some time because it's less straining on his threa than if a warlock sent out ball after ball of flame. As each level of magic ascends, the amount of will, or gaize, required from a person's threa to conjure the spell is increased. A threa is best described as a reservoir. Magickers and the Gifted both have threas that can be strained and even emptied. Whenever this happens, feelings of sickness overtake the user. Magickers and the Gifted are similar but very different..."

Arlahn turned the yellow page and continued reading.

"... magickers all have a set of principle confines for their abilities. In a sense, all magickers possess the same powers, but some possess different disciplines of those powers with differing potency. For the Gifted, it's an individual association, entirely different and unique to each Gifted person. Furthermore, the Gifted are blessed with a strength to absorb magics into their body, transferring it into more gaize for their threa. This fact makes the Gifted unique in the world of Tehbirr. It should be noted that occasionally there are those who are blessed with being twice or thrice Gifted. But these individuals are extremely rare."

As Arlahn read quietly aloud, his voice became monotone and he slowly felt his eyelids growing heavy. They closed for a moment and he slipped into a short and shallow sleep.

Jerking himself awake, Arlahn's eyes burst open. He looked back and forth at the other people in the room, but no one seemed to notice his sudden movement. Closing the book, he replaced it on the shelf and strode out of the library. Hunger was eating away at him now. All he'd had all day was the apple and by now his body had surely consumed its energy. His stomach growled its anger at him. Arlahn looked down at his flat stomach and smiled quaintly when it irked again.

He left the library and walked into the evening streets. The sun was just visible over the horizon and torches were being lit all over the city. The Prince made his way up to the gate of the palace.

"Arlahn!" a voice called out from his left. Raphael came walking over to him, bow in hand. "I don't like it, little brother. Hitting the target outside the bullseye is a disgrace."

"I hit white just as much as red myself," Arlahn told him as they continued into the palace. "No one's ever called me a bad archer."

"I have. But that's beside the point, I need to find another way to shoot."

"Just use a crossbow like most men," was the answer Arlahn provided, knowing full-well Raphael's distaste for them.

"Don't be foolish, Arlahn. You don't need any talent for that, you just point and shoot. They're much too slow to reload anyway. A real archer would bury five arrows in crossbowmen before any cranked the draw string back."

"Then just carry like, ten of them all over your body." Arlahn played further, pretending to have them draped around himself, pulling one off, shooting and dropping it to instantly have his hand find another. Over the years, he had learned to poke back at his brothers, though it was usually in the form of a playful tone or harmless gesture. His japes were never cruel or ill in intent. "Or just make a speed-shooting crossbow."

A spark ignited in Raphael's mind then and a mad-genius smile reached his face. "You might have just given me an idea with your foolery."

"Foolery or genius, brother? Besides, I found the answer to all my problems a long time ago." As he made fun of his brother's enthusiasm, his stomach growled angrily, and Arlahn looked down at it. "Food!" he exclaimed.

Raphael chuckled. "I would've gone with sex myself, but every man has his tastes I guess."

They entered the palace's dining hall where dinner had already been set out waiting for them. Hectore and Annabella were eating with Marlyonna, Raphael's betrothed. The two blonde women were striking. Annabella was over forty years of age now and was still considered the most beautiful woman in the empire. Placing the fork beside her plate, she resumed her regal posture. "Raphael, Arlahn, why don't you come and join us for supper. The kitchen prepared more of that delicious doe you brought home the other day."

The two men exchanged a nod of agreement, courteously acknowledged their company, and sat down. The five tucked in to the delicious food and engaged in conversation. Hectore mentioned travelling to PJ's mountain to Annabella, and although he would have gone no matter what, he asked her leave. Raphael was interested to learn that Arlahn intended to train in the camp. But Arlahn grew uneasy at the conversation and brought up the speed-shooting crossbow idea to his brother again.

"Don't give him another bone to chase after, Arlahn." Marlyonna said in a joking fashion. "Once your brother gets a taste, that's all he'll want."

"One, it can be done. And two, you always think of a way to distract me, Marly," Raphael smiled with a devilish wink. "I'll have to re-design it, but I like a good challenge now and then." As Raphael began giving an overview of his ideas, Kael entered the hall through a side door.

They soon noticed that he was accompanied by a beautiful young woman holding his hand. "Family," he said anxiously, "this is Luzy." Kael smiled at the woman and she smiled back at him then turned her attention to the family sitting at the table.

"Hello, it's nice to meet you my King and Queen, my Princes."

Arlahn looked at her with amazement. Kael had brought home pretty women before, but this girl set the bar higher. She too was blonde, with emerald eyes that shone as brightly and radiantly as her smile. She seemed somehow familiar though, but he couldn't put his finger on where he may have seen her. Arlahn looked at the happiness in his brother's demeanor, felt it exuding from his body.

"Please sit, enjoy a meal, my dear. Welcome to our home." From the head of the table, Hectore gestured to the two empty chairs at his left, beside Arlahn.

Kael sat at the end so that his date could more easily converse with his family. As Luzy took her seat next to Arlahn, it hit him. She was curious little Luzy from Elder Rufus' lessons, always so smart, so logical.

Over dinner, their guest fell in love with the Rai family. This was in large part due to the flattery of being the centre of attention. Virtually all of the conversation was directed at getting to know her, but Luzy could tell that the family's interest was genuine and not just a test to judge her worth. She told them that she had a younger sister and loving parents, who had moved years ago to live on the outskirts of Pellence after taking to an Eastern settlement named Silver Streams.

At the end of the meal there was a long silence, which Kael broke when he turned to the king. "Father, I would like for Luzy to stay with us. With your permission."

The king sat back into his chair, which dwarfed him, and looked at his guest, thinking. "Ask your mother for such a matter."

Kael turned to his mother with a boyishly hopeful expression on his face, his icy blue eyes crying out for her to tell him "yes." Annabella glanced with loving, but disbelieving eyes to her husband. She knew he knew all along that she would say yes. It was merely a formality. Annabella would never turn down someone in need, the power of generosity was never lost on her, and after having a meal with the young woman she knew that true passion had sparked between her and Kael. "Of course she may stay with us, I'll have an extra armoire brought to your room, Kael." Annabella leaned over the table closer to Luzy. "It's full of old clothes that once looked as good on me as they will on you." She cracked half a smile and winked. The release of tension in Luzy's shoulders was visible. She blushed and couldn't conceal her beaming smile any longer.

"Kael, your family's incredible. This is my childhood dream come true."

*****

Blond curls hung over his face as he sat staring at the page on the oak desk. Raphael pushed his hair back and rested his forehead on his palm. He was lost in thought.

Over the short years of his life Raphael had become many things: a hunter, a brilliant strategist, a voice of reason amongst the city council, and all before he was thirty. When he was sixteen, he led the defence of Corduran with his brother at his side. At the same age, he won his first archery tournament and every one he'd ever entered since.

Now he had turned his ambition to inventing. For years, Raphael was considered one of the most proficient archers in Pellence, he was pinpoint accurate and quick to nock the next arrow. Still, he wanted to be unparalleled.

On the page, he had drawn out an elaborate crossbow, sketching the item in incredible detail and adding a few unusual modifications. The most noticeable of which was an addition to the loading mechanism, a small front mount was added along the body and it boasted a new trigger, a semi-lunar groove, for your index finger. Notes explaining these modifications and their function were scribbled alongside calculations in the margins.

Raphael didn't know how he was going to build his new weapon, but the concept alone had sent chills over his skin; integrating machines into weapons in a way that the world had not yet seen. He had already finished drawing up another variation to his incredible tool. The drawing looked simple, it was to be crafted around a drum, with several criss-crossed lines going every which way. He could build this one in a month, he surmised. But the revolving crossbow he'd planned originally was proving a more formidable task. The size and weight were his biggest obstacles.

Eventually, Raphael pushed the page forward and sat back in his chair. He had a headache and pressed on the pressure point slightly below his sharp brow. His breathing calmed and steadied – in moments he was relieved.

Getting up, he walked through the open curtains out onto the balcony. It was evening and there was a cool breeze in the night air. To the west, the clouds were a sea of red from the setting sun.

Incredible, Raphael thought. The sun is what fuels life. The earth, magic, and even a person's Gift, yet no one knew what it really was. It was just a bright ball that circled around Tehbirr, basking it with life.

"Raphael, how was your work?" He turned and saw Marlyonna had entered the room, "I brought you some tisane, it's just the herbs in hot water. No honey, the way you like." She smiled and gave him the cup.

"Thank you," he said gratefully, sipping it.

The tisane tea was a special blend that Marlyonna had discovered by chance. It was a blend of natural herbs, but among them was a rare leaf she had once accidentally mixed in, mistaking it for mint. It had helped Raphael feel a sense of reconciliation and harmonized his Gift with his thoughts. From then on, she began cultivating the plant herself since it was hard to find, and Raphael insisted that she use it in her tisane.

Marlyonna paced over to the large desk and began slowly going through the pages, observing them as she ordered their stacks. There were pictures from all different angles with descriptive notes pointing to areas of importance. Some pictures were within boxes to signify an enlarged view of certain mechanisms. "Sometimes I try to imagine what's floating through your mind," she told Raphael, holding a page in her hand before placing it on top of the pile. "Drawings like this help to give me an idea. But there are times when these ideas fly over my head like birds do the clouds."

Raphael sipped his tisane and went to her. "I've been given a Gift. And it's my duty to use that power for the good of my people. I've already designed some new machines to help with our defences."

"You are a genius, my love," she said firmly. "And not just when it comes to war."

"There's just one problem. This new weapon is proving more difficult to design than I thought. It's like a crossbow, meant to fire by squeezing this bit of metal. With a pump here, I'll have nocked another bolt from the ring and drawn back the bowstring. But I can't seem to reconcile how to do it just yet…" He pointed to the trigger and front mount on the page. His mind was already back at work.

"Mmhmm," Marlyonna hummed, uninterested. She spun him around and planted a wet kiss full on his lips. "But do you accept my submission?"

Raphael met Marlyonna's gaze and saw the fiery passion in her eyes. Before he could say anything, she leaned in and kissed his lips again. Pulling herself slowly away, she cocked an eyebrow and started backing up, taking his hand.

It broke any spell his work had on him, and Raphael followed her in pace. As she backed into the edge of their bed, Marlyonna sat down gently. Raphael took up her face in both hands and kissed her passionately. Their lips connected again and again, their tongues playing together as the moment became sweeter and more sensual. Raphael's hands went from either side of her neck down to her shoulders, where he pushed off the top straps of her gown.

Marlyonna's hands raced over him, yanking and pulling and ripping at the belt on his waist as his competed with the laces of her top. Her modest breasts fell clear in time with the dropping of his pants, and Raphael pushed her back onto the bed, kissing his way from her lips, to neck, to clavicle until finally he found her perfect, coin-sized nipple. But there wasn't just the one, so he pleased the other with a circular lick before taking it gently between his teeth. Marlyonna quietly moaned and gave a quick gasp of pleasure. Her hand brushed through his golden curls and she squeezed a handful of it, pushing him gently downward toward her prize. Raphael never stopped kissing on his way down. Marlyonna began to softly moan again when their lips connected once more. "You… are…" she began to say between rapturous breaths and uncontrolled shuddering in her thighs. She never finished her sentence, needing to bite down on a pillow instead.

Chapter 7

The sound of pounding hooves approaching their perimeter roused the attention of most of the men, who were eating or lounging around campfires, but it was much too conspicuous to generate any sense of panic. They watched with silent stares as the rider quickly manoeuvred his steed toward the large black pavilion in the west end of their camp, recognizing him as one of their own immediately. Obviously distraught, the man dismounted and stormed into the pavilion that belonged to the general, Evris.

The tent was large, given the circumstances. It had been erected carefully, using the ruins of a windmill as part of the structure. Inside, the room was cut into two, with a black curtain hanging down the middle. One side had been made into a bedchamber, while the other, the one the rider was standing in, was sparsely furnished. Lanterns sitting on the long desk where Evris sat were the only source of light, and they lit up the room dismally.

"We were undone, Lord," the rider told his leader, a tall and wizened old man.

Evris raised his eyes from the sheets on his table and looked at the man before him.

"Show me," he told the young soldier, beckoning him to sit.

The dark-haired man walked closer and sat across from Evris. Drawing himself up to his full height, the general rounded the desk, casting a shadow that covered the entirety of the tent before him. He placed one cold, slender hand on the soldier's shoulder and palmed his forehead with the other. The two men waited in silence for a moment. Evris stood as still as a statue as the other man watched him unevenly. He opened his mind and accessed his Power. The *suuluuk* granted him revelations of the people he touched. Although the memory would play out in real time (and could last up to several minutes) in his mind, the vision was almost instantaneous in its completion when physical contact was made.

Togut was this man's name. He knew instantly when he gained entrance into his subject's memories. Togut had just finished winning in a game of knucklebones. His prize was a fat, old ring that they had taken from a young couple they ambushed earlier on the forest path. We should have moved on after that, he thought. Well, Togut thought. He heard the sound of horses' hooves clapping against the beaten path behind him. Together, he and the group of scouts withdrew from their game. Togut saw the three riders come into sight. They stopped and waited a moment before the closest one asked, "Why is the path blocked?"

Togut watched as his leader, Grosmon, walked out to talk to the other. He was an officer of the Damonai army and assigned a scouting mission into the far lands. But that greedy old fool was going to get them killed before we had anything real to report he was drawing far too much attention. This is not our country... yet, he had thought. Togut moved silently to his horse. He and his comrades had spread out across the pathway, all six of them. He watched the newcomers swing down from their saddles, then turned his attention to his leader, who was walking ever closer to the swordsman. The fool, he was getting too close. Togut was twice the hunter this man was, yet still he had to follow him like a senseless hound.

His attention was broken by the sound of Grosmon's voice. "Sharp as a tack this one is, eh fellas?" When the swordsman drew that menacing blade, Evris felt the fear that coursed through Togut's body as he heard the metal sing. He looked at it through Togut's eyes with great wonder.

"Please, there's no need for bloodshed. Just let us pass and we'll part peacefully," the unarmed rider pleaded.

That was when the swordsman buried the blade into the ground where it danced back and forth, every second or so catching a ray of the sun and blinding Togut.

"These men don't bargain," the swordsman answered his fellow rider after demanding silence.

Grosmon had almost closed the distance between them, talking all the while. Togut noticed his leader take up a small dagger in his hand from behind his back. He prepared his wits for the conflict that was likely to ensue.

"The chances of you leaving here are..." Grosmon's right arm flashed up fast, but the unknown swordsman was faster. With one swift movement, the dagger sat snugly in Grosmon's heart. In his peripheral, Togut saw other men advancing and he started moving forward with them. We are Damonai, he told himself fiercely.

The spearman on Togut's left fell to his back, a black arrow piercing his throat, and he heard the archer jest to the swordsman, who was now brandishing the massive blade.

The sword caught Evris' attention more than the conflict that took place. It had inscriptions on it that he could not make out, yet they seemed familiar. Through Togut's eyes, Evris saw the swordsman stab low into another of his *fellow bandits, the one Togut had won the ring from. Within moments, two more were fell, one having misplaced his head. At that, Togut raced to his horse and jumped onto the saddle. He sped towards the three death-bringers, making sure to put himself between the archer and his ammunition to avoid being shot. An hour later, when Togut safely assumed that the riders would be gone, he doubled back and rode hard for two days, barely stopping for food or rest.*

Evris slowly opened his eyes and removed his long, veiny hands from Togut's shoulder and forehead. "Togut," he said, his deep voice reverberating around them. "You were right. You are twice the man that fool Grosmon was. You'll be twice the leader."

Evris could see Togut's shock. He had served Evris for several months now and they had never exchanged words or even a mere glance. Togut had no clue of what had just transpired, that when Evris used his *suuluuk* he was given unrestricted access to the man's memories. But it was more than that. After his Power surfaced, Evris had served in the Damonai's HolyWar. It was then that he learned to control the *suuluuk* and retrieve specific memories. During these experiences, it became more natural for him to accept rather than resist the feelings and thoughts that also belonged to his subjects. I know you now, Togut, better than you do yourself. Evris thought to himself. You can't hide or lie in my presence. I know your fears and I know your flaws.

"Twice the leader, sir?" the man said with puppyish glee.

"Yes, you'll rest here for a few days, and then you may select a dozen men, as you see fit. I want you to find these riders. If these men are as dangerous as to make six of our soldiers look like practice dummies, we had better prepare more adequately for the next encounter. A dozen should suffice. When you do kill them, bring back the greatsword. Now leave me. I have other business to attend to."

Togut, clearly alleviated, got up and saluted his general with a fist on his chest. Evris returned the gesture, and Togut turned and left, ducking under the tent flap. Evris eased himself back into his chair, took a deep breath, and straightened his posture once more. Beside him, his acquaintance materialized back into vision once again. "I would have killed him at word 'undone' if I were you," the deader claimed. "I guess that's why I only work with my Wraith, if at all. Failure isn't tolerated."

Evris had known Mordo Lobo for a long time, but there was no such thing as becoming friends with the Shadow of Death. Their dealings were always strictly professional, business as usual. Mordo had just admitted his envy of Evris' Power before Togut returned – he confessed his delight at the idea of being able to read his deadees' life stories, only to use it to humiliate them further before delivering them to their makers. But Evris' Power transcended the histories of mortals. With a mere touch, he could review the entire history of anything, any object. In his mind's eye, he could quite literally project the evolution of its energy field in reverse. Because of this, Evris probably had a better insight than anyone into the origins of creation, but inevitably all histories led to a time and place of such utter chaos that even Evris could make no sense of it. He had used his Power to gain favour with the GodKing Tumbero by acting as a spy in the early years of the invasion. Beginning in the northern land, Melonia, he joined a council, convincing the others he was sent by King Arlahn. With a few mere handshakes, he had learned important names and dates, supply schedules and sentry routines, information that was instrumental to Tumbero's success. Later, in the short span between wars, Evris had served as a greeter, searching those who took audience with his GodKing. He'd read their histories and scan their minds for any suggestion of wishing harm on Tumbero. Not that the GodKing needed help if anyone wished to die by his hand. That man radiated his Power.

Mordo, however, the greasy haired creep, had warmed up to Caliph Hennah by earning his name, DeathShadow, among the Damonai soldiers. But he was no real shadow of death. It was more of a sham than anything to Evris. How could a man defend himself if he could not see his attacker? Evris would much rather face someone using his mind and wit to his advantage. He could think of no one better than Mordo to personify the concept of "dishonourable." As such, Evris always used extra caution when dealing with him.

"Mordo, the men I saw in my vision just now..." he began, ignoring the deader's remarks, "...they moved well. The three of them were expertly trained, yet only two of them engaged in the killing. The third acted only in defence. But these two killers! They wore hoods but looked to be twins. What power and grace! A man wielding a claymore and an archer!"

"Did they seem like they had Powers?" Mordo asked, suddenly interested.

"It wouldn't surprise me in the slightest. The speed, the strength. My men would not have perished if these killers were not endowed with some form of Power," Evris said with obvious admiration.

"And there was a third companion in the party?" The tone in Mordo's voice growing more serious.

"Did I not say that already? Why is that important?"

"Hennah told me she's given birth to only one set of Powered twins, twins with a younger brother. You were just looking at the Rai children."

"These men weren't children, Lobo. I promise you that. I reckon they could maybe even stand against you," Evris told him. Evris had seen more, knew more than Lobo ever could. More than that, he had long passed his prime years and understood that all men had the same enemy in the end. Time is the true shadow of death. And it was only a matter of Time for Mordo as well. He was not as immortal as he believed. While Mordo killed, Evris calculated.

A part of Evris had always wanted to touch the man so he may see his past. He was intrigued to learn the reasons for the deader's soullessness. Perhaps he was born this way? No. Something must have made this monster. The other part of him was both disturbed and intrigued about what else he would see.

Mordo's eyes snapped into Evris'. "No one can stand against me, Evris, you know that. You'd do good to remember it," Mordo told him coldly. "Send that man, Togut, to search for these boys. In the meantime, it's the Caliph's orders to separate the rest your forces into search parties, small groups. They're looking for a hidden camp, so I won't imagine it will be an easy task. They start in a week. When they find it, send for me. I'll tell you what Caliph Hennah has planned next."

"A hidden camp? Belonging to whom?" Evris demanded, knowing his right to the information Mordo held.

"Do you remember the one we called Howler? Who rode alongside Demonblades?" Mordo asked.

"Yes. The other leader of their Brotherhood. He's still alive? I thought Kragos killed him."

"He's alive. Only until the DeathShadow finds him. A little birdie told me he has a place where he's still training boys to play at war."

"He raised peasants into warriors. You'd do well not to underestimate him. As I recall, that was Tumbero's undoing," Evris warned the overzealous killer.

"Yes, yes. But I am not Tumbero." Mordo's tone was arrogant.

No, you are not. You are a shell of what he was, Evris thought. But he bit his tongue and let it pass.

"What was so special about the blade you're getting the little lackey to fetch for you anyway?" Mordo asked.

"There were markings on it. Almost familiar, seeing them reminded me of the Divine Blade."

The last two words caught Mordo's attention. "Really?"

"If the blade and the GodKing's Guardian are both here, then Caliph Hennah has a remarkable well of information. It seems she knows a great deal about the world and its Prophecy even before it happens. With your apprentice growing older each year, a GodKing will emerge again very soon, and Demonblades and his Howler will be revealed to the world as false prophets. How have you made out with finding the Guardian's Blades?"

"Ten years of running around like a chicken with its head cut off. If the guardian needs the blades, let the guardian find them, is what I say. Either way, Wraith is ready for whatever comes next. Most stories end up with the blades in the ground, but we've dug for them and found nothing. How important can they really be? It's the man behind the blade that matters. Not the other way around."

"If the Caliph has had you looking for ten years, then I'd say very important, probably required," Evris told him, knowing his Caliph's patience.

"I have to make a stop in Pellence before I return to Wraith and continue our business in Esselle. If anything urgent happens, send Bohr out to find me. I've been working over a new informant in Esselle. A mer-chump that claims he has a way of getting ahold of a Prophecy Tablet. Apparently there's one in their fortress vault."

"Rali's been hiding it from us," Evris said, remembering the turncloak that sided with Demonblades in the middle of his rebellion.

"Pellence is well-guarded," Evris warned him as a habitual formality. "What brings you to the heart of the realm?"

"Hennah wants me to release another Powered from the pampering clutches of his life. I want to go after Demonblades but Hennah says he's too well-guarded, even for my *nsuli*. You stay here. Organize and mobilize the troops. Not all at once like a fool, but slowly."

"I know Mordo. I was your age now when we marched on Saintos the first time."

"Maybe that's why you failed."

Evris could do nothing, say nothing.

He watched the deader turn, reach the door, swing it open, and he was gone. Evris wondered if Mordo ever used his Power to spy on him. He wouldn't put it past the man to *pretend* to leave, just to sneak back in, veiled in his *nsuli*, laughing inwardly while he watched him. Either way, Evris knew where his allegiance lay and always carried about his business with Mordo Lobo accordingly, horrible as that was sometimes. Still, the thought that he could still be there, watching him, was unnerving.

Chapter 8

Hectore unhitched his horse. He had packed enough food and grains for himself and his horse for a week's travel. He looked up across a rampart to his bedroom window and silently wished his wife well in his absence, then rested his foot on the stirrup and pulled himself atop the white stallion. Rubbing the beast's neck, Hectore kicked his heel and the horse began to walk.

He was almost outside the outer wall's gates when Arlahn came riding up alongside him. He had extra gear in the pack attached to his gelding. "I'm coming with you!" he yelled.

"If that's what you want."

Arlahn almost began to recite the rebuttal that he had planned for his father's refusal. His brow was already furrowed. When Hectore's words finally registered, Arlahn's expression quickly changed to one of satisfaction, and he struggled to conceal a smile that he knew would look childish.

Hectore saw no harm in it. Pientero Jessonarioko was Hectore's most trusted friend. The thought of rejection hadn't even occurred to him. Sure, PJ would agree to train Arlahn, but the real question was, was Arlahn truly ready for PJ?

Hectore knew all too well the intensity of PJ's training. He had seen more men than he could count literally crack from the pressure. But the King revered the austerity of PJ's regime, and he thought it likely that it was the only good thing to result from the man's past.

When Pientero Jessonarioko was a young settlement chief, Tumbero, the evil GodKing raided his lands. The raid was utterly unexpected, vicious, and calculated. Pientero was quickly subdued at the outset and staked to a cross to die while he watched his people butchered. It was the GodKing's demented way of flaunting the chief's failure.

PJ watched the GodKing's soldiers cleave his men to the ground and force themselves upon screaming women before killing them as well. The carnage ensued for an hour while the GodKing and his men scoured every corner of the settlement for riches and sustenance. Every few minutes, they would find a child or two hidden away by some prudent mother who now lay dead in the street. The relative isolation of their screams made them seem even more tragic than the mass murder that preceded. Being witness to such evil is enough to contort a man's soul to any manner of ends: madness, sociopathy, apathy, suicide. Then, with PJ beaten, dehydrated, and unconscious, the GodKing and his men left him there to rot, likely thinking he was already dead. Yet somehow, he'd survived, coming back from the very brink of death. He accredited his saviour to divine intervention from a fallen angel. It's a wonder that PJ emerged with his wits, let alone a newfound strength.

After that horror, PJ swore that he would never be held back to watch such evil again. He roamed from settlement to settlement, gathering every willing soul who was old enough to either know battle or learn it. Together, the men had trained day and night, mastering every form of combat, unarmed to ranged, swords to axes to spears. From that moment on, they had been known as Pientero's Brotherhood.

Hectore met them by chance. PJ rescued him, in a sense, and once he found out the King's true identity, he suddenly had more purpose. Motivated by the prospect of restoring the true HighKing to the throne, PJ began to fight for more than mere survival and revenge. He believed Hectore was brought to them for that reason. After that, they learned about the Ancient Prophecy that the Damonai had uncovered, and Pientero refused to believe it was about anyone but Hectore. In truth, it was PJ that had convinced the world that Hectore was the God returned.

When he assumed his reign as HighKing, Hectore gave PJ and his men a strategic tract of land, isolated high in the mountains of Tehbirr's Spine to conduct their business. The Brotherhood was Hectore's elite regiment of soldiers; warriors, bred for the sword and able to thrive in any condition with their extreme dedication to survival practices.

If Kael and Raphael were not generals in the king's own army, they would have fit in all too well with Pientero and his Brotherhood. They would have been his champions, had Hectore not wanted his boys close to home. PJ had been overwhelmed by Kael's strength and how determined he was to gain new experience. During his stay there, Kael pushed the limits of nearly every exercise, always thirsty for more. PJ had also once told the king about his respect for Raphael and the young man's appreciation for attention to detail. Raph had brought with him a game of Battlegrounds and taught the King-in-the-Mountain how to play. By the end of their first visit, Raphael had PJ doubting certain tactical advances.

Hectore rode beside Arlahn as they passed the city's gate. The massive wooden doors to Pellence, each six-feet thick and forty-feet tall, stayed open, as they did every day. In times of war or states of emergency that warranted a curfew, the giant doors would be closed and sealed. Even with the strongest men in the gatehouse, it would take at least fifteen minutes to close them.

For more than an hour, father and son skirted the crop fields surrounding Pellence. Every farmer they passed gave them a casual greeting, and both Hectore and Arlahn returned the courtesy. They had worn "street clothes" rather than any royal dress to avoid unneeded attention, so Hectore was pleased with how cavalier the country folk were being about their passing. Most didn't recognize who they were.

At the forest's edge, they took to a wooded path and rode for the entire day without distraction. Arlahn was finally able to question his father about the black leather vest with the golden eagle pendant that Hectore wore almost every time he travelled outside the city walls.

Arlahn had seen him wear it so many times since he was old enough to remember, that, to him, it was rather mundane. But as of late, his eyes had become more tuned to identifying the finer things, and he could suddenly tell that the vest had some special character.

"It's a special vest, son" he answered. "It was made by Dannisera Moren, someone whose Gift had fully matured by the time I was your age. But not only that... Somehow, it came to be enchanted. Dannisera insisted that she did not know the source of the enchantment, but that it must have come from some spirit creature unseen to her eyes. I was never satisfied with this story because you know I like it when things have an explanation. But it's too remarkable for me to ignore."

"How do you mean?" Arlahn asked plainly. Hectore stopped to face him. He strafed until the two horses' shoulders were touching.

"Do you see the eagle's look? If you watch closely enough, the eyes are somehow animated. It's strange, you don't really see them move, but somehow they do. It's forever watchful. When I wear this vest, I feel like I have the sight of an eagle. Every movement in the forest undergrowth is that much clearer, every impression of a footstep hidden in the dirt is as obvious as a dog wearing a hat. I see things I don't otherwise see. What's strange is that I see them with my mind, not with my eyes."

"Amazing," Arlahn answered, astounded. "Can I try it on?"

"I never let anyone wear this vest," Hectore replied. "Because I know nothing about its enchantment, I don't trust what it will do to anyone else, or what anyone else might do to it. Please don't take it personally, Arlahn. Your brothers have asked me the same thing, and I gave them the same answer." Arlahn looked disappointed, but he had half expected it. Now that he thought about it, he had never seen anyone else wear that vest in his life. "I'm quite certain that I would not be alive today were it not for this." With that, Hectore closed the conversation.

Some time later they stopped in a clearing and dismounted, walking their horses around for a few minutes to settle their heart rate.

After feeding the horses some oats, Arlahn removed a pot strapped to his pack and walked over to a knee-deep stream to scoop up some water. In the meantime, Hectore collected several long-dead saplings that he could easily break over his knee. He snapped off about ten short logs then laid two down parallel to one another, one length apart. He laid two more across the ends, and so on until he had a crude wooden box. While Hectore layered dry leaves, twigs, and sticks inside the box, Arlahn returned with the pot of water and two folding stools which he had fetched from their gear. Hectore looked up at him with a nod, knowing that his hips and back would appreciate a proper seat that didn't bounce on him. He sparked a piece of woollen steel toward the kindling and gave it a gentle blow. Within minutes, the larger pieces had caught and the two relaxed for a silent moment while a small fire formed.

Once the flames had died down into a nice coal bed, Arlahn walked back down to the stream and grabbed two small boulders. He dropped them into the coals and laid the pot of water across them. When the water was boiling, Hectore produced some semi-dried roots and salted fowl, which he dropped in the water.

They poured half the pot into another for Hectore and ate in silence, which was a change of pace for Arlahn and his father. Although the starch from the roots thickened the broth slightly, and the salt from the meat added some flavour, the soup was still quite runny and bland. Both men knew that didn't matter though – calories were calories, and that's all they needed. They rather appreciated a simple meal for a change.

"The ride's been good to us so far," Hectore claimed "Let's hope it stays that way. We'll need our strength for the climb."

"Kael took me climbing the day before we left. And Raphael told me all about what to expect. He said some footholds aren't as strong as they look, that sometimes they just crumble in your hands, that Kael would have fallen once but with his strength he held on for life with his fingertips. He also said there was an easier path, one he mapped out entirely in his mind before attempting with lots of easy three-point contact. There's a moss patch near its beginning."

"I know of the place Raphael told you, that's where we'll start then. I trust him. Besides, it's been many years since I've personally come to this place—" Hectore paused to do some quick mental math, then continued,

"Kael and Raphael's Gifts came around at a young age, but has it really been nine years?"

The question was rhetorical. Arlahn spooned the last of his soup. Standing up, he brought the empty pot to the stream and cleaned it.

Behind him, Hectore was still pondering on his question, reaching further back to tally up his entire life. He was a thing of legend once, defying death at every turn, accomplishing impossible tasks to unite a continent. What happened to him? How could he have grown so lazy for so many years? *I conquered his evil and retired to happiness and a family*, he told himself wordlessly. His last great feat of heroism was to save the life of the Corduranese Princess, Annabella… What could be a better ending than that?

He had shot her with an arrow – almost. There was a struggle. One of Tumbero's captains was holding a knife to her neck, and a low tenor came from Hectore's bow as he loosed the arrow. Annabella's neck was grazed by the metal tip and the captain's knife just broke her skin – but so little that it was bleeding less than the arrow's cut – as his body fell to the ground. They had known each other briefly before her capture, under different pretexts. Annabella was a medic for Pientero's Brotherhood, and Hectore was just an upstart soldier back then, both unaware that the other had royal blood in their veins until her capture. It wasn't a story of love at first sight between Hectore and Annabella. It was on the return home, he had later learned. Annabella first saw the confidence and swagger in the king's demeanour when he convinced an army of two hundred men that his Brotherhood was lurking in the trees, "Twice as many in number, each with an arrow notched and ready to fire!" Hectore could still recall the uncertain look of doubt on the men's faces as their eyes frantically scanned the forest. Thankfully, Hectore's reputation and knowledge of the Brotherhood won the day and he escaped with his bluff.

He looked at Arlahn, who was petting his horse's neck and talking to it. *Would Pientero accept him?* Hectore thought. Arlahn was the most kind-hearted and loving person he had ever met, which was saying a lot coming from a man who travelled across the continent. Arlahn was able to interosculate with seemingly anything, like he was trapped in some nighttime tale and everything was strangely full of hidden significance. Pientero was a simple man, a warrior through and through, hard as the granite of the palace's walls. The complete opposite of Arlahn. The king watched his son a moment longer. It was as if he was in tune with the world around him, like there was some intricate network of tangible connections between absolutely everything, and he could feel their movements, of which he was a part. He affected them and they affected him. And if some form of evil disrupted the benevolence that was intrinsic to their natural form, it threw Arlahn out of sync like snapping a string. Not in the moment though – Arlahn always maintained his composure in the heat of the moment, no doubt a trait inherited from his lineage. It was always afterwards when he was alone that he wept or trained or found some other way to release the frustration he incurred from witnessing another's evil doing. It was part of his being. That innocence that he'd had as a child never left. He was pure and absolute in his love of everything. As if there was no wrong that couldn't be righted, clemency was never misplaced with Arlahn. On the contrary, he forgave sometimes even before he begrudged. It was a gentle quality that Pientero would not understand. And Hectore worried that he might destroy it.

That night, they made camp in the clearing and slept close to their fire with their horses. In the morning, Hectore was the first awake, but Arlahn was the first one ready. Eager to start, he climbed into the saddle.

"Come on, we should get moving, the mountains are still a few days away, gauging how far we've come and what's left," he told his father as he looked out to the high mountains.

"We've travelled a little over a quarter the distance. It's not the ride that worries me, it's the climb." Hectore mounted his white stallion.

Gently tapping their heels to their horses' hinds, the two began slowly walking down the trail, the walk soon transforming into a trot and gathering speed.

*****

Kael and Raphael were sitting on ebony stools with thick cushions at a table in one of the palace's courtyards. Sunlight bathed the area, adding to the beauty of the flower statues that surrounded them.

The men, however, paid no attention to the beauty of the falcon soaring beside them, or the details of the hedgehog opposite. They were too engaged in their game of strategy: Battlegrounds. A ten by ten grid board was on the small round table, the board filled with little game figurines.

The rules to the game were somewhat complex, but to the seasoned veterans of Battlegrounds it seemed simple and moves were made quickly. The game began with an entire row of militia, the row behind it, at the end of the board, housing four symmetrical pairs and a king and queen in the two middle squares. A turn was completed by moving a game piece; if an opponent withheld his advance, he forfeited his immediate turn but accumulated an extra move on his next turn. A player could play a maximum of three turns at once. Movement consumed one turn and attacking two. Militia could kill diagonally and forward but were limited to moving forward or backward, one square per movement. Each pair of pieces along the back row had required movements. Towers could move forward and sideways, any length of the board. Magickers diagonally, any distance they pleased, and their attacks affected two adjacent squares. Cavalry moved in an "L" shape any direction which was available to flank opponents. Archers could move diagonally and forward, but only at a maximum of two squares. The king was the most valuable piece, he could travel any distance forward, back, diagonally, and side to side. If the king was killed the game ends. The queen could also move any direction but only one or two squares a turn. If the queen died first, however, the king was crippled by his loss and thus, could only move a maximum of two squares a turn from then on. Sometimes it was greatly advantageous to take the queen first, other times the king could be killed opportunely.

Raphael *always* won, but Kael never gave up. This was their third game of the session. Each time Kael would attempt a new strategy, Raphael would outmanoeuvre and overcome his brother's game plan.

The Golden Boy, they had called him since he was a young teenager, partly because of his tactical genius in the annual Battleground championship from the age of twelve, and partly because of his full head of long golden curls that fell down past his ears. It was fitting that he almost always won the game with his archers when he was an exceptionally deadly archer in real combat as well.

Kael moved his tower down three squares and took Raphael's mage. Raphael recovered by taking one of Kael's militia with a clever cavalry flank, exposing his king to a multitude of threats. He began talking to Kael.

"So what do you think of Arlahn going to the Brotherhood?"

"The other day we sparred and he moves well. He seemed to know what he was doing. He's getting a lot better, anyway. I just wonder how it would translate into a real fight – you know how training is totally different. Real battle is instincts," he replied, waving his hand aimlessly. "The training there is hard, and I don't know if he'll be hard enough to fight back. He's too gentle in his core, too trusting. I mean, this is the same man who saves spiders and bugs rather than just killing them."

That reminded Raph of a story and he smirked. "Yeah, remember when we were younger and he found that old dog in the alley? The one with the broken leg, that Wender took."

Kael started wheezing a hard laugh at the memory. "And we told him that Pubes was the perfect dog name!"

Raphael began to laugh too. "Those first few days after the dog was gone, he went around the whole palace asking everybody. 'Where's Pubes? Have you seen Pubes around?'"

By then Kael was almost crying with a full-hearted smile on his face. "What a bunch of bastards, ha-ha!"

"Oh well, what are brothers for?"

The two smiled at their fond memory before Kael remembered the game. Making his moves, he continued, "Speaking of brothers… Do you remember what we did to Balanor and Balanus the day we arrived? I doubt Arlahn will be the most popular man in the mountain."

"Maybe they moved on and won't notice him?"

"I wouldn't bet on it."

Raphael gave a crafty smile. "Maybe he'll impress us all. Imagine if his Gift manifested while he was in the mountains. It could be anything, Kael." The thought roused a sort of fanciful excitement in him. They both always hoped the best for their baby brother.

Kael was forced to use his king to kill the cavalry piece. "I wouldn't bet on that either. Maybe Arlahn's Gift will surface, but I don't know if he has one – he's lost or broken or something. I heard father speak of it once just after he was born. I didn't see who he was talking to though. Never really knew what it meant until now, I guess."

"Really? I've never heard of this," Raphael cut in.

"Remember after he was born, Ma didn't leave his room for months."

"Ohh, yeah. I think I do remember that now." Raph's eyes gazed into the distance as he recalled the memory.

"It was a long time ago, we were young. I actually forgot about it too. Don't know what made me think of it. It doesn't matter either, he's still our brother."

"Hmm," Raphael grunted absently. "Well, I hope he does alright. I tried to help him where I could."

"How?"

"With the climb. I told him to look for the path beside the Freefolk Chieftain in the mountain, next to the moss patch. The same one we took if he can see it properly."

"No one sees things like you do, brother," Kael told him.

Raphael used his own king to move diagonally across three-quarters of the whole board, landing him before Kael's king and removing any hope of retreat. Then he advanced his archer forward so checkmate was inevitable. "The king or the archer, brother. How do you want to go? Either way, game," he said casually as Kael lurched forward to replay the moves in his mind, disbelief on his face. "On another note though," Raphael started – Kael was still studying the board, struggling to understand where he went wrong – "with our King father gone, we share ruling over Pellence. I'd like to discuss some serious business. After a little bit of thought, I think I have some plans for how to improve our defences; a few new inventions that would change our army."

"Go on," Kael said seriously. His ice-blue eyes met his brother's and Raphael began explaining his ideas to his intrigued older twin. Among them were simple modifications to existing weaponry. Enclose the rams and combine them with siege towers to smash a gate and storm the wall simultaneously. Build saucers to put the catapults on so they can swivel their aim. Then he began talking of new inventions altogether. Starting with the speed bow Arlahn suggested.

"I already have an idea of how it can work. I just need the time and parts. There's also a variation of it, much larger, one that we can use on our walls that'll let two men fire fifty arrows in a few heartbeats."

That seemed to impress Kael. "And what would you need to build one of these weapons?"

"Bowstrings for starters, lots of them, cranks too and some other little things the smithies can make. Oh, and a drum for each one..."

"A drum? Like bong-bong?"

"Yes," Raphael replied, sensing his sarcasm.

"You'll have to design that one on parchment. My mind never could picture things the way yours does. Good games though, brother. Tomorrow we'll summon Zeph and the others and talk more of this."

After the matter, Kael went back to his bedchambers where Luzy had been painting her nails, waiting for him. She welcomed Kael with a huge embrace that lifted both her feet from the ground for an instant. Kael could see her biting her lower lip as she finally pulled away. Knowing how excited she was to see him made him feel something special, he couldn't put his finger on it. Despite all his royal and military maturity, he was still a young man and had the same sense of romantic anxiety all young men felt around a beautiful woman. Perhaps this is what love really is? he asked himself.

Luzy pushed herself up on her toes and kissed Kael's lips. That made him feel something else, and that thing he *could* put his finger on. "Did you and Raph have fun?" she asked him.

"Yeah, sure." Kael gave her a brief smile. "If you call losing three games of Battleground in less than ten moves fun. I just can't figure it out, Luce. His mind flexes like a cat's spine. He has this idea for our army..." he began. "It'll be amazing."

"Amazing at killing you mean? Don't men ever talk about peace? Don't you think fighting only makes things worse?" Luzy sighed, blinking away forlorn thoughts, and then looked back into her prince's blue eyes. "I know my history, I know wars have been necessary, but isn't the main purpose of a war to achieve peace? Doesn't that part always seem to get left out?"

Although she had never seen a real battle, Luzy had read about their horrors. She had grown up hearing all the stories of the heroes of war and the prophesied King. But she always wondered, "Why does there have to be a war for a hero to be born?"

"Unfortunately my dear, evil is rooted in some men and they just insist on renouncing any idea of peace," Kael told her. "Sometimes they just feel more entitled. But when groups of bandits attack innocents, how do you protect them without drawing swords of your own?"

"I guess evil just begets more evil," she concluded with a tone of finality. She was innocent in so many ways, but Luzy was smart above all else, Kael noticed. Not fast and inventive like his brother, but comprehensively understanding in another respect.

Kael could tell that Luzy was no longer interested. He smiled at her and wrapped his arm around her shoulder, walking her to the door. They left the room and made their way down the wide corridor. The walls were decorated with other regional forms of artwork: paintings and carved out scenes. Luzy complimented their beauty, pointing out that her sister wouldn't believe their extravagance. They continued down the stairs into the grand foyer with its high arched ceilings and black and white marble floor.

Leaving the palace, Luzy turned to Kael and asked him finally, "Where are we going?"

"To buy you a gift," he told her plainly

"No, you don't have to buy me anything."

"But I want to," he persisted.

Luzy smiled happily at him and fell back into his chest as they walked down into the market. "See, you're *my* hero already."

*****

That night, Hectore and Arlahn made it to a hunting camp where they settled in for the night.

Long ago, the great hunters of old had gathered and built such places in the forest for their trips. They were usually small buildings that were simple but had all the necessities. A kitchenette and a small table with four chairs filled one corner, while bunk beds for eight lined the walls. In the hearth, a fire was pre-built as per the rules of all such camps. Whenever a party left at the end of their visit, they always prepared a fire, never knowing when or who would be visiting next. The hunters of old had agreed that no man should have to worry about gathering wood in the cold dark of winter. There were other rules outlined on a pennon that hung in each cabin. Arlahn had committed the rules to memory long ago, but he approached and read them to refresh his retention.

> "Enjoy and respect Nature and the Wild.
> Do not shoot to injure an animal, torture is cruel.
> If a fire is left for you, leave a fire.
> Appreciate sacrifices made from the Wild in your name.
> Be courteous to other hunters.
> Weapons and anger do not mix."

And finally,
> "Enjoy the outdoors in its beauty, breathe in its peace."

The two lit the fire and cooked up a hare Hectore had brought down with a well-aimed arrow. They were about to start eating when a knock came on the camp door.

Father and son exchanged a look and Hectore grew cautious. He rose, gathering a cook knife and concealed it in his hand before he went to the door. He gave Arlahn a nod, and the Prince drew his pearl dagger and sat on it, keeping the handle slightly exposed. "Come in," he said, ready.

The door slowly opened, and two young men dressed in travelling clothes entered. When they saw the knife in the king's hand they raised their own. "Easy folks. We don't want trouble. Used to be places like this were a sanctuary for cold autumn nights."

Arlahn regarded them. They both had dark hair and darker eyes and were dressed in strange tunics that resembled the overgrowth of the forest and chestnut-brown pants. One was clean-shaven and the other was attempting to grow a beard but failing at it. They didn't seem threatening and so the king replied, "And it still is. Welcome."

"We just wanted to cook our partridge and rest our heads, you won't know we were here," the clean-shaven man promised. "I'm Tamis, this is Gringoll."

And so the two hunters sat with the king and prince and shared a meal, but when they asked the two where they were headed, Hectore quickly responded, "I'm taking the boy to his uncle in Corduran."

"Ah yes, the Golden Port," the hunter acknowledged. "What brings you there?"

"Gold. What else brings a man to Corduran? How about you?"

Gringoll, the hairier of the two men, didn't speak much and was eating silently, so Tamis answered. "We're from around here. Live in a small village up the way. Trails can become treacherous at night though. No need to risk our horses' ankles over some partridge."

When it came time for sleep, the hunters, seeming much too trusting or not at all concerned, both rolled their backs to the Rais and closed their eyes. Within minutes, they were both snoring as Arlahn sat up with the King.

"Get some rest", his father advised him. Arlahn gave the hunters a look, remembering the bandits from the days before. Hectore read the concern and told his son, "I'll watch them for a bit, you sleep for now."

Reluctantly, Arlahn went to the furthest bunk and lay down. He didn't like it, but after the hard day in the saddle and sleeping in makeshift camps on the ground, sleep came easily to him when he put his head down in the soft bed. He fought to stay awake for his father's sake but every time he'd shoot his eyes open, they'd beat their lids back down on him. He remembered waking once in the middle of the night and thought he heard whispers but again sleep consumed him.

The next morning when Arlahn woke well-rested, he saw the two men had left before the sunrise. His father had breakfast cooked and had just finished building the next fire. "Good, you're up, eat. We have one more day's ride ahead of us. Then we climb. Are you sure you're ready for this?"

*****

Kael sat beside Elder Rufus amongst the council during the meeting his twin brother had called. They were to discuss his inventions with the heads of the realm. For most of it, Kael had sat quietly and allowed his brother to do the speaking. There was no dispute or argument made against Raphael's mention of building such machines, they simply listened to his enthusiastic explanations. He had surprised Kael with another idea, though Kael still questioned the concept.

The council took a fondness to his ideas of improvement, especially the battle-minded Zeth, who saw the real value of such additions and added his own touch of genius to the enclosed rams. He mentioned that the palace had a few fire-resistant blankets in its storehouse. They would cover the enclosure for the drivers' safety.

Zeth had been promoted to Knight-Commander with the retirement of the old scout, Halder, who was seeking out his refuge with his hawk friend in the quiet of the forest, away from the crowds and swarms of Pellence.

During the meeting, Raphael asked his brother if he would be willing to visit some of the most reputable smith workers to secure their business on his behalf. Kael was happy to contribute to his brother's ventures. Their support for one another ran as deep as their bond as twins. Only wanting to see his brother succeed, Kael knew Raphael needed a precise quality of ironwork for his machines to operate properly. The only time he spoke out against Raphael was when he expressed his idea to relieve a magicker of their growth and preservation schedule, so they could put together his inventions faster. Kael refused the idea in the name of their father like a perfect emissary with an immovable notion, knowing their citizens hunger was a constant concern for their father. Even when Raphael complained that the grain and storehouses were full, Kael still refused him. As a consolation, Kael agreed that he would help Raph as much, and in any way, as was needed. But Raphael was particular when brokering this deal, making sure there was a clause that his brother couldn't embellish that his Gift had been hijacked, leaving him weak and helpless. In short, Raphael made him pledge his effort.

Now Kael was obliging his end of the bargain. He donned a brown leather doublet and filled up a pouch full of silver and a single gold coin in case he needed any for the day, then made his way out of the palace and strolled like another civilian amongst the crowded streets. He was accompanied by his newest friend, a scout named Bregan, the Cheif-Kalendare Brandigit's son, who suggested a smith close-by to Kael, praising his work for the short duration of their walk. Kael was sold and took Bregan at his word. The scout had an appreciation for fine things, much like a younger version of himself, Kael had concluded, minus the *kjut'tsir*.

"You can wait outside. I'll only be a few minutes," He told his "guard." The company was more a formality for Kael. He was possibly the last man in Pellence who really needed guarding.

He entered into a shop with a sign dangling on two hooks that displayed the smithy's mark. The heat contained within was thick. Kael felt like he had walked through a translucent wall. Amongst the smoke, the permanent stench of endless labour hung in the air. On one side of the interior, the walls were lined with hooks, dangling on them the tools of the blacksmith trade. There were four different sizes of each set of tongs, round-ended and needle-nosed. Beside them, were different sized wrenches and hammers. Measuring tools and handled boring drills were scattered on the benches along the walls. There were innumerable chisels with a myriad of tips, from as broad as an axe to as fine as a needle, unorganized and piled high, overflowing from a battered wooden crate.

However, on the other side of that same shop, some of the finest pieces of ironwork Kael had seen in a while were displayed. He noted a menacing hauberk and several fine longswords. Some had tags signifying owners that were to return for pickup. He found horseshoes and arrowheads by the dozen in neat piles. There were simple visor-helms and riders' half-caps, fine breastplates and shiny greaves, lobstered gauntlets and studded vambraces.

A younger man with dishevelled, dirty hair in a black apron was stacking horseshoes in one arm, while another older man in a similar apron worked on them by the large smelter at the centre of the room.

"Are you the owner here? I'm looking for a blacksmith," Kael asked the man pounding on a horseshoe.

"Well my name's Jonnimack," he said as he finished his work and placed the shoe in a bucket of water where the heat jumped off in a loud "hisssssss".

Kael loved the sound and envied that smithies heard it all the time.

"And if you didn't know this was a smith's shop, that there is what we call a door. It's how you get out," Jonnimack said, pointing with the head of his hammer, as if he were explaining directions to a simpleton.

He doesn't recognize who I am, Kael realized, and the Prince decided to shroud his identity unless it was required. He was curious how this was going to play out. He announced, "I have these orders from my brother. It's for plans to design some kind of bow thing we're going to put up on the walls."

Unslinging a rigid leather bag from his shoulder, Kael flipped open the flap and produced a stack of papers in his hand. The blacksmith placed his hammer down and wiped his hands on his apron before accepting the offer.

Jonnimack sifted through the top ones, stunned by their detail. Each page was full of designs and directions. Among them, the genius prince had also provided a legend page with assigned part numbers to each individual piece. Inside, he gave information on every piece that needed to be crafted from iron. There were specific sizes, lengths, and dimensions, along with a total count of how many of each he required for one invention. The blacksmith kept that sheet and handed the rest of the pile back over. Kael promptly replaced them in his document satchel.

"This should be all I need. How many o' these you building?" he grumbled as he looked over the order.

"He wants to outfit all four walls with them. Probably around twenty for each wall would be a safe start."

The blacksmith was surprised at the size of the order and suddenly disheartened because he would have little time for any other customers. *He thinks he's losing good business for my brother's toys*, Kael mused. *He may not yet deduce who I am. I'll only reveal myself to be Prince if he denies me. But he may also just do it because I asked, and I should appease him for that.*

In matters of their own, Hectore had taught his sons to be frugal and take only what was needed, but paradoxically, he also instilled a generosity in his boys, encouraging them to reward a man's toils with recognition, appreciation, and when it was deserved, compensation.

The man paused for a quick second to tally things in his mind. Then, still somewhat disappointed, he announced, "I can do it, yeah."

The apprentice was walking by with a stack of horseshoes in his hands when the blacksmith slapped them from his arms in passing. The whole collection fell and scattered to the ground in a short cacophony of deafening clatter.

The apprentice looked in disappointment toward the smith. "Well, that was uncalled for."

His response was a loving tap to the back of the apprentice's head. Then the blacksmith spun the young man round with a hand on his shoulder to introduce him. When Kael looked, he noticed a particularly unique feature in his face. The lad had two different coloured eyes. One was a tawny brown, the other bluish green.

"Billiem here can give me a hand, won'tcha Billi?" the smith said, clapping a thick, calloused paw on his apprentice's shoulder.

"Only cause you're my boss, Master Jonnimack," the apprentice joked good-heartedly.

"I am the boss. That's what I thought! Go copy this order down and bring the original back to this man. And clean this mess up before you get back to work," he japed with a master's tone, and the young man carried on with his duty, retreating back to the cleaner table and taking up his quill and ink.

"He's a good lad. Poor guy just lost his mother to a sickness that took her in days. I felt bad when he came to my door and told me that's why he was looking for work. But the kid's a natural with a hammer in his hand," the blacksmith admitted fondly. "Billi, show this fella your helmet."

Billiem stopped scribbling with his quill and smiled at the master. He dipped into a side room and came out with a most peculiar helmet, which he handed to Kael for better inspection.

The piece was remarkably well done. It was the shape of a theatrical jester's mask, with details that were as cold as the metal. The wide smile that was so friendly on flesh turned intensely sadistic on steel.

"It's fine work," Kael told him, handing back the helmet, "I like it."

"Okay, now you've shown off your beauty, get back to work," Jonnimack ordered the red-haired youth. He obediently returned his work in the side room before going back to the table, parchment and quill in hand.

"I'll get him to start making casts for the common parts so we can mass-produce them," the smith explained.

"Excellent, we'll pay you twenty silvers for each complete set you make."

At the sound of his value, the blacksmith's demeanour flipped as quickly as one might roll a coin over. He grew a large yellow grin across his face and the Prince knew he had his smith.

"I can definitely work for that," he said, his voice seasoned with greed.

"How long will it take? Do you know when I can expect the first set of parts delivered?" Raphael had mentioned something about trying to make it a surprise for father.

"In that much of a rush? I guess I can make a set by hand while my boy's getting other things ready. I could have this stuff for you in a fortnight, I'd say, but then you have to build it. I saw those plans, too many lines for me. I heat and I pound. Even the kid's better with words and numbers on paper than me."

Then, as if he was showing off his legibility to his master, Billiem appeared page in hand. "Eh Jonni, read this?" Billi held the page for his master to see. Jonnimack didn't even attempt a glance at the page, he just stared stone-faced at his apprentice. Billiem handed the original back to Kael giggling. "He can't read the words, never learned 'em, hehehe, hehehe, hehe."

His short repetitive laugh brought a smile to the smith's face, who shook his head before feeding him another loving tap across his red hair. "There're still shoes all over the floor."

So the apprentice bent down on crouched knees and began gathering his horseshoes once again, mumbling, "Where else would you keep your shoes?"

Kael was enjoying the exchange between master and apprentice, but he had other things to do. He replaced the order back in his rigid leather bag and slung it over his shoulder once again. "A fortnight seems like a long time... can't you do it faster?"

"Have you ever seen a cow's liver?" the blacksmith asked in a seemingly random transformation of topic.

"No," Kael lied, he had but was curious to see where the expected answer would take him.

"Well you can stick your head up a cow's arse and have a look. Or you could just take the butcher's word."

Kael understood the analogy immediately and praised the entertaining blacksmith with a smile. "Alright then, a fortnight and I'll return with your twenty silver." He turned to go.

The blacksmith took up his hammer and resumed his work. On his way out, Kael stopped at a large hunk of a shiny, reflective metal displayed on a dais at the store's entrance. He'd somehow not noticed it on his way in. He stopped at the piece and out of pure curiosity, Kael turned back to the blacksmith.

"What are you planning on making with this?" he asked, laying a hand on the top and feeling its surface. The metal absorbed the warmth of his hand and reciprocated it back into his nerves.

Jonnimack stopped his pounding again and shook his head "That there is adamantine. You can't make anything with it. It's a pity, its strength is its weakness. We've gotten our smelters as hot as the sun and the damn stuff won't bend."

"Hmm," Kael noised in audible apprehension.

Then, for no reason at all, he got an overpowering urge to slap the metal. He swung his arms out and sandwiched a chunk between his hands, as one might do to a man's ears in a fight in order to disorient him. The metal gave way and surrendered itself to the power in Kael's *kjut'tsir*. It squeezed together and contracted, lengthening out the way dough would beneath a baker's pin. The blacksmith's eyes grew as big and white as chicken eggs.

"How'n the hell'd you do that?" he asked with equal parts amazement and surprise but sprinkled with a touch of dread.

"I don't know. Can I buy this from you, though?" Kael said.

"Buddy, you can *have* it after that. That was un-fuckin'-real, never in my life..." His expression told Kael that what the blacksmith had seen was still registering in his mind. "... Billi, come see this."

He knew something special had actually happened when Billiem came over and imitated his wide-eyed surprise when Jonnimack told him about it.

"Who are you, anyway?" Jonnimack the blacksmith asked.

The Prince's question from earlier was answered. He doesn't recognize me as a prince at all, Kael realized. So he continued his casual behaviour and replied, "My name's Kael Rai."

When the blacksmith heard the last part of the name, he dropped his forge hammer to the ground and it bounced to the stone with a thud. "Well pluck me out the chicken house. I didn't know I was talkin' to a prince. I half-wondered how you got clearance to mount hardware on the walls. Billi, go get your helmet, the Prince said he liked it."

Kael stopped the boy, smiling again at the blacksmith's boisterous character.

"You keep your hard work. It was a refreshing change of pace speaking with you, Master Jonnimack. Next time be the same man you were today. There's too much formality in a prince's life. Thank you for the gift," he said, heaving the hunk of metal into his arms. It was lighter as a whole than he anticipated.

When he entered into the streets, Kael realized that he was unsure whether the blacksmith would take his last words as advice or direct order.

On the way home, he lumbered blind with Bregan guiding him through the streets, drawing looks and giggles from passersby. Once back in the palace with the chunk of adamantine, Kael carried it to his bedchamber where he had every championship award or trophy for a melee tournament that he'd ever entered on display – even those for which he'd disguised himself as a commoner, so the opposition wouldn't relent. Kael set the chunk of metal in the corner before he noticed Luzy following him in.

"There you are," she said from behind him.

He turned to accept her welcoming kiss.

"What have you got there?" she asked him, noticing the attractive metal.

"It's called adamantine. It's too strong to be forged apparently," Kael explained, placing a hand on the top of the mushroom he'd created.

"Oh." Luzy's mind quickly put the pieces together. She understood what that meant and valued it as worthless, just a shiny rock. "But if you can't forge anything, what are you going to do with it?"

Ideas and designs were already moulding into shapes in his mind. He observed his handiwork from before, catching Luzy's beautiful reflection in a smooth portion of surface and admiring her.

"I'm going to make a suit of armour with it," Kael claimed as if he didn't understand what he'd been told, but she knew he wasn't as unintelligible as that.

"And how are you going to do that?" she asked him with a challenging look on her face.

"With my Gift."

Chapter 9

He had always been her favourite, her scalpel for surgical accuracy. He prided himself in that. He was DeathShadow.

Mordo Lobo was a deader by nature, and Caliph Hennah Asa, supreme leader of the Damonai, had always found ways to sate his urges. If he hadn't been sent out on a mission, he was in charge of training his apprentice, teaching him the art of stealth and deception. Even though Lobo had the Power to become invisible, he still comforted himself by moving in dark shadows, the darkness becoming home to him after his life as a human hunter.

He had always been malicious, even as a child. Even before he was able to will himself invisible, he had killed. When he was a young boy, he started by killing his first chicken. In the days to follow, carrying a knife at his hip grew to feel natural, and slowly the number of his victims grew as well, until finally, his father's yappy dog was the target. Mordo's father had no idea of his hidden aggression. He was more organized and much cleaner than most boys his age, which had helped him hide his secret.

When his father was off working, Mordo used to pick on other boys in his village and beat any who opposed him. But one day, his father returned early from felling logs and saw Mordo bullying another boy.

Mordo would never forget that child. He was older and bigger, but his harmless demeanour made him an easy target, with his unique, mismatched eyes that were two different colours. Mordo remembered the boy's father had drowned in a river, and he was threatening to throw him in the water. When it came to blows, Mordo's father rushed in and pried him off his victim. Somehow, this boy threw a ball of blue flame from his palm, and the fire swallowed Mordo's father before his eyes. Mordo fell to his knees, clutching his father's burnt corpse. He remembered how skin peeled off his father, clinging to his clothes and hands whenever he tried to move him. Occasionally, when a certain breeze blew past him, Mordo would still catch a whiff of the horrible stench of charred flesh.

That night, Mordo had gone to the boy's house and thrown a lantern through the window. Then he ran to the edge of the forest and watched until it caught ablaze and people began screaming in the pandemonium. That was when he felt his first sense of true inner harmony.

The burning of that house marked the first few moments of the rest of his life. With nothing left for him in the village, he decided to never return home again. Throwing a small travel pack over one shoulder, Mordo began to make his way into the dark of night, stopping eventually to huddle in the cold under an uprooted tree. Loud howls echoed from nearby, but Mordo remained silent, the calls urging him somehow to travel north.

He began to live in caves and old abandoned hunting camps, risking trips to settlements and other towns only when his hunger demanded until Hennah Asa found him for the first time.

One night, she entered one of the hunting camps unannounced, wearing a tattered cloak, her grey hair wild from riding all day.

"I've been looking for yew," she told the skittish youth sitting at the table as he ate a mouse that he'd found in the cabin. "I was told yew were de one who was meant to 'elp me."

There had always been a strange aura surrounding the Caliph Hennah, like she was some great thaumaturge, an energy that Mordo felt grow in the air as she approached.

"Who are you?" he asked the woman.

"My name is Hennah," she answered, taking a seat opposite him, her accent coarse. "Hennah Asa, and you are de one from de village."

"How do you know that?" Mordo remembered asking her, paranoid she'd come looking for him.

"I know a great many tings young man. Tings dat I need your 'elp with."

"My help with what?" the young Mordo asked her with cautious eyes.

"With Godly work. Tell me, how did you come by dose clothes?"

"I stole them," he admitted.

"But how did you steal dem?"

"I took them," he explained to clear the confusion.

"You just took dem, hmm... Strange dat no one saw you take anyting dough, almost like you weren't dere. But stranger tings 'ave been known to happen in dis world. Dat could be why I was supposed to find you. You 'ave a Power. I'll 'elp you learn how to use it. And if it's what I tink, it can be quite useful," Hennah told him.

"Why were you supposed to find me?"

"I was told you were tasked to make a great delivery."

The power behind her words warmed Mordo Lobo, filled him with purpose and reason. From that night on, he shared a unique sense of communion with Hennah.

And so his employment began.

It had taken time, Mordo wasn't ready until the end of the Rebellion War. But Hennah's patience was endless. In the beginning, she seemed to know and understand the young killer even better than he knew himself. She granted him knowledge of his *nsuli* and taught him that killing didn't have to be without meaning, that if he let her, she could mould him into a purposeful assassin. "One dey'll write into de hist'ry books," she promised.

That was three hundred and twelve deadees ago, none of whom were Mordo's childhood nemesis with the mismatched eyes. Hennah Asa tried to teach Lobo the importance of humility but with the Gift to disappear at will, Mordo Lobo had never run from a fight and was yet to meet an adversary who could repay the favours he'd dealt out all these years. He had no reason to doubt himself. He'd killed babes in their cradles and generals in their armouries. Hennah always had someone who needed DeathShadow cast upon them. He never questioned why his deadee was selected. Mordo only knew that she assigned him jobs that required no witnesses, a request that he turned into his signature trademark.

It was dark in Esselle, quiet for a city of its size this time of night. But this was a city of academics. The studious minds had laid their heads down to rest.

Mordo strolled down a quiet street and passed the only origin of sound: a lively tavern. Inside, a few of the Essellian men and women were singing and drinking. He walked past and continued to go unnoticed through the wide empty streets.

He was remembering his last deadee, number three-twelve.

On his return from Evris' camp, Mordo had stopped in Pellence before making his way here to Esselle. He was in a hurry, so his killing of the woman Hennah had told him to release was barely planned.

Gaining entrance into the city as a delivery man, he sought out her identity. Rasha was an aristocratic mistress in the city, mother to a burly lad named Billiem. Once he found her, he followed her for an afternoon and cast his shadow the first chance he got. As she received a rose from a paramour and gave it a sniff, Mordo crouched in an alley and veiled himself in his *nsuli*. Taking out a poisonous dagger, he crept up and pricked her finger. Just as he expected, Rasha assumed it was a thorn from the flower and sucked at the fresh blood. With his work done, Mordo made for the city's gates in a rush for Esselle and his apprentice. She would be dead by now, he knew. Once the poison began coursing through her veins, she would have had a few days at the most, and there was no known cure.

His act wasn't empty though, it was necessary. Hennah had explained to Mordo that in order for a person's Power to rise from the depths within, the person needed to undergo some form of personal catharsis. In a way, this justified the deed as a worldly service to the emotionless killer.

Through an unseen exchange of potent emotion, he woke the potential of another Power.

After killing a general here in Esselle once, Mordo had learned that his Wraith would be that great delivery Hennah had spoken of their first night. But right now, he was making a delivery of another sort, one that Hennah had told him was to be delicate in its handling.

He passed the barracks where he'd fought that general. His death was the climax of a series of terrible assassinations. Mordo remembered hearing of it at the time and smiling inwardly; to him, it was as if the community was praising his handiwork. And without the general at his side, the king was powerless against the many local noblemen seeking to advance their positions. The whole affair was the rock falling into the water. Mordo's work as of late would be the ripples to follow.

He arrived at his destination and saw a glow of light shining from within the building through a quartered window beneath the roof's gutter. Mordo entered the shop without knocking and found the merchant Pical sitting behind his clerk's table, counting coins and arranging them into neat, ordered stacks. Before Mordo was noticed, he willed himself invisible.

When he slammed the door behind him, the frightened man leapt up from his chair. Pical was stocky, with short sandy hair and brown doe eyes. Eyes that were wide as eggs as they scanned the room attentively. Suddenly DeathShadow appeared right in front of the portly merchant.

His hand shot out and snatched Pical's throat. Rushing him back, Mordo slammed the man against the far wall.

"Lobo... please!" the merchant squealed out behind the clenched grip.

"You know why I'm here," Mordo uttered angrily in a low growl.

"I can explain... please," Pical pleaded, his face flushed red.

If the man proves his loyalty, Mordo figured, he could keep his life for now. Perhaps there was more to it. Mordo's narrow eyes stared into Pical's. He stepped back, banging the merchant's head against the wall with a thick thud then threw him to the ground. When Pical sprang up, gasping for air, he was alone in the room once more.

Pical's expression turned to terror and he stood nervously whimpering excuses at first. His heart was pounding out of his chest. Then, a few of the coins from his desk began to clink as they fell from an invisible pocket.

"I know the last shipment of trade carts deviated from the path," Pical managed through his fear, the first intelligible sentence he'd spoken.

"That's not a good start," the deader interrupted, coming back into sight, "especially when you're the mer-chump that's supplying our information on those carts."

The deader stepped toward Pical, hurling a chair out of the way, and hammered a right cross into the portly man's cheek. The blow threw the merchant around in semi-circle and he collapsed on a mantle that held an ornate sword. Pical took the weapon up, ripping it from the sheath, which went flying to the ground.

He turned and swung. And hit nothing. The stupidity behind futility, Mordo thought.

The room was empty. Again.

"Come on..." the merchant pleaded. "You think I betrayed you? It were Wender. He mentioned somethin' to some guards about the roads becoming dangerous... they must have changed their route last minute. I don't have any investments in those carts. I wouldn't give a shit if I had one to give to these people. All I care about is gold. If I cared about them why would I find the tablet and your blades?"

For a moment, there was complete silence. Then the merchant felt a hand on his wrist and with a twist, he dropped the sword and fell to his knees in pain. Lobo appeared, sitting on top of him, Pical's twisted wrist was wrenched back up into his shoulder blade and Mordo's knee was pressed hard into his back. "Did you find them?"

"I got one," Pical confessed through his agony.

Pical had someone check out their lead for finding the blades before but it turned up empty. Mordo had been upset to learn his efforts were fruitless back then, perhaps this time he would kill him after all. He threw the merchant free. "What did you find?"

"Not the blades," Pical said, rising and rubbing his shoulder. "But I got the tablet. Hennah said it was worth a fortune."

"Where is it?" Mordo asked impatiently.

"It's close by, do you have my fortune?" the mer-chump asked with a greedy glint in his eye. He fixed his dignity and sat down across from the deader.

"You give me the tablet, and I'll bring you your fortune. That was the deal. If a mer-chump's not going to make good on his word, I'd say his head doesn't look good on his neck."

At that, Pical noticeably swallowed a lump. "I'll get it."

He left the room, waddling through the arched doorway that led into the back warehouse of his shop. The merchant had secretly been paid to track down two sets of items, one was the famed Guardian's Blades for Wraith, and the other was a deal Hennah had arranged.

Mordo retreated and seated himself in the chair across the table. He disliked merchants and only dealt with this swindling weasel because it came as an express order from Hennah. She had sought out the man's services in the acquisition of a valuable prize for the Damonai, a secret tablet that she recently learned was kept guarded and hidden deep in the vaults of Esselle. A hunk of wood with some scripture on it, as far as Mordo was concerned.

Mordo wished he could have bypassed this clown and stolen the tablet himself, hidden in his *nsuli*. But Mordo was still only a man. Even if he could become invisible, he couldn't sustain that invisibility forever. He couldn't get through locked doors or walk through the sentries that guarded them, though he could usually pick a lock if given the time and kill any man that came at him.

Pical returned several moments later carrying a package, wide, thin, and flat, wrapped in a rich blood-red pall. At least the fool chose a good colour, the deader thought.

"Is that it?" Mordo asked, wondering how something so inanimate and worthless could be so valuable to Hennah.

"The Prophecy Tablet from the vaults of Esselle," Pical said as he sat back down behind his desk, hiding the package on his lap. "No one but the Warden of the West, Nakoli Rali himself, knew this was here. No one but him and my associate."

"And who's the associate?" Mordo asked, curious to know who it was that could accomplish the theft.

"It wouldn't be professional of me..."

Mordo stared blankly at the man, imagining all the ways he could slaughter him. "Do I have to sink into the shadows again? You people never learn."

"His name is..." Pical began.

The door burst open, and two men entered the room. One man, finely dressed in the navy-blue uniform of a justicar, escorted another in shackles. The prisoner stood only six feet in height but was several inches taller than his captor.

"Mick!" Pical shouted, equal parts outrage and fear. "What brings you here at this hour?"

"Pical, good evening. I'm here on business," the justicar greeted the merchant then he shot Mordo a glance. "Who's your company?"

"I'm an old business partner," Mordo answered before Pical could ruin his story. He gestured to the coins on the table. "I'm here to collect some gold before setting off to trade in Corduran."

"You're a sailor then? What's your boat's name?" Mick interrogated Mordo, but the deader remained composed. He was a born liar, and he'd heard countless stories during his travels, which only filled him with more fodder for his deception. Adopting the half-insulted nature of a sailor, he guffawed and retorted, "It's a ship! 'N her name's Catallina."

"You named your ship after a cursed magicker?" Mick asked.

"You may think she's cursed," Mordo answered coolly, "but I've been lucky with her so far. You said you had business?"

"Yes, right." Mick dragged the prisoner forward a step. "This man is Darius. He's a known fugitive and lately he's added grand thief to his résumé."

"Allegedly," the man said with a little smirk, looking over at the merchant through his shaggy black hair.

"Shut up!" Mick told him abruptly before continuing. "Did he come in to sell anything in the last week or so?"

"No. Never seen this one before," Pical told him with convincingly after a quick inspection.

"Do you know of any colleagues who were perhaps bragging of a 'big score' lately?"

"No. Never heard anything," Pical echoed, same as before.

"What is it this man allegedly stole?" Mordo asked, feigning interest.

"I'm not at liberty to say, but he took it from the castle's own vaults," Mick answered, unknowingly revealing the identity of Pical's associate to Mordo.

"That's why it wasn't me this time, Mick," Darius argued. "I wouldn't willingly go into that place. There're too many stupid guards and their stupid faces, always punching mine 'cause they're jealous I sleep with women and not dogs. If I wasn't in chains—"

"The chains don't stop you, thief," Mick interrupted. "I've caught you four times before and every time you've gotten out somehow."

"Then you must either be really good or really shitty at your job," Darius quipped.

"Shut it, Darius!" Mick dealt him a quick shot to the stomach, which had the desired quieting effect.

"Hmm. Well, I'm sorry Mister Deddick, my partner and I run an honest business," Pical said. "But if we hear anything about this, you'll be the first person I send for."

At that, Mick gave a curt nod, apologized for the intrusion and assured handsome compensation for any helpful information. Before he turned to leave, he said, "I'll let you two finish your business. It's getting late."

Mordo was surprised when he heard Pical improvise himself. "Oh that's alright. We were just finishing for the night, weren't we Mordo?"

He gave Mordo a jubilant look that the deader wanted to slice off, but instead he clenched his jaw and began to rise. "Yes, I suppose that's enough for tonight."

Pical quickly moved the tablet that was perched on his lap onto the floor and followed the trio to the exit. He made sure the deader was outside and held the door tight to his portly body. Mordo turned back from the two others. "I'll be back tomorrow to pick everything up, alright?"

"Sounds swell," the merchant told him with one last fat, triumphant smile.

At that, Pical immediately closed the door and barred the two locks. He let out a sigh of relief and wiped the perspiration from his hairline, then returned to his desk and his neat gold stacks. He sat down in his chair and smiled like a giddy girl who had seen a prince. A fortune! he thought. A bloody fortune for a piece of wood!

Pical gently cleared a space between the coins on his desk and picked up the red covered plank, laying it out carefully on the table as he uncovered the ancient bark.

It was ornate with elegant scripture that was impressively dark. The entire thing was as hard as stone and felt the texture of antler.

Pical was admiring the piece when a chill licked a finger down his spine. He walked over to the window, grabbed a pole from the corner and used it to push the high slanted glass closed for the night.

Returning to his desk, Pical leaned the tablet beside him for the time being and sat back down to resume counting coins. He reached across the desk for a loose pile when the table fell upwards into his face.

A palm had grabbed him by the side of the head, slamming him down into stacks of coins, flattening his neat columns into ruin. Another hand shot over the fat man's cheeks before he could cry out for help.

Behind the merchant, a skinny hooded monster clad in black stood leaning on him. The figure was slight in build, similar to either a teenage boy or a slender woman. In that moment, as DeathShadow's messenger, the creature could have been both, or neither, merely a phantasm shrouded in cloth.

"Don't squirm or scream," the voice advised in youthful tones. "It's always pathetic when they scream."

Wraith put more pressure on the helpless victim, who did, in fact, begin to squirm and make more noise.

Wraith took Pical's head up off the desk and rapped it into the coins and wood once more.

"You have all we need." The figure loomed closer to Pical's squashed face. "DeathShadow calls, and his Wraith answers." Now the intruder was close enough to whisper in his ear, "No witnesses."

With intense speed and extreme precision, the young apprentice quickly let go of the mer-chump's mouth, snatched a throwing knife from a sheath at their thigh and planted it in Pical's neck. He gasped and struggled, flopping underneath Wraith like a fish out of water for a few seconds but eventually he settled into everlasting stillness.

Not wasting a second, the apprentice gathered up the tablet from the table and vaulted to a rafter in two impressive strides up the corner of the wall. Wraith clamped down on the wooden brace with one hand, carefully pinched the tablet between knees, and hauled itself up. Reaching over and opening the window, sliding the red wrapped tablet down to the ground where Mordo caught it, then Wraith shimmied over until they could squirm its lithe frame through the opening.

As Wraith landed soundlessly on the ground, Mordo told his student to return to their safehouse outside the walls and await him there.

The deader made his way to a familiar location.

Mordo walked up to the door, but it opened before he reached it. Hennah was seeing a woman and her child away with a smile on her face. Sometimes Mordo almost believed she cared for the people of Esselle, but her blood was Damonai and she loathed all Sainti people. She wore green robes and her hair was a grey spider web. "Needy, weak scum," Hennah whispered under her breath, and it became Mordo's turn to smile. That was the Hennah he knew. He followed her into the foyer before she could close the door.

A young teenage girl sat waiting for the magicker's services, and Hennah walked past her, swinging her hand.

"You'll be de lass one t'night," she said and led the girl into a room. Mordo walked into Hennah's office in the back and waited.

Moments later, the magicker came in, cleaning her hands off with a white rag. After they quickly exchanged courtesies, Mordo recapped his meeting with Lord Evris. She was interested when he mentioned the Divine Blade but otherwise said little.

"Tell me what elss yew learned t'night," Hennah ordered once Mordo had finished speaking.

"It was Pical who told the Essellians about our ambush. He tried to blame it on a man named Wender," he told her. "No witnesses, Caliph."

"Chris suspected it was de merchant. I had done right in choosing you to be de trainer. A smart student you've bred, DeathShadow. You should be proud of your Wraith," the old woman said. "Do you feel better now dat death eez touched?"

Normally, Mordo's thirst wouldn't be quenched unless he was the one delivering death, but there was a separate, though slightly weaker, kind of satisfaction knowing that his protégé extended his touch. It was akin to smelling the fruits of his toils rather than tasting them. "I do," Mordo replied blankly.

"Good, den we can turn our attentions toward de apprentice."

"What about Wraith?" Mordo asked.

"Chris has indeed become anudder shadow in our forc's. And now it'z time we send your Wraith out on its own. De Guardian always finds der way to de GodKing, it is known." She noticed the red package behind the deader and asked, "Do you 'ave somet'ing else for me, DeathShadow?"

"Pical got the tablet. I met his thief tonight too. But he was already apprehended by a justicar."

Mordo had contemplated killing the justicar Mick Deddick and keeping the captive as his own. But murdering a justicar in Esselle would have grave ramifications, and he couldn't afford to foil his work by initiating a city-wide search for a killer and escaped convict.

He handed the tablet to Hennah who took it with delicate hands. She held it out at arm's length, admiring it with bewitched eyes. "Dis iz purfict, DeathShadow. Now I 'ave one more delivry for yew."

*****

Mick Deddick studied the cold body of Pical, sprawled on his table in a pool of drying blood. Strange, he thought, it didn't look as if a single coin was missing from his piles – robbery wasn't the intent. Whoever had killed Pical came after he had left with Darius and Pical's partner, Mordo. Mick recalled his introduction to the man. Mordo seemed friendly enough with the merchant, but perhaps there was more to the meeting. Mick was suspicious by nature, understanding that things were not always as they seemed.

He was a young man, twenty-five years old, with dirt-coloured hair that matched his bushy eyebrows. His pointed nose was sharp and he had a small brown mole in one eye while the iris colour was a mash of brown, green, and grey. Standing five and a half feet tall, he was slim and athletic.

"A man named Mordo was here last night. I left with him. He claimed he and Pical were partners. Check the inns and stables, track him down. I'd like to speak with him again," Mick told the junior justicar, who nodded and left.

Now alone in the room, he noted the way that coins had been thrown all over the ground. Mick knelt down with his elbows on his knees and looked at the deceased in slight disbelief. Pical had grown a respectable influence in the city. He was rich and generous to the right people with his wealth, making him seem amiable to most.

Three times in the recent past, guards had found dead gang members, including one day last month when an entire crew had been found seemingly executed in the streets.

Mick stopped his aimless search when the image of the crime scene flashed before his eyes once more. Several men in the alleyways had wounds similar to Pical's, consistent with a small knife. Was there a connection between the two events?

The sudden drop off in gangs had caused the nobles to re-strategize their policy, expanding their grasp for power. Then someone had possessed the skill and audacity to steal a treasured artifact from the vaults, crippling Warden Rali's credibility as palatine – a position that was always questionable due to his Damonai heritage. With city officials busy investigating incidences within the town, bandits began intercepting trade caravans, leaving other Essellians short-handed. Soon the majority of the populace would find food scarce. Mick had learned this from an old merchant, Wender, who had information about the ambushes and prevented the last attack by diverting the shipments last minute.

"Did you know this was going to happen?" Mick asked Pical's body. "Did you know more than you told me last night?"

Silence was his only answer.

The junior justicar returned. "I've sent some men to look for this Mordo down by the stables and in every inn."

Mick stood, seeing nervousness touch the younger man. "What is it?" he asked.

"It's Darius, sir."

Mick already knew what was coming next. "He's escaped again? How? We had guards posted outside his cell all night."

The young man shook his red hair. "I don't know. His shackles were still clasped. I've never seen anything like it."

"This wasn't his first time," Mick barked in annoyance.

"There's one last thing, sir," the junior added.

After a lasting moment of awkward silence, Mick demanded, "What?"

"He uh... relieved himself on his shackles before he vanished."

"Of course the prick did," Mick sighed in momentary defeat, recalling Darius' words: "You must either be really good or really shitty at your job."

"Next time I catch him, I'm just going to kill him and be done with it." Mick buried his anger by imagining the story being told at an inn, chuckling at Darius' audacity before pushing his thoughts back to the present.

Mick gave the corpse one last look. He began to explain his thoughts to the junior justicar. "Usually when you find out why, you find out who, but this is different. Random, but still connected somehow…"

"Connected to what?"

"Remember the gang last month? They had the same wounds as Pical here. Precise, lethal," Mick explained then ordered, "Tell the guards they can fetch the physicians and scientists. This murder was straight-forward."

"Do you think they stole something?" the junior justicar asked.

"Look at all the wealth here. If the murderer was here to steal something, it wasn't gold."

Mick contemplated the possibility of the artifact ending up with Pical. What else could be worth more than gold? he wondered. Did Pical and this Mordo lie to me last night? Finding either Darius or Mordo might answer that. Perhaps they were working together, thief and con man.

"What are you thinking sir?" the red-haired youth asked.

"That I need to speak with my father and Warden Rali," Mick answered.

He left the merchant's shop and walked toward the castle.

The architecture in Esselle radiated a forlorn beauty. As if built with the most meticulous of hands, from the most precise of measurements. It was said that the stonemasons poured their love into nothing but their trade.

Esselle was a very old nation, and the castle was no exception. It was the second oldest known structure – second only to the Palace of Pellence – famed for its bewildering libraries and graceful elegance. Mick came up to the crowned castle gate. The battlements were almost thirty feet high; an angular bulwark surrounding the entire structure. There were small octagonal turrets placed in all corners of the oddly shaped perimeter, which resembled a shining star from the heavens, he had been told.

The castle itself had been partially repaired and rebuilt here and there after the Damonai invaded years ago. The large iron-banded gate before Mick was ten feet wide, a foot thick, and fifteen feet tall. When Mick banged on it twice, a man poked his head over. In the brisk autumn air, his seasoned face held little warmth and less welcome. "Warden Rali ain't planning on seeing anyone today. Now bugger off."

Mick straightened the blue tunic of the city justicar. Growing a touch irritated, he called up, "My name's Mick Deddick. I'm a senior justicar and my father Baulim's in with the Warden already. Now open the gate or I'll see you digging latrines. I see the gold in your crest, I know you're an officer, but do not misplace your authority with me."

Suddenly the stern look on the guard's face washed away and pleasantness filled his weathered features, as if he was happy Mick was angry with him. "Baulim's your father!?" he exclaimed. "Why didn't you plowin' say so? I was with him when we smashed this very gate. You sure you're his son though? Look a touch small."

"I am his son. Now open the gate."

"Alright, alright, don't get your scrolls out of order."

Before Mick could counter the proverb, the officer coughed lightly and ordered the gate open.

He walked in and the guardsman descended to meet him.

"Normally Warden Rali's skeptical about people who just appear at the gate. What was it you wanted you talk to him about?"

"I think I might know what's going on with the murders. There was another last night, the merchant Pical."

"Shame, he was supposed to bring in some damask for my wife," the officer said, thinking aloud. "Anyway, the Warden will want to hear your theory. Come, I'll show you the way." The officer gestured, leading Mick ahead.

Together, they walked up to the castle door and batted on it once, then twice again, almost rhythmically. The thick wood cracked open and a maid greeted them both as they entered the building.

She was pretty, wearing a simple white smock, and had her long brown hair bound in a bun behind her head. The maid bowed and took the officer's shield. Mick felt awkward so he simply nodded to her and smiled as he walked past.

"You knew my father..." Mick began to say to the officer, who took over the conversation from there as he led Mick through the castle, regaling him with a boisterous story that could only come from an elder. In it, the officer, Baulim, and the late-general Raphael, who was mysteriously assassinated within the barracks years ago, were the primary forces in winning the day, with little mention to the HighKing Hectore or the Poet of Battle and details of their triumphs.

"The Pellencians believe that victory belonged to the Poet and the king, but we Essellians know it was really your father who won the day."

Mick dismissed much of what the man was telling him as exaggerated reveries of past accomplishments, yet he still couldn't help but feel pride at the mention of his father's heroics. Mick had always wanted to be a great warrior like his father but Baulim had forbidden excessive weapon training. "Speed and strength will last through your youth," his father would tell him, "but knowledge and intelligence will last a lifetime."

Just as the conversation was running stale, the two rounded a corner and were suddenly before a great set of doors. A pair of banners bearing the Essellian crest flanked them with sentries bearing halberds posted beneath.

The officer approached the soldiers and tapped his fist to his chest, bowing his head. "This is Mick Deddick, son of Baulim. He's a justicar and has news for both his father and the Warden." One guard acknowledged them and mentioned that the Warden was currently attending to Baulim, while the other guard checked inside quickly before allowing them passage.

Mick walked past the professional stillness of the guards and into the large room. There were frescoes of virgin landscapes that incorporated real flowing waterfalls on the walls, as well as statues of past kings and palatines lined in rows. The centre of the room was clear, as it was often used as a space for entertainment. Behind it, there were thirteen stairs up to the throne, which itself was six feet tall, designed with the same beautiful architecture of its surroundings.

Yet it was empty.

Instead, the Warden was sitting in a wooden captain's chair at one of two long tables in the room. To his right was Baulim. Mick couldn't help but notice that more ash had settled in his father's hair of late. Nakoli Rali gestured and Mick, following his bidding, approached the table and sat opposite his father.

He noticed how vulnerable the Warden looked now. His age seemed exaggerated by his proximity. It would not be long, Mick thought, noting the rheumy joints in his shoulders and knuckles. Dressed in a gilded white robe, the Warden looked fragile, like a porcelain doll with grey hair.

Mick exchanged a look with his father, who gave him a courteous nod.

Rali spoke first. "I hear you have news for me. I hope you've recovered my artifact."

"No, my lord, not yet," Mick said dipping his head in shame. "But there is something." He told them of his night apprehending the thief Darius and questioning various merchants on his way to the prison cells. Neither man had heard of Pical's death as of yet so Mick informed them of his previous investigation and explained his theory relating that incident to the gang members found in the street. "I just don't know how someone can be killing all these people without leaving any evidence, or witnesses."

Baulim, who had remained silent until now, leaned back in his chair and stroked the beard on his chin twice in thought. "Nakoli, what do you remember about the Council of Deaders?"

The room became darker, heavy with a grave seriousness in the air. Nakoli stared hard at Baulim with a sternness clouded by hate, then he sighed defeat and looked down at the woodgrain before him. "The Council of Deaders was just a rumour when I came over from the Damonai. The idea behind it was to find and train the Gifted, though we called them Powered, to become assassins. Tools for Damonai purpose."

"I thought only the Rais were Gifted?" Mick asked.

"Not just the Rais," Baulim told his son. "True, historically they are mostly Gifted, but there have always been a few others who are blessed by the gods with Gifts."

"What kinds of power do these Gifts hold?" Mick said, having never really known about their influence.

"The GodKing Tumbero himself was one of the Gifted," Rali told Mick. "He held the Power to pry into one's mind. And once inside, he could play with thoughts and emotions like a puppet master. I've seen him make brothers kill each other with pure hate and make a man mate with a horse and believe it was the best sex of his life. Gifts must never be overlooked. Their powers can't be calculated or measured, but their presence is instrumental."

"You think the Damonai convened this Council of Deaders?" Baulim asked his old advisor.

"Maybe," Rali answered. "They could be planning on invading again. It's quite coincidental with the Prophecy Tablet going missing from the vaults at the same time. Perhaps they're trying to bring about the prophecy. They'll have a new GodKing to lead them soon."

"Doesn't that mean they'll intend to usurp Hec?" Baulim asked.

"Your old friend Hectore may already be dead," Rali pointed out.

"No!" Mick protested. "Hectore has Kalendare watching him at all times, an elite unit hiding as servants and commoners in plain sight. How could they hope to kill Hectore in his palace?"

"The Palace of Pellence is a respectable stronghold Nakoli, have a little faith in our king," Baulim added.

"I've placed tremendous faith in Hectore. But if a stronghold keeps people in, we call it a prison," Rali reminded Baulim. "And I know too well what kind of beast the Damonai are. Snakes."

Chapter 10

It was nighttime and the forest was sleeping in the dark. Stars and the beginning of a new Red Moon shining bright bode well for the travellers. Arlahn and Hectore were on their horses, discussing Kael's new woman, Luzy. Hectore was surprised to hear that Arlahn had remembered her from his time spent in the late Jofus Rufus' sessions. She had been one of the most intelligent kids in class but was always so shy.

Their conversation ceased as Hectore began to recognize his surroundings. They were at the base of the mountains, just inside the tree line. Maples stood tall all around them; the colours of the leaves were breathtaking in the pale moonlight.

The horses walked slowly now, and the riders steered them clear of the forest.

They had reached the base of Tehbirr's Spine. Arlahn and Hectore dismounted and took up their reins to lead the horses closer. Arlahn looked up with bemused eyes. To either side of him, the Spine stretched out as far as his eyes could see. Above him, the peak faded into blackness and the whole thing stood almost vertical.

From this close, the sheer size made Arlahn feel as though it was leaning out like an angry bully would over a small child, looming and taunting, ready to tumble and collapse and bury him. And I haven't even left the ground yet, he thought. There were plenty of handholds though; that was the only good he could see for the treacherous trip he had ahead of him. Arlahn walked closer to the mountain face and placed his bare hand on the cold rock, looking up. "It's going to be hard enough, but I can see some places where we can rest on our way up."

He looked back to his father as if an apple had fallen from the mountain and struck him on the head. "What will we do with the horses while we climb?"

"We'll leave them in our camp tonight and start first thing in the morning," Hectore told Arlahn to his relief.

"Where are we going to make shelter?"

"One's already here..." Hectore said as he walked away from Arlahn and stalked along the base of the mountain, "... we just have to find it... There!" he claimed, pointing with a gloved finger at a large slanted boulder.

Hectore led his horse to the massive rock and waited for Arlahn to follow. It was leaning against the mountain. Arlahn arrived beside his father, and only then when he was standing close enough, did he notice that it covered a mouth in the face of the mountain. Hectore drew a single sword and wedged it between the two rocks. Holding the hilt, he turned to Arlahn, "Give me a hand!"

Arlahn grabbed hold of the flat of the blade, and the two pried the large boulder back until it propped itself upright. Replacing the sword and taking up the reins once more, Hectore led them in on foot.

Arlahn followed his father's lead into the crack in the mountain, it was fifteen feet high and not wide enough for two horses to walk abreast. It was a one-way path. Darkness grew as they advanced deeper and deeper into the crack. Thanks to the black catacombs under the palace, darkness no longer bothered Arlahn, but the horses began to shiver and were reluctant to move on. Hectore patted his stallion's neck and whispered words of strength and courage. Arlahn did the same, having learned the skill from his father years ago.

Almost forty paces in Hectore spoke and his voice had a slight echo. "Arlahn, take my reins."

Arlahn shot his hand out in the direction of the voice, he couldn't see anything in the blackness. His hand touched something that his mind quickly identified as his father's forearm. He followed it to his hand where Arlahn felt the leather straps fall into his grasp and he held them tightly.

A moment later, fire leapt up from a torch that Hectore had lit with his flint. Arlahn squeezed the reins in case it alarmed the horses. They were standing inside a cavern. Hectore did a quick lap, illuminating four more torches anchored to the walls. The space was around twenty feet wide and another thirty deep. The two riders unpacked their horses and removed all dressings. Hectore pulled the unique "Y" shaped scabbard housing his two blades clear, a shorter gladius that hung around his waist and a deadly katana slung over his back, walked over to the shelves lined along the western wall, and placed them down gently. There were sacks stuffed full on the rest of the shelves and large oaken barrels lined up in a row along the ground. Hectore reached into one of the burlaps and pulled out some dried meat. Studying it a second, he seemed satisfied and bit into the meat, ripping a piece away. He chewed a moment and swallowed hard. "Magic can do amazing things, can't it? Preserving food for months, even years at a time can be incredibly valuable to building a prosperous future." Arlahn cursed himself for his naivety about things to which he should have paid more attention. Hectore opened several other bags until he finally found what he was looking for. There were turnips and onions, potatoes and carrots, salted beef, salted cod; enough food to feed a small army of men. When Arlahn thought of where he was, maybe that was its exact purpose.

Arlahn walked around the room. His eyes had now fully adjusted to the light of the torches that were sitting in racks around its perimeter. Against the northern wall were two massive low-cut barrels and a tub full of water, and beside them were large beds made of straw. In the corner, Arlahn spotted two huge, round bales of hay, while Hectore was pouring out grain and oats into two separate buckets and unbuckled his horse. Arlahn now understood that the horses were to remain here while he and his father travelled over the mountain.

The cave air was dank. The only time Arlahn had smelled air like this was when he was a child, wandering through the secret passages of the palace with his brothers.

"What's so different about Pientero's training from your own, Father?"

"Pientero can teach things that I have no real grasp of. He finds your potential and draws it out of you. That's his Gift, if he ever had one. He can show you the difference between chance and opportunity," Hectore told him, breaking up some herb into his pipe

"What did he do for you?" Arlahn questioned.

"Everything."

"That's not an answer, Pa," the son told him, unsatisfied.

Hectore sparked a match, lit his pipe, and hauled a toke before he spoke again.

"I was eighteen when Pientero found me. I had experienced my Gift before, but I never had control of when this power would come and go. I was headstrong, but I wasn't good in a fight. One day I was caught stealing from a Damonai merchant and when I ran into the forest, PJ and his men descended on my pursuers like savage ghosts. One moment they were there, the next gone, with only the blood of the enemy on the ground as evidence. After that, PJ took me in and trained me. He pushed me harder in ways I never thought imaginable. Then, when he found out who I was, he began to show me how to lead. By the end of the war, at the peak of my strength, he had taught my body and mind so well that I could stand naked in the middle of a frozen lake with a blizzard around me for three days and never be cold or hungry. My mind could make my body metabolize food and consume tissue to produce its own heat. I don't know how it works, it's just part of me."

They stayed up and spoke a little longer before eventually turning in for the night. Arlahn always hardly believed the stories of his father's life – how incredible his accomplishments were!

The next morning, the two men bid their horses farewell and left the cave while the animals were eating too greedily to notice their retreat. At the entrance, they unencumbered themselves of any unnecessary weight, leaving their packs just far enough inside the crack for the darkness to be absolute. All they would bring were two small sacks containing a few necessities, which they could tether to their belts. Arlahn also strapped his pearl dagger in the sheath on the small of his back. He never went anywhere without it. Together they heaved the massive rock back into place, leaning it over the crack.

The morning broke cool and clear, the sun quickly drying the night's dew. In the daylight, Hectore and Arlahn studied the face cut in the mountain, planning their ascent.

Arlahn told his father Raphael's advice about the Freefolk Chieftain and the moss patch. When he'd first seen the Spine, he hadn't grasped his brother's vague description of the face in the rock. But bathed in sunlight, the mountain took a slightly less haunting shape than in the previous night's darkness, and he easily found the long solemn face of a Freefolk Chieftain naturally cut in the stone.

Before they began to climb, Hectore sat down on a nearby rock and pulled a small pouch from his pocket. From another, he took out his long, curved wooden pipe. Breaking up the herb in the pouch, he packed the pipe and lit it.

Arlahn watched his father exhale the white smoke and saw a wave of calm wash over his body. The king hauled another toke from the pipe and closed his eyes. Arlahn had seen his father smoke for years, but this new herb from the cave had an effect on him. He was about to say something about it but decided against it, and the silence grew peacefully.

They sat together a minute, enjoying the morning sounds of the forest close by. Chickadees sang to one another, while squirrels hunted for fallen nuts and chased each other through the bare branches overhead. Then Hectore opened his eyes and raised himself from his seat on the rock. "Are you ready to do this, son? It's a long way up. In many ways, this is your first trial."

Plucking a seed of doubt from his mind, Arlahn took a breath. Kael had taught him that the trick to climbing was to keep yourself as tight to the wall as possible, so your legs do the work. He walked over to where he had stood the night before and set his hand in the same shallow crevice. Lifting his foot, he placed it as high as he could on the surface before him. Arlahn crouched a bit and sprang up, his other hand snatching a hold.

And it began.

Raphael hadn't lied to Arlahn when he told him there were many three-point holds. But he never mentioned the size of them or their placement during the climb. Arlahn found himself putting his weight on three fingers more often than he liked in the beginning.

Still, he was thankful for the advice, the mountain face was treacherous and surely impossible to reach the top in some areas. Slippery moss and jagged holds that bit into his skin were all around him. When he had looked up from the ground, Arlahn counted at least three ledges where he and his father could rest a few moments, and he was already looking forward to the first's salvation.

Like two spiders, the king and his son ranged the first portion of the mountain. Their path was far from direct as they found themselves moving lengthways here and there. They even had to double-back down the mountainside once and come up further left to get to the better holds. The experience of climbing down was much worse, having to look down for each hold. Arlahn tried to focus on the rock before him, but at times his eyes would wander to the depths below. Once, he swore the bottom of the mountain fell another hundred feet down, stretching out what he'd climbed already to twice its length. He focused himself back on the rock before him and continued climbing.

The mountain was jagged and beginning to get cold with the stronger breezes higher up. Arlahn could feel the skin on his fingers start to split and crack. He was holding on a small ledge of rock with his left hand and another smaller one with his three right fingers. He reached with his left up to the next hold, his fingers clinging to the nub, but when he put his weight on it the rock pulled away from the mountain.

"Watch out!" Arlahn screamed frantically to his father below. Instinctively, his hand shot out and grasped the first ledge as he watched the rock fall and skip right beside Hectore, tumbling down the hundred and seventy feet to the bottom. That fall would have killed you, he thought, pulling himself closer to the rock. He rested his forehead on the cold stone and took a deep breath. He looked back at where his next hold once sat and now there was a pock mark in the rock, the perfect size for his hand. Lucky, he thought.

"Trying to buck me off you already? I won't make it that easy!" Arlahn told the mountain in defiance as he continued climbing.

Another twenty-five feet up and Arlahn finally topped the first ledge. It was only two feet wide at most, but the Prince was thankful to sit for a few minutes. Leaning back, he reached down to help his father up. Even though Hectore was over twice Arlahn's age, he moved with the same strength and vigour as his son, and when Arlahn peeped back over the edge, he was startled to see the hand of his father slap the stone before him.

They rolled onto the ledge and sat with their feet dangling, breathing the cool mountain air deep into their lungs. "Well that wasn't so bad," Arlahn said between gasps, rubbing aches and cramps from his forearms and fingers.

"Yeah, but that was only the first half!" Hectore jested. Their breathing slowed after a couple of minutes.

"Pa, what was that stuff you were smoking down there?" Arlahn finally blurted out. "I've seen lots of different herbs and tobaccos before but that one didn't look familiar at all."

"Oh that, it's something PJ left for me. It's a rare herb that only grows in these mountains called Yenmaraj. It's an incredible plant really. *You* don't have to smoke it, you're still a young buck, but obviously I do. It helps me… concentrate." Then Hectore's look became more defiant. "I can't always go around being Hectore the Hero, I'm getting old. I can feel it in my bones, this climb is proving that to me."

"Everyone gets old, it's just what happens with time."

"Not everyone," Hectore spoke more inwardly.

Arlahn was wondering what his father was thinking about. He could always tell when Hectore was lost in memories of his past. Sitting up, Arlahn nudged his father who caught his gaze.

"If you think that, you should smoke another one," he told him. "Your songs and stories will be heard hundreds of years from now. Like our tales of Juliessa, or Isla who slew the giant Lukza. Her story has been told for almost a thousand years."

"You've always loved that tale."

"It is a classic," Arlahn argued.

"We're all mortal 'til we're immortal," Hectore said to no one in particular before turning back to the Prince. "It's funny how the world remembers our accomplishments, but never our determinations."

"That's what I was telling you!" Arlahn said enthusiastically, but he grew serious before he asked his father, "How come you never tell your story? You never talk about your past. What happened that's so bad?"

Hectore had never confided this to anyone. But there was an innocence that beckoned understanding in his son, a trustworthiness that was offered with comfort and love.

"Do you really want to know?"

"That's why I asked," Arlahn said solemnly.

"The GodKing Tumbero was a brutal man, ruthless in his mission. He had your grandfather killed, stole my crown, waged war on our people." Then Hectore swallowed before admitting something he never had. "But when I cut him down... I killed my brother."

"WHAT!?" Arlahn spat, sitting forward in shock.

His father sighed deeply, staring into oblivion ahead of him, before clarifying, "My father had a bastard with a Damonai woman. And when Tumbero was growing up, all he ever heard was that his father was a king. It made him different, entitled I guess... I sliced a hole in his neck, Arlahn. I watched my brother die... But the part that haunts me deep down, is that I shouldn't have wanted to."

"How come you've never told anyone before?"

"Once the deed is done, it can't be undone. Talking about it couldn't change anything." Hectore got up and gestured to his son. "Alright, let's go. Now that we've started, we have to finish. If we wait too long, fatigue will set in and I don't want to sleep here tonight. I'm pretty sure there's only the one way down, and it didn't end well for that rock."

Before Arlahn started scaling the mountain again, he looked out over the ledge. He was two hundred feet up now. Bumps swam to the surface of his skin and his hairs began to stand on end. Breathing in deeply, the cool mountain air filled his lungs. He calmed his nerves and stepped up onto the rock ledge.

The next portion of the mountain Arlahn knew was the easiest, albeit still hard. They shimmied along the ledge to the far right of where they had rested. It was a good eighty feet long and shrank from two feet to only inches wide in some places.

With the wind snapping at their clothes, they hugged the wall and slid foot beside foot. That was when Arlahn's first distraction came in the form of a seagull. The ledge was a mere six inches and the bird was skirting the mountain with broad flight strokes. It was either brazen or unaware of the two climbers and grazed right by, batting the Prince's nose with a pump of its wings, sending a gust of air into his eyes, making them tear up. The disturbance caused Arlahn to lose his balance and he fell out from the mountain. In a split second, his father grabbed his chest before he could fall, heaving him back into the rock.

"Are you alright?" Hectore asked.

Other than the poop in my pants... Arlahn thought. "I'm fine," he answered, blinking away the tears.

Arlahn gathered himself before he continued. When he did resume his shimmy, it was painstakingly slow as he tried to remain resolutely sure of his balance.

The next obstacle was an overhang that came too far down the face of the rock for them to slide past. The Prince was forced to hold on to the far side and swing himself out over the abyss behind him, over to salvation. After that though, the ledge was forgiving and offered little obstacle until they reached the end where, instead of continuing to reach up almost vertically, the mountain leaned back into a natural grand staircase.

They climbed another seventy feet hand over foot up the steep mountain stair until finally they found a thick runnel at its apex. More of a chimney cut into the wall before them, the space was just wide enough for a man to climb in sideways and raise his knee almost to his chest. Keeping all of his pressure at a downward angle, Arlahn dug one foot into the wall before him and kept the other resting just under his rear and began to crawl upward through the chimney. The process was very slow but luckily the chute had undulations from years of drainage and his feet were always firmly planted. After a minute of crawling straight upward, Arlahn found his weight beginning to lean forward – the runnel was angling. He dug into the rock with his hands and squeezed tight around the ribs to resist slipping back down. Arlahn could feel water trickling around his hand. That was when his foot slipped out from under him, and he began to slide down the chimney, frantically panicking as he realized he was going to fall into his father. He would send them tumbling down the stair, over the ledge and out into the abyss. It wasn't just Arlahn who was going to suffer for his failure, but his father as well. He was going to kill them both.

*****

The hard rock dug into his knees, beating against the bones underneath as he slid. Arlahn's arms sprung out and slammed themselves back into the ribs of the chimney. His nails cracked and broke under the impact and his arms felt like they were going to snap like dead branches. Grinding down the chimney another two feet, he stopped just before kicking his father in the face. "Son, are you alright?" his father asked, looking up at his boot with some unknown and impossible plan of rescue written on his face.

"I'll be fine," Arlahn answered through winced pain. He had to push on, the only way forward is up, he told himself.

Soon, it was over. He'd climbed back up the few feet he slid down and proceeded with the change of angle cautiously until he found himself crawling flat into a shallow pool. He'd uncovered a small niche that was hidden from the ground. Turning around, Arlahn checked on his father, who was crawling closely behind him without complaint. How is he still going so fast? Arlahn wondered. Where is this strength coming from?

Escaping the runnel before him, Hectore went to his son and rolled up his pant leg. His right knee was bruised and a trickle of blood was flowing from below his patella. The king flushed the wound with cold spring water and inspected it with a few prods and gentle squeezes. "It doesn't look broken at least."

"I don't know if I can keep going," Arlahn said angrily in defeat, as though the mountain was starting to conquer him back.

"We must keep going. Once you start the climb, the only way back is forward. First, we're going to take a little break and eat. Keep flexing and stretching that knee though, or else it will stiffen up on you."

They had stuffed some food in their pockets before the climb and chewed now on the salted beef from the cave. In this moment, Arlahn contemplated that it might be the tastiest thing he'd ever eaten.

"What if I fail?" the Prince asked and his father sensed the doubt in his voice, "I almost fell and killed you back there."

"If you don't try then you always fail, son. We didn't fall back there because you didn't give up. Don't give up now."

Arlahn looked at his father, voicing his previous thoughts, "How are you capable of keeping up?" Hectore began packing another pipe. "You're twice my age and you still beat Kael in duels and Raph in archery. What is your Gift really?"

Arlahn had heard stories and eventually came to know some of his father's shaded past. But most of the accounts were from second parties. Rarely did Arlahn hear his father talk about himself in a past tense, especially in a boisterous manner. He had never really learned the true nature of his father's Gift. Only that it made him the closest thing to perfect as there was. Last night's conversation had been the closest he'd come to talking about it.

Hectore drew in a contemplative breath and exhaled one of smoky capitulation. Arlahn could tell it had been so long since he'd spoken of it, he was forgetting how.

"I was touched with the Gift of *sciong*. Harbinger could explain it best."

"Who's Harbinger?"

"He's just an old friend," was the king's answer.

Just another old friend Arlahn had never heard of. Before he could ask about him his father had already begun again.

"He would tell you that my Gift is the power of complete concentration, an absolute synchrony between my body and mind. People wonder how I can hit a flying partridge in the eye from sixty yards. I wonder how they can't. It's been a part of me for so long that I've learned to channel and control it. When climbing something like this mountain, my Gift gives me perfect balance and control of my weight. When I deal Judgement, an array of circumstances jump before my mind so I can understand from an objective view, see all the possible outcomes."

"What about in battle?" Arlahn ventured deeper, having never heard anything like this from his father before.

"Battle." The word brought a tiny smirk to the corner of the king's mouth. "In battle, the *sciong* is so powerful that I have seamless control of my weapons, as if they were part of me. I focus so hard during moments of adrenaline that for me, the only way to describe it is that the world around me and Time itself slows down. I dictate movement in all directions and I'm precise enough to slice the wings off a fly. I have complete control over my surroundings. I see my opponent's moves in the tiniest twitches of their posture, it's like I know their thoughts as their body hints them to me. Again, I don't know how it works, but the Damonai army would attest that it does."

Arlahn could barely fathom what his father was telling him. He couldn't imagine having a power inside of him that was so supreme.

By now it was high noon, and the sun was burning bright and hot down on the two men resting in their oversized nook. Through a vein in the mountain, a trickle of water was draining out to pool beside them. It was cool and Arlahn bathed his knee in it several more times before standing and stretching it out once again. "You ready?" he asked his father.

"Whenever you are."

The mountain above was corrugated and had a thin crack, no more than two inches wide, reaching upwards with a slight turn to the right, topped with a thick ridge. Arlahn knew he could hoist himself up on the ridge and continue with more holds. Slotting his right-hand thumb down in the crack, he swung his body beside the wall and slotted his left hand opposite. Pulling down, he slipped the edge of his foot in the crack and hauled himself upward hand over hand. At first, he was clumsy and fell back down, but Arlahn quickly regained himself and tried again. Slowly and surely, he made his way up, ensuring he had a tight grip with his upper hand before submitting the lower.

Gradually, Arlahn and Hectore continued the climb up the mountain. Foot by foot, they made their way higher, until at last they reached the small ridge to hoist themselves up to more holds. Both men took a quick break and looked down. Arlahn stretched out his cramped fingers by opening and closing his hand, rubbing the bloody joints and cracking them. When he began to climb again, he started moving very cautiously. Arlahn checked every hold before putting the full force of his weight behind it; if he fell now, he wondered if death would come before impact. He had heard of such occasions where the heart implodes and kills you peacefully right before landing in a splatter. Arlahn would occasionally glance down to see his father shadowing him, using the exact same holds.

They were at the third ledge now, a cool three hundred and forty feet up. Arlahn could feel his insides swimming against his belly and begin to crawl up his esophagus, but he swallowed the acid back down. The only benefit to being this high up was that there was a healthy cut in the mountain that they could rest on to enjoy their view.

"How long do you think it's taken us?"

Hectore shrugged, weariness beginning to set in on the old man. "Couple of hours maybe. Prepare yourself though. This last part is the hardest."

"Why do you say that?"

"Because it's the last part," his father told him "Everyone always gets complacent at the end. It's important to keep your wits about you."

"I'm not worried about being absent-minded when I'm over three hundred feet in the air. It's you I'm worried about up here."

"Me?" Hectore sounded almost insulted. "Why?"

"You talk about complacency, what about crazy? You're half a fool to come here."

"Then what does that make you? Asking to come with me."

"No doubt a full-blown fool," Arlahn said to the king's pleasure. "How many times have you made this climb?"

"Seven. And every time I swear to myself it will be the last."

After a moment, Arlahn grew more serious. "Why did you come, though? The realm needs..."

"The realm has your brothers," Hectore interjected. "Sometimes the king gets to do whatever he wants. And right now, it's visiting an old friend."

"You're the king, you can do whatever you want, whenever you want."

"Oh is that so? Have you forgotten your lessons as a child?"

"No," Arlahn relented.

"Then why don't I?"

"To be fair and keep our people happy. Sacrifices by the privileged lead to great things for all," Arlahn answered. He remembered the conversation better now. He was barely eight, they had been walking outside the second wall visiting farmers when he had asked why they didn't have all the food on the farm. "The farmer's the one who rises every morning and plows and tills his crops until they're nurtured into food. To come and steal that away in a day would destroy the man. Instead, the crown taxes only what we must in order to feed the other citizens," Hectore had explained. That same day, Arlahn learned that his father had implemented the conscription they had in effect. He believed every citizen of Pellence, man or woman, should know how to read and write, defend themselves, and offer first aid when needed. It also gave some people direction, while it taught self-discipline to others.

"Are you worried about the bandits that are around? You said it could be something worse," Arlahn asked suddenly.

"I'm afraid the Damonai are planning something," Hectore sighed. "That's the other reason for my visit to the mountain. Our family helped found this Brotherhood and every member of our family is part of it. Now it's your turn."

"Even mother?"

"Your mother was one of the original medics Pientero had, a member before me, even. She was taken from us before we knew she was a princess. One night, the Damonai came down on our camp and caught us off-guard. The camp scattered and she was among many prisoners taken."

"That's how she ended up a prisoner in Pellence during the war." Arlahn knew the rest. His father and Pientero had their best fighters don their armour to misdirect the Damonai's attention during the final attack launched on Pellence. Meanwhile, the king, Pientero, and a few others used the distraction of battle to infiltrate the palace where they rescued his mother and retook the heart of the city. "Did you love her before that? When you first met, I mean."

"Honestly, I don't know. I thought she was a redhead she had so much blood in her hair that day. We first met when she reset a broken bone in my arm. She wasn't very gentle, so I wasn't very nice. But there always was something about her eyes... We realized our love eventually, though." At that, the king's expression hardened. "Are you only going to talk about the past? When do you leave your own legacy? I think it starts at the top of the mountain."

They continued onward and upward, like two monkeys clinging to the side of the rock. The pair were sound climbers but began to lag in pace from before. Arlahn could feel his strength wading and wondered how long before he was atop. Just then, when things had already begun turning on them, the mountain itself began to angle outward. The Prince reminded himself of Kael's instruction: "Keep your hips tucked in and the weight on your legs," he told himself.

About three hundred and eighty-five feet up, Arlahn clamped his right hand down on a hold, the fingers of his left hand wedged in a slit in the rock. He moved his left foot and reached over his left hand with his right, positioning his fingers tightly in the shelf crack as he pulled his right foot up. Suddenly, the grip on his left foot slipped away from the face, swinging out over the chasm below him. Feeling a jerk of weight on his fingers, Arlahn clamped down for dear life and held himself a moment. The moment grew longer and longer, and he felt himself grow heavier with it. Hair whipped across his face and covered his eyes and mouth. He began to scream, first in frustration, then in his effort as he dangled. His fingers had locked into position on the rock, but blood dripping from them began to slick his grip. Arlahn tried to reach a hold with either of his feet, but the swinging exaggerated his weight. So he dangled there, almost four hundred feet in the air, helpless. Arlahn could feel the blood work its way between his skin and the rock. He knew it was over.

His strength was failing him. He had failed.

He couldn't make the climb and now he was going to pay for his over-ambition. Arlahn's fingers began to give. He couldn't hear his father screaming or the wind whistling hard beside him. All around him, the sound drowned out into a sweet, peaceful quiet.

Chapter 11

Mick felt the cool breeze of the night as sleep eluded him. He had been on the road travelling with his horse for just under a week now. His lower back muscles felt cramped and his legs were tired.

He had been given a message of great importance to deliver personally to the HighKing Hectore Rai from Warden Rali. Baulim had handed him the sealed parchment. He'd told his son that its contents informed Hectore about the theft of a Prophecy Tablet. As Mick had turned to leave, a palm clenched his shoulder and spun him round into an embrace. While they shared close proximity Baulim informed his son. "There's no mention of the Council of Deaders in the letter. That knowledge should remain with you. Our suspicions about the Damonai should be spoken to the king only."

Letting go of his embrace, Baulim had offered his son farewell one last time with an affectionate pat on the cheek.

Restless, Mick threw his sheepskin blanket off him and sat up. He pulled on a long-sleeved cotton shirt and rubbed his eyes before looking at his hound Kovi, who was deep in sleep himself. Occasionally, his teeth would show and his paws would twitch as if running.

Silently, Mick got up and dressed himself a little warmer, pulling on his sheepskin-lined, leather jerkin and attaching a wool cloak over his slender shoulders. He walked over to a tree and began to relieve himself.

Mick's memory wandered back to when he was ten years old. He had walked out from his room in a chainmail top with his leather jerkin atop of it, and a helm that was much too large for his head so it sat awkwardly, making him feel uncomfortable. Underneath, he wore iron greaves over brown leather leggings.

Baulim laughed, "And what's this?"

"I'm joining the True Blade recruits," Mick said clumsily in his oversized helm.

"Ah son, you don't have to do that."

"You were a soldier!" he started his debate.

"You're my son, you're not me. I want you to accomplish great things, but none of them should be battle. There's nothing great about war. You have a sharp mind, use that instead."

"But others will think I'm a coward, you were a great general, don't you think I'd make a great general?" Mick doubted himself back then.

"I was only great at arising to the situation and accomplishing what needed to be done, but my times were different, Mick. We had no choice, it was fight or die." Baulim placed his huge hand on his son's small shoulder. "Now please, take off that armour and breathe comfortably. Why don't you consider a future in construction or banking? The cities grow larger in times of peace, it's good, honest work."

Mick had approached a carpenter the next day and offered to work alongside the man in order to learn the trade. When he proudly returned from work, his father met him with the news that the girl he had infatuated himself with, Jassyka Grent, had disappeared in the night, her family slain. There were never any witnesses.

The act had caused Mick to take up criminology as he tried to piece together what had happened. The house was one of those neighbouring the outskirts of Melonia, and the scene inside was horrid and bloody. Three little boys, all dead.

More and more, Mick dove into studying crime. The next case he had solved was a theft. The victim had claimed that two men assaulted his caravan, stealing his goods, and butchering his oxen. The crime had been orchestrated beautifully, but something happened to Mick that day; his instincts led him to the truth. The merchant victim had surmounted quite a gambling debt, and Mick interrogated the man until he eventually broke down into tears, admitting that he was faced with a choice: his wife or his business.

Mick was promptly inducted into the justicar service of Warden Nakoli Rali. Two months later, the wife of the merchant was found, beaten to death. The husband had flown into a drunken rage when the two had argued about his business. After that, Mick had become almost obsessed with solving crimes. At a young age, he'd exposed himself to villainous men of all sorts and dangerous situations but in doing so propelled himself through the ranks, becoming the youngest ever senior justicar.

Pushing the memories from his mind, Mick shook off the last few drops and turned to his camp. He startled Kovi awake with a hushed yelp as Mick noticed the man sitting in his makeshift camp.

In his early thirties, Mick guessed, the short, lightly bearded man had sandy hair and was wearing a fine green tunic edged in gold. His legs were covered with dark leather leggings and doeskin traveller boots. The man had tucked his feet beneath him, his hands busy playing with intangible threads in the air, manipulating the physical world around him. In a matter of seconds, he had effortlessly pulled a circle of rocks in to surround the fire burning before him.

"Can I help you?" Mick asked, startled by the newcomer and his spectacle.

At first, the man didn't answer but merely tended to his flames, only when they were in flickering in symmetry did he speak.

"I ask myself that same question of all you world-born men."

Mick grew suspicious. "Do you know me?"

"In a sense..." The figure's features became clearer as golden-orange flames reflected off his face. "... I've seen your path, though your branch leads to an extinguished end."

Now Mick could see him, he appeared to be just a few years Mick's elder. "What are you talking about an extinguished end? Who are you?"

"Call me what you like. I have been here a very long time..." the man answered lamely, as if he'd repeated the words beyond meaning. "... so long that I forget what my *amiro* called me. I've witnessed the birth and extinction of entire races, felt the magnetic poles change and the climates reverse. I've lived through Juliessa's war of nine armies and the Great Western Plague, I've seen history's repetition, grown tired of the world's theatrics."

"Why are you here then, drifter?" Mick asked, considering his questions carefully, not sure what to make of this possibly insane stranger.

"Drifter! That's a new one, didn't think I'd hear one of those." Then he sighed and Mick felt his forlorn. "I've been waiting for the prophecy to be fulfilled, for Him."

Mick nodded with mixed feelings of bewilderment and disbelief. "Who?"

"That's not important to you. You're just the messenger."

"What makes you think I'm a messenger?"

"I know. I told you, I've seen your path," the man took his eyes off the fire and met Mick's before continuing, "entertained your branch on the Tree of Life."

"So you've read the Tree of Life? How do I know anything you're saying is true? You could be completely daft... The Tree is a myth, the only proof it exists is that someone *claimed* the Prophecy Tablet came from it," Mick argued.

"I saw the Prophecy come off it. Your thoughts and feelings are irrelevant, Messenger. You're on your way to the HighKing." Without waiting for Mick's response, the sandy-haired man continued, "Tell him Harbinger has seen that war is imminent. The mountain will be found. He must send his twins there if it's to survive but one of them will not."

Mick closed his eyes to commit the instructions to memory but before he could open them, he felt two fingers touch his forehead and heard mumbled words. Without realizing it, sleep came crashing down on him.

Now, a phantasmal voice echoed between Mick's ears once more. "You and your new mate will need each other for what's next. Trust your instincts."

Before Mick opened his eyes, he contemplated his memories. Was that a dream? The man's encounter was so brief that, for a moment, Mick questioned whether or not he should accept that the events had even transpired.

The man was a mystery, came and left out of thin air, and commanded Mick with the words of a seer. Mick could vividly recall a cold disconnect in his voice. What was he talking about, trusting my instincts?

Feeling a shadow fall over his face, Mick opened his eyes expecting it to be his hound Kovi. Instead, a pair of legs filled his vision. He followed the hard-worked leather boots up. They belonged to a huge man, bald but bearded like a lumberjack. Covering heavy arms, a bearskin cloak hung over his shoulder. He snorted and asked someone, "This 'im?"

Mick saw another man drag a hostage out from a tree. The man's black hair fell over his face, but Mick recognized Darius almost immediately.

"That's him!" the thief said.

The looming presence darkened with seriousness, he picked up his mud-crusted boot and dropped it on Mick's face, snapping his head back into the hard-packed earth. Mick's vision blurred and his eyes rolled back, the next thing he felt were unknown men yanking him from the ground and carrying him along.

*****

Arlahn was about to give up and let go when he felt something. It was a hand clamping down on his ankle.

His father raced to where he dangled as fast as he could, completely disobeying the rules of three-point contact and risking his own life. He ran along the mountain face for three steps, catching a jut of rock before lunging as far as he dared toward the Prince. His hand clasped onto his son's ankle and his momentum swung them both into the mountain long enough for Arlahn's foot to find salvation.

"Have you got it there, son?" Hectore yelled up.

Arlahn planted his other foot sideways onto a thin ledge then gripped with his remaining strength. "Yeah, do it!" he answered, knowing what his father had planned.

Using his son's ankles as holds, the king worked his way past the Prince to where the overhang was minimal. He climbed up and worked his way back right over the top of Arlahn. There was a jut of rock another foot above the Prince that the king found himself on, just wide enough to lie down and grab hold of his son's hand.

Arlahn wiggled his way up onto the rock and sat for a minute feeling his fingers. "You saved my life there, my fingers were about to let go."

"But they didn't," Hectore replied grimly. "Enough alright! Or you'll beat yourself before the mountain does."

The Prince obeyed his father's command and suppressed any more doubt he had. He looked down at what he'd already accomplished then looked up to the last bit ahead of him. I can do this, he made himself believe. Arlahn took a short break before he got up and grabbed hold of the mountain again.

Arlahn had only climbed a short while when he reached out to grab a large, round hold and it fell away from the mountain. He fell back to his position. "What the shit?!"

It was the only hold he could grab onto for the next three feet, and it was already a strenuous enough final move after such a grueling climb. Now, the rock was smooth all the way to the top, insurmountable. "No, no, no, nooo! Why do you hate me, mountain?"

He looked around himself for another way to go. One foot up and two to his left was a tangle of roots, sprouting through the grey stone, another short distance from the roots, a watermelon-sized protrusion stabbed out from the surface. Arlahn rolled his eyes, letting out a deep sigh and thought to himself, this is insane.

He threw himself to his left, his right hand dragging along the grey mountain beside him. He felt the roots brush through his fingers and began to panic, when an inexplicable and life-saving gale of wind suddenly rushed up. With the wind helping Arlahn defy gravity for a split second, it spun him around, and he accepted the change of movement, clamping down on the roots with his left hand like a bear trap. He swung on the root, turning the front of his body away from the mountain to reach his right arm around the protruding rock and grab the far side. The gravity of the situation hit Arlahn like a stone wall. Here he was, over four hundred feet in the air on a sheer cliff, hanging face-out with only one hand secure, trusting the weight in his left hand to roots – feeble, thin things that really shouldn't be trusted. His back pressed up to the rock as he tried to cling to the mountain face. He moved his feet, but they found no friends with which to make their acquaintance.

Hectore watched with amazement for the first few moments, until he too realized the gravity. "Arlahn! Be careful." Worry written clear on his face.

Arlahn was looking up at the final ledge, it was two feet above where his hands hung, sticking a tongue out at him in a mocking fashion. He had come all this way, and even though that top crest lay just above him, it may as well have been miles away.

He was stuck. Again.

Just then, the roots grasped tightly in his left hand started coming loose. Arlahn panicked, but his body didn't freeze, instead his strong lineage shone through like it always did in such moments, and he reacted. Pushing off the bare mountain face with crunched legs, Arlahn hurled himself up with all his remaining strength, letting out a great cry as he launched upward, spun one hundred and eighty degrees in mid-air, and grabbed the ledge above him by its mocking tongue with both hands.

With one last release of energy, Arlahn pulled himself up onto the smooth surface until his elbow broke the crest, then hefted his upper body, and swung his feet up the rest of the way. He rolled over, away from the ledge and took a moment to gather his breath. Remembering who was following him, Arlahn suddenly crawled back to the edge. "Pa, don't even think..."

Without hesitation, Hectore had sprung himself from where Arlahn had been stuck, over toward the roots – unaware they were about to give way. The king snatched up the feeble strands and they began to pull away like loose threads from a seam, only to miraculously hold at the end of their length. Hectore was just beginning to slip away, when his momentum swung him far enough to reach the jagged protrusion from which Arlahn had pulled himself up onto to the ledge. But Hectore calculated his approach so that he was at least facing the cliff. He let go of the roots as they fluttered down behind him and clamped down on the protruding surface with both hands. His body jerked hard one way and then the other, like a ball bouncing on a string, but the king lived up to his Legend yet again and held on. Dangling now, he looked up at Arlahn who was in utter shock.

"Could have warned me, you know," he said as nonchalantly as possible given the strain he was under. Arlahn reached down and took his father's wrist before the king let go of the rock to take his. At first he struggled to pull his father up, but soon he had both hands over the ledge and he hauled his father to safety with two great tugs.

They looked over the long drop down and rolled onto solid ground once again. "I can't believe you did that!" Arlahn said, closing his eyes as he took deep, exhausted breaths.

"Ah, people make too much fuss about some things I do," the King responded.

Arlahn was about to get up and reply when he heard something. It sounded like... tension? Like squeezing fresh leather or the tightening of wood?

He opened his eyes and was initially blinded by a gleaming reflection. When it came into focus, he saw that the tip of the reflection was a mere inch from his eyeball and razor-sharp. Four more archers stood around them with arrows nocked and drawn back. Arlahn froze up instantly, only his eyes grew until the glare forced him to squint again.

"What business do you have atop the mountain?" the archer in Arlahn's face asked menacingly. His beard was dark, and he had a small forked scar under his left eye.

With a tilt of Arlahn's eyes, he saw his father beside him, being pulled up to his feet like a prisoner.

"Unhand that man!" Arlahn commanded, though the man wrenching the king up paid him no mind. Arlahn saw that their other captor looked exactly like his own – twins.

"He may be your king," the archer in his face said, "but we have our own in the Mountain."

He backed away enough to allow one of his Brothers to wrench Arlahn up.

How did he know that my father was the king? Arlahn wondered, then heard his father's words echo in his mind once more. "No one can find PJ unless he wants them to. That's the way it's always been with him. You don't find him, he finds you."

Before Arlahn could protest any further, one of the men tossed a black sack over his eyes and he felt a sharp rap on the back of the head.

*****

Serah-Jayne never truly understood her Gift, her *amrak*, but she did understand the magnitude of power she possessed. Diyo, the man who had raised her, in a sense, had taught her all about the world, all its history. It always seemed majestic to her, but majesty was Diyo's way. Sometimes he'd even speak of the events to come, and they would always occur the way he had depicted them to her. He was a man of incredible magic tricks, she thought. He fooled the inevitability of mortality that Serah-Jayne felt weighing heavier on her bones and joints each day.

She was crawling into a cave that was dark and dirty. There was little light, though her eyes had adjusted quickly enough.

"Oh, the things I do for you, Diyo," she said aloud to herself, assessing her past with the man.

Serah-Jayne had lived alone for many years, in fear that if she ever returned permanently to a densely populated area, something terrible of magnificent proportions would happen. Occasionally Diyo would visit, and he would send her out on errands to different cities all across the world. She enjoyed the travel and the feeling of purpose he bestowed on her.

He had tried his best to describe the change in her when her Gift had first manifested. "The *amrak* lets you control things, Wildflower," he'd said, taking her hand in his he produced a small copper coin from his pocket and held it up. "If I were to flip this coin, you just being here would determine which face would land up."

"Please Diyo, it's hard enough without you jesting." She started to grow annoyed with him and pulled her hand away from his.

"I'm serious my dear, look." He pressed his thumb under his forefinger and placed the coin on top of it. "Head or imprint?" he asked and flipped the coin up into the air.

It spun countless times, and Serah-Jayne thought of the least possible outcome: *standing on edge*.

Then the coin bounced twice on the table between them and settled standing up, improbably, a gilded Rai face staring at Serah-Jayne. "You thought of it standing up, didn't you?"

"That was just a freak chance," she countered.

"That's how I should have described it from the start! Oh I hate it when your human words get mixed up in my mind and I can't think of the right one." Diyo took the coin and placed it in her hand, folding her fingers around it. "So long as you are here, the outcome of this coin isn't determined by chance, but by you."

Serah-Jayne stared into the man's old, grey eyes. Without a response from her, he began again with his explanation.

"It's because you affect the outcome of every event that would otherwise be mediated by chance. It's like, when you're around, the dice that are normally thrown by Nature are instead thrown by *you*. Although it may not always seem so, *everything* that happens in this world happens by chance. The reason it doesn't always seem so is that *most* things tend to do what they're most likely to do, what you'd *expect* them to do. But underlying everything is a complex sea of probability that makes almost *anything* possible, although these things are most often very unlikely. But *you*, Serah-Jayne, you can control these waves. If you wanted to, you could make rain fall up, walk through stone, you could freeze fire."

"How is that possible?" asked Serah-Jayne.

"It is your Gift."

It is my curse, she thought impulsively.

"It's part of who you are," Diyo added, reading her mind. "You were born this way, Wildflower, and you will live a life of great importance because of it. It's a complicated thing, and you must try to control it. Once you can, all the power of chance will be at your fingertips."

Serah-Jayne remembered the rest of the conversation that night. She had begun piecing together more and more of her past, up until the day she'd fallen asleep as a young girl and awoken to the destruction of everything she had come to call her Northern home.

Serah-Jayne was getting older now; more worn and colder, and lonelier than ever. She missed Diyo and his warmth. She had been glad when he'd called on her one night in her hunt cabin.

Diyo had sent her to the mountains of Tehbirr's Spine, tasked to watch the king and his son climb safely up a mountain that led to a hidden camp Diyo had told her of. The two were careless and she had to splash the waves of fate for their sake on more than one occasion.

To their credit, they had recovered well from the bird skirting the mountain, but soon after she had to intervene again. As the Prince began grinding down the chimney, she had avoided him sliding down by holding the rock solid, keeping the weak undulations from collapsing under his knees.

The end of the climb was the last time they both truly required her assistance. The boy's fortune became dangerously turbulent, the tree of possible outcomes that flashed before her mind's eye was sparse and overwhelmingly fatal.

Foolishly, the son threw himself out from the mountain. He reached for some roots, but Serah-Jayne saw them slip free of his grasp. She gathered the air below him and willed it forcefully upward. The Prince did the rest. Snatching the thin stocks in his left hand, he had swung along the mountainside toward a rock that was jutting from the face. The weight of the boy on the shrub strained the thin roots and it was ready to give way. Serah didn't even have time to act before the boy vaulted himself to the ledge above. But as soon as the young prince had peaked the mountain, that suicidal father of his mimicked his son's senseless performance and this time Serah-Jayne had to use her Gift to save the man's life.

By virtue of her Gift, she persuaded the roots to hold once more. Lucky bastard, she thought. It was true what Diyo had said, that Serah-Jayne could make almost anything possible, but using her Gift was still not easy, and the more she had to strain against the *natural* flows of chance, the harder it was on her. Then there was the blacking out, but that was something else she didn't understand altogether.

Shortly after the king had thrown himself to the protrusion, the shrub had fallen out from the rock and fluttered its way down to the ground. Fate's original intention.

Chapter 12

Annabella was wearing a long white, slim-fitting gown trimmed with silver and beautiful golden embossments leeching from her shoulders. She sat in front of a mirror on a backless ebony stool, hands folded on her lap. The dainty, aged thief Tod was standing behind her, combing her shining blonde hair, untangling the day away. He volunteered to remain in the service of the Rai family and had reformed into a model helper. Annabella refused to refer to them as servants, and the word "slave" was worse than most insults to her.

She was silent, eyes cast off to mountains and the wooded hills beneath them. Marlyonna and Luzy came in quietly, already looking like sisters of a sort, both fancifully dressed in green and yellow gowns that were embroidered and trimmed with gold and silver lace. They had been into the wine and each held their own silver goblet, with Marlyonna carrying a second for the queen.

She placed the cups on the makeup table, wordlessly relieving Tod as she took up the comb. The queen didn't move for her wine, and Marlyonna saw the worry in her eyes through the mirror.

"What's bothering you, Anna?" she asked in an affable tone.

"It's the king."

"He hasn't been gone long."

"I know I should only expect him to just be getting there now, but he's growing old, Marly," the queen told her daughter-to-be in the mirror before her. "He smokes more and more because he says it helps him feel better, but I know it's killing him at the same time. Pientero has a way with him too. I'm worried that he'll get Hec into trouble without knowing it, say *something* that'll make him want to be a hero again." Annabella looked to a mouth of darkness in the tree line. The night sky was full of stars. "I'm afraid something will happen to him."

"My queen, the king is more than a great man. He'll return to you as always, I'm sure," Luzy said with a smile to reassure the queen, but she feared it would be to no avail. She sat on a short, pillowed bench with one leg tucked under her.

Annabella sighed, professing to the girls what it meant to be with your *amiro*. "When Hectore and I consolidated our bond after our wedding we became one in many ways. I had heard that finding your *amiro* was like choosing the right snowflake in a winter storm. And there's only one for each of us. But when those two souls find one another, it's as if their very fibre is weaved and meshed. Impossible to break or fray. I can, in a way, feel my husband's being. We live as one and if the stories are true, we'll die as one." It's why dealing Judgement was so hard for her. Hectore was nine parts warrior, one part lover, while Annabella was nine parts lover and one part warrior. But at times that one part could swell and overcome all impulses from the other nine. In those moments she felt her husband's shame, like he had failed the people before him. "He's weary and should rest. But I can feel him pushing on to get home to me."

"That is so beautiful in such a sad way, Anna," Marlyonna told her.

"You are well-loved, my queen," Luzy added, again hoping to bring some cheer to the room.

"And that can go a long way," Marlyonna agreed.

"Even the townsfolk have noticed you haven't smiled as much since he left." Luzy comforted once more. "Last time I went to the orphanage there was a little girl who gave me a hug and kiss for the dumplings you supplied. She ran towards Kael and he backed away and bumped into a boy who'd caught a grasshopper." Taking a sip of her wine. "Honestly, I don't know what jumped higher, the bug or Kael. On our way back he called me brave for going there. Can you imagine? He's so strong."

"It's a different strength to show compassion." Annabella told Luzy.

Luzy sipped her wine again, "He said the children made him uncomfortable, I think he's scared to hurt them but he's gentler than a cat with me."

Annabella was smiling once more, her mood restored. "I'm pleased that you and Kael get along like Hec and I."

"I love him, Your Grace. I hope he's my *amiro*," Luzy confessed, suddenly becoming the picture of gentility. "He's everything you dream of finding in a husband when you're a little girl. He's handsome, caring, smart." She bit her lip for a moment and announced, "I'd like to make a trip home with him. So he could meet my family."

"I'm sure those arrangements can be made," Kael said as he ducked his head into the door, gently knocking on it.

The women's laughter had echoed through the corridors and Kael's expression gave away that he was unsure what he would find in investigating the source of the noise. His ice-blue eyes glinted from the lantern bracketed to the wall.

Annabella spun in her chair to face him, motioning for her son to take a seat. "Kael! Come in, please. Sit."

Stepping into the room, Kael sat down next to Luzy on her bench and looked his mother in the eyes. He was concerned, his words hesitant. "May I speak with you, my queen?" he asked courteously.

"Of course."

"Ever the perfect soldier, eh Kael?" Marlyonna teased as she grabbed Luzy's hand and took her from the room. "C'mon Luzy, we'll get you ready for bed. This sounds serious."

Kael waited for the door to softly close before he broached the subject. "It's Arlahn. I remember when I first arrived in Pientero's village with Raph." He took up his mother's soft hand, it was cold to the touch and he could feel the warmth of his own hand flood into her skin. "They're a different people there altogether, it's changed from when you served. All they do is live and breathe survival and war."

"That's no different from when I served at all," the Queen told him. "Except we did it for real, Kael. We know the Brotherhood in the mountain, why are you so concerned?"

"Arlahn's a good brother, he's a strong man, but there's still a tenderness in him. It'll just get taken for weakness in that camp. And those men prey on weakness. Some people in the mountain will break him if he stays up there for too long. Has Raphael ever told you of our first day?"

"No."

Kael began to tell the story of when he and Raphael first arrived in PJ's village.

They were sixteen years old, and yet the pair had been too quick up the mountain for the normal welcoming party of the Brotherhood. Both boys' clothes were ragged and torn from the treacherous climb. Kael was laden with much more gear than his brother, but still walked in stride with Raphael's quick pace the whole time. Finally, they stopped among a dense stand of pines and cedars along a mountain path they'd found. Kael swung his pack from his shoulder and plopped it on the ground. Unhooking a leather canteen from the side, he pulled the cork and drank swiftly from it. With his thirst satiated, he wiped his face with the back of a hand. "There's only a mouthful left," he said and handed the rest to Raphael, but his brother didn't drink from it just yet. He was busy noticing the company arriving through the foliage.

They were approached by a small group of men from beyond the trees, burly men with barrel chests, long hair, and thick beards. A scruffy-faced man leading the pack stepped forward. "So these are the new recruits, they look a little young for our training," he said, even though the boys were right in front of him.

"And you look a little old for a beating," Raphael answered, irritation clear in his voice. If there was ever one thing that drove Raphael off edge it was prejudice of his character, physical or mental.

Angry now, the bearded man glared into Raphael's face and saw the reciprocating emotion. "Is that right? C'mon son!" The man punched one hand against the other, cracking his fingers, and began walking toward the young blonde man before him. "Let's see who gives in first then!"

Suddenly he was cracked in the jaw by a right straight punch and staggered back, clenching his teeth. The man looked over to see Kael standing between them. He had his fists at his side now and his posture was measuring and ready, proud and firm. After no one else came at him, Kael stood up straight. "You will never refer to me or my brother as 'son' again, understood?"

The man was clearly embarrassed after being almost knocked to his knees so easily by a young man. He ran at Kael full of emotion, swinging a heavy right haymaker.

Kael ducked under and snapped a left hook into the man's kidney, and as he winced and bent over, the Prince landed a right uppercut into the man's solar plexus. He grabbed hold of the man's chest with his left hand and repeated three strong crosses into his face. Kael didn't hit him with full force, but still the man's cheek cut open on the first blow and his knees buckled.

Another thick-boned and scruffy-faced man emerged from the crowd. He was coming up on Kael from behind, full of hostility. Raphael stepped in, spraying water from his mouth into the man's face, causing him to reflexively close his eyes. Raphael swung his bow hard, as if scything grain. The hardened maple shaft slammed across the man's jaw and he was stopped instantly, falling back on his rear. It took more than a moment for Raphael to register it, but the man he had just struck down looked exactly like the man that Kael had just embarrassed. They were twins as well, only they were the identical kind.

Finally, a deep voice bellowed over the crowd. A path opened among them as if curtains were being pulled open to the morning sun. A tall man dressed in pelts of brown fur walked alone through the crowd. He had long black hair tied in a ponytail at the neck, and dark, dark eyes. He walked with authority and it didn't take any longer than a first glance for Raphael and Kael to know that this was Pientero.

"Balanor! Balanus! You two deserve that beating, attacking the climbers and not one minute after their arrival," he snapped quickly in agitation, pointing back through the path he had cut in the crowd. "Go back to my quarters and wait for me there," he ordered.

No man would deny Pientero Jessonarioko's power, he simply took it. The twins obeyed the command and walked past the staring eyes with their tails between their legs.

Once Balanor and Balanus had left sight, the crowd dispersed, no longer interested in the two young men. No one really knew who these two young newcomers were. To the rest of the Brotherhood, they were just a couple of new recruits. Pientero turned back to his guests with a smile. "A kingly greeting, eh!" His voice full of sarcasm. "Come, I do have some questions for you before we start."

"That day, Raph and I made powerful enemies among the Brotherhood," Kael told his mother. "Balanor is strong, no doubt a superior by now, and he'll do everything he can to shame Arlahn, just to spite me and Raph."

"A cut on the cheek will heal in time, but a cut through a man's pride..." Annabella's voice trailed off as she understood why Kael was concerned for his brother. She forced a smile and looked back into her son's gaze. He was disappointed in himself for that day all those years ago and she saw it. It had never occurred to him before that Arlahn was the one that would be punished.

"You shouldn't burden yourself with such thoughts," the Queen told her son. "It wasn't you who climbed the mountain this time. Arlahn can befriend anyone or anything! Remember Wender's dog?" Smiling, she recounted the time when Arlahn was younger and had befriended a sickly mutt that passed away soon after.

"Raphael and I were just talking about that the other night actually." Kael smiled sheepishly.

"Arlahn cared so well for that dog after he found him in the alley. I have no doubt that you and Raphael know how to handle yourselves when push comes to shove. But Arlahn has other virtues that may not be as glamorous, but are useful, nonetheless. You'd be surprised at the power of diplomacy in those very same situations, if you'd ever be so willing to try to use it."

Kael forced a smile, knowing his aggressive demeanour. "Yeah, Arlahn does have something special about him when it comes to caring. Maybe he'll do what I couldn't and end this feud between brothers."

A silence fell over them then, as if they were contemplating the possibility of Kael's words.

Comfortable silence, thought Kael. But he was the first to break it. "Raphael finished his designs for a few of his inventions. Tomorrow we're going to start building them."

"That sounds like a busy day. I hope you two will make time for those beautiful girls."

With that, Kael rose and Annabella with him.

He stood like his father, full of pride. "Speaking of which, I should go to bed. I don't want to keep Luzy waiting too long."

Annabella pushed herself up on her toes and kissed his forehead gently. "Goodnight, my son." She smiled at him full-heartedly and watched as he opened the door and slipped through into the flickering ruddy corridor.

*****

Togut had been given direct orders from Lord Evris that night in his tent. "You'll rest here for a few days, and then you may select a dozen men, as you see fit," he had said after he touched him. Afterwards, Lord Evris sought him out once more and told him that their targets were the princes of Pellence, the sons of their sworn enemy, Demonblades.

Togut had always thought himself a smart man with a good sense of judgement. That was why he kept such information to himself for the time being. He walked among the soldiers in the camp and selected a few of the least conspicuous men. Evris' army was full of men who seemed to have their brains off tilt in their skulls. They were warriors and barbarians, rough men. Togut was looking more for the opposite. He was planning a strategic infiltration route and needed more civilized-looking men and those who had some degree of control over their impulses. They were still strong, quick to temper and deceptive at heart, but you wouldn't recognize it just by looking at them.

A fine bunch, Togut thought to himself. Gordun the axeman was his close childhood friend whom he'd trust to the end. They had grown up together and joined the GodKing's army with dreams of success. When Togut was given permission to commission twelve men, Gordun was his first thought. There was perhaps no man stronger in the entire Damonai army.

A few others Togut had trained with volunteered when they heard the news. He knew they were all good soldiers, all of them. When it came time, he needed only to select another four men, and he did his best with what he had left from the army camped among the Sainti ruins. Three of the four men Togut took were brothers, one nimble, one powerful, and one sly.

Togut himself headed his group of scouts back toward the path where he'd had his encounter with the princes of Pellence. When they arrived at the site, he suddenly remembered that there were no bodies left from the attack, having noticed this when he'd doubled back from his escape. Togut cursed, thinking now that he may not find what he came for. He began walking around the site until finally Gordun voiced his thoughts, "You've always had a flair for the dramatic, what are you looking for Togut?"

"When I was scouting this area and we were attacked by those sons of bitches, my captain carried a generous purse and a map," Togut answered.

Most men in the Damonai army didn't recognize the significance of a map. But most men didn't think like Togut. He didn't just follow like a senseless hound anymore, he was going to lead. And in order to lead, he needed to have direction around the unknown lands of Saintos.

"After they killed him, they must have cleared his body away. I'd just as soon leave and make do with what we've got rather than look for the fool's rotting corpse, but I have plans for that money and need his map."

The men all dismounted and began searching the ground.

It was a good ten minutes until a man found evidence in the shape of a black leather boot. Togut went to the location and looked all around him, spinning full-circle, but found nothing else. Then a wet drip fell on his shoulder from up above. He looked up to a horrific, gory scene. Twisted in the overgrowth of the trees, bodies had been lodged into branches high up. After a week, faces mutilated by carrion birds had rendered most men almost unrecognizable. Eye sockets were hollow and black, noses eaten to the cartilage, cheeks missing rotten flesh.

"I found the bodies!" Togut claimed to the squad and they arrested their search to gather at his position. "But I don't think we'll be getting anything from them."

He looked up and revealed the corpses in the branches.

"How the hell did they get them way up there?" Gordun asked aloud.

"These men weren't just men," Togut told him, remembering the swordsman. "One was a beast."

"But he couldn't have just heaved fully grown warriors into the trees," Gordun stated like it was fact.

Togut was unsure, having seen the man firsthand, and remained silent.

"Well, we only need to find the leader's body, right?" the biggest of the three brothers said. He clapped his nimble brother on the shoulder. "Palor can climb anything, can't ya bro?"

The slender man named Palor looked up and scanned branches. "Yeah, I can get up there."

It did make sense that if anyone was to climb the tree it was him. Palor was tall and lanky, and although he wasn't the strongest of the bunch, his length and lightness afforded him certain advantages.

Togut began circling the tree, looking up at the bodies. A third of the way around he backed away from it, pointing up. "He's the third man up," he said as he recognized his former leader.

Palor removed his sword and handed it to his bigger brother as the other men gathered round.

"Someone give him a boost," Togut ordered.

Gordun moved to the tree and readied himself. Palor stepped into Gordun's cupped hands and was hoisted to the lowest branch, and he began climbing the tree.

As he rose, the stench grew stronger until it was almost unbearable. He was beside the first of the dead soldiers. The man was a mess. His nose, eyes, and lips had been ripped away from the flesh, his clothes torn to shreds. Skin had been pecked at relentlessly and black dried blood was everywhere. This particular one had an arrow in his armpit and a long open wound on his back that housed a new cultivation of maggots.

Palor almost hurled right there but instead pushed himself ever higher, breathing only when he needed to and turning his head away from the rot as he did so. He passed a headless corpse and climbed as quickly as he could to reach the leader Togut had pointed to.

The man was propped up, almost sitting looking down into the valley. His face – or what was left of it, rather – had a look of bewilderment on it, made worse by the fact that his left eyebrow and eye remained, though it bore no lids. His cheeks were relaxed and his mouth was open, but there was no tongue. Wearing torn clothes with a dagger sitting firmly to the thumbguard in his chest.

Palor perched himself on a thick branch and rifled through the dead man's clothes as quickly as he could. Suddenly, he heard the jingle of coins under his left hand.

Taking a quick gasp of air, he reached into the man's pocket and produced a small leather pouch with a thread weaving through the top of it tied in a knot. As he pulled the bag from the man's pocket, he dislodged the corpse enough that it fell. Tumbling down through the tree branches with loud snaps and cracks, the body pounded to the ground onto his back and settled twisted, staring up at Palor with his dead eye.

Togut found the bloodied map in the man's breast pocket, as Palor dropped the bag and began climbing down as fast as his long frame allowed him. The bag landed in Togut's other hand. Opening it, he saw the gold and silver pieces glittering inside.

Palor fell the remaining ten feet to the ground, bending his knees deeply to absorb the impact.

"Well done, Palor," Togut told the climber. He flipped a silver piece to each of the men in his party. The purse was heavier than he had expected, and it was a good way to build trust with his men. Togut unfolded the map and gathered his bearings.

"We should head for the city of Pellence. These brothers were heading in that direction. According to the map, we stay on this path for about a league and take the west fork. Let's go."

The men followed Togut as they marched through the woods beside the trail to avoid unnecessary encounters that could be reported to an authority. No, that was not his fashion. Togut would move silently, infiltrate the city keeping a low profile, and gather information before he made his move. He was a thinker, and he knew what the princes were capable of. He would need to take them by surprise.

That night, they camped in a clearing. Two fires had been lit, and men were sitting around them both. They were not permitted horses for the mission and each man was exhausted by day's end. Togut had arranged for a nightly watch, with new watchmen being replaced roughly every two hours – the routine worked well.

Each fire had a cauldron hanging over the flames and men were cooking warm stew with some of their dwindling rations.

As Gordun handed Togut a bowl, he leaned in close to his ear. "We're running low on food," he spoke in a hushed voice.

Pulling away, his eyes met those of Togut, who acknowledged what was said and gave a slight nod. Gordun turned, picked up a stick, and plunked down.

Togut appreciated the discretion. It was not a matter he wished to speak of openly in front of the other men. Empty stomachs usually beget bad moods. He hadn't realized how hard he'd pushed his horse to get back to Evris. The journey back, with some many more people travelling alongside him, took longer than he'd anticipated.

The two sat together on a fallen tree. Gordun stretched out his legs while Togut finished his stew, and they watched as the climber approached them.

"What will we do when the food runs out?" Palor said.

"You have keen ears," Gordun told him.

"Aye, they've kept my brothers and me alive a few times," answered the climber.

"Tomorrow or the next day we'll reach the city of Pellence. I'll restock our supplies and continue our search," Togut answered.

"Maybe we can find a settlement on our way," countered Palor.

"Not unless there's one along the road." Togut shook his head, "The map's old, they didn't draw any settlements on it."

"I see, when we reach Pellence then," Palor said before walking away.

For a moment, the two men sat in silence, watching the climber stroll over to his brothers at a fire. Gordun threw the twig he'd picked up. Then he spoke, "So, you're just going to walk into Pellence undetected?"

Togut glanced at his old friend and said nothing at first, only grinned. "Something like that."

Gordun stood up, placing one of his thick meaty hands on Togut's shoulder to help his ascent. He knew he'd learn Togut's plan sooner or later, and he was too tired at the moment to digest it. "You and your damn flair for the dramatic."

Chapter 13

Arlahn came to with the black cloth still before his eyes, though now little lights danced in his vision. His captors were spinning him around in circles slowly, until they weren't, and his consciousness grounded things once again. The Prince felt his movements restricted as well, strapped to a chair, he realised. The air stunk of thick incense and he heard bodies moving about, though none of them spoke a word. In the distance, he could hear a commotion, a large crowd screaming, though he was too far to hear words.

Finally, without warning, Arlahn felt a prick stab into the back of his neck. The shock made him jerk his head away and he demanded then, "What do you want?"

"What is it *you* want Arlahn, son of Hectore?" came a deep voice in response.

He was caught off-guard. How did they know who he was? He and his father travelled wearing simple clothes to avoid detection.

"There was a man with me. What happened to him?" he asked.

"I wouldn't worry about anyone but yourself."

He felt the pinch bite into his neck again and he took it without moving, squeezing his jaw through the pain and silently cursing his torturer.

"From now on, when I ask questions, you give me answers. Not more questions. Understood?" the voice behind him was so deep that it resonated off the walls until it filled the room.

He heard what sounded like the singing of those strange meditation bowls priests used back in Pellence. The ringing chime reverberated through the room until it settled into silence.

"Breathe this in," the voice commanded.

"Why?" The Prince began to hold his breath in protest but soon surrendered. What was he to do, not breathe? The scent was an earthy fragrance that was welcoming like a woman's perfume but stung at his veiled eyes and lungs like smoke.

From outside, Arlahn heard a large hush fall over the crowd and a lone voice boomed out a few words before a long, haunted silence began.

Then the deep voice finally answered, "So you can tell me no lies."

*****

Hectore watched as one of the Brothers cracked Arlahn in the head. After which they had respectfully unhanded the King and greeted him accordingly. He had recognized the mountainous features on Tamis and Gringoll the minute they had arrived at the hunt camp in the foothills of Tehbirr's Spine. That night, after Arlahn fell asleep, Hectore roused them quietly from their fake slumber with a touch. They spoke for a few minutes after verifying their identities and the Brothers took off.

Now, Hectore followed the group along a narrow path until they crested a hill and down in the valley below them was an entire community. He looked out at the buildings, all whitewashed wood and one story tall. The ground of the compound was grey, sandy dirt and there were footpath entrances spaced every twenty feet around the entire perimeter. At the heart of the community were twin high-ceilinged buildings that acted as halls and storehouses for the mountain men.

The king heard strange noises coming from within the city, and he walked down toward it. Shouts and taunts suggested a commotion, and through a few breaks in the buildings he saw a crowd gathered. Confused, Hectore quickened his pace toward the barbaric screams coming from the twin buildings.

He turned a corner and saw a crowd of people dressed in warmer mountain clothing filling the space between the two structures; their fists in the air and their screams jumbling incomprehensibly. Hectore started to push his way to the front of the crowd, slipping through the men and women like a snake through grass.

In the centre of the massive circle were two men. Pientero Jessonarioko stood tall, over six feet, long silver hair clasped at the base of his neck with a gold-trimmed leather strap, and dark, furrowed eyes. He was bullying another man of equal size, tossing and smacking him around like a dirty, old rug.

"On what grounds?!" Hectore bellowed out as he stepped clear of the crowd.

"Steer clear of this, King!" PJ roared. He blocked a punch with his forearm and threw an overhand right into the man's jaw, hauled him up, and pounded him back down with another thunderous blow.

Infuriated by his response, Hectore marched over to where PJ was wringing the other man's collar with one hand and pounding him into unconsciousness with the other. He caught PJ's arm with his own as it swung back and their elbows locked into one another. For that moment, breaths were caught in lungs, eyes glued open, the world stopped.

PJ glared back at the king with fiery eyes that burned with rage. But Hectore stood firm and kept his icy gaze chilling to the bone. Finally, PJ lowered his hand and threw the man to the ground.

"On what grounds?" he spat. "This… This traitorous whoreson tried to poison me!" Hoofing the man's ribs with his boot, who rolled onto his back with his arms crossed over his chest.

Hectore was shocked at the accusation. The man must have the wits of an ant to try and poison Pientero Jessonarioko. "Why would he try something so base?" Hectore asked in the man's defence as he was pushing himself feebly back onto his knees.

"Because he's a fucking weasel without honour! That's why!" Pientero fed the weasel another boot to keep him down. "He wished to dethrone me while I slept. The laws of this settlement are clear. We've never needed this one till now. If a man wishes another dead, the duel is put down. Where's the duel, Hec? Where's the fucking respect!" A glob of spit jumped from PJ's mouth through his rage as he advanced toward the man. But this time, Hectore resisted him with a hand to his chest, heels digging into the ground.

After Hectore had become the HighKing, he gave Pientero rights to the mountains and supreme authority of the area during his absence, essentially making Pientero the king-in-the-mountain. But Hectore was here now. And it seemed the mountain had need of him to be King for this matter. After a second look from Hectore that warned Pientero of his trespassing, he once again submitted to the king and turned away.

Hectore held out his hands for momentary silence then announced. "If Pientero challenges the man to a duel for treason, he may not refuse, and that will be his punishment."

Pientero walked over to the closest Brother and pulled the sword from his scabbard. Returning to the man he had beaten, he stabbed it into the ground beside him. "Duel then," he said coldly.

Pientero began walking to another soldier for his sword when the weasel took up the weapon and ran at him. PJ turned at the last second and slapped away the stabbing blade. Now the warrior king was furious, he didn't even think about searching for a weapon. He faced his opponent with his hands raised, curses and promises of death raging from him. "This time you're not saving him!" he called out to Hectore and the king simply shrugged and disappeared back into the crowd.

The men circled each other once. The traitor had youth and strength to his advantage; Pientero had unending experience to his.

The traitor came at him with textbook form, but Pientero was still too powerful for him. The man lunged with a thrust, quickly followed by a backhand then forehand slashes. Pientero ducked and began weaving right and left, each time guiding the blade away with the palm of his hand on the flat of the blade. Pientero then launched his own combination of blows, ending with a devastating elbow that snapped the man's head back and sent him staggering. Thoughtlessly, the traitor came at Pientero with a telegraphed attack. Again, PJ side-stepped, and as the man followed through with his wild stab, he grabbed the base of the sword's blade with one hand and drove one knuckle into the bone on the back of the traitor's sword hand, forcing him to release the weapon. Using the momentum, PJ continued to spin the man back around and countered with a solid boot-heel into his chest.

The warrior king closed the distance and, holding it by the blade, he plunged the sword down into the man's chest. Coming up again with bloody fingers where the sword had bitten through, Pientero looked round at his people. They weren't scared, but rather shocked and in awe. Most were even comforted by having the distribution of power restored. Silence filled the mountain valley.

"This man was a traitor!" the king-in-the-mountain declared before his people. "He tried to poison me in my bed. You should all sleep better knowing that he is no longer among us. This is why we don't take in strays from the lower lands."

The crowd felt no sorrow for their fallen member, as if none had known him. Pientero walked back through the circle, brushing past Hectore on his way. "Follow me," he told him without stopping.

He's still used to command, Hectore reflected as he followed the mountain king through the crowd and into the streets. They finally entered a house that looked just like any other and Pientero beckoned his old friend to sit. The place was handsomely furnished with plush cushions on the chairs and a rich burl-finished table. PJ sat at the table and looked at the king with forgiving eyes. "I'm sorry, old friend," he said. "My emotions got captured by the moment."

"There is no need for apologies, brother," Hectore told him, taking the seat across. "Sometimes our emotions better steer our way through a situation," he pointed out. "I just wanted to be sure it was justice and not malice that I saw out there."

"That man was a traitor, Hec. And since Dofi, I've never had a tolerance for men of the sort." Dofi was a general who had worked with Tumbero against Pellence. He was one of Hectore's father's most trusted men before he arranged King Arlahn's coup. Pientero had known all too well about the man from tales even before he heard their truth from Hectore.

"I believe you. Now how about offering me some water? The climb was harder than I remembered."

"Ah, then you have forgotten what I taught you all those years ago," PJ claimed as he reached for a clay jug and two glasses.

"Don't give me that shit! I'm just getting old, same as you."

Pientero gestured an insult, and Hectore smiled. "Don't think I didn't notice how long that fight took."

"Barely a minute!" PJ retorted.

"Yes, but the old Pientero Jessonarioko would have ended it with the first swing of the sword!"

PJ began to laugh, pouring the water he told the king, "Maybe I was giving my people a show?" Then he slid the king his cup. "Ah, maybe you're right, but until I can't do what I do, I'll always fight."

"That was never in doubt, my friend." Hectore raised his cup in cheers.

Then the salt- and pepper-haired man leaned over the table and spoke in a lower voice "That man today, Hec, there was something different about him."

"What do you mean?" The king looked puzzled.

"He came to us a few months back. Scouts found him alone, he said some bandits raided his farm and kept to his story long enough for us to believe him and welcome him into our home. But when he was attacking me, his form was trained — only not by this camp. That man knew war before he found us. And the poison he was going to give me is completely untraceable. My men would have thought I passed in my sleep." PJ sat back in his chair. "Luckily I had a friend warn me of his attempt."

"So you believe he was sent here?" Hectore didn't want to think the worst just yet. But his nightmare was solidified when Pientero grew as grave and replied, "I do. And you and I both know who makes long, deceptive, cowardly plans."

"The Damonai," Hectore voiced it, though he dreaded hearing the words aloud. "Then what I feared is true. I've been getting reports of bandits in the woods around the outskirt settlements, Tall Oaks and Silver Streams mostly. I'd hoped it was just young hoodlums and the local authorities would handle it. But the region's being scouted out too. My boys noticed it the last time they were out hunting after they met a group of these bandits."

"Then it's good that you came, we can start preparing the Brotherhood for war. I was beginning to think I wouldn't get to see another battle. Kind of a sad thought, almost."

"I can't stay, but I'll bring this news back to Pellence. Summon the Wardens and tell them to ready their arms. It looks like we'll have to throw the Damonai back on their side of the Spine again."

"Ooh, I like when you come around, Hec. Fires get started, water starts boiling, shit gets done!" Pientero grinned at the defiance in the king. Then, with a more composed timbre in his voice, he asked, "But why are you really here? My scouts said they met up with you at a hunt camp the night before last. An' get this, another pair told me they saw a lone traveller. Big man with a black butterfly axe, sound familiar?"

"Kind of sounds like Jole," Hectore said, suddenly reminded of his old magical comrade from a past life.

"No way that crazy bastard's still alive all this time though. Not when you wrestle bears like he does. You think he survived after he left us?"

"We did," the king answered with raised eyebrows then took a gulp of water. "I came with my son Arlahn. Your men welcomed us after the climb. I trust he's alright?"

"He'll be fine. He's just answering some questions," PJ reassured him. "You think it's time for him to become a Brother?"

"He does... And I do too."

"Why the hesitation?"

"His Gift. It still hasn't manifested."

"So the boy's a gimp then?" PJ said, downing the last of his water. "I wonder why that Wytch Hennah called him Doom?"

Hectore took offence to that. Every time he heard the word "doom" he heard it in Hennah Asa's throaty accent. "The Wytch is crazed. The boy's perfectly fine. He's a quick learner and he's got a strong heart. He's been training with his brothers since he was old enough to walk in their shadows."

Pientero deliberately contemplated for a long minute, reading his friend with a look as he did so.

"Well," he said at last, "I don't know if you noticed, but no one else in this camp has one of your fancy Gifts and these are the finest soldiers in the world. Only these men and women have been with us since the war, Hec, some of them were even born in these mountains. It's all they know. We don't eat creampuffs and sleep on fluffy beds here. Your boy will have to be able to handle it. He thinks he's ready, we'll see how he does tonight."

At that, Hectore was alleviated but strangely unnerved.

*****

    Jole was used to being alone. His entire life had been one lonely journey for the most part. There were times when he interacted with others, but not often. He had lived and fought in the king's Rebellion as a soldier for the Brotherhood. But even surrounded by men he would dare call his friends, he never felt a sense of belonging. Jole remembered that the only few who ever attempted friendship with him were the group's leaders, Hectore Rai and Pientero Jessonarioko, a man as strong as he, named Anvar, a pair of brothers, Raphael and Kael, who were best friends with Benson and Annabella Wellcant. Hectore was inspiring, the way every leader should be, never asking anyone to do something he wouldn't have done himself. Pientero, he remembered, was more seasoned at the time and had grasped vital knowledge in his travels. The man somehow had an understanding of magic and taught Jole many of the spells one could use with practice.

    It was always afterward, when he wasn't fighting or killing men, that he wanted distance from them. Once he had known love, or so he thought. But that woman left him in a Cooperith town. Rasha was her name. She said she loved me, but she loved the singer more, Jole thought resentfully.

    He had often been called a giant of a man, though he wasn't exceptionally tall. He was still a clean six feet, but it was his frame, thick and heavy, that radiated his power.

    Dressed in a sand-coloured, wind-battered overcoat, Jole topped a hillcrest and looked out over the low valley. He scanned the terrain for the contingent of savages he had been tracking. They had been moving purposefully on horseback, mostly in single file. The hoof marks overlapped, so it was hard to tell exactly how many there were. Ten men would have been a tasty amount for the bestial man to engage into combat with. Fifteen would have him full, but twenty men would have seen him actually challenged. Jole pushed on with no fear for the impending doom. Odds had never stopped him before.

    His whole life he had beaten overwhelming odds on more occasions than he could remember. So much so, that he had almost grown accustomed to it. His body was covered with scars and nasty gashes from countless battles, not all of which were from weapons or men. He'd fought with all manner of beasts throughout his life, but there was no beast as deadly or vicious as man. Other species, Jole had learned, could be bargained with, dominated, or avoided altogether. Most animals had one set of rules, laid out by the Wild. Man was more unpredictable, with more rules laid out by other men, rules that were easily broken if they were even followed to begin. Jole better understood the rules of the Wild so he sought out life among it, alone. Loneliness didn't really bother him, however. He had never properly grown a sense of community.

Finding himself without a home as a young boy, Jole had grown up in the lush terrains of Saintos, travelling to nearly every realm during that time to survive but keeping mostly to the solitude only found deep in the Neddhiwan mountains. He had vague memories of a caregiver from when he was younger, but every time Jole tried to remember more, his eyes would water and he'd smell fire smoke. He didn't know if this person he remembered was his mother or a distant relative, they may have even been fantasies he burned into his mind from having watched normal children with normal lives from some dark corner of an alley. Jole knew nothing of his heritage. He grew up living in caves and abandoned shelters and sustained himself by foraging when the seasons were generous, and with rubbish and carrion in desperate times. Living this way, he quickly learned what survival meant – adhering to the rules of the Wild. A lesson that his very presence on this hilltop proved he had learned well.

Jole carried a traveller's pack over his shoulder and one weapon: a two-handed battle axe. He had found it in the high mountains of Neddihw in his youth. It had a matte black haft with a butterfly blade. There were foreign markings along the haft between set gemstones, he never had learned their meaning.

How Jole ended up alone and how he came about the axe were the same story in a way. His father had drowned when he was clearing a dam and it gave way without warning, so Jole lived alone with who he figured was his mother as a young pup. One day, another child in his village said something about how Jole's father must've been weaker than beavers and a fight broke out. When the boy's father came to break up the fight, Jole's first fireball leapt from his hands through his emotion. It swallowed the man before his son's eyes and Jole ran away as the boy cried. He had bumped into a girl with a streak of blonde in her hair, he remembered. She wasn't much younger than Jole but she claimed to have been sent with a message: that he had been chosen for some great delivery. When Jole made it back to his village that night, he found his home ablaze. A neighbour came to him and apologized, telling him that his mother had been sleeping inside.

After all these years, Jole didn't remember much of their conversation but two things she said stuck; the mention of the great delivery and that she called the weapon Omega. And so, it was named.

Shortly after, Jole got caught up in the middle of a war and since then he had never found his peace again. But I at least delivered Rasha to her brother, he thought, I have done something right.

He hefted his axe and balanced the shaft on his shoulder. His eyes narrowed when they finally found a pillar of smoke against the moonlit night. Jole had learned about his magic as a young child. It was probably the reason why his people had abandoned him, he thought. He took a deep breath and closed his eyes hard. Then he opened them quickly. What were once eyes, so healthy, were now balls of intangible yellow light. A black slit through the centre of each gave him the look of the feline giants in the mountains.

The world he now took in appeared through a cataract haze. Jole still stood atop the hill and gazed into the valley, only now the terrain seemed even darker to his eyes – it usually did when he willed the magic to his vision. In the night, everything almost blended together, except for living things. Under the pillar of smoke were blazing figures of bright white light. *People*, he told himself.

Jole watched them as they moved around. He was still a fair distance away, but he could now tell for sure that there were definitely more than eight and less than fifteen, ten or twelve probably, he figured. Better than he anticipated. He'd killed twelve men at once before.

Closing his eyes again, Jole blinked away the magic. It was a strange thing to him – *magic*. He could feel it in himself. It was a warmth that swam through his veins. A feeling of utopia that would oscillate along with gut-rot and feverish chills. When he used too much of it at once the feeling would turn into a migraine that ruptured his skull.

Jole felt the cold steel of the axe shaft sliding down his hands as he lowered it from his shoulder, the hilt thudding into the ground. He looked at the butterfly of blades around his hand. They were as long as his forearm, thick and heavy, with multi-coloured gems beset in a pattern on the flats of the blades. It was a beautiful, yet menacing weapon.

Taking up the axe in one hand, Jole walked down the hill toward the group he'd been following. He came upon a cave and stepped inside cautiously. It was empty.

Content that his potential campsite was isolated, Jole flicked a flame from his finger, which instantly licked a fire over a pile of kindling. He walked back out of the cave into the forest, returning with a large forked stick. Pulling a short skinning knife from his pack, Jole sharpened points into the wood.

When he was done, he set his traveller's pack next to the fire, pulling a black bag from it, and a dead rabbit from the black bag. It was already cleaned. He speared the rabbit meat onto his stick and held it above the fire, slowly turning it until the skin was golden brown and dripping.

Jole sat and ate in complete silence, thinking. He had been following the riders for a few days. In that time, they travelled in almost a straight line, strategically. Jole didn't know what their intentions were, but a group of that size only moved with such speed for a few reasons. Jole knew of their ill intent. He had found three dead bodies on their path, two children and an old man. The old man had been beaten brutally to death. The two boys were lying on the ground close by, each with gashes across their throats.

At first, when Jole had found them, he wondered what could have prompted such an act. And when he found the trail of multiple hooves, he began his pursuit. Jole was a man of action, unable to see the world in the intangible shades of grey. For him it was only black or white. Pleasure or pain, good or bad. It was that part of him that had brought him together with King Hectore during his rebellion. The two men shared common views on many things. Of all the people he had met during his years, Jole believed Hectore Rai to have been the best of them. He understood why people had called him the prophesied King and why hundreds of thousands of men followed him in the end. There were few men Jole would openly call friend, but he was proud to call the king his friend, although he hadn't seen or heard from him in decades.

Sometimes in the presence of too much commotion around the king, Jole had grown very anxious. When a magicker becomes anxious, the surrounding area can become very dangerous, very quickly. This was another lesson he'd learned throughout his childhood, and eventually he was forced to leave the king's side. Keeping his emotions in control was crucial to controlling his magic, and Jole was a sympathetic being. It was the injustice and pain of foul deeds that fed these emotions, and all around him, he could see men being used by others, treachery and pain being delivered for personal gain. There was no order like there was in the Wild.

But in the next few days, Jole would close the gap between himself and this party, find out why they killed an old man and two children, and restore order to his own personal Wild.

Chapter 14

Arlahn was forced into a door and shoved down hard onto a chair. Then a hand ripped the black cloth away from his head. Long hair fell before his face into his eyes and he shook it clear.

He saw the man holding the black sack in his fist first. He was probably more bear than man. Tall enough that Arlahn had to crane his neck, a bastion for a chest, tree trunks for arms and a great beard that collared his neck. He was bald, and when he took a step back Arlahn could see that he only had his left hand. The other arm was a stump, cut off part way up the forearm. "He answered the questions well enough, my king. This one's got some strength in him yet," the man claimed in his deep voice.

Arlahn noticed the other two men in the room then. His father sat on the far side of a large table, opposite another man, who Arlahn could tell was Pientero Jessonarioko at first glance. He basked in confidence and glared at Arlahn through grey, bushy brows. Eyes black as night felt like they were digging into the Prince's soul.

"Stand!" he commanded the Prince. "Come closer."

Arlahn obliged without hesitation. Pientero rose to tower several inches over him. PJ sensed Arlahn's anxiety, but he also felt little intimidation in the young prince. To PJ, this was most important; any trace of fear of what was to come was intolerable. He was satisfied with what he saw and gave the Prince a few hits on the shoulder, measuring him up quickly. "Tell me, Prince. What's the greatest strength of a good army? Is it the strength in our arms? Or the quality of our weapons? The strategy of our plans maybe?"

Before Arlahn answered too hastily, he took a moment of contemplation, proving his adolescent maturity. There were many factors that were the ingredients to a good army. All the aforementioned were prime examples, and Arlahn considered them along with the possibility that Pientero had given him the answer in the question. *Perhaps he wants me to tilt for good leadership?* Arlahn wondered, but when he looked at his father, he realized he was contemplating the question wrong. He had overlooked the most basic principle. His answer came to him – the difference between fighters and soldiers, a mob and an army. "The greatest strength of an army is their discipline."

Pientero liked that answer and graced the Prince with a little smirk. "Good." He sat back down. "You've met Anvar already. I'm Pientero Jessonarioko."

Arlahn acknowledged the huge man before him more appropriately as Anvar greeted Hectore, clasping his forearm left-handed.

"Good to see your strength kept up all these years, Anvar," the king mentioned as he squeezed the big man's forearm. Anvar seated himself at the end of the table between the two kings.

"One more question. If a sickly boy is out alone on a winter lake and falls through thin ice, what would you do?"

"I would try and save him," the Prince answered, noble intentions in mind.

"Then you would die trying, or not save him at all," Pientero told him gruffly. "In the winter, if a mother bear and her cub starve for food and run the risk of death, the mother will eat her cub. It's not because she doesn't feel for her baby, but because she knows that if she were to perish, the cub would soon follow and that would be the end of it. She could always have another cub, but only if she survived."

The king-in-the-mountain glanced across the table to the HighKing. "He's soft, but soft is easier to mould. I'll take him." Then he gave the Prince a quick look. "You can sit back down."

Arlahn did as he was bid on the chair in the corner and seemed instantly forgotten by the trio at the table. So for the next two hours he merely listened as the three men engaged in conversation. He paid great attention to all the details of their discussion. First, they spoke more of the deception and complexity of the Damonai's war plans. Then they remembered the heroic deeds they had accomplished as the Brotherhood of old during their rebellion. Suicidal recon in enemy camps, run-ins with near-legendary beasts, outnumbered twenty-to-one in fully armed fights. The fact that both leaders were still alive was a mystery. In some of the stories Arlahn heard, it seemed as if one would deliberately leave the other for death, yet they always both escaped. He was captivated by their tales but inwardly dismissed most as hyperbole. The whole scene seemed too much like a fantasy to Arlahn. In their house, PJ was talked about like a hero in an epic novel. And now here he was, sitting right across the table from his father, within spitting distance, joking and laughing and farting just like any other man. Yet to Arlahn, to the world, he was *more*.

The people of Pellence would have marvelled to see Kael and Hectore train and spar together; mention of anyone else as equal in battle would be heresy. However, most residents of Pellence hardly recalled Pientero's existence, mostly because anyone fighting the Poet of Battle didn't survive to recount such tales.

Having suddenly erased himself from the world after their war, he was more a myth than anything now. Once upon a time, Pientero was well known throughout all the lands west of Tehbirr's Spine, but now he was a story to be told around campfires to beady-eyed children. Almost thirty years, he had lived in these mountains, Arlahn knew, and during that time had no interaction with the outside world, as if he'd just walked off its surface one day. He simply remained in the mountains, training the best fighters in the realm.

A fight between the two kings in front of Arlahn would mean the death of them both, he was sure of it. It was a godsend that they were both fighting the same evil in the end. Each man literally had the capacity to turn the tide of war, Arlahn knew that from experience now and was beginning to understand why. Although he never actually saw Hectore in real battle, after learning his Gift, the mere prospect of it gave Arlahn a chill. Father beats on Kael like a practice dummy, and Kael beats on all of us like we're the dummies. How would Pientero stack up? Arlahn wondered. Was this man truly the HighKing's equal, even without the possession of any Gift?

"The Damonai rally behind the Gifted same as the Sainti," Anvar pointed out. "I guess this next war depends on who's got what Gift and who uses theirs best. If there's another Tumbero, there could be trouble."

"I'm a different man now!" Hectore proclaimed. "We'll handle whatever comes at us. We did then. How many arrows did I have the night we took Pellence?"

"Nine. I remember," Pientero answered, "You took down twenty-four men with those arrows, killing your way to your queen. But you were a different man, you just said it yourself. Remember what you would do back then? The heights you went to? And I've been over that night a thousand times in my head. If the storm hadn't started when it did, we may not have won. It was the luckiest situation we could have hoped for."

"We build our own situations PJ. You taught me that," Hectore responded stubbornly.

"Well, we'll have to be careful from now on is all. But if a war is coming, we should make the Brotherhood known again to the Damonai. I'm sure they didn't forget how we whooped 'em. We can't let our presence be forgotten."

"If I recall, the fact my presence was forgotten was one of our most powerful weapons," the king answered in debate.

"Yeah, I guess that's true too, huh? We can continue this talk later though, in private," Pientero concluded.

Turning to the Prince as if he had just remembered his presence, Pientero gave him a look. "You'll stay here for a time." Pientero rose and Arlahn knew he should follow. They made their way to the door. "Your father will take your horse home for you." Outside the door there was a lad a touch younger than the Prince. He saluted Pientero when he recognized his approach. "Take the new recruit to Jassyka's. He'll stay there for his time."

"Right away, sir."

Arlahn remained close to his new cicerone. Every building looked the same to him in this place and if he took a wrong turn he'd be lost. "You were the one from the hunt camp, Tamis right?" the Prince said, recognizing him suddenly.

"That was me, yeah. Scoutin' for King PJ. He sends us out to relay activity on the lower lands." They stopped in front of a door close to the far side of the compound. "Here we are." Tamis pulled down the latch and entered.

A young woman looked up from her table, where she had been drawing with coal and parchment. She was petite with black, shiny hair, wearing a leopard-kin jerkin and tight black leggings. "No!" she said.

"Jassyka, this will be our new recruit."

"No—" she interjected but Tamis continued as if not hearing her.

"He will stay with you, and you will show him around."

A look of annoyance flushed her expression as she shook her head. "No."

"You didn't see this one coming, did you?" Tamis asked in a joking manner, grinning playfully.

"If I did, he wouldn't be here."

"But I am standing right here," Arlahn reminded them, beginning to feel insulted.

"Good for you then. You didn't splatter on the climb."

"Right, well," Tamis said, sensing the tension. "I'll leave you two love doves to get acquainted." And he was gone.

Arlahn walked fully into the room and his eyes met Jassyka's. They were dark, almost black, the same as PJ's. He could see her annoyance and tried to smile to lighten the mood. It didn't. He stood there awkwardly for a minute until finally he approached and peered closer at her parchment.

Jassyka pulled the piece of papyrus closer to her. She took up a stick of coal and began scribbling on her picture, rubbing it with her thumb or middle finger occasionally.

"What are you drawing?"

"Something from my dream. Leave me alone," she told him with hostility.

It was only then when Arlahn noticed all the pictures on the wall beside him. There were dozens, and they were all beautiful. Most were sketches of notable landscapes and wildlife, castles and village markets. Arlahn walked over for closer inspection and they renewed his curiosity about her newest picture. But as he tried to get a look at her drawing, Jassyka stopped and huddled closer to the page, hiding it. She was looking at him suspiciously out of the corner of her eye like a threatened lioness would while protecting food.

Arlahn wanted to attempt a conversation with the girl, but he had the strong impression that she wasn't interested. He kept getting ready to speak but remained quiet. Eventually, his presence became awkward and Jassyka finally addressed him.

"You answer Anvar's questions yet?" she asked Arlahn suddenly, trying to distract him.

"Oh yes, Anvar and I had a lovely chat, me with a stinky sack over my head and him with his dagger."

At that, Jassyka almost smiled. Arlahn thought about talking about it but she had already brushed him off and was back to her drawing. After a moment, she told him, "There's partridge by the hearth if you want. Pientero would want me to offer you some for tonight. But starting tomorrow, you grow and hunt your own food."

Arlahn thanked her before sitting and eating in silence. He savoured the partridge's flavours. Jassyka had seasoned it perfectly with salt and pepper, garlic, and onion and cooked it in wine instead of oil, he could tell. He finished and thanked her again for the food before he yawned tiredly and stretched out his arm. It cracked at the elbow. The day had been long indeed, the climb had begun at dawn and taken him until almost early evening. He recalled the times the mountain tried to kick him from it. But I beat you, he thought. Reaching the top to find an arrow pointed at his face had redefined "surprise welcome", Arlahn should have anticipated as much from Pientero.

Now he was in his new home for the next while, a small square cabin. Arlahn looked around and noticed a doorway next to the kitchen with a sheet hanging over it. Dipping in, he saw only one cot on the far wall of the second, smaller room. He walked over and was about to sit on it when Jassyka spoke up, "That's my bed!" she told him in an overpowering voice. She had appeared in the doorway behind him and marched over to sit on her cot. "You sleep on the ground for tonight. There're a couple of pelts in the basket by the hearth. Tomorrow Anvar will teach you to build your own cot."

Arlahn looked at her in disbelief. Did she not know he was the Prince of Saintos? The third son of Hectore, the Prophesied King. His entire life people had admired him for that alone, name and title. They would dance on the spot if he asked them to. But this girl was defying all he'd known. "Don't you know who I am?" he almost demanded then.

"I do, but I don't really care. In the mountain you're just a visitor. This was my home first." She did have more right to the bed, Arlahn rationalized then, having always being a victim to seniority when it came to his brothers.

And so he eased his way onto the bearskin carpet and did his best to cover himself with three small pelts. Arlahn closed his eyes and soon drifted away into sleep.

He woke up sore as the sun was cresting the mountaintops to the east, dressing himself in a long blue shirt under a leather sheepskin-lined jerkin and cream-coloured leggings.

Arlahn noticed that Jassyka had already awoken and was gone. He glanced around his frugal new home then walked out into the forest. Stopping beside a thick pine, Arlahn relieved himself, yawning the morning grogginess away.

He was walking back to camp when he found his father getting ready, saddling a mountain pony. "When do you leave?"

"Now," his father told him, cinching the saddle. "I have lots to contemplate and discuss with your brothers and the Wardens."

"Is it important? Should I come back with you?"

"No," the king said sternly. "You stay here until your training is done. Piege will let you know when that is."

"How are you getting home?"

"I know my way through the trails," Hectore answered with unquestionable confidence.

"Kael said they're like a honeycomb or mole's burrow, more of a maze than a path. If you knew the way, why did you climb with me?"

Hectore smiled and clapped his son on the shoulder before climbing into the saddle. "I'll see you back at home, son." And he tapped his pony's flanks and walked down the trail back toward the mountain alone.

"Hopefully I won't grow up crazy too," Arlahn said to himself as he watched him go.

He wanted to follow his father, but he couldn't go missing the first day he was in the mountain. Resisting himself, Arlahn walked back into the white settlement and made his way toward the big central buildings.

Arlahn was about to pull on the iron latch when he heard Jassyka's voice behind him.

"What are you doing?" she asked him wittingly.

He stopped and turned to her with a cocky expression. "I'm going to start training?" Turning back, Arlahn pulled the latch.

"Funny. That's not where we train. That's where we eat," she answered.

He let go of the latch and faced her. "Okay then, where do we train?"

"Up there. The thin air works us harder." Jassyka looked up to a mountain crest. Arlahn could make out a structure on the ridge, a domed gazebo hidden amongst the pines of the mountains.

"Good," he answered and began walking directly toward the building on the far-off clifftop.

"You're going there now?" Her voice was starting to get annoying, he thought.

"I want to start training. Something wrong with that?" Arlahn was getting frustrated with her, and he was so accustomed to remaining calm. What was this mountain doing to him already?

"Well, it's roughly a league to the training grounds, and once we've arrived, we train hard. You'll want to eat before you go." Although he must have liked what he heard on account of the rumble in his stomach, Arlahn was still set off by her snootiness.

Jassyka passed him and walked into the building before Arlahn got the chance to say anything. It was probably for the best. He didn't know what he would say, but it wouldn't have been pleasant. She was cold to him last night, and now she was advising him, who did this girl think she was? Are all women here like her? Arlahn thought.

Once inside the building, he recognized it to be some sort of mess hall where the Brotherhood would gather to eat as a family. He saw men and women seated on both sides of long benches, eating a hearty mountain of breakfast: various fruits, eggs and potatoes, toast and fried ham. Arlahn felt eyes linger on him. He was a new face here, never seen before among this community of Brothers and Sisters. He was about to sit when Jassyka came to him and handed him an apple. "This is where the Brothers eat. You're no Brother, yet."

"Is this all? I thought I was training hard?"

"Count yourself lucky for that much, Babyboy," one of the Brothers told him from a bench. Arlahn saw that he was seated beside his mirror. The twins both had coarse beards and close-cropped raven hair. The one who spoke had a scar below his left eye, the archer that welcomed him atop the mountain. His mirror added something that Arlahn ignored.

Pientero showed up then, as if emerging from thin air. At his arrival, the japes hushed below earshot. "That will be sufficient for your morning, Arlahn. Training your body will come after. First, you'll train your mind. Find Anvar and begin your lessons."

*****

Kael sat down to take his first break of the day. He donned a brown cotton top with his sleeves rolled partway up his arm. Sweat crescents stained the fabric beneath his armpits and the base of his collar. A bead rushed down the side of his face and he wiped it away with the back of his hand, accepting a drink from a field-hand.

Raphael had commissioned fifty men to begin the construction of his new defence weapons. Among them, Kael was highly depended upon for his ferocious efficiency. He was invaluable. He made his work look effortless, burying nails flush with wood by simply pressing them in as if they were buttons, using drills like corkscrews, making holes that would normally take minutes in mere seconds, or carrying huge two-man logs in each hand, all without ever slowing in his production.

"You're not taking a break already, are you?" Raphael teased, approaching with a roll of papyrus in his hand.

Kael smiled. "Just letting everyone else catch up. You shouldn't be afraid to help out yourself brother. It'll help you feel included."

"You live through your strengths, Kael, I live through mine," Raphael answered. "Organizing all of this is my contribution."

Kael swung his arm in dismissal at that, stood up, and went back to his work. Around him, the construction teams went about working on their respective designs.

Some men were sawing pieces of wood to proper length while others planed them down to the appropriate size and dimension, other groups still worked on assembly. All for which Raphael had provided detailed instructions on parchments that looked like architectural drawings. Two-man teams had been assigned to operate hand drills, taking turns to make sure never to slow down, drilling holes in exact locations for the long bolts that would hold everything together.

"It is going well," Kael admitted, stopping to gather another handful of nails. "Better than I expected."

"That's *my* effect," Raphael told him.

"How do you figure? You haven't lifted a finger all day!" Kael remarked.

Raphael stopped a man carrying one of the completed archery drums back to a finished pile. "How many of those drums has your team finished?" he asked the man.

"This is our fourth, sir."

Raphael turned to Kael with childish jubilation on his face. "Four already? How come you're working so fast?"

The worker had the small features of a chipmunk and made a face when he shrugged his shoulders. "I guess we had everything right there for us all day. Once I got here, I was sent straight to my foreman. I got my duties and all the tools I needed. Since then, I' been on a rotation with six men, workin' most o' the hour, breaking the last few minutes in the shade to drink lots o' water."

Raphael thanked the worker and sent him to continue his duties. "See, my preparations are the oil between the gears."

"Then get out of here and go check the rest of your 'gears,'" Kael told him.

"Are you sure you don't need any help nailing?" Raphael teased. "I hear it's thought-provoking work."

Kael responded by pressing another nail into the wood until it disappeared beneath his thumb. He turned back, "I think I'm alright."

As Raphael walked on, he passed a group of men surrounding their schematics laid out on a workbench, rocks placed on each corner to keep the wind from stealing it away. He heard disagreement amongst them and moved into the crowd. Two men were arguing about an issue assembling one of the pieces for the bowstring drum. They couldn't agree on how the schematic was telling them to weave the strings through the design. Raphael took a look, removing the rocks weighing down the paper and flipping it around to put it back down.

"This might help," he said.

Both men had a moment of sudden clarification and voiced this with a simultaneous "Aaahh."

Raphael chuckled, shaking his head as he walked away to further inspect other crews. Behind him, he heard one of the men start to explain. "So, we start from here..."

He noticed Kael had stopped working and was in full conversation with some Raphael had never met. The Prince laughed full-heartedly and clapped the man on the shoulder. He was in a black apron and had the dirty look of a smith to him.

As Raphael approached, his brother urged him over. "This is the smith I told you about, Jonnimack."

The smith introduced himself. "Your brother really made me look a fool when we first met," he told Raphael. "It was a good thing there weren't many people in my shop that day."

Kael was still laughing. "Yes, just you and your apprentice. How is the boy anyway? It was Billiem, right?"

At mention of the boy, Jonnimack's expression grew proud. "I'll only admit this 'cause the little bastard's not here, but he's taken to the kiln unlike anyone I've ever seen. He'll be a smith worthy of my shop sooner that I thought. Anyway, I came here to bring you somethin' that we've been working on."

Kael smiled, he loved surprises. "You've brought something else? I showed you the adamantine that he gave me, eh Raph?"

"Yes," Raphael answered, knowing of the shiny piece. "That's quite the metal, I'm told. What prompted this second gift?"

Not four days after Kael had made his order with the smith, he'd received it. Jonnimack had originally quoted much longer, but he had claimed a set of molds for the pieces had "magically" shown up on his table after the second day. The Princes were so satisfied with the early delivery that Kael doubled his original payment.

"After you replaced most of my steel with silver, I had some free time on my hands before my next shipment. I made you this with my last bit of stuff," Jonnimack said as he moved aside to reveal a wain being hauled by a mule into the work area.

Raphael wasn't sure how Kael commanded such respect from the man. His brother didn't really know him, as far as Raphael understood, least of all well enough to receive gifts. But he wouldn't complain about being a benefactor of the smith's generosity.

The wain rolled over to the trio of men and the smith walked over to the back. He dropped the tailgate and threw aside a canvas cloth.

Kael and Raphael's eyes gleamed, taken aback for a moment as they stared with open admiration. Jonnimack crossed his thick, hairy arms over his chest and claimed, "Not bad, huh?"

Kael approached the back of the wain and reached out. His fingers felt the cold steel, traced an edge to the pointed, reinforced tip. He grabbed the object and dragged it clear of the cart, holding it to shine in the sun like a trophy between him and his twin.

It was a battering ram's head, but unlike any piece of metal that capped a ram either of them had ever seen, fashioned to look like the ancient sigil of the Rai family. They were staring into the face of a roaring lion, its snout and fangs exaggerated into piercing ends. Coming out from behind the beast's ears were a set of furrowed wings, as if a bird was landing in its flight, which also sharpened into menacing points. The tip of the wings caught the sun, reflected it brightly off the polished steel.

"This is beautiful, Jonnimack!" Raphael told him.

"It really is," Kael agreed.

Jonnimack blushed. "I'm glad you two like it. Now you already paid me enough for what I've done. So this is just a gift."

Raphael told him he'd put it on the first fire-retardant battering ram they finished.

That began a small tour of sorts around the workplace. Together, the Princes paced through the projects that were underhand. They went through the design and function of Raphael's drum-bows, with Raphael explaining things in simple terms to ease the smith's understanding.

The last item on the tour was still covered in canvas. When Jonnimack asked what was under the cylindrical cover, Raphael would only tell him that it was a surprise.

The tour ended when the princes' two paramours arrived, and Jonnimack excused himself and returned to his shop. Luzy and Marlyonna welcomed their princes with kisses, Luzy playfully commenting on Kael's sweat-soaked top.

"Are we done for the day, brother?" Kael asked his twin with an arm around Luzy's shoulder.

Raphael thought hard about losing his brother's efficiency, but most projects were ahead of schedule. "I guess you can have the afternoon off."

"I'm leaving anyways. That's enough for me today," Kael told him as he turned Luzy around and walked away.

Raphael watched him go. He knew there was no telling his brother what to do.

*****

It had been a long day of rude awakening for Arlahn Rai. Back home, he had been an accomplished soldier, fast and purposeful with a blade, he could hold his own in a duel with just about anyone in Pellence. But above all, he was well-respected. But in these mountains, the world was inversed, their training styles completely unorthodox. He was a baby again. And the Brothers quickly learned to remind him of it. His place in the Rai lineage earned him the name of "Babyboy" in the mountain. Sometimes it was just "Baby" and others called him "Babyface." Either way, the whole mountain, Pientero included, took up the name for him.

"A rank befitting your experience, no doubt," a Brother named Balanus announced when his twin Balanor had come up with the label.

Jassyka had taken off to the mountain crest with the rest of the Brotherhood shortly after breakfast, while Pientero delivered Arlahn to Anvar on the edge of the main compound. He was in a storage building on a north-east corner. "Did you have a full breakfast? Har! Ready to start?" Anvar asked the younger man after courtesies were exchanged.

"Whatever you need me to do," Arlahn replied, in an affable, willing tone.

Anvar tossed a handful of linens into his face and the Prince caught them before they fell. "Good. Sew these up. If you can sew up a sheet, you can sew up flesh." He produced a needle for the Prince in his left hand. "There's plenty of thread in the basket," he said, pointing behind him with his right stump of an arm to a long, rectangular wicker basket. "After you've finished patching the sheets, come find me outside."

Arlahn questioned the true reasons for this needlework but he refused to complain, so he took up the needle from Anvar, sat down, and quietly went about stitching the white sheet in his lap back together. He had learned needle and thread for the same reason in his father's conscription. It had gifted him back then with patience and his focus taught him grace.

After an hour at the needle, Arlahn found Anvar in a section just beyond the yard with old scrap lengths of shaved wood scattered everywhere. He was rifling through the piles, tossing select pieces into a neater one.

Arlahn presented the quilt to Anvar who looked it over quickly and said, "Not bad. I've seen cleaner, but I'm sloppier myself, what with the one hand and all! Har har!" His roaring laugh brought a smirk to the Prince's lips, and he forgave the big man then for his torturous questions when they had first met. He was simply doing his duty, Arlahn rationalized.

Bringing him to his neater pile, Anvar said, "Now you're going to build a cot for your hut. I'll learn ya how. Grab that wood and follow me."

Anvar led Arlahn into a tool shed where he instructed the Prince on how to go about making the cot, sawing his pieces to length for legs, a frame, and bracing. Without nails in the mountains, he was forced to bore out holes in some pieces of wood while he tapered and whittled ends of other pieces to fit those holes. By early afternoon, Arlahn had hammered his crude cot together and it was back in the sleep room of his cabin.

When he returned to the tool shed, Anvar led the Prince into the woods beyond camp, not far beside the scrap lumber yard. "There's somethin' special in these mountains, Babyface. C'mere, I'll learn ya." He hopped over a fallen birch and came up beside a mound of fresh earth.

"See these mushrooms?" Anvar pointed at some tall, skinny mushrooms with purple dots on their tops, growing in a mound, "The only other place these grow is in the hills way north of Melonia. When you eat 'em, they give you a pantuur's energy, fight or rut all night on these. And these ones right here close-by..." he pointed at stunted mushrooms this time, with fat tops and yellow dots. "Eat some o' 'em, and you die! Har har!" Anvar's eyes doubled in size and his half-crazed cackle made it seem like it was a game at first. Arlahn could barely believe this was the same man who had questioned him with such deathly seriousness. Anvar sounded so sure about such things, it was as if he'd planted them all himself. Arlahn would come to find that this *was* the big man's garden, of a sort.

After his short lesson, Anvar opened up the Prince's eyes to the world around him. There were all kinds of vegetation growing from the earth or clinging to the barks of trees. Each species was somehow partitioned from the other, but they grew in healthy groups all over, and their uses were just as various, Arlahn knew.

The rest of the day was one long, educational conversation, bringing them further into the forest down a natural path of brown earth. Anvar guided Arlahn through the mountains and along the way he would stop to "learn" the youth a thing or two about which other mushrooms, spices, berries, flowers, and plants were safe and which were harmful or poisonous. He boasted about how these mountains contained every type of medicine for every type of illness. Anvar knew how to concoct healing pastes, how to grow food, and when it was ripe for cultivation. As they spoke, every now and then the big man would encourage Arlahn to try some of the vegetation that grew in the mountain. They would also stop for Anvar to point out convenient places to build shelters or plant traps.

Some of the traps he'd come across had snared rabbits, goffers, and even birds. Their journey found him with nine small game altogether. On the last discovery, Anvar told him with enthused pleasure, "Har har! That's enough for a small batch o' stew."

The trail took them alongside a curtain of rock. They stopped down the path when they found a mouth in the wall beside them. Anvar brought Arlahn into the cave and over to a rock face with a constant but rapid drip. Without saying a word, he stabbed his hand violently through the stream of water three times and revealed it to Arlahn to be bone dry. When Arlahn tried, it proved much more difficult than he initially anticipated. *Would all my time in the mountains be hard like this?* he wondered, stabbing again and again into water. Perhaps his new nickname was more fitting than he cared to admit.

When they re-emerged from the cave, his teacher continued down the path at a steadier pace this time. Somewhere along the way, they had begun climbing. Not like the mountain face that was Arlahn's first trial. Compared to that, this was a hill.

They came out of the tree cover when the ground gave way to a clear-cut open area.

The training ground. *Finally*.

All around him, two hundred men and women sparred and trained together. Arlahn came to realize that in the mountain all weapons were equal. And why not? His father always stressed the importance of opportunity, and Raphael had taught Marlyonna how to use a bow better than most men.

Instructors moved through the rows of trainees carrying out their exercises. People were dueling with every manner of weapon, all over the yard. In the corners of the grounds, Arlahn noticed that some Brothers were carrying heavy rocks to build crude sentries, others cut wood or did some other form of static exercise.

The Prince approached a barrel where wooden practice swords were kept. He fingered a hilt and drew one out, feeling its weight in his hands as he tossed it from one to the other. Arlahn squeezed the grip tightly and then loosened it so the wooden sword almost fell from his hand. Then he spotted the king-in-the-mountain instructing the young men with an undisputed authority.

When Pientero noticed the Prince holding the wooden practice sword noticing him, he called the youth over. "Baby! Come show me what you know."

Arlahn was about to stroll over, wood in hand, when the king-in-the-mountain added, "Leave the sword."

He dipped the practice sword back in the barrel and came over to Pientero. "What weapon do I use first?"

"Weapon?!" Pientero snapped, as if the word had insulted him. He held out his large, overworked hands, presenting them to the Prince. "These are the only weapon you need!"

At that, he leapt forward between a sparring Brother and Sister roaring, "COME AT ME!"

But *he* came at *them*.

Before they had a chance to coordinate their attacks, Pientero quickly spun and booted the Brother's shield, pushing him back half a step.

The Sister came at him with a high thrust of her spear, but he leapt free of the attack. Landing a right backhand slap to her cheek before taking her up by the shoulder, Pientero's left hand grabbed hold of her control arm and he tossed her forward, directing her spear toward the Brother's groin. The Brother recovered just in time to slap the low point away. PJ snatched up the defender's shield with both hands. Spinning and reefing it away, he sent the Brother sprawling through the air, only to come around swinging, bashing a blow into the Sister, driving her too, to the ground. The king-in-the-mountain turned back to Arlahn, tossing the shield into the Brother, and raised his hands, same as before. "See, your hands might control every other weapon. But they're always your best. And remember... everything is a weapon, boy."

"Another thing to remember, Babyface," Anvar said, leaning in close. "It's not the size of the cock in the fight. It's the size of fight in the cock. I used to love watching your father take down the biggest men on the battlefields. The roars afterwards made us invincible."

A small group of trainees had gathered to watch, and PJ scolded them for stopping their own training, threatening to keep the watchers out mucking latrines all night.

After that, Pientero instructed Jassyka to take Arlahn aside and train with him, although when he said, "train with him," the king-in-the-mountain really meant "beat him." Arlahn was not permitted a practice sword. Pientero's display proved he would need to learn to alleviate his attacker of their weapon before he earned the right to his own, as his new King had explained to him.

The petite roommate of his was fast, much faster than he was used to, her quick, consecutive blows always finding vulnerable openings in Arlahn's defence. A few times he would manage to grab hold of her shield, just to catch a swat in the leg or poke in the belly. Or he'd almost get her sword but would end up pushed back with a punch from the shield's edge. Eventually, he concluded that the only defence was to just never get hit. Saying it was one thing though. Saying it was easy. He had a score of bruises that would protest the difficulty.

Still, Arlahn was grateful that Jassyka wasn't as physically strong as some of the Brothers he'd seen. He caught a glimpse of the twins Balanor and Balanus training together, and they were ferocious toward one another. He wondered how much more brutal their attacks would be if someone unknown to them were their training partner. Someone like himself, who they didn't seem fond of already. He didn't quite understand that one, didn't know what he had done.

His first supper in the mountain humbled Arlahn even further. When he entered the main mess hall back in the camp, a hush fell over the crowded tables. It was where the Brothers eat, Jassyka had told him in the morning. But when he grabbed a tray with some hot mutton stew in a bread bowl, Balanor swatted it from his hands. The stew splashed on the floor, spitting some over his foot, and the plate bounced and rang in the echo of the hall. "This food is for the Brotherhood, Babyboy. You eat in your cabin."

Arlahn looked down at the food, he grew furious but didn't move. Too many unknown eyes glared at him. He was so hungry. He gave the Brother Balanor a stiff look that was exchanged with one of granite. But Arlahn was too exhausted for another physical beating, so he took this blow to his pride. The Prince dipped his head and hobbled back to his cabin to eat nothing. *This is where the Brotherhood eats. And I'm not a Brother*, he mused.

Alone at first, Arlahn sat at the table in his cabin, brooding over the recent events that had brought him here. He could go out and forage for some of the edible berries and mushrooms he'd encountered earlier in the day, but he wanted to hit something right now instead. Frustration fed his hunger for the moment. Perhaps he should just sleep.

After a few calming minutes, a knock came to the door and the light-hearted scout, Tamis, poked his head in. He had snuck out another serving of supper for the Prince. "You should eat. You have to keep your strength up."

"Thank you," Arlahn told him earnestly.

He appreciated the warm meal and again the food was delicious. He was halfway through when he asked the scout, "What's the deal with those twins? Is it me or are they just a couple of donkeys?"

Tamis giggled and recounted the story of Kael and Raphael's arrival. Arlahn had never heard it before.

"I was just a little one, only good for gathering, when your brothers came through. But I remember those four always hating each other," he told the Prince.

After the meal, Tamis left to return home for the night. It had been a grueling day to say the least. But soon, Arlahn would wake up and do it all over again. *And in a few days, I'll be conditioned to it,* he told himself. As he eased his aching body down on his cot, the Prince closed his eyes and dreamt of a better place, home.

He woke from his slumber in the middle of the night, sat up on his meagre, handmade bed, tucked away into the corner of the sleep room. The linens he'd sown together were his permanent blankets now, just as he'd suspected, and they failed to keep him warm. Looking to his right, Arlahn saw that the bed of his new roommate was empty. Curious, he got up and dressed himself in simple clothes and his warm cloak. He could feel that the night outside was cool. After pulling on his leather boots, Arlahn strolled out from the small white house he now called home.

He walked through the white city of the mountain and marvelled at it, counting the number of nuanced buildings he passed in each direction to remember the way back to his own. This place had remained a hidden stronghold for almost thirty years, and it housed the most famous company of soldiers in Saintos: the Brotherhood. Though most of the world still spoke of the Melonian Guard or the Essellian TrueBlades, Pientero's Brotherhood had carved itself into history with the rise of the lost HighKing. Arlahn smiled thinking of his father. In that moment, he wondered where he was. Perhaps making camp for the night, or if he'd rode hard all day, he could have even made it back to the hunt camp.

Arlahn walked on for a little while longer, lost in thoughts about the world beyond him. There had always been an endless well of questions, yet where were the answers? *Who created this place? Why am I here?* He had always felt a great connection to the things around him, but he could never transcend that bond into further understanding. Emotions were often stirred within the Prince, but he could never find their origin.

Picking up a stick, Arlahn began tapping it to his side in a rhythm as he strolled along a path in the night forest. Silver moonbeams shone through the overgrowth around him, lighting the area in thick slants. Some twenty paces ahead of him at the edge of a hill, he saw a huddled silhouette sitting cross-legged on a boulder. He guessed who it was.

Coming up alongside her, Arlahn noticed that she had been drawing again with her length of coal. He peered over her shoulder and saw that a tall, dark figure stood in the centre of her papyrus. He was standing powerfully, with a sword in one hand, and something unrecognizable – though she had drawn it to look as though it was shining brightly – in the other.

"Who is it?" Arlahn asked her finally.

Startled, Jassyka jumped and swung around, slamming a chop into the nerve in Arlahn's leg. The pain was shocking, his lower leg cramping up instantly. Looking up and realizing it was her new roommate, Jassyka made a sound of frustration, half sigh, half growl. "I don't know. Don't ever sneak up on me again." She swung back to her original position.

Arlahn stood a moment, rubbing his shin, and then sat down beside the artist. "Why did you draw him then?"

Jassyka remained silent for fear that her anger would surface. Unaware of her feelings, the Prince continued, "I've been looking at your drawings back in the cabin. You do justice to the places I know. I've seen the great Bridge to the North, the ruins of Gor Dunas, the forests of Cooperith. I've even seen my home in one. Have you ever been to the palace?"

"No," she answered. Arlahn thought that was all she would say on the matter. It was her favourite word, it seemed. But then Jassyka spoke again.

"I drew him to get him out of my dreams, just like everything else. Will you stop bothering me now?" she asked.

A breeze pierced through Jassyka's thin tunic and she stopped drawing for a moment to huddle over for warmth.

"I didn't know I was bothering you," Arlahn answered, removing his sheepskin-lined cloak and draping it over her shoulders. Then he sat back silently and Jassyka noticed he was steadying his breathing, looking at the stars.

Curious to know what the Prince was thinking, they exchanged a couple of uncomfortable glances before she inquired, "What?"

"Do you think some of them are gone?" he asked her, his voice much smoother now, more like a poet's.

"Do I think some of what are gone?"

"The stars... My brother Raphael, he has this unbelievable Gift for understanding, seeing things the way they really are, almost from another perspective. He says that the stars we see at night are merely the light from a billion other suns. That the light is travelling across incomprehensible distances, and because it takes so long to get here, we're seeing the star as it was many years ago. It could be that the star there..." Arlahn pointed to an easily distinguishable bright star, "... has exploded and is merely plasmas and energy now, yet the light from the star that once existed there is still on its journey to us. Do you understand? It took me a second explanation before I got it."

"I understand that we see light," Jassyka said, unimpressed. "But the stars are gateways to the Graceland. Each one is for a great hero of this world so that they can always turn back and watch over Tehbirr. Such a place is reserved for your father, I'm told, another for our King."

"So the story goes," Arlahn said, dropping the matter. Sitting up, he gazed at the freckles on her cheeks, following them to her nose, until finally he met her dark eyes. He knew the story from his childhood, but Raphael had told him differently after reading about it in a text. He somewhat longed for and admired her misguided beliefs, realizing that he was no longer the little boy he remembered being.

Looking to change the subject, Arlahn noticed sudden glints of multi-coloured light flashing in the valley down below. "I've seen those in the country before," he said, pointing to a bright red flash that soon turned purple, then green, "they're called rainbowflies."

"We called them lightningbugs where I'm from," Jassyka put in.

"You're from Esselle?" he asked, surprised.

"How did you know that?"

"Rainbowflies are lanternbugs for Melonians. Nightlights to the Freefolk of the South. And along the Spine they call them torchflies. Only Essellians call them lightningbugs," Arlahn told her.

"Lightning bugs make the most sense, 'cause they only flash for a second or two at once. But I understand why you would call them rainbowflies."

Arlahn found himself surprised that Jassyka began talking and let her continue. He wanted to find some sort of common ground.

"All their colours are so pretty and alive. I come here when I can't sleep, when I need to draw, or sometimes I meditate. The lightningbugs are my favourite things to see. It's not every night they come out, but I love to watch them dance. Their trails of light are the only thing disturbing the tranquility down there."

Arlahn didn't want to disturb her, this was the first time she ever regarded him with any civility, and he was impressed at how well-spoken she was, but Jassyka noticed she was trailing off and stopped herself. To avoid any awkwardness, he stated the obvious, hoping to get her talking once more. "They're so lively and vibrant."

A short pause.

"Sometimes I wish I could reach out and touch them, so that I could dance with them," she wished aloud. For all her coldness, Arlahn was realizing that Jassyka was not much different from himself, with her own hopes and flaws and, as he would find out later, her own demons. For some reason, she tried to keep them guarded.

"Do you dance?" Arlahn asked attentively, his voice still soft and gentle.

"I do. It's good footwork training. Don't tell me you know how to dance."

"Have you ever seen a prince dance?"

She hadn't. But that didn't mean they didn't. Did it? She stayed quiet. With a smile that Arlahn used to conceal a shiver, he got up and paced away. Jassyka took note that his movements were as gracious as a cat's.

That night, when she came into the cabin, she stirred the Prince awake with her entrance. He dismissed the loud sound of the door but rolled to face the room as Jassyka walked over and draped the cloak on him as an extra blanket. Arlahn's eyes opened and he acknowledged the deed with a hushed, "Thank you."

She slipped off her top before climbing under her own furs. He closed his eyes to once again accept slumber when he heard her whisper a unique prayer that was virgin to his ears.

"We are the king's Brother, we stand by his side. With a shield to protect all that he prides. We are his shadow in the dark and his sword in the light. When he calls us to arms, we rise up and fight. We are his right hand of justice, our coming is swift. Our deeds will outlive us and that is our Gift. We are legion, we are family. We are all mortal until we're immortal."

*****

Hectore came out from a narrow opening in the mountain. He had just released his mountain pony to return to the Brotherhood. The animal was smart, and the King had no doubt it knew the way, it had been sure-footed the entire ride.

He was wearing a royal-blue long-sleeve shirt with his enchanted, black leather vest, a woolen cloak hanging over his shoulders. The sun was shrinking in the distance and the ink dot clouds floating across the sky were painted with the deep shades of gold and red and purple that only a setting sun can provide.

Hectore walked alongside the mountain base for a few minutes until he was finally standing in front of the large angled boulder. It wasn't until he was standing here now, alone, that he realized the gargantuan size of the rock. He wasn't going to move it, not alone anyways. "You're too worn up, old man." An unwanted voice whispered in his mind.

He should stay here for the night, but he would only stop to gather his things and continue on. He just wanted to get home; he missed his wife.

Flustered, the King laughed at his current predicament. "Should've kept the pony," he voiced aloud.

Sitting down on a nearby rock, Hectore pulled his long, curved wooden pipe and a leather pouch from his belt. He set the pipe between his legs and pinched out some herb, packing the pipe. With the end between his lips, he flinted a spark to the herbs and they smouldered instantly. Hectore sat back and hauled in long breaths of smoke.

Getting up, he turned and looked at the large boulder. It seemed to taunt him. He couldn't move the rock out of place in order to free his horses inside, but that didn't restrict him from entering the cave, he concluded. Hectore crouched down and squeezed his aging body through the small triangular gap between the boulder and the mountain face.

Once inside, he could see that the torches still meekly lit the path to the room ahead. As Hectore walked into the large hollow room, his white stallion rose to its hooves.

He saw anxiousness in the beast at his sudden appearance and reached out to its neck. Patting it, he whispered "Calma, mi Bere. The way is shut, but I'll be back for you."

With that, Hectore poured more grain out into a bucket. The water basin was still plenty full. He gathered the scabbard with his two swords and a few other possessions from his horse's pack, mainly food. Hectore was game to walk back to a settlement if he had to, although the journey would take a few more days, he knew the horses were safe. He would have plenty of time to return to Pellence. And when he did, he could just send his other two sons for the horses. Kael alone could no doubt hurl the boulder aside effortlessly. Then Raphael could ride back on Arlahn's mount. It pays to have sons, Hectore thought, the best investment one could make.

Emerging from the crack, he looked back up at the sky. A large cloud had moved in front of what was left of the sun, and Hectore could see the mountain top one last time in the fading light. "Good luck, son. Find your path. We're all mortal 'til we're immortal."

Hectore strapped his elaborate scabbard to his back and around his waist, one hilt jutting out from his shoulder and the other at his side. Swinging his cloak over his back, he started a steady pace down the path and into the forest. He just wanted to get home; he missed his wife.

The air of the forest was sweet in the King's lungs. Cool breezes made the leaves of the trees dance their happy dance, occasionally catching one in their clutches and pulling it to the ground. How peculiar, he thought, how fertile the ground beneath his feet was. Maples, cedars, elms, and oaks surrounded him now like an endless army, and that was just a handful of the trees that grew in Saintos. Most of the lands of Damonos had been salted two hundred years ago, from what he understood. The rest was dead bogs and eyries, with few in between. He had never been there but the few Damonai he had met and known to be kind had told him their land was seriously, literally haunted by shadow monsters; things that come out only at night to kill and eat their prey, things that haunt grown men and fall to ash beneath the blades of those brave enough to fight them. Imaginary evils, Hectore believed, invented by the Damonai to justify their move on Saintos and his father.

He took up a trail that would lead him back to Pellence. While he was walking, Hectore had plenty of time to think of his past; the things he had done, great things that swelled him with pride. He had fought champions in single combat, representing an entire army, rescued a council of Sainti rulers from the clutches of the GodKing's generals, besieged his home, the Palace of Pellence, to save his *amiro* and wife. Hectore was once a boundless source of energy, it seemed. But the things he did were not always so impressive. Among his deep regrets and shames were the times he had stayed silent and bore witness to all the beatings that his friends endured during his time as prisoner under false identity. Friends who were repeatedly questioned on the whereabouts of Hectore Rai. He also regretted his helplessness when he had left a woman and her baby to perish in their burning home. And last of all, the underlying source for all his torment, a secret that, until recently, found him as the sole surviving carrier. The fact that when he killed the GodKing Tumbero, he had struck down his half-brother. Tumbero was perhaps the only other person in Tehbirr who had known of this connection. But he had to be stopped, Hectore told himself, I needed to stop him.

"You would have torn down all of this if I had let you," he justified aloud to the trees around him.

As Hectore walked along the wooded path through the foothills of the mountain, the surroundings reminded him of one of his earliest accomplishments: retaking the fallen city of Illium from Tumbero, where he had, by chance, intercepted the slave caravans out of the city in the process. He freed thousands that day, men and women who would join his cause.

His leadership, courage, and skill had been proven as Hectore led a victorious ambush in the forest, only to push his attackers into submission of the castle. At that time, he was unstoppable to anyone and anything. A man determined to end the GodKing's tyranny. Rumours burned through the lands like wildfire of a man who had defied the evil GodKing Tumbero, and the heralds rallied to the fallen Rai that was rising up. Pientero made sure they knew of him, that they knew a lost king was returning to his throne.

Hectore stopped for a short break, which he did often to keep his strength up. He sat down and leaned against a tree. The sun had sunk and night began to blossom around him. He reluctantly decided he would make camp.

He just wanted to get home; he missed his wife. But Hectore wasn't twenty-five anymore, not that endless bundle of energy. He walked around the forest and finally found a natural lean-to shelter between a small rocky crag and a large uprooted tree. He sniffed the air carefully and decided that overnight rain was unlikely.

The king quickly sparked a fire and prepared a light serving of boiled oats. Hectore preferred it sweetened with honey but settled for the plain taste. He spooned his bowl clean, drawing now his leather canteen. Wandering over to a nearby stream, the King dunked the canteen under the cold running water, allowing it to fill. He thought about boiling it first, but since the water was freezing and fast-moving, he didn't bother.

The sensation of water rushing over his hand triggered the movement of his bladder. Hectore rose from the stream and waddled over to a tree. As he stood there, paralyzed by the strange enchantment one only feels while urinating in the woods, something in the far distance caught his attention. A blue flash lit up from beyond the trees, then he heard cries and the echo of steel singing against itself.

It was battle.

The nobility of his character washed over him like a tsunami over the low land. Hectore raced back and pulled his katana clear, leaving his gladius in the scabbard. Forgetting all else behind, the king raced toward the beams of light and clashing of steel.

Running into a clearing, Hectore almost tripped on a body that lay dead on the ground. He looked around to find three other bodies, two of whom had small holes burnt through their chest and black pits for eyes.

Hectore saw a flash of blue beam again in his vision. But he didn't see the actual source of the light, only a man, who fell back dead, seared by heat.

The king looked up, one man was standing defiant in the clearing among a group with brandished weapons. He sent forth another ball of blue flame from his hand that swallowed a sixth man. The magicker was a giant, not overly tall but built like a stone wall. Hectore could seldom recall meeting another so big since… but could it really be him? The king couldn't believe his eyes. He watched a moment in appreciation as the six-foot giant handled his weapon. Then he noticed the battle axe. Omega was its name, Hectore knew. It was the kind of weapon you only saw mounted on the wall of a room like the palace's own Great Hall. A trophy, not something you'd ever expect someone to actually wield. *He still controls it with the same incredible balance he did all those years ago*, the King noted. A cohort of heavily armed soldiers was coordinating themselves to bring down the magical giant. But he parried an attack with his haft, spun, and hacked into another body, which fell forcefully to the ground.

Hectore quickly evaluated the situation and added himself to the uneven team of one. Twenty-five men would challenge any one magicker to his limits, even one with a deadly axe. The king walked into the battle, his sword poised, to stand beside the huge axe-wielding warrior.

Noticing Hectore's approach, the cohort reformed in a huge semi-circle around the two.

"Funny I found you like this Jole. Piege and I were just talking about you!" Hectore told the man at his flank. A clamour of profanity came from the surrounding attackers all at once. "I see you kept your knack for making friends."

The large man beside him let out a grunt. "Killers. I had 'em," he answered. "Never thought I'd see you again…"

"You could have just visited instead of this." Hectore nodded toward the group of enemies before them. He felt a change in his posture as he surrendered himself to the *sciong* and began subconsciously sizing men up in front of him, ordering their threat as both individuals and as the whole. Jole merely tightened his grip on the long shaft of his axe. The king turned his attention to the enemies who were closing in around them and the sortie in the bush began.

In that moment, it was as if all the years of his life were erased, and a youthful strength swelled in his muscles. Hectore was young at heart again. He parried the first enemy's blade into the second's neck, and both bodies dropped dead together. Such was his efficiency in battle. Every movement was carried out through his *sciong*, producing the most lethal art a man could dance. Hectore's blade flashed up and down, left and right. As if choreographed, he moved easily through a group of bandits, ducking and weaving, blocking high, stabbing low, twirling, and slicing deep through leather and flesh, sinew and bone. After his next series of moves, ten warriors were dead, four of which had fallen from friendly weapons redirected. The last man fell to the ground trying to stuff his entrails back in his belly.

Hectore looked over to see that the giant magicker Jole had downed five men and was fighting several more. One man turned and rushed at Hectore, their swords clashed, and the attacker leapt back from his counter.

Keeping his distance, the man took note of the death around the king and realized that Hectore was beyond skilled with his sword, making him reluctant to attack stupidly. He began stalling for time. Smart, thought Hectore. He realized the man was hoping his comrades would finish off the giant first. Hectore wouldn't afford them the chance. He stepped in, feigning an attack with his blade that brought up his enemy's sword in defence. Then he slapped the defensive blade out of the way before bringing down his own, shearing off the man's sword arm below the elbow. Finally, his screams where cut short at the neck and the man fell. Hectore turned to re-assess the situation.

Eight soldiers surrounded the magicker Jole now. He slammed the ground with the butt of his axe, and with a thunderous impact, the earth shuddered, and three of the closest men were thrown from their feet. The giant immediately lunged forward, cleaving the matte black butterfly blade into the middle man's exposed chest, as Omega expelled fire outward from the flats of the blades to engulf the downed men on either side.

Hectore felt the shock of the wave as it threw him off balance, making him plant his sword to keep from falling. He saw the bandit in front of him stumbling forward and lunged to meet him. Booting his blade clear, Hectore stabbed into the man's chest with his sword. The weapon lodged itself and he tried to pull it out quickly, but it was wedged between his victim's ribs well.

Hectore saw an enemy behind Jole raise his sword for attack while the giant was still busy dealing with two others.

The king let go of his pinned sword. Spinning for momentum, he took up the dead bandit's blade with both fists then hurled it through the air. Steel twirled and glittered through skinny slants of twilight, passing the giant to plunge and nestle a foot into the swordsman's neck, freezing his posture.

Two of the last three warriors split from the giant to take a stab at the unarmed king. Hectore ducked under a slash, caught his attacker's wrist, directed it to parry away another sword, then quickly snatched a dagger from the man's belt and plunged it into a chest. He stomped a lunging blade-point to the ground and hammered a thunderous cross into its wielder's jaw.

A sharp pain took him in the back of his head, and he tasted the metallic tang of blood on his tongue. Hectore heard Jole bellow something from beside him. Darkness followed. He just wanted to get home; he missed his wife.

Chapter 15

The sun was shining bright at its apex. Alone on the cliff's edge, the large domed gazebo reflected the light into Arlahn's eyes. He had learned that it was a storehouse for the mountain-men's training gear, organized in an orderly fashion, and continuing up the spiral stairs that spanned half the interior's perimeter.

All around the storehouse, trees and shrubs had been cut and removed, creating a massive training ground. Every day, two hundred Brothers and Sisters were paired together to train hard and work out in the bailey for hours on end, their ranks partitioned into trainers and five superiors. The thirty or so residents in the remaining mountain populace were outperforming other various tasks while their muscles healed for a day. They would tend their gardens and stack up chopped firewood and maintain the camp where it needed maintaining. There was also a group of twenty-odd sous-chefs, randomly selected to help prepare the day's meals every morning.

Sweat glistened off of Arlahn's wide chest. His body was just now maturing into that of a man, and he had a good build from years of training with his family. But although the Prince was no bone rack, his frame didn't exactly portray an image of dominance either, he was quite normal. As a soldier, however, he was athletic and quick-witted.

A bead of sweat trickled from the bangs of Arlahn's shoulder-length chestnut hair. It perched on his brow and he could feel it hanging there, then it dropped. It was only early afternoon and already his limbs felt like lead.

Arlahn was nearing the end of his first week in the mountains and, as he'd hoped, it had gotten easier over time, but it still wasn't easy.

On the morning of the third day, matched up with the young scout Tamis, Arlahn had finally earned his sword. He had stepped over a low cut and stomped his foot down on the blade, ripping it from Tamis' fingers to the ground. Then he bulled the younger scout over and quickly pinned Tamis' wrists with knee and hand. Once Arlahn did earn his sword, it remained his for the morning. He didn't know how to fight like the Brotherhood yet. But he could always scrap with the best of them.

From then on one weapon replaced the other. Arlahn trained five of the first six days in the sparring yard, only being selected to tend other duties once, during which he started his own garden. This required him to revisit

Anvar's introduction to the nature in the mountains with the offering of help from the same scout, Tamis, he'd earned his sword from.

For lunches, the training group would eat porridge and honey, eggs, and some bread. Some added to that and ate different nuts, berries, and other fruits mixed in a leafy salad. They drank mostly goat milk or water in the mountain, with the only alcoholic exception being the strong, honey-based mead. Other spirits were alien to the mountain. Arlahn had learned that if they couldn't cultivate it themselves, the Brotherhood wanted no part of it, with the only exception being water. After lunch, once the food had settled, they would carry out the rest of the day's exercise with renewed vigour.

When they resumed training in the afternoon, Arlahn was told to trade in his morning weapons (sword and shield) for his partner's (a spear this time) before they would start again. He had never used a spear before, but Pientero appeared whenever he sensed it was time for instruction, times he had an uncanny knack for sensing. He explained the basics of the weapon in childish detail, then demonstrated how to distance yourself and where and how to hold the spear for a solid thrust, and when it was okay to have one hand gripping the haft or two. Arlahn took in everything the king-in-the-mountain said with enthused interest.

Every day, he had practiced a new weapon, trading with his day's partner after lunch, which he still ate alienated from the others. Each new weapon introduced to Arlahn left him with several new bruises, scrapes, and even a bleeding cut here and there. Pientero would reserve a few minutes each day with him to instruct him, as he did with the spear. Afterwards, his roommate Jassyka had administered an ointment on the cuts to accelerate the healing and prevent infection.

Now it was the afternoon of day six and Arlahn was training with just a large brick in hand. "Anything can be a weapon," Pientero claimed. Balanor approached, bow in his hand. He had been instructing the day's group of archers as a superior on the edge of the training bailey. "Babyboy, see if you can at least *hit* one of those dummies." He punched Arlahn's chest with his bow hand. "I hear the bows in Pellence are toys."

Arlahn took the hit and the bow, forcing a smile. It was made of wood; a lot heavier than the short, recurved Pellencian bows. He walked over to the line of bowmen. Arrows were stabbed into the ground in rows all along the front of them.

The targets were standing in the field at various distances. They were not round conventional targets with the concentric circles that Arlahn was used to in Pellence but dummy men, stuffed with straw, scattered all around; some exposed, others partly hidden behind objects and shrubbery. Arlahn nocked an arrow and drew back the string to the corner of his mouth, taking aim some sixty yards away. "Breathe in as you draw, exhale as you aim, and let the string roll off your fingers to fire!" His father's lesson repeated in Arlahn's mind.

The arrow flew toward the target. But at the last second the dummy jumped from its location and the arrow sailed on.

The Prince instantly felt cheated and said as much, turning to Balanor.

"It's not cheating. In the real world, people do unexpected things, like move."

Doing just that, Arlahn ripped an arrow from the ground and fired it instinctively, imagining he was Raphael back in Pellence, shooting at a flame with his father. This time, however, when the dummy jumped in a similar fashion, the arrow sailed past and into the target behind.

"You're right, should I do it again?!" Arlahn asked arrogantly, forcing a smile and trying to feel as cocky as he sounded, though he was unsure of what sensation had just taken him.

It was only his sixth day in the Brotherhood, but he felt like this was a long time coming. After hearing the story about his own brothers' arrival to camp from Tamis, Arlahn understood that Balanor and his twin Balanus had some kind of problem with him, and they were constantly snickering remarks and trying to provoke him.

Balanor grunted and walked away, shaking his head.

"Should I do it again?" he imitated in a mocking voice to his twin, "Little shit." Balanor couldn't stand the Rai brothers. He stopped beside Balanus, a second well-built man with a hardened, square jaw. "Next time he smiles like that I'll smash his teeth out," Balanor complained.

They exchanged looks and Balanor took up a bow and nocked an arrow. He drew back hard and loosed it. The steel tip hammered home into the heart of a straw man.

The more level-headed Balanus replied, "He's King Hectore's son. Did you not expect him to know how to use a bow? I swear that sometimes, once you're angry, you're as useless as teats on a bull. His brothers are freaks, I admit, but this one's just a pup. Look at him. Would you have even noticed he was here if PJ hadn't made the announcement?" Balanus explained to calm his brother. "He eats alone, he trains alone. He'll destroy himself before anyone has to."

Some believed that only Balanus could speak to his brother in such a manner, but it worked. Sometimes he just needed the simple facts slammed back into his face.

Balanor's tension eased and he continued on firing arrows with precision, but he periodically looked over at Arlahn between shots to think up some slander. One of those times he looked over to see Jassyka standing there, staring at him. Her look was stern, as if she had heard their conversation.

"Come on people! We're calling it a day. Tomorrow is a day off," Pientero announced to the training camp.

To Balanor's dislike, Jassyka walked forward to join the Prince for the return walk back to camp.

After the week's long exercise, Arlahn was both pleased and grateful to hear that they were finally awarded full rest on the seventh day. He wasn't sure what he'd do with his free time, but he was happy for it, nonetheless.

That night, as Arlahn slowly eased his bruised, cramped body into bed, he breathed a deep sigh of relief. Maybe he was just going to sleep for the entire day tomorrow. His eyes closed and his hard, wooden cot felt like a goose feather pillow. Sleep was just becoming his friend when the loud call of a wolf woke him.

Only it wasn't a wolf, it was a horn, proudly blaring, urging the camp to rise. Arlahn looked over and saw Jassyka bounce up and begin getting dressed in startling urgency. Her alarm and energy stirred the Prince up and he dressed himself quickly as well.

Jassyka told him to hurry as she tied up the last of her bootlaces and took off through the door. The Prince simply grabbed his and carried them along, following her to the beginning of a mountain path where Pientero stood, dressed in the black of night as if it was the mid-afternoon.

"You're up. Good. Jass was always one of the fastest."

"What's going on?" Arlahn asked, tying up his boots.

Pientero explained the horn blast was the call for a camp-wide run. "You never know when you're going to have to summon more energy, lad. Sometimes you have to duel at the end of the run before you're done. In wartime, the enemy waits until you sleep before they attack, they don't ask if you've had a full breakfast."

As PJ continued his explanation, more and more Brothers began taking up a jog into the forest behind him.

"There's a set circuit through the paths, keep to it with your Brothers and you'll be fine. Stray from it and you'll get lost. If you get lost Baby, you might die before we find you. It's happened before. So keep up."

"Shouldn't I be running now then?" Arlahn asked, sure he understood.

"Probably," Pientero said, unsure if he had answered a rhetorical question.

Arlahn took up a full sprint at first, but when he quickly caught up to a group of runners going at a much slower pace, he realized the run must be long. He fell in with the small group and stayed with them. He was looking for someone familiar, but they were all new faces to him. There were about ten of them together for the majority of the run. Sometimes a few would break ahead of the group at a quicker pace. The path before Arlahn went on and on the longer he ran. He stayed beside a Brother who at least didn't try to shrug him off and coasted quietly along. Focusing on his breathing and watching his footing in the night trails was enough for Arlahn at the moment. Slowly, he fell behind from his running partner, eventually losing him altogether. He knew some were behind and decided to stop for a quick breath. In moments those stragglers came up on him, and he found himself struggling to keep the last Brother in sight for fear of taking a wrong turn and getting lost.

Trying to keep pace was the only reason Arlahn stayed the circuit and came out of the mountain that night. He broke free of the clearing and ran over to the building, touching his hand to a storehouse. Everyone was doing it, and he realized it signalled his finish. Hundreds had arrived before he did with only a few more sluggish types left coming out behind him. Gasping, Arlahn bent over and could feel his heart pounding in his chest. He was exhausted before the run. Now he felt like he could sleep where his body fell.

"Walk around," Jassyka told him as she strode up herself. She had her hands behind her head and she was calmly breathing in the cool night air. "Like a horse. It's not good to just stop running after a long one like that."

Arlahn reached for words but they got caught in the dryness of his throat. He nodded his acknowledgement and began pacing back and forth.

A few minutes passed and the last of the other Brothers and Sisters came into sight. One of them – Arlahn could see it was Tamis – stopped at a tree before the clearing and bent over. His back arched up and Arlahn could tell his supper had just come out of him. He staggered dizzily out of the forest and made his way to the storehouse. Arlahn admired his perseverance. Tamis was perhaps his only real friend here at this point.

Jassyka helped him out of obligation to her roommate, but even she hadn't chosen to accept him yet.

After a short rest and a quick drink, the men were all lined up again. They were arms-length apart forward and sideways, standing in perfect formation.

Pientero came to stand in front of them. "People, you've done me proud! Each day you grow stronger! Faster! Harder to kill... Soon, we might get the call to war. It's important that we stay strong! That we stay vigilant! We're all mortal until we're immortal!"

A cry went up from the soldiers. With one voice and a hundred voices, the Brotherhood spoke the final line of Jassyka's nightly prayer, "We're all mortal until we're immortal!" before they fell silent. That seemed to finalize the speech.

The crowd started scattering and moving back to beds and warm furs. A few of the men pleaded with the beauties to help show them the way. Pientero began to walk through them, his dark eyes scanning their hard faces. When he picked out the Prince, he ordered him, "Walk with me."

Pientero led him into the woods, down another path. All around the mountain village there were footpath entrances leading in every direction. Most paths had their own destination but forked into neighbouring entrances, if you knew where and when to turn. For the most part, they spread out and wound like a labyrinth or some unholy maze. Arlahn heard Pientero mutter as they chose one and entered, "Stay close, for every path into this village, there's ten that lead out."

"You don't give in easily... I like that," he continued after a moment. "Think you could've kept up with Jassyka if I hadn't stopped you? Don't be discouraged next time if you don't, no one beats her in the run. Probably 'cause she's got a lot less bulk to carry than some of the others. How do you find living with her?"

Arlahn had no complaints as of yet. He mentioned how she had offered her partridge the first night when he was hungry from the climb.

"Has she been sleeping well?" Pientero asked, concerned for the girl.

Arlahn never expected that he would have needed to take note. "She sleeps every night, at least. One time I found her outside drawing. Why?"

"She has trouble sleeping sometimes. Drawing helps her."

They had walked up a hill, along a wide stream, and finally to a waterfall. It was a sight to behold. Fifty feet up, water poured over the edge before them and hopped down the mountainside, from step to step, landing finally into a large leaf-shaped pool. The water streamed from the tip further down into mountain.

Pientero walked over to the top of the waterfall where a beautiful plant grew beside the rushing water. It stood knee-high from the ground and had white petalled flowers all over thick bushy stems.

Slipping out his knife, PJ took a stem and cut it at the base. He removed the white flowers and tossed them in the air, watching them spin their way into the pool and down the stream. Pientero stood and held the plant out for Arlahn to better observe. "Do you know what this is?" he asked.

"Yenmaraj?" Arlahn guessed, his father did mention it was native to these mountains.

Pientero snapped his finger and pointed his approval. "That's right, Baby. How did you know that? Your father's been teaching you my secrets, hasn't he? That's okay, I always kept a couple for myself." He gave a wry smile. "Do you know what it does?"

Arlahn had some vague ideas but couldn't articulate them the way he would have wanted, so he shook his head, unsure.

"This herb is only found in these mountains, as far as we know. It can be eaten, smoked through a pipe, brewed in a tea... It typically induces psychophysical effects that are experienced differently for each individual depending on how you take it."

Spoken as if from a text, Arlahn thought.

"Were you listening?" Pientero asked him.

"Yeah, psychophysical effects..."

"You heard what I said, sure, but what does that really mean, Baby?"

The Prince remained quiet, humbled further, cursing himself that he didn't have Raphael's Gift of *mniman* to better understand.

"Hearing is letting the words pass through your head, listening is understanding those words. If you don't know something, Baby, ask."

The king-in-the-mountain continued his lecture. "It means that if I eat this, it could make me super strong and feel no pain for a while, whereas if you ate the same bit of plant, you might find you have the most unbearable water-shits. Smoking it helps your father concentrate. I retched up like a seasick dog when I tried inhaling the stuff." He handed the herb to the Prince. "Keep this one, bring it home and boil it in a tea for Jassyka, that'll help her sleep, she'll appreciate it."

"Why does she have trouble sleeping?"

"She has visions in her dreams. Sometimes they're... disturbing for her."

"Visions of what?" Arlahn asked.

"That's not for me to say." Then PJ chuckled. "She probably wouldn't want me telling you about the dreams as it is."

Arlahn was curious but dropped the matter for the time being. He had the whole day off tomorrow. Who knows what he might get her to confess to him in that time? The Prince understood the proper way to play with his words. His strength in such situations derived from his empathy; his ability to genuinely connect with others.

"Come, it's late. And all this talk of dreams is making me tired."

Pientero started to jog toward the compound, and Arlahn was impressed with the speed and vigor of the older man. He trudged after him and they emerged into the quiet camp together. After bidding the king-in-the-mountain goodnight, Arlahn found his cabin in the corner of the compound and laid down in his makeshift cot. His bones and muscles were so sore it felt like a giant pillow. He realized that night, as he lay with his thoughts, that in the mountain, he would be like a three-legged wolf in the Wild. And like a three-legged wolf in the Wild, he'd have to scrap and claw and fight even harder for what was earned.

*****

Jassyka rose later than usual on her day off. She was awake and attentive as soon as she opened her eyes, which was her sign of a healthy night's rest. She had come to appreciate dreamless nights more and more. Brewing the leaves Arlahn had returned with one night helped her find peaceful rest. Her curse occasionally authored horrible visions when she closed her eyes for slumber.

She got up and saw that, for the first time, the Prince had beaten her from the bed. Having his presence superposed on hers had peeled back layers to the Prince that remained unseen to others in the mountain. Because of this, Jassyka didn't refer to him as some form of baby, like the rest of her peers.

Jassyka wanted to refresh her soiled training clothes and decided that would be her task for the day. She bundled up her gear in a loose duffle sack, grabbed her washboard from the counter, and left her home.

She was walking toward the footpath that would see her to a pool when she spotted her roommate. He was with Tamis and his sister, Aideen, going through a garden, learning which foods were ripe. Jassyka regarded the Prince as she watched him crouch over, pluck a tomato from the stalk, and bite into it like an apple. He had done alright during his first week of training, she thought. She had to admit that on the first day, she didn't think he would have withstood her beating for as long as he did before asking for a break. She had stopped putting so much force into her blows after a while when she started to pity his failed attempts to disarm her. Jassyka was too quick and skilled for the Prince to take away her sword, but he worked hard the entire day and took his beating without a single word of complaint; not even when Balanor knocked his food over in the hall at supper. She respected that he didn't make a big fuss as most entitled people did.

But later, he had found her drawing and babbled the stars into something she couldn't begin to grasp. It showed her a sense of maturity and depth about him that she didn't recognize in the other men of the mountain. Jassyka couldn't tell if she was frustrated with his unannounced intrusion into her life or attracted to him somehow. Her aloofness had become almost reflexive to her, a default behaviour. But the Prince had broken her guard, even if it was just for an instant, with the lightningbugs. He also seemed to have read her mind when she'd caught the chill that night. In her head, she had wanted to ask him for his cloak but would never voice the words – that would be like relinquishing some kind of intangible point to him. Still, without hesitation, he gave her his cloak, as a simple act of goodwill, and it was crystal clear that he neither sought nor expected any reward. He didn't even ask for a thank you, which she never did actually give him. In fact, Arlahn had even thanked her when she returned it, Jassyka recalled now. She had met few people like that in her life, save maybe her own mother. Perhaps there was more to this prince than what she had assumed in her initial judgement.

Jassyka slung her stuffed duffle over a shoulder and started her way down the footpath. As she walked, she became acutely attuned to her surroundings. Jassyka always hunted for a fresh catch whenever she travelled the trails by day, and she was looking through a break in the trees when, out of the corner of her eye, she caught the Prince following her from a distance.

She dismissed him and continued her hunting down the path. Jassyka heard him closing distance behind her when something ruffled the leaves in the forest at her side. She shot up a hand to halt his loud, careless movements. Her wrist flashed down then out, sending forth an eight-inch throwing blade. The blade found its target and the partridge jumped once to attempt flight before it fell back to the ground. Moving like a gust of wind, Jassyka was on it, snapping its neck to finish it off.

"You need to work on your guile, Rookie," she told Arlahn through the trees. "And you're lucky partridges are a dumb bird."

Jassyka took up her kill by the talons and carried it along with her. Returning to the path, she continued her way toward the river to wash her laundry.

"I saw you were going to clean clothes," Arlahn pointed out and she noticed him adjust a similar duffle over his shoulder.

"I'm not cleaning yours," she told him, assuming the Prince would want it done for him.

"That's fine. Just show me where and how. I'm a quick learner."

Jassyka took him to a river where the water rushed over the ledge into a leaf-shaped pool.

"I've been here before!" Arlahn announced when the atmosphere became familiar to him, pointing out an herb growing near the water's edge. "Pientero brought me last night, that's where we got the Yenmaraj for your tea."

Jassyka had appreciated his gift. In return, she showed him how to use the washboard and they set about cleaning their clothes in silence.

"So Jassyka," the Prince started, breaking her peace. "I've gathered you're from Esselle. How did you end up here?"

Jassyka scrubbed harder at the washboard with the clothing in her hands. Again, the Prince had prodded her with a subject that beckoned response.

"I found Pientero in the mountain about ten years ago," she told him.

"You found him? I didn't think that could be done," Arlahn said, soaking another garment in the current.

"For most people, it can't. I had visions of this place."

"Visions of what exactly? King PJ told me you dreamt things sometimes."

Why would the king-in-the-mountain confess her secret to someone without her consent? she thought, suddenly bothered. She told herself that it was because the man was concerned for her, having been more of a father than teacher to the girl. With Arlahn living with her, PJ was using him as an extended way of providing care.

"I dreamt this place, over and over," she explained, scrubbing at the board. "I saw the white houses, Pientero, and a wolf every night until I found it. Once I got here, I started dreaming about other things."

"Other things, like what?" Arlahn asked gently.

"Right before you got here, I saw a man try to poison Pientero. I see things that are about to happen or are happening right now, somewhere else. And I dream things that happened a long time ago. Sometimes it gets confusing though, like fantasies. I see my childhood maid still alive, laughing and dancing in beautiful dresses with handsome men, but it can't be real. She's dead." Jassyka was surprised to find herself divulging anything to this stranger. But there was something deep within him that she trusted... or maybe it was just the warmth of his cloak on a cold night.

"It sounds like even you have a Gift," the Prince told her. She heard the slight touch of jealousy in his voice.

The word Gift made her chuckle. "A curse is more like it."

Arlahn dropped the issue then, and this time the silence made Jassyka feel uncomfortable. In a rare display of openness, she asked the Prince, "So, what's it like?"

"What's what like?" he answered, taking up another garment.

"I don't know, growing up in a palace, being a prince. You must have stories about home."

"Being a prince is like anything else, I guess. There's the good to it, and there's the bad." He scrubbed the washboard as he took up conversation. "There's lots of responsibility being a prince or princess. My father always says being on the throne means everyone else is looking up *to* you, not *at* you."

He handed her the washboard before he continued, "You're always being groomed to become a king or a queen. Those responsibilities sometimes force you to do things you don't always like but that you've already learned must be done," Arlahn told her with the icy, stern tone of his father, remembering the first time he'd witnessed his father deal Justice. Softening his voice, he carried on. "When you live as a commoner, you care for the well-being of your family and those you call 'friends.' But when you're a king, my father told me, the entire kingdom is your family and you have no friends. He said that, 'The people's hunger is your hunger; their pain is your pain. If a man gets convicted of murder and is punished to death, you oversee that execution, and it's not as easy as some people think, no matter how filthy his deeds are. In a part of yourself, you still feel like you've failed.'"

"I see." Jassyka understood the Prince's words, but her training in the mountain had hardened her. She passed back the washboard. "But death is a more than reasonable punishment for murder. A life for a life."

Arlahn didn't protest that, putting aside his clean top and taking up another soiled one to scrub in the rushing current. "What I miss the most about home is my family. Watching my father and brother have archery competitions. They light a candle and stand back thirty yards, whoever shoots out the flame wins. I miss chasing girls with Kael, but I guess that's over now too. I miss thinking of pranks with my sister-to-be and talking with my mother about the past."

"I've heard stories about how Queen Annabella was a medic for PJ once." She stopped to regard his words. "Here in the mountains, we're all considered family. Do common men not care for the others in your city?"

Arlahn felt disappointment come over him when she asked that. He stopped his work for a moment.

"No, they don't. I think it's because of how many people live there," he answered as if it hurt him. "When you ride into Pellence, there are four walls that surround the entire city."

Removing the clean garment and setting it aside, he passed the washboard to Jassyka once again. "Each wall you go past brings about another type of character. Inside the first wall is where you find the humble, field-working class like farmers and lumberjacks, the candle-makers and seamstresses. Inside the second wall, the buildings grow a second floor and you'll find a few rag-tag taverns and businesses. There's also some small playgrounds and pools for the kids to play in. The third wall is where the city really takes its shape; most buildings there are three or four floors, some of them higher than the wall. There're lots of alleys and neighbourhoods connecting everything, like the footpaths here. That's where you find the nicer inns and brothels. The palace and its grounds are inside the fourth wall, at the heart of the city. There're thousands and thousands who live there, so they use coins to purchase their possessions and luxuries. They don't care for the one who knitted their dress or painted the canvas that hangs on their walls. They don't appreciate when cooks slave hard all day to prepare their delicious meals. They're too important and valuable for such appreciation, some people think anyway."

Understanding this, Jassyka empathized with the sadness in the Prince's voice. Arlahn continued, "I know people in a richer district who heat the water supply that flows from the aqueducts into Pellence. They have men chop wood and stoke fires all day in massive cauldrons, just so they can make heated pools. Isn't that a waste of resources and manpower? Come winter, those fires could save lives."

"Pientero has always been the leader of this place." His word is iron and as sharp as his blade, Jassyka thought as she grabbed another linen from the shrinking pile beside her. "He preaches that if you fail to respect your

Brother, he won't respect you. That it's mutual caring that makes a Brotherhood strong."

"He's not wrong, but you all live together in this small community. Each person plays a role in your survival. Everyone's appreciated for whatever they do, whether it's sewing furs, planting corn, or extracting the oils you cook with. In this place, you *need* each other, because the currency here is service. It's *given* rather than *exchanged*. You all understand that your turn to take will come when you have to give something up."

This prince was clarifying unconscious connections in Jassyka's mind that she hadn't even considered to consider before.

"The rest of the world just isn't like that. If the payoff isn't immediate, or otherwise guaranteed, then there is no exchange. And that's why people don't care for each other the way this Brotherhood does. The only time two people *need* each other lasts no longer than the time it takes to trade coins for bread. Pellence, when stripped of its grandeur, is just like any other city: walls and buildings, friends and strangers, so many people just trying to live." Arlahn's eyes looked toward Jassyka, and he grew shameful before speaking his next words. "Greed is what drives most men in cities. It's very different from life in these mountains."

"I'm glad I found my way here then, to the Brotherhood," Jassyka voiced her thoughts.

The Prince was open now and as he realized that he hadn't pressed the girl about her past, he asked her, "What about your family before the Brotherhood?"

Now he would be expecting her to say that much about her past, Jassyka would oblige his curiosity a touch.

"I lived on the edge of Esselle. My father was a nobleman. Ironically, he was actually quite the opposite. He used to beat our maids. How noble is that?" she asked rhetorically. Jassyka remembered her father, vile and loud. In front of his colleagues, he turned into a round-cheeked suck-up, but alone he was a bipolar sociopath. "He was a horrible father," she explained, anger beginning to boil within her. She closed her eyes and caught a lump in her throat. Somehow, Jassyka got her story out.

Her father, Stevano Grent was malicious. He cheated, betrayed, and lied his way into position. Jassyka hated him for it. Her mother was killed when she was a little girl, and she always suspected it was a consequence of one of her father's foul deals, pushing her disdain for him further. Jassyka recalled when he would yell and beat her best friend, a servant girl named

Christianne. She could hear his voice now as clear as she did from the other room years ago.

"Do not speak unless spoken to! You will follow at my side but don't let me see you unless I order it. You'll fetch me whatever I need, you'll make my bed, prepare my food, help me bathe – and you *will* keep quiet while you do as I say," he'd order. Jassyka would hear the slap of flesh on flesh and knees dropping to the floor. Seriously? she remembered thinking, a beating for something as trivial as speaking, for requesting fundamental needs? The poor, beaten Christianne could only wipe her tears and whimper, with "Yuh-yuh-yes, milord," becoming her fiercest reply. Anything else would earn her another backhand across the face.

Arlahn was appalled. His father would have never allowed such a thing to occur if he were there. Suddenly, he understood the true meaning of his father's guest seat at their dinner table. When Arlahn asked Jassyka if she had ever confessed to someone of authority, she shrugged her shoulders. "Who believes a child over their parent?"

She still remembered holding her friend tight and hiding her when her father drank himself into violence. The fragile maid would whisper her yearning for freedom, for strength to Jassyka. She saw the life in the servant girl's beautiful blue eyes fading, felt her spirit crumbling day by day.

One night, Jassyka ran away, knowing that she could no longer bear a life with her asshole father as the sole authority. A little over a kilometre out, guilt turned her back for her brothers. She had two younger that she expected to need convincing and one a year her elder who would come willingly. She opened the door to her home and saw that all three of them had been slain.

"I remember my two little brothers. They were on the ground beside each other, holding hands. And whoever the monster was that killed them had hung my older brother Doffrey from the chandelier in our entrance. I still see him hanging there in my dreams sometimes. Twisting slowly with the gust of wind from when I opened the door."

As she told her story, Jassyka had become more and more detached from its specifics until she was just a voice saying the words, absent of emotion. Arlahn was horrified by the details and contemplated moving toward her for a hug. But when he saw the icy disconnect in Jassyka's eyes, he withdrew his approach.

Jassyka was staring blankly ahead of her, but the Prince's movement caught her attention and she looked at him before her empty voice continued, "I didn't check the house. Christianne found me and said a ghost was killing everyone. We ran into the darkness until we were so far away. That's when three bastards found us. They said something about a time together. Christianne told me to run and threw herself at them, and I ran. I never even turned back. I just ran. That night was when I had my first dream of this place, Pientero, and the wolf."

*****

The lone scout came back over the hill. He broke from the path at a destination marker and emerged into the nearby trees. Togut and his group were waiting for him. Palor had turned out to be an excellent scout. Twice he had warned Togut of travellers, and the men avoided unwanted detection.

Togut huddled the party beside a fallen tree and had been telling them their role in his plan.

"Pellence's first sentry is just over the ridge, the city can't be far beyond," Palor announced. "The path to the ridge is clear. But I spotted two soldiers manning the tower."

The men moved through the woods alongside the path and eventually came to the ridge. Once there, Togut ordered them to remain and bid only Gordun and Palor to follow.

When they neared the summit of the next hill, Togut told them to drop to their bellies, and they crawled over the second ridge under hawthorns and trees.

Before them sprawled the great city of Pellence. This was once the home of their GodKing Tumbero, until he had been usurped by a threat that they hadn't seen coming. The Damonai had named that lost king Demonblades. The man, who slaughtered thousands, had killed Togut's own father. It was his inspiration for joining the Caliph's army.

The city was grand, set atop a long hill. Massive walls were spaced far apart in four curtains, that each looked to be about fifteen feet thick with turrets placed every seventy-five feet down their length. After the third wall, the tops of buildings sprouted like seedlings out of soil, and at the summit of the hill was a beautifully built castle the Palace of Pellence, Togut had heard it called. Even from this distance, it had a commanding presence among the city's structures. It was black and white, Togut could see, but other details blended into the overall shape. Backing away on their bellies, the men retreated a safe distance from the ridge before huddling once more as a group.

"Okay, we've been searching in the woods for days now. They most likely went back to the city," Togut began.

"How do you even know they were from Pellence?"

Togut didn't want to divulge this information just yet, but he saw there was no avoiding it with his men. "Before we left, I talked to Evris. He told me that these brothers were the Princes."

"So there's twelve of us out here. How do we get in there to kill them?" Gordun declared.

"That is a good point," Palor stated.

Togut looked around at the men and smiled, thinking: we draw 'em out. "Leave that to me boys."

"What?" asked Gordun.

Togut began stripping off his clothes. Unbuttoning the top two buttons, he pulled his shirt over his head and tossed it to Palor. Then he pulled off his boots and leggings and finally his small clothes until he was as naked as a shaved cat.

"Okay, what are you doing?" Palor asked, his arms full of clothes.

"Everybody trusts too easily in Saintos, especially the unfortunate."

"Flair for the dramatic, this one," Gordun voiced.

Togut found some muddy ground and rolled himself in it like a sow. When he was done, he stood up and approached Gordun.

"Whoa, that's close enough Togut," he said, taking half a step back.

"Punch me!" the naked man ordered.

Without needing to hear it twice, Gordun cracked his leader above the eye with a thunderous right hook.

Togut spun with the blow and touched his hand to the ground to keep from falling. "Damn. That might as well be a medak paw."

The big man chuckled.

"Okay, one more. With the left this time though, and maybe not so hard, I still need my senses afterward."

Gordun happily obliged again and punched his leader's face. When Togut came up, he had blood dribbling from both blows and, combined with his nakedness, he looked like he'd just been run through the mud behind a carriage. He smiled at his men one last time, then Togut looked at the destination marker and read some of the arrow signs. "Pellence, Silver Streams, Corduran." Silver Streams, he decided, it wasn't on his map and he assumed it was a smaller town with less notable folk.

"You know what to do," Togut told his men before starting down the path.

As they watched their leader walk toward Pellence, Gordun leaned in next to Palor. "I always wanted to punch him in the face."

Chapter 16

Jole stood up near the fire, walked to the mouth of the cave and leaned in its entrance. Staring into the moonlit sky, his mind replayed the events of the night.

He had swung round, axe firm in hand, ready to decapitate the soldier behind him, but a flash passed him by, and he saw steel drive itself into the man's neck. Jole watched the man fall to the ground. He had turned to see the king unarmed. Hectore was fighting the way Jole remembered he could fight; unlike anything he had seen before. He'd watched how flawlessly his new companion dispatched ten enemies in a matter of seconds. None of his movements were wasted, all were either lethal or self-preserving. His twin blades glinting and gleaming in the moonlight. The king's grace was beautiful, almost melodious.

Hectore stomped an incoming stab to the earth and hammered his attacker's jaw, dropping him to the ground. But behind him, the last survivor of the enemy warriors was preparing to swing his broadsword hard at the king's head. Jole had pulled out the thrown sword from the dead man's neck – who was conveniently sagging semi-upright against an uprooted tree – and hurled it at the large warrior behind the king. The blade catapulted into the warrior's chest, hilt first. He had stunned the man, but the swinging broadsword carried through, taking the king in the back of the head before he fell to the ground.

"No!" Jole roared out. All his life he had never met another that gave him the same sense of kinship as Hectore Rai had. He was the type that would unexpectedly come to his aid, like he just had.

Letting out a terrifying war cry, Jole had rushed over and bore lone the survivor down. The enemy shuffled away on heels and palms, consternation quickening his movements, but Jole placed a boot on his chest and brought Omega down, splitting the man's skull as if cutting wood.

Over twenty-five bodies littered the earth around him but Jole only cared for one. Kneeling, he'd rolled his saviour to his back, placing two fingers on his throat.

... thump... thump... thump...

There was a pulse! Though it was fading quickly. Jole checked the back of Hectore's head.

The sword's hilt thundering into the man's chest had been enough to throw off his aim, and it was mostly the flat of the blade that struck the back of the king's curly-haired head. But there was still a flap of scalp peeling away from his skull.

He was unconscious and blood had begun to soak into his hair.

"Did, we... get 'em?" the king had suddenly asked between wheezing breaths.

"Aye brother, we did, now rest." The king closed his eyes and rested his head on Jole's arm, still breathing erratically.

"Please be enough," Jole whispered to himself. He took a deep breath and joined his hands, no words were said, though his mouth was moving with quiet whispers of good intentions. The giant placed his hands over the wound in Hectore's hair, the blood trickling out through his fingers.

There it is! Warmth flowed from his hands and blanketed the wound. Then he'd lost control of his magic. The wound in the king was ravenous and began sucking out his power uncontrollably, faster and faster.

Jole began to lean over and his eyes rolled back into his head. He fell away from the King and stumbled back on his ass. What the hell was that? he'd thought.

His vision became blurry and he blinked hard. Slowly, the trees, moonlight, and dead bodies all came into focus. Jole began to check his companion but fell back on his hand again. He was dizzy and uncomfortable suddenly.

Waiting a moment for the feeling the pass, Jole swung round and peeled back Hectore's hair where the sword had pierced. The cut was still open, and a fresh gush pulsed out of the wound.

Jole had tried to stand but dizziness pulled him back to the earth and he puked yellow foamy liquid from his mouth onto the mud before passing out for a few minutes.

When he came to, he managed to get up and noticed that his barrel chest felt considerably lighter. Jole took a breath of relief as he glanced up into the starry sky. Then he'd picked up his saviour and walked deeper into the darkness of the forest.

He soon found what must have been the king's campsite and placed him down next to a small fire that had been reduced to coals. Stoking it back to life, Jole added branches that had been gathered earlier.

He looked around.

An empty scabbard was lying at the foot of a nearby tree and, leaning up against its base, Jole saw the traveller's pack. Grabbing it, he'd swung the pack over his shoulders, picked up the unconscious king again, and summoned the remainder of his drawn magic to aid his vision through the dark.

Jole entered the mouth of a cave and carefully laid his comrade on the ground to start a fuel-less fire on the rock beside him. He checked Hectore's wound one more time and, satisfied that the bleeding had mostly stopped, he'd laid down and passed off into sleep.

It had been three days since the night of the attack and the king hadn't so much as babbled a few syllables of undecipherable nonsense since the time he'd asked if they had won their skirmish. He was still unconscious. Jole had tried healing him once more but again the dizziness came over him and he passed out. He didn't understand his magic and for some reason it wasn't working on the king. His memory brought forth a sudden recollection of his unconscious friend in another life. When they first met, Jole had found Hectore in a bear den. He'd used his fire to ward off the bears, but when a ball had accidentally caught the king it melted into his body rather than consuming it. After Jole had asked him why he wasn't charred and dead, the younger version of the sleeping man had told him that magic helped nourish Gifts.

Jole left the cave entrance to gather enough wood for a real fire. He couldn't maintain his magic for much longer and the king needed warmth. Walking in the sun helped replenish his strength, but he was uncharacteristically exhausted since he had drained his threa of its magic. When Jole returned with an armful of logs, he rummaged through the travel pack. To his great surprise, he found a small leather pouch containing a rare leaf that he had seen only a few times in his life but recognized immediately: Yenmaraj. The amount he had in his hand was worth a small fortune.

Jole held the herb between two fingers and watched the king sleep for a moment. He had rolled one of his spare shirts for a pillow and blanketed Hectore with his large woolen cloak.

When he checked his temperature, he saw the patient was still mildly feverish. Jole was still exhausted himself and contemplated who had it worse at that moment. The king was sleeping, otherwise unaware to his pain for the time being, as his mind lay in another realm. Jole, on the other hand, was entirely conscious of the weakness he felt. Headaches would come and go like the winds, throbbing as if his brain was trying to break free of his skull. He was weak and he was sore, and he hated feeling both. He could barely hold his arms up. This was always an uncomfortable feeling for Jole. He was like a maple tree tapped of his sap and had to wait for it to slowly return.

"That was a long enough walk, I think," he said, suddenly satisfied with the few minutes he'd spent gathering logs.

He shuffled next to the small fire and looked at Hectore. During the fight, this incredible man showed no sign of his age, yet now he looked very age appropriate. Jole could make out the creases around his eyes and off his nose, he guessed that the King was in his fifties by now.

Jole crawled and laid his back against the wall before his head swam another lap. He closed his eyes and drowsed against the wall. Being stirred awake when he heard a noise. The king had begun tremoring so much so that it had hitched the cloak off his chest, now only covering his waist. The convulsions continued for another few seconds before stopping as quickly as they'd started, and when Jole went to check the wound he saw that the thick red gash had begun scabbing where the blade had sunk in, the flow of blood all but stemmed. But surrounding it was a dire spiderweb of blue veins. That bade bad omens, even the magicker knew. Infection. Jole left Hectore to be at peace, there was nothing more he could do for him now.

Still, he worried for his patient. Since the night of the fight Jole's magic had been scarce and was becoming utterly useless now. He looked again at the signs of infection, gnawing its way into the King's skull like termites through wood.

On the fourth day, Jole couldn't resist the temptation of the rare herb. He made a light tea with some of the Yenmaraj he'd found in the leather pouch, and it swelled in his chest with comforting warmth, soothing the entirety of his being.

Jole checked his patient, who was still sleeping, and being confident that the king was stable, he decided to take a walk. He stepped into the forest where the sunbathed the trees, thick slanted pillars of light beaming through the overgrowth.

Jole saw the forest through new eyes under the influence of the Yenmaraj. Though difficult to put his finger on it because the sensation was so subtle, the world seemed more animated, as though he could see the life coursing through the foliage. He stopped in a clearing of trees where the sun shone brightly on a giant moss patch.

"You would make a nice bed," he told the fluffy moss like it was an old friend.

Jole took off his grey wool jerkin and folded it on the ground. Then he lay down on the soft moss blanket in the glorious warmth of the sun and took a nap.

He woke up when he heard an echo come from the cave. The giant rushed back to root out its source when he found the king in another seizure, his body thrashing about with disregard for its surroundings. The scene was upsetting and Jole pitied his friend again. Then, suddenly, the king stopped thrashing. He stopped moving altogether. Jole fell on his knees and checked. And then he knew, Hectore had stopped breathing. He was dead.

*****

Serah-Jayne could play with fate gracefully, like a musician does a harp, to affect the actions of things around her. She could pull and strum the strings but never pluck them from the harp completely. Sometimes the consequences of her Gift led to death, but she was always more of the editor, rather than the author, of the victim's undoing. Even with all the horrors she'd witnessed, Serah-Jayne had never grown accustomed to seeing a corpse.

Which was why Diyo had asked her to see the Prince safely up the mountain, but Serah-Jayne was lonely, and thought she might as well see the king back to his queen. She dared not follow the king and his son into the village of the Brotherhood. If one of the Brothers' scouts had found her sneaking around, they'd likely kill her. She might have been able to plead with the king to spare her, but then the Brothers would never let her leave the mountain. Leaving the Brotherhood was a luxury that the Poet of Battle afforded to the royal family alone.

So, she waited, and she patrolled the foothills of the mountains, hoping to intercept Hectore on his return. But it soon became clear to her that he must have either decided to sojourn with the Brothers or had slipped by her with a different route. At last, somewhat distraught, she decided it best to give up and report back to Diyo. But as Serah-Jayne picked her way through the forest on her way home, she suddenly heard the clash of battle. Following the sounds, she ran to the edge of the tree line and looked at the moonlit clearing. She watched as King Hectore and another man, who she recognized but couldn't place from where, were fighting a score of soldiers. Although they were greatly outnumbered, the bodies on the ground told her that the king was a phantom of his former self. When

Serah-Jayne saw the big man's axe, she suddenly placed the memorable weapon, Omega. Once she realized the weapon, she remembered the man.

The two men were both terribly deadly. Serah-Jayne watched the fighters with a spectator's awe. The king's grace was almost hypnotic, fluid yet unpredictable, with an efficiency where none of his movements were in vain. The axeman throwing magical fire from his palms between heavy swings of Omega. But their enemies were numerous and she could feel that the tides were turning. Serah-Jayne quickly tapped herself into the dance of chances that were surrounding the fight. Soon, she was connected to the fates of the men before her, holding them like marionettes, only the strings were elastic, vibrating of their own accord, and so numerous that they were uncountable.

Hectore was about to catch a blade with his neck when Serah-Jayne intervened and turned the blade flat in the man's swing. The blow knocked the king unconscious, but he would survive, she thought. Then she watched as Jole tried to use his magic to aid his companion. Foolish man, Serah-Jayne thought. She tried not to worry, telling herself that he was not meant to die in the woods at the hands of a group of petty brawlers. No, this King Hectore, that she had helped many times from behind the curtains, was destined for a much more glorious path.

That was why she was in this cave, now, days later. The king and the giant were around a short bend in the darkness. It had been four days since he incurred his wound, and Serah was staying close by to make sure it didn't worsen. Only it did, into infection. His body would begin convulsing from time to time and Serah-Jayne had done her best to quell his thrashing.

That was when it hit her. If she could affect the outcome of anything then maybe she could use her ability so that Hectore's Gift wouldn't absorb the magic and he would heal like anyone else. She played out the dynamics of the probabilities in her mind.

Over the last few months, she was really beginning to grasp the true nature of her Gift. Serah realized that she first needed to get a feel for the *potentials* that dominated the situation and their interactions with the things she wanted to influence. She still hadn't fully come to terms with this concept, but she knew it had to do with the forces driving the dynamics of the situation. They could be an arrow falling under gravity, the flow of a river, the wind in the air, a man's intentions. Then, to tap into her Gift, Serah had to decompose those potentials and interactions down to smaller and smaller scales until she could sense their purest form: pure probability, jostling about like raindrops on a dirty window. Only then could she draw her finger over the water to paint the picture in her mind.

The king began convulsing and thrashing about again in another seizure. She hugged the shadows and crept into view. Within moments, the giant came rushing in and hurried to the man's side. Although her eyes were fixed on the two men, she no longer saw through normal vision. Her mind reached out to the subtle energy fields of the giant's magic. She could feel their domino effect through vibrations of the very space that separated them. Serah followed the vibrations to their target: the dying king. She sensed the potential sink into the king's threa, which was swallowing up their power.

It was well known to magickers that the Gifted were immune to the effects of magic. But she knew Jole wasn't a conventional, educated magicker. Serah-Jayne cleared her thoughts, and through the divination of her Gift, she assessed the landscape of probabilities that surrounded the king. For several moments she was dumbfounded by what she was feeling, like she was on a boat with plenty of wind but no sail. Every other outcome she had sought to control had been fundamentally different from this one. Every other time she'd used her Gift, the potentials she pushed and pulled on had tangible sources, she was persuading physical *things*. But this time, it was different. The threa was not physical. It seemed to her that the threa was not entirely *within* this world, but rather like it was straddling this world and another that was outside the reach of her senses. It felt like she had no control, like there was nothing to push against. There was only one thing left to do. Serah didn't know if it would work, and failure would seal the king's doom. Her reluctance was making her want to run.

But inaction would see the infection run its course, so she stayed. Carefully, her mind found the pathetic string of air being drawn into the king's lungs. Gently, she squeezed until it stopped resisting. It was a delicate trick for her to begin with, but the gravity of the situation made it feel almost impossible. *She* had just killed the king.

*****

Annabella was attending court in the throne room when she suddenly collapsed. Her sons rushed to her side and Kael sent Raphael through the building screaming for help. Fortunately, an aging physician was in the palace and attending to the queen within a short moment.

She had fallen limp and already looked paler than usual. The physician blew air into her mouth and then pumped on her chest repeatedly. He did this twice more before the queen choked in a breath and began coughing.

Once Annabella began to breathe on her own Kael checked that she was alright before he helped the old man to his feet. "We were lucky you were here," he said.

"What brings you to the palace anyway?" Raphael asked him graciously.

"I was seeking an audience with his Grace. I was recently removed from my position by a younger healer in my settlement. I know I still have the talent, so I was coming to the king for help to start a new business here in the city. I needed some funding just to get established and heard his Grace was generous with those who help others."

"He is," the queen answered, having regained her colour. She sat on the second stair to the golden throne. "And I am too. Forget about your business in the city. You have mine. What's your name?"

"Sol."

"Well Sol, this will be your new home now. Welcome to the service of the palace." The queen gestured to one of the court officials, who immediately understood her order to take Sol to administration where he would be added to the palace ledger and have a check of his background in the Sainti records.

The rest of court was called to an end and the hall quickly took their leave.

Now, the queen was seated along the edge of the fountain in the palace's inner courtyard. The structure consisted of three tiers of angels, depicting promises of the place after death, the Graceland. Atop the third pedestal stood a tall, beautiful stone woman, water flowing out of the ends of her hair to course over her body.

Annabella passed her hand through the pool at its base, watching goldfish swimming under the water, their red-orange scales glittering in the sun.

She was thinking of Hectore. It was the morning of the tenth day since he'd left, and she had felt a halt in his progress right before she collapsed. For ten days, Annabella had been busying herself with the two daughters-to-be that had taken up residence in the palace, and she had talked to her sons about their ideas for castle defence, taking note that Raphael was especially excited.

Her blond-haired son came walking into the courtyard to check on her then. He had seen his mother sitting alone from one of the many balconies overlooking the square.

"How are you feeling?" Raphael asked her.

"Better, thank you," she answered.

He approached the fountain and sat down opposite his mother. Annabella smiled at her son, the Golden One, they called him. And Kael's the Beast, she reflected, fine names for leaders. She looked up at the statuette. "She's beautiful, isn't she?"

Raphael shrugged, "I guess she's as beautiful as stone can be."

"Do you know who that statue is, Raphael?"

"What do you mean?" he asked

"This fountain was a gift from Dannisera Moren. She was a friend of my mother's in Corduran when I was a little girl. When my mother wed, Dannisera made this statue of her. And after your father rescued me, it was an act of good faith from my people to give it to him. My parents were killed saving me and my brother during the Damonai's siege on Corduran. You could imagine why I loved her so much. When the statue arrived here, there was no convenient place for it, so your father tore down a crumbling, weathered man that stood on the pedestal and had my mother's statue retrofitted into this fountain."

Raphael looked at the fountain again through new eyes. Now that he saw his late grandmother in the stone, it hardly looked the same anymore. "He wanted you to know that she lives happily in the Graceland," he said.

"I believe that was his intention. Your father is a sweet man."

Annabella turned and looked at Raphael's deep-blue eyes. "Raphael, something happened before I fell today. I stopped feeling his presence..." she started.

"I'm worried about him too. I told him to take either me or Kael, but he insisted on going alone."

"Old habits die hard," she said with a look of concern as she thought about her husband. "He thinks he has to take the world on alone. He never would travel with any more people than he needed too. It was fine when we were younger. One time, he even convinced a small army that there was five hundred men in the trees when it was just the two of us. People used to think twice when they came across him. But now he and I are growing older. I feel it in my body, and I know he can too. He smokes his herbs to help him feel young again, but they don't last. I'm worried about him, Raphael. Can you send out a search party?"

"No one knows the way to the mountain. I'll tell Kael to start preparing for the morrow," Raphael obliged, noting genuine concern in his mother. He rose swiftly and bowed to kiss her forehead. Then he turned and left the courtyard.

Annabella rested a moment on the statue's edge, reflecting on her life with Hectore and the love they bore for one another. She passed her fingers through the water once more, looked up at the monolithic woman and sighed. Concern framed her eyes as she wistfully whispered, "Where are you, Hectore?"

*****

Hectore was dreaming of the time when he was still held in captivity by the Damonai before his Gift first manifested. He was only fifteen then, and he had spent most of his youth locked in this decrepit dungeon. He had been brought there years before and it showed – he already looked to be worn many years beyond his age. His clothes were torn, his hair was shoulder-length, greasy, and matted. His face was covered in dirt. He was imprisoned. He was the lost and forgotten King.

His father, Arlahn, had been betrayed by Dofi of Melonia, the two-faced turncloak of the GodKing Tumbero, someone Hectore's father once called friend. Hectore had been held captive for almost eight years. During his time in the dungeon cell, he had seen many prisoners come and go and often wondered when he would be called for execution. Only they never called him. He learned much later it was because Tumbero knew he was his half-brother and was keeping him for some sacrifice.

Still, Hectore dreaded the day he'd meet Tumbero. A guard once told him that the GodKing personally executed the men from these dungeons.

The sound of the victims' cries was chilling. He could hear it resonate through his cell every now and again, and he imagined that the GodKing's ultimate sacrifice would be much sicker than an execution. For the executioner, it was just a job. For the GodKing, it was a hobby, and hobbies are usually pursued with much more... passion.

Hectore rose up from the hard, flat slab of rock they expected him to sleep on. Although it offered little more comfort than the floor, it was the only object he had in his cell with which to occupy himself.

Hectore had fashioned a key from a left-over chicken bone. That meal had been a godsend to him at the time, the first meat he'd eaten since his arrival, despite its slight rancidness. For the most part, all they ever fed him was some kind of slop that seemed to be a mixture of used dishwater and expiring horse feed.

In this dream, he would escape the same way he did all those years ago.

After taking the guard by surprise, he picked his lock using the bone-key, his chest heaving in exhilaration, Hectore stumbled from his cell and looked at the long stair ahead of him. He took them three at a time and shoulder-rushed the door.

When he charged through to the other side, Hectore suddenly found himself outdoors, on the balcony of his bedchamber, back at the palace. It was cool, like a spring evening, wind pulled at his clothes and caught the breath in his mouth.

A man was standing with his back to him, resting his hands on the railing that was held up by dozens of little stone men. The man turned and Hectore's face went white.

He'd instantly recognized GodKing Tumbero standing before him; black curly hair, grey eyes, and the cut Hectore gave him still dribbling blood on his neck.

"Why'd you kill me brother?" he asked with soft melancholy carrying his words. "You could have let me live, my part in His story was done."

"What do you mean? You killed our father, stole his crown. You locked me up!" Hectore defended himself.

"That crown was owed to me," Tumbero said. His posture suddenly took on the air of a man asking his brother for forgiveness. "I only did it because the Witch of the Woods thought those prophecy tablets were about me. She thought she could make me a god."

"But they weren't about you, Tumbero. You died. I fulfilled the prophecy."

"No, brother. Through the release of death, His plan is revealed. I know more now than I ever did in the flesh. Your story's similar to what was written. But you've only been told so much. The whole thing is vague and cryptic. But you're like me, Hec. You're not Him. Your knowledge of the prophecy was inconclusive. He can't die brother... but you will."

Before Hectore could contemplate any of what his dead brother was telling him, the world slipped out from around him, and the brightest light he'd ever seen began swallowing up his surroundings.

*****

There was a strange feeling that overcame sensation. As if being suspended by nothing in the space around. Floating through a time seemingly filled with places, drifting through a place where time didn't exist.

Chapter 17

Since her collapse, the queen was filled with dreadful disturbances whenever she thought of Hectore. She never knew what to do in such times when she felt so helpless. That was why she had joined the war when she was younger. Annabella had become a medic in Pientero and Hectore's Brotherhood so she could keep herself busy. The fact that she was helping others was kind of secondary. She found herself ashamed that she wished for such a distraction to take her mind from her King.

Annabella didn't want to hold court without Hectore anymore. She didn't want to do anything anymore. Marlyonna and Luzy often had tea and biscuits brought up to her and they shared an afternoon together one day. Yesterday, Luzy brought her on a charitable mission in the city. They stopped at a school, orphanage, and hospital to offer gifts and help to many who crossed their path. But the whole time Annabella was smiling, a gnawing feeling ate at her stomach.

Today was the fourth day she dealt with her nausea, she simply sat on her ebony stool, wistfully looking at the path to the Spine, hoping her husband would ride through.

Annabella wore a royal-blue dress trimmed with gold, delicately embroidered around the collar and cuffs. Her humble, braided crown sat soundly on her head. The crown he'd won for her.

She toyed with the idea of visiting with her sons and checking on their inventions. But the two had been enveloped in plans, building, and test trials, ever since the blacksmith had appeared with an early delivery of their parts.

Her two daughters came in, talking about whether or not the thief servant Tod preferred men or women. Marlyonna had known him better and tried to explain his preference to Luzy. But her sister-to-be thought he was pretty enough for any girl. "Too pretty," was what Marly told her new.

Marlyonna wore a sun-yellow dress trimmed with black lace. Luzy's light green eyes beaming, complimenting her green satin dress trimmed with silver. It held tight to her figure and looked magnificent. She asked the statue before her, "My Queen, maybe we can go for a walk through some shops?"

"I know you'd rather go hawking, but a walk might distract you for a few hours," Marlyonna added. "Maybe we'll find some big fancy hat we can get for Hectore's return as a joke."

Once Annabella agreed, the women called for a carriage, and Zephoroth came trotting up with his black hair tied at the neck. "I'll be your escort today, Your Grace. Brandigit's going to dress as Kalendare."

"Wonderful," the queen said with empty acknowledgement.

The carriage pulled out of the palace's gate and strolled into the city. Once inside, Luzy plopped down on a cushioned seat opposite the queen and asked, "Please Anna, tell me how you and the King met."

"I didn't know who he was at first, just another boy with a broken arm. I was a medic in Pientero's Brotherhood. I found him getting ready to try and reset it himself. He's always been so used to doing things by himself, especially back then. I stopped him before he broke it again, took up his arm, looked him in the eye, and popped the bone back into place. He called me a 'sonuvabitch,' but it was just the pain, and I was used to hearing that stuff from the soldiers."

The carriage stopped and the three women climbed out into the sun. Busy crowds of people were moving all around them like ants in a farm. Everyone doing something, Annabella thought.

They entered a corner shop that belonged to an old friend of the Rais, with Brandigit following as a casual shopper and Zephoroth a loyal hound at their heels.

"Hello Jersay," the queen said when she walked in and saw him cleaning a glass counter. He turned and tossed his cloth in the air behind him when he threw his hands up. "My Queen! It's always a brighter day when you stroll through my store."

"Brighter for your purse, you mean," Annabella joked truthfully with the old man.

"Better my purse than Wender's, how is that old fart? Still breathing, I hope?"

"I haven't seen him in quite some time." The queen remembered the old merchant who had sold her Arlahn's Ritual Gift.

"Travellin's more dangerous than settin' up shop. I told 'im that. Oh well, what can I do for you, my Queen?"

"We'll just browse for now, thank you," she answered.

They spent some time pacing around the store, looking at all the glamorous jewellery and clothing and other fancy vases, trinkets, and combs.

Luzy had called them over to a vase with the Southern Freefolk painted on it. She was telling them of a history she'd learned from Elder Rufus when a bowl fell from Jersay's hands and shattered on the floor. Annabella,

Marlyonna, and Luzy saw Jersay staring at the entrance. They turned and were just as surprised as the shop owner by the sight before them. It was a naked man, lightly bearded with short, cropped black hair, holding a simple rag over his parts, and doing quite well to hide his vitals and maintain some dignity.

His body was smeared in mud and he was bleeding from a few cuts on his face, as he was escorted inside by Brandigit's son, Bregan.

"I found him just beyond the wall like this. I told him he should get dressed first, but he refused. He insisted on talking to the queen. Clearly, he's unarmed."

"My queen! I only ask you hear my story," the man said then, starting an approach toward her.

Leaping out from behind a nearby wristlet stand, Brandigit cut the naked man off, pushing him into a counter, and knocking over some jewelry. He had produced a dirk and was holding it tightly in his fist, close to the man's body. "Not another step toward her. State your business and let's see if your words are faster than my knife."

The man raised his free hand in submission. "I just wanted to speak to the queen."

"Then speak," Zephoroth said, hand on his hilt, clad in the full Sainti armour. Annabella noticed a few other Kalendare meander closer to the shop, darting glances in the direction of the commotion.

"What is your name?" Annabella asked, ever courteous, even to this naked man.

Brandigit relaxed his grip on the man and let him tell his story.

"My name's Togut. I was out on my farm when men came out from the corn stalks. They butchered my animals and killed my wife. I was in the barn when it happened. One of them found me in there and came at me. I only got away 'cause I hit him with a cowbell. I came straight to the city to ask you to send your sons out to find these men and bring them to justice."

Annabella wanted to refuse; ever since her collapse, she'd had an ominous feeling that she couldn't shake.

"There *have* been other bandits before," Annabella whispered to Zephoroth. "My husband's alone. Only Kael and Raph know where he is."

"The king should never be discounted, my Queen. But if it would please you, I will send for your sons to go out for him when we return to the palace."

"They're already preparing to leave," Annabella said quietly. She asked next, "What about this one though?"

Zephoroth saved her from denying the man herself when he turned to him and said, "The Princes have been busy lately. They have more urgent matters to attend to."

"Still," Annabella started, "I won't just refuse you help."

And Brandigit sealed the decision when he volunteered to check into the matter. "Tell me how many there were, and where it happened."

"My farm's up the road, place called Silver Streams."

"If we leave now, we can be there by sundown tomorrow," Brandigit promised the man.

"And you guys will... do whatever you guys do?" Togut asked the Kalendare following him out of the store.

"We'll see them brought before the king for Judgement."

After they had exited, Luzy turned to the queen concerned. "He said Silver Streams, right? That's where my family's from."

With the events bringing a close to their shopping, the women returned to their carriage and strolled back home.

Later, in the palace, Kael and Raphael were preparing to ride out to the Brotherhood for their father. Within an hour, they had horses saddled and bridled, and Kael was saying goodbye to Luzy when she told him, "I might go back home for a visit, just to see my family. But maybe after you find your father you can come too. We live on the east side of the big mill..."

"... in a brown house with a red door," Kael smiled, "I've heard all about it. I can't wait to see it."

*****

With the king dead, he lost connection with his threa. Serah-Jayne dreamt that the magic that coursed into him began dancing about, liberated. Jole's own magic was now true, and his change in posture suggested that even he could feel it had found its target. Now came the moment of truth. Serah-Jayne released her grip, allowing the myriad outcomes of the situation to follow their natural dynamic. She watched the king with such intention that she couldn't breathe. Her heart dropped when she saw no response from him.

In what felt like an eternity, but what must have been no more than ten seconds, Serah-Jayne stood on the brink of indecision. Yet there was nothing to decide. There was nothing she could do. Her energy was spent. She hadn't really done much, but she did it with such intense care that she was utterly exhausted. All Serah could do was watch, watch the king slip away forever, and she knew the course of this world would change irreversibly from this very moment. Because she had killed the king.

Serah-Jayne began to weep as silently as she could.

Suddenly, the giant sprang to his feet. Serah was stricken with such terror that her knees buckled. He must have heard her and sneaking spies in caves were probably not his fancy.

But his attention was not on her. Jole was hovering over the king, checking his vitals. He had just realized that the king was still dead despite having healed his wounds. Running about the cave, he began tossing items here and there. Within seconds, he returned to the king with a pair of bellows. Jole inserted the end into the king's mouth and, with one massive hand, he pumped the bellows slowly. With the other, he pressed on the king's breastbone over and over. Serah-Jayne watched intently and cringed twice as she heard the snapping of bone beneath the giant's powerful hand. Then she heard a surprisingly full-throated groan come from the king. Although he winced in pain and held his chest, she could see plainly that his breath was stronger than it had been in days. Jole was immediately on his feet again, throwing things about, this time getting water, blankets, and some other things that Serah-Jayne assumed were the artifacts of a healer. She finally took a deep breath and watched their following exchange.

Jole was jumping around in the excitement of *his* apparent triumph and hooting with over-joyous pleasure. Only when he noticed Hectore trying to rise, did he remember to be cautious of his environment.

"Whoa, take it easy brother. You've been ill. Rest for a while," Serah heard Jole advise.

The king listened and laid back, leaning against the rock wall. He managed, "Where am I?"

"In a cave, about two leagues from the Spine," answered the giant. "I brought you here after I found your stuff at your camp."

"What happened? I remember throwing a sword. Two more of them came at me. I had no weapon..." he trailed off in thought and gazed at his companion's face.

"I'm surprised you remember anything at all," Jole replied, looking at Hectore with eyebrows raised. "You took a nasty blow to the head, but that won't stop ya, will it? You still move the way you used to. I see that hasn't left ya. Still ain't seen anything like it."

Hectore began to lean for his pack then sagged back into the wall. "Can you fetch me my pipe? And the pouch with the herbs in it?"

Jole fell clumsy all of the sudden and he stumbled for his words. "Oh! Sorry King, but after I tried healing you the first time, I passed out and puked. When I found the Yenmaraj in your bag I made a tea with it. It helped me feel better. I hope you don't mind... Is something wrong?"

"Just a dream I had. And don't worry about the herb, Jole, Pientero left it for me. He has plenty where he lives," said the king. "But a cup of tea would do wonders for me right now, is there any left?"

"Of course," Jole obliged bringing a cauldron closer. "The Poet's still alive? I heard he died in the final assault on Pellence."

"We dressed up our best fighters in our armour to draw the Damonai's attention." Hectore grew sad at the memory of his long-passed friends, remembering his sons' namesakes and their fatal destinies. "Raphael's brother Kael was killed. Raph became a general in Esselle, but he died years ago now, assassinated in the castle barracks."

"It must have been a good fighter that took Raph down. He was stronger than me, and I don't say those kinds of things," Jole said, then flicked his fingers toward the coals. Flames licked up from the ashes.

"You're a magicker, that's right!" Hectore said, reminded by the act, pardoning his own absent-mindedness. "But magic doesn't affect the Gifted, how did you heal me?"

"You had infection in your wound," Jole told him. "My first few tries to save you didn't work. But you died so I had to try again, that time you healed almost completely. I don't know why."

"I died?" Hectore asked, shocked. "No, I was only dreaming."

"You were dead, Hec. Like a fish outta water too long."

"Then you're quite the magicker, Jole," the King said. "One who never ceases to amaze me."

The two sat in conversation, sipping their tea and regaling each other with stories since their last encounter. Hectore explained that he had three sons, two were Gifted like him and showed great promise, the third was off training with Pientero. Jole's story was less uplifting. When the king mentioned Jole's woman, the big man grew sad. Jole had found out Rasha was also sleeping with a pretty singer when they were together. He had accompanied her to the Cooperith town Laika and never saw her again.

Hectore eventually stood and walked to the cave entrance. He must have felt significantly better because he turned back to Jole, who was still seated, and urged him up.

Serah-Jayne smiled to herself. She silently thanked whatever wise soul bestowed the healing arts upon this seemingly brutish giant and slid from the cave back into the deeper shadows of the forest. She knew now that the king would survive. And she knew that Diyo would be proud.

Serah made for her horse that had been tethered a safe distance away. It's a wonder, she thought, how little gratitude or appreciation I receive for my services. If only I started charging, I would be rich. Only problem is I never stick around to collect.

Approaching the saddle, she was about to vault up when she heard a noise come from behind. She turned around in time to see a thick elbow coming at her and then nothing.

*****

His head was throbbing. His vision was white and blotchy at first before it slowly cleared. Breathing was painful, nausea rushed to his head and his stomach churned. He was going to… yup, he couldn't stop it.

The spasm was involuntary and Mick toppled face-first to the ground, a mouthful of bile spewing out to mix with the forest floor. Behind his back, he could feel the rough tension of rope squeezing his wrists together whenever he tried to move them.

He rolled to his side and lay there a minute, taking deep breaths through his nose and out of his mouth. Finally, Mick sat up, wiping himself clean on his shoulder. He could see a company of men pacing around a campsite. Some sat indulging in food and conversation, while others carried out duties – erecting tents, digging latrines, or cleaning equipment. Along a toppled ancient ruin, a single black pavilion had been erected.

The men were grizzled-looking, garbed in mostly lightweight black or brown clothes that were weather-beaten and tattered or donning heavier black plate armour. Mick saw the sigil they bore here and there on a shield or breastplate, but it was unknown to him. It resembled two men, one in gold, standing proud before a vagabond in silver, who was pleading on his knees.

Damonai? They must be.

Across the clearing, Mick noticed another two bound men. Darius was sitting obediently on the ground, the other lay motionless beside him. He could see red staining the neckline of the old man's tunic.

Pain swelled in the senior justicar's skull and pierced into his nose. It was broken, he knew. Slowly, he recounted the last things he remembered – the strange exchange with the mysterious man, Drifter, whom Mick still thought may have been a figment of his imagination. But the boot that had fallen into his face before he passed out, landing squarely on his pointed nose, was certainly a piece of reality.

The huge man who had delivered that vicious boot came wading over and stopped above him. "Thought I might have killed you. Woulda been a shame, eh? You know that man?" he asked, pointing out Darius across the makeshift compound.

Mick sat there a moment, looking over at the thief, when he grasped the words of the fey man sitting at his campfire the night before. "You and your new mate will need each other... Trust your instincts." Right before he was booted, Darius had confirmed Mick's identity. *They were looking for me, but why?* he thought. Mick decided he would find the answer to that question. His eyes gazed up and met those of his captor.

"Aye, I know him," he answered, measuring the weight of each word before speaking it.

"What's your relationship with him?" the man interrogated further, crouching down so that he was closer to his captive.

"That depends on your definition of relationship," joked Mick, knowing Darius found his own wit irresistible. He was sure the thief would have given a similar answer. *He's interrogating the wrong man*, Mick thought, *I've been doing this for years.*

"Do you love him?"

"Definitely not!" Mick exclaimed. "I... work with him."

Upon hearing this answer, the man seemed unconvinced. Mick felt his stomach churn again and struggled to control his composure. A second wave of bile came creeping up his throat, but he muscled it down with a straight face.

"What do you mean 'work with him?'"

Mick's mind raced to link together a story. In a matter of a heartbeat, he'd fabricated his lie. He knew he would have to sell it, and to convince a skeptic, Mick had learned from experience that you must show him proof. "I'm a justicar of Esselle. But go over and ask him, he'll tell you five times he's gotten out of my cells. I've been letting him go. He brings me a cut of all his scores, says it's fifty percent, but I think he's cheating me."

The interrogator stood once more and stared at Mick before walking over to the dark-haired man. The two exchanged a few words and several glances toward him before the bald warrior wrenched Darius to his feet and dragged him across the yard.

After being thrown to the ground, Darius japed a remark about his sex life being as rough, and this earned him a thunderous blow from a lobstered gauntlet. Red swelling took to his cheek instantly, but Mick swore he saw a smile hidden within Darius' winced pain. He knew their ploy would work then. Darius was elusive in his own, respectable fashion. It had taken Mick the better part of a year to catch him the first time, longer than any other wanted man. On several occasions, he'd escaped while being cornered, somehow vanishing into thin air.

"Enough!" barrelled Mick.

"I'll decide when it's enough," the bald man replied unfazed, punching Darius again in the stomach.

"Alright, alright..." Darius answered, touching his swollen cheek gently to a shoulder. "You could have just asked nicely."

The leader grunted and raised his hand. Darius prepared himself for another blow, but this one never came.

"Where were you going?" the captor's gruff voice demanded.

Again, Mick's mind was racing through plausible stories. He knew they would have found his father's note, so he started with that. "I was on my way to Pellence. But first I was supposed to meet my friend here in Corduran for payment."

"You're right about him cheating you. Said you've been getting a tenth of the profits. Called you a chump too."

"I think it was *stupid* chump, actually," Darius added.

"You're a dead man, thief!" Mick threatened hollowly from behind his bondage.

"Tell me about Pellence," the bald man said. "What were you doing there?"

He's looking to catch me in a lie, Mick knew. So he told the truth. He briefly outlined his meeting with the Warden Rali. And just as his father warned, he excluded any mention of the Council of Deaders and stuck only to the highlights in his letter: "An item of grave importance has been stolen from the vault." Mick sold the man his story easier than a vendor sells water in the desert. He was impressed at how simple, subtle changes of details came to him. His mind worked the same as when he played the game Battleground, three moves in advance. Surprisingly, Darius was almost as perceptive as Mick in catching minor details in stories and the two quickly grew the give-and-take dynamic of old friends, mentioning commonly known barmaids and grumpy landlords.

"Alright," the thick-chested leader told them. "I believe your story."

At that, Mick and Darius shared a look and hid quick breaths of relieved exultation.

"But tell me why I shouldn't kill you right now?"

As if he'd encountered this situation countless times before, Darius took over the conversation, speaking without any apprehension. "Well gold, of course."

He quickly adjusted his legs under him to seem more composed, professional, and convinced the man that he had a special talent for finding secret places around the world.

"Drelnum, maybe you can use him to find those blades Mordo's after!" a voice called from behind a tree. A tall, weathered, middle-aged man stepped out then, dressed in a sun-faded brown leather doublet that matched his hair and eyes.

Drelnum, the bald warrior chief turned to the newcomer. "You hear everything, Tracker?"

"That is one thing I can do, yes," replied the man.

"Then hear this. Fuck off. You'd be in ropes too if your Power didn't make you useful."

The man named Tracker bit his lip, shrugging the comment off with a shake of his head, and carried about his business, walking off into the camp.

"What blades are you after? Boranius'?" Darius asked, almost eagerly, Mick noticed.

"We can be of use to you," Mick told him in an attempt at self-preservation. "I track the inventory down, and he picks it clean. It's what we do."

Drelnum cursed Tracker for putting salvation in their minds. He pointed to the lifeless prisoner across the compound. "That merchant Wender was a sort of guide to get us closer to Esselle and our Caliph. Yesterday he refused to help us any longer, so he became useless."

"But we're still *full* of uses," Darius commented.

"We'll see," came Drelnum's ominous answer. "DeathShadow will be here in a few days, he can decide what to do with you." He ordered them both tied to trees near his black pavilion. A nearby soldier with a thick blonde beard obliged his leader's orders and came over. While being bound, Darius mentioned something that earned him a punch to the stomach from his captor. When it came time for Mick to be tied up, he complained about equality until Mick took a blow too for good measure.

"That just means he likes you," Darius joked as the bearded chief walked past him into the heart of the camp.

He spat out some blood and waited until they were as alone as they would be. "That was lucky, ya?" the thief whispered over to Mick.

"He was about to kill us!" Mick raged, struggling to keep his voice below alarm. "And what the hell was that about? Equality, not fair? You're a donkey."

"Calm down and I'll get you out of this."

Mick was furious, but he forced himself to take a breath. "How did you know they were looking for Boranius' blades?"

"Because I got the commission for them already," Darius answered.

"What? Who would send you to look for those?"

"That fat merchant, Pical. The one you dragged me in to see my last night in Esselle. I didn't know that it was for these guys though."

"Let's hope we don't end up as dead as Pical," Mick said.

"Pical's dead?" Darius asked, disturbed, seeking rhetorical confirmation. "Oh well, I still say we got lucky."

"Lucky?!" Mick struggled to free himself to slap his new prison-mate. "We're prisoners tied to trees! Where's the luck in that?"

The first sentry guard approached. Stabbing the butt of his halberd into the earth, he leaned it into his shoulder with both fists squeezing the haft. His stare was fixed on them as if they were the only light in pitch black.

"Don't worry," Darius told Mick before giving a coy smile. "I'm right where I want to be. We just had to survive the day."

That was when it occurred to Mick. Five times. Five times he had escaped lockup in a castle cell with real security. Some rope in a forest wouldn't hold this evasive thief. Despite his contempt, Mick suddenly realized that Darius was his only chance at survival.

Darkness came, but sleep was next to impossible. There was a knot in the trunk jabbing into Mick's lower back and his wrists had chafed bare. It was only after the rest of the camp slept and the sound was reduced to the crackling of dying fires and crickets, that the senior justicar's eyes finally closed heavily for the first time.

Something startled him awake and when he opened them Darius was on the ground with the sentry behind him, smothering the air from his throat with a forearm.

How did he get free? Mick looked at the bindings that had once held Darius. The rope was still wrapped in circles around the tree, just like his manacles.

Darius swept up the sentry's dagger and, holding a finger to his mouth to suggest silence, cut Mick's binding free. Mick nodded, rubbing his wrists, waking instantly with a burst of adrenaline.

Keeping to the shadows, the two men moved through the sleeping camp. Darius kept the dagger firm in hand. Once, a drunken soldier stumbled from a tent right before them, but he was too occupied trying to relieve himself cleanly to notice them slip past.

They had made their way to the edge of camp when Mick stopped Darius. "Hang on, there's something we need."

"You're not going back to take shit, are you?" Darius japed quickly.

At any other time, Mick would have hit him, perhaps even killed him, like he'd once claimed he would do. But after their recent experience together, he couldn't help but quietly chuckle, shake his head, and call the man an idiot.

"I knew you'd like that."

"Shut up," Mick told him quickly. "We need a horse if we want to get away for good."

"Good idea, stay here," Darius told him and took off back toward the black pavilion at the edge of the camp, leaving Mick alone in the forest. He hid behind a wide tree and waited for the thief's return. Moments later, he came back with a saddled black mare. Darius climbed atop and offered a hand down to Mick.

At first, they walked for a minute, remaining silent in the forest. But as the distance between them and the renegade camp increased, they jumped the horse into a canter and started down the path into the night.

*****

Swordsman and axeman, scavenger and King, together they marched through the forest as friends. It took Hectore a few minutes to gather his bearings. He was taking his time as he was in no rush, and though his body had healed physically, his forehead was pounding. He stopped to take a break and the large man laid his axe carefully next to him on the log as he sat as well.

The king felt worse now, returning to his previous state; the effects of the Yenmaraj were wearing off. An outstretched hand offered him a tin canteen, and Hectore took it, drinking the cool, fresh water. He stopped to take a breath.

"Why were you fighting all of those men?" he asked.

"All my fifty some years I've travelled alone across most of Tehbirr. But no matter how beautiful the land is itself, the hatred in men turn its beauty into tragedy. A little over a week now I found three dead bodies, one was an old man, the other two were just children," Jole spoke as if he was talking to himself. "Bandits seem to be growing in number these days. I hunted them down and served my own justice."

"The punishment fits the crime." Hectore believed that to be true. "Why so many though?"

"When I first found them there were only twelve," the axeman started. "Something went wrong the night of the attack. They must have caught on that I was trailing them and sent for another party close by. As I caught them in the clearing, the second group came out of the trees."

Hectore sat silent and pensive for a moment, knowing that the problem was ultimately his to solve. The Damonai, he thought, have they chosen a new GodKing? They were a strong breed and, ruthless as they were, they chose their leaders with great care. A new GodKing would have to be a man of impressive proportions, someone Gifted, just as Anvar had concluded in Pientero's cabin.

A moment later, Hectore stood up again and the men continued their hike through the night. "You should come with me, I'll take you to PJ's Brotherhood."

Jole had no other motivations to chase at the moment so he agreed.

They emerged from the woods in front of the large slanted rock at the base of Pientero's mountain. Hectore looked at the heavy boulder. Lucky, he thought, they could have come out anywhere along the Spine but were exactly where they wanted to be. He told Jole what lay behind it, and without being explicitly asked, the giant knew what the king wanted him to do.

Happily, Jole waved his hand at the rock and heaved it upright almost effortlessly, revealing the tunnel entrance. Hectore led the way into the dark tunnel. From behind him, a beam of light suddenly illuminated the narrow, crooked path. He looked back to see that Jole had formed his outstretched hands to resemble a sun. From it, a beam of light radiated outward.

"I'm not keen of the dark," he confessed.

Two minutes later, they walked into the large room inside the cave and Jole saw the shelves full of bags, jars, and other containers, the water basins, and two horses stamping with an exhausted excitement, whinnying and clumsily tangling each other's reins and stepping on each other's heels.

"They've been alone here far longer than I'd anticipated. They may look like a couple of idiots right now, but they're really two very solid steeds, and well-trained." Hectore walked to his white stallion, sixteen hands tall and powerfully built. He spoke gently to the beast, rubbing its neck. The horse seemed to understand him and calmed himself under his touch.

Hectore walked over to the shelf and strode alongside it, looking at the emblems drawn on each bag and jar. He pulled out a jar with a red cross and applied a white salve to his chest beneath his doublet, before grabbing a bag with the picture of a green and white leaf on it. From it, he produced a generous handful of Yenmaraj and placed it in a leather pouch, much like his own. He walked over to his old friend.

"Here, consider this a thank you token," he told Jole, extending his offer.

The man lifted his hand and answered, almost dutifully. "I don't need a reward for helping you, my King."

"Consider it a token of our friendship, then."

Admiring the persistence of the king, Jole grinned and accepted the leather pouch. Even Jole, after his years of seclusion, knew that refusing a reward once could be considered courteous, refusing it twice was simply offensive. But who refused a king at all? Hectore was not your average King though, Jole knew, his humility was too grounded.

A token of true friendship, Jole knew the king meant. The thought almost made Jole feel sad, he'd never really had a real friend, someone who showed as much sincerity as the king.

Tucking the leather pouch into his pocket, Jole walked over to the other horse. A chestnut gelding, it was nothing when compared with the King's stallion, but a good horse, nonetheless. This horse, he thought, better suits the needs of a soldier, more agile and manoeuvrable. Jole didn't like riding, but he would make the attempt; the king had asked him to come.

"This is a fine horse," he told the king, who was saddling his stallion now.

Hectore turned his head swiftly, the black and silver curls bouncing from the sudden movement, and he had a wide smile on his face. "But you're leaving it behind."

Jole didn't understand, though he was used to not understanding the intentions of other men.

Taking up the reins in one hand, Hectore explained to the magical axeman. "Pientero's Brotherhood is on top of these mountains. You should find him. He'll take you in. Anvar's there too, I remember you two got along."

"What are you going to do?"

"I'm afraid I'm already a few days late for my return to the palace and it's a full week's ride."

"Oh, of course," Jole said, picking up the saddle that sat on a stool close by. He put in on the chestnut horse and strapped all the buckles in place. Then he handed Hectore the reins.

Following Hectore's lead, they emerged into the sunny grounds once more. The king climbed smoothly into his saddle and looked back at Jole. "Mind closing that back up?" he asked.

Jole swung his hand and the huge rock lowered back into place.

"You make magic look so fun," Hectore told him. "Once you're up into the mountains, take the path ahead of you. Follow it to the second fork then take a right. Take a left at the next junction, then you'll pass two forks from the path before you take another left, the camp is out of the next right-hand trail. Confusing I know, you got it though?"

Overwhelmed, Jole asked for a second explanation to help commit the directions to memory. "PJ's scouts will find you before you find them, and they're not hospitable to unannounced guests. When they find you, give them this sign." Hectore gestured the face of a wolf with his hand. "Then say the words 'We're all mortal until we're immortal,' and show them the crest on the pouch of Yenmaraj. That should be enough to convince them, hopefully."

Jole bid the king farewell and watched him tap his heel to the horse's flanks and start a canter into the woods. Looking toward the top of the Spine, Jole let out a breath. "I never liked climbing."

He took his first step upward into the air and a flat rock floated beneath his foot, then another. Continuing, he ascended on stairs that chased one another like they played a game of leapfrog.

Chapter 18

When he first came to this place, Arlahn had been pushed into acceptance of his new role. To these hardened survivalists, he was still a baby. So at first he was attentive and focused. He wouldn't initiate general conversation among the other men and women, but he would merely ask questions to improve his understanding.

He did have his small group of companions; his roommate Jassyka, the young scout Tamis, and his sister Aideen had become fond of him. Anvar and Pientero, two undisputed authorities, were fond of his tenacity and spirit as well. The mountain poured knowledge onto Arlahn like water and he soaked it up like a sponge. After a few introductory lessons and some practice, the baby learned to crawl. After that first week, he saw he was learning to walk. And once he could walk, like all babies, it wouldn't be long before he was running alongside these mountaineers.

Running like he was right now, in the predawn gloom.

Arlahn had initially been awoken by his roommate, opening his eyes to see her lying in her cot, hitching her blanket about. She threw it down to her waist and started pleading in childish fear, "No. No. No don't, don't. No don't. Please."

That was when the horn blew out like an injured wolf howling at the moon, waking the entire camp. "AAAAAAOOOOooooooooooooo."

Jassyka sprang up at the sound, eyes shooting open full of terror, screaming out, "NO!"

Arlahn rushed to her side to check her, but she pushed him away. "It was just a dream. Come on, get up, we have to run. PJ doesn't believe in excuses."

They took to the path together, and for once Jassyka didn't speed off ahead of him. The pair jogged leisurely alongside one another and Jassyka began to explain that the horns came without schedule, but Pientero only sounded them four times each moon so that nearby travellers who happened to hear the sound dismissed it as a wolf calling out.

Together they kept to the circuit that Jassyka had long since memorized. This time when Arlahn emerged back into the far side of the compound, he saw that duelling was expected.

There were weapons laid out neatly for selection. Jassyka urged him to follow her, and once they had touched the finish point, they went back to choose their weapon. Arlahn took up his favoured sword and dagger combo and Jassyka found some stilettos.

The Prince had come a long way in a short time under the tutelage of the king-in-the-mountain. Now, he and Jassyka were about par in their skills and neither one of them really dominated the other in their bouts. Arlahn was still learning though, and each time he sparred with her, he grew more accustomed to her unorthodox, acrobatic fighting style. He'd picked up the subtle tells in her stratagem. Like when Jassyka came at him, she always led with the opposite foot of her attack hand.

They walloped each other a few good times until they were satisfied and the Prince was slightly winded.

Balanor saw the spar and approached with his own sword and shield in hand. "I'll show you how to get your ass beat, Babyboy."

Arlahn was about to retort his own comment when Jassyka appeared in Balanor's path. "That's enough, Balanor. We only have to duel once after the run. That's the rule."

"But I want to make the baby wail." He glanced behind her at Arlahn. "What are you looking at?"

"A cocky prick," the Prince told him in a rare act of defiance. He was growing more strength in his spine among the Brotherhood. He needed to.

Balanor began storming at him, but Jassyka placed two hands on his chest. She ground backward in the grey sand slightly before she gained the traction to shove the superior Brother back a step, roaring at him, "Enough!"

"I don't know what I did to you," Arlahn started, "but if you hate my brothers so much that you want to fight me about it, I'm not scared."

Balanor spat, "You say that. But I don't see you in front of me."

"Jass," Arlahn said. She was staring up at Balanor with coldness in her eyes. Like a pantuur being challenged, she wouldn't be the first to relinquish, she never wanted to surrender. Finally, she turned back to the Prince.

"Move."

Balanus and others began to gather and form a circle around the two. Men were cheering for Balanor to clean the forest with the baby. He felt little loved in the moment but allowed no sign of uncertainty to show on his face. Arlahn swallowed, flipped the dagger around in his left hand, and took a step closer to Balanor, prepared for the fight.

"What the hell's going on here?!" a voice boomed from outside of the circle.

Men parted like curtains and Anvar was standing there. He had a coil of hempen rope in his left hand and a tarp draped over his shoulder.

"Babyface, didn't I just see you duelling with Jass?" he called out in his resonant voice. "That's enough for now. I have to learn you something. Come with me."

Relieved, Arlahn gave Balanor another glance. The twin had eased his aggression when Anvar called the Prince over, but he warned the Prince in passing, "Next time, Babyboy."

Arlahn walked out of the crowd and replaced his weapons in the pile.

He went to Anvar, who handed him the coil of rope, then flipped the tarp on his shoulder. "You've come a long way with your fighting, but that's not the only way to survive. I've seen you in the gardens with Tamis and Aideen. Heard you started hunting with Jassyka in the bush too. And at night you sleep in your shitty little cot back home, har! That's all well and good, but when you're fighting a war, sometimes you don't have time to stroll through gardens or hunt. You need to learn how to build camps on-the-go and trap for your food."

They started down another foothill in the mountains and were soon lost in the wilderness. There were pines and maples standing in formation all around. A short way off the path, Anvar saw the surroundings fit to begin his next lesson.

"I mentioned before that you can build traps to catch your food while you're busy with other things. You ever build a trap?"

One look gave Anvar his answer. "Of course not, har! You princes either hunt or have your food delivered on platters, don'tchu! Traps are a real survivalist's pride, har har! Hand me that rope. I'll learn ya."

Arlahn did and Anvar told him as he accepted it, "Nice rope like this can be almost all you need out here."

He taught the Prince how to build a few of the simpler traps one could use in the wild. There was the spring snare that caught the game and strung it up in the air with a noose around its ankles. This trap was common in Tehbirr, but Arlahn learned that it was good for large game as well. Anvar showed him a deadfall trap that looked like sticks and rocks delicately angled into each other. When an animal disturbed the trigger, it would dislodge the fragile support and the large flat rock would fall and squash smaller game. Anvar kicked his over for an example of its simple function.

The next trap, Arlahn thought was genius. The two trappers entered into a clearing and he saw it immediately, his mind piecing together how it worked before Anvar said a word. There was a thick stake in the ground that housed the contraption. A small landing branch was drilled in near the top of the stake, ideal for a bird. Draped around the branch was a looped snare, its end passing through the stake and down to a rock. They approached it and Anvar voiced the explanation.

"When a bird lands on the branch, it breaks this little twig here," he said, pointing to a knotted twig that kept the rock from falling further. "The rock falls down, pulls the noose taut. Poor little birdie doesn't have a chance. But they sure are tasty."

When Anvar showed the Prince out of the clearing, they came onto another path. The maze of trails was finally starting to become familiar in the Prince's eyes, but he still wouldn't wander through them alone. This new trail led to a beach with dozens of canoes shored upside-down along the white bank.

"What are we doing here?" Arlahn asked.

"Sometimes game doesn't cooperate with your traps," Anvar told him and they diverted from the path and started along the rocky shore. "When that happens, you can always fish! Har har!"

The one-armed teacher brought Arlahn to a point and showed him another trap that seemed trivial in its simplicity.

Five feet into the water, the Brotherhood had built a sort of wall in the shape of a kidney bean, with a fat log lying in the middle of the only entrance.

"Fish swim the banks at nighttime. They're not the smartest neither so they follow the log into the wall and most of 'em are too stupid to even find their way back out, har har! Doing the fish a favour, too bad it's not that easy to fix the stupid in people, eh? Har!"

After a few more minutes of instruction, the two started to return back down the path toward the mountain compound, or at least Arlahn assumed that's where they were going.

"So now you know a few tricks to help keep you fed." Anvar again veered and wandered into the woods. "But at night you need someplace safe to put your head down."

Anvar now "learned" Arlahn how to build a few shelters on-the-go. There was the simple "triangle-frame" design with the rope between two trees, the canvas tarpaulin draped over the rope and staked down in the form of a triangle. Another was the lean-to, which was self-explanatory. Besides, Arlahn had already built them with his father on their journey to the mountain. The last shelter they found was called a wicki-up and was almost like a large cone of kindling, but it was made of poles and brush and vegetation and large enough for four to six people.

By the time they had finished visiting their last shelter, the sun was setting fast over the hills to the west. That didn't stop Anvar though, he continued to explain two more shelters that were environment sensitive. A sun-tarp for hot days on open plains and the quinzhee, built with snow. The quinzhee was the most laborious of the homes one could build, but in the cold of winter, its insulation was invaluable, Anvar explained.

When they were finally ready to begin their trek back to camp, Anvar stopped Arlahn with a strong left hand on his chest. "I didn't learn you how to build a camp in the bush so you could go sleep in your cabin. You're gonna find a nice place out here for tonight. Set up camp."

Suddenly Arlahn smiled inwardly, he had come to expect this in the Brotherhood. Their training was perpetual, synchronized to the beating of their hearts.

That night, when Arlahn settled down into his simple lean-to, he reflected on the events of earlier that morning – seeing Jassyka in one of her nightmares – and wondered what she saw when she slept.

After he had closed his own eyes for the night, he dreamt the most vivid and confusing dream he could ever remember...

He saw a man terrified in a dark room like a cave. His bad fortune leading him into delirium, he was screaming and hooting at the walls, shuffling through a travel pack. When Arlahn noticed there was a man lying on the ground beside him, he saw it was his father. He looked pale, Arlahn thought. He took a step toward him, tripped under a root and fell. The world flipped on itself and when the Prince looked up everything was different.

Now, he was standing in a room that was in utter turmoil. There was a couple he didn't know strapped to chairs. Arlahn was standing behind a table with a blonde woman, whose face he couldn't see, tied to it. The couple in the chairs had been beaten badly. The woman had blood crusted to her face, hiding her identity, and the man's had been partly filleted. Arlahn struggled to hold his eyes open, horrified by the gore. He started walking toward the table to identify the last victim, but as he approached, his foot froze to the ground.

Arlahn looked down and watched his foot slowly pry itself off an invisible stake, pinning it to the ground, and took a step forward.

When he looked back up, the world before him had turned into a waterfall, and he was somehow standing on top of the water pooling at its base. He preferred the tranquility and peace of this scene to the previous gore, until a powerful gale of wind began surging up around him, tugging, flailing, and inflating his loose clothes. It became so commanding that it actually reversed the flow of falling water.

After a few seconds of watching the water climb itself, a doorway was revealed behind in the rock. Arlahn took a step toward the entrance and it fell away, water pouring down on him. He closed his eyes as he braced against the cold drenching his body.

It was over as instantly as it started. When he came up and opened his eyes, he was standing in the centre of an oval arena. The hot sun was shining bright on him and he heard brass instruments playing a tune. There were thousands in the crowds cheering around him. He began to spin, trying to recognize his unfamiliar environment, but as he spun, the face of the world countered his rotation and settled into something else.

Arlahn was suddenly in a room built out of black and white granite. The walls were partitioned by giant murals whose displays were hazy and distorted beyond recognition, like the backdrop of a window when you focus on a single smudge. The mural before him appeared open and black like the starry night sky. Above it, perched the only photo that was somewhat clear, a huge black and white picture of a man's downcast face, as if in prayer or consuming thought. Arlahn focused his eyes on its details and swore he saw something else when the blackness started consciously clawing through the white until it hid the photo entirely. It leached out from the mural, pooling onto the floor and walls, consuming everything in its path until it became absolute and Arlahn saw no more.

*****

It was evening, though the sun reflected brightly off the moon, visible in the sky. The new moon already had a healthy slice shaved from it but still provided sufficient light for a column of soldiers, who patrolled down a hard-packed road with the forest growing thicker around them.

Togut was leading the men with this Brandigit bastard. He wanted the Princes, but he had once heard that any good leader could change his plans on-the-fly. So that's what he would do. He remembered the destination marker was around the bend they were riding and knew his men were lurking in the woods beside it.

Back in the city, he had been so proud of his cunning deception that he almost blurted out his plans by saying, "And then you guys will die..." But he recovered with, "do whatever you guys do" in time. Again, Togut praised to himself. That was smooth.

When the group was at the marker, he called for their leader, Brandigit, to halt.

"There was something I wanted to ask you," he said, turning to the brown-haired scout, noticing that his armour had no collar.

"The longer we delay, the further they get. What is it? We're in a hurry."

"Well that's good," Togut told him, "because I wanted to see if your blade was still faster than my words. Now, boys!"

Togut's plan was executed beautifully. His four crossbowmen couldn't have timed their releases better; one of them caught Brandigit in the shoulder and he slumped on his horse. The attack came without any forewarning and it came quickly. Togut's men leapt down from branches onto riders, unhorsing them, as Palor tossed him a sword. The rest of the attack was over just as quickly as it had begun, the sound of steel clashing barely echoing through the forest. The leader Brandigit managed to take one of the men down before Togut cut his throat from behind. Two more of Togut's party died clumsy deaths during the assault. Now the weakest of the fighters were rid of him – they weren't of any importance to him. He was pleased they were dead; three fewer mouths to worry about. Togut ordered the surviving men to strip the Pellencians of their armour once they were dragged clear of the path. Each man would have his own suit, save Palor, who preferred his scout's garb.

They pulled on chainmail shirts and black leather vests. Each vest bore a winged, snarling-beast pin, clipped on the left breast. Then the men put on the greaves and gauntlets, and finally Togut decided they looked like Pellencian soldiers.

But Togut's plan had changed. He wasn't going back into the city to find the Princes. His ears were keen. He heard the bitch Queen whispering about the king being alone, that she was going to send the Princes out to find him. If Togut could either track down the brothers or the king, he'd just need to stay with one long enough to lead him to the other. Once all the royal bastards were in one place, he thought, they will all die royal deaths. This was too good to be true.

The men slaughtered the extra horse and ate him that night.

Now they were full and eager for instruction. So Togut began instructing.

They had been riding casually through the forest undisturbed for days now, since they looked the part of native soldiers. Having refused the Pellencian garb, Togut made Palor continue to scout ahead. He came back into sight and pointed over into the woods. Togut's eyes sharpened and, though he could barely make it out, he saw the first orange light through the trees. Once he caught the flicker, he knew it was a fire.

Palor came closer to Togut, his voice was just louder than a whisper, "There's a man camped at that fire, just one, not two brothers. He's old." Palor patted the crossbow in his hands like it was his pet. "What do you want to do?"

Togut reached for a theory in the back of his mind. If the queen said that her husband was out alone, maybe, just maybe this was the king.

Demonblades.

The temptation was too much for him. He looked at Palor's skinny face and the stubble that tried to hide his dimple chin.

"I think we should go talk to him!" Togut declared.

He walked out into the clearing, brazen as could be, and soon his eight other men followed him.

The man at the fire looked at the newcomers with welcoming eyes. "Men, what brings you out here?"

Togut and his soldiers tethered their horses at the edge of the clearing and approached on foot.

They sat in a two by four formation across the fire from the lone traveller. Togut looked at the old man and felt the need to break the silence before it grew awkward.

"We were sent out here by the queen," he said, removing his helmet. It was a test, he was curious how the traveller would take the news, and he was pleased with the look on the man's face.

"Anna? Is something wrong?"

Who else would call the queen by her first name?

"Not in Pellence, my King," Togut risked.

"Have there been any more bandit attacks?" Demonblades asked. That gave Togut his story.

"Yes, my King. A group fell down on your sons... There was news they were taken hostage."

"That's a funny joke. The other week I watched Kael handle six men at once in training."

"Training doesn't help when you don't see the arrow coming, Your Grace," Togut intervened quickly, crushing the seed of doubt in the man before him.

"You're serious." Demonblades noticed then. "Well c'mon," he urged as he sprang to his feet. "We have to get back to Pellence. Organize our moves, find my sons."

Togut didn't understand the hype around this man. After all, he was just a man. He wasn't as big as Gordun or as quick as Palor, why did he command such fear within the Damonai?

Behind the king, a rustle stirred in the undergrowth. It was the scout Palor, Togut knew, getting into position. If he gave the signal, Palor would shoot a bolt into the king's back.

"What was that?" Turning toward the distraction, Demonblades exposed his back.

The temptation grew insatiable in Togut. Demonblades had killed thousands and if Togut ever had a chance at avenging his kinsmen, his father, it would be now. Childhood games had been built around this moment, *the man who defeated Demonblades*. He would be rewarded with riches and concubines forever from the Caliph Hennah Asa. Her hate for the man was well known. Togut fingered the hilt of his sword, then gripped the handle. All he had to do now was draw it clear and stab the king in the back.

*****

They had been walking since their second day together. The pair were arguing about their speed, urging the horse constantly between a trot and a gallop, when neither rider nor horse noticed the gopher hole in the earth. It was only wide enough to catch a horseshoe, and it did. The black mare's ankle broke with the momentum and it tumbled over, sending both riders to the ground. The two men gathered what gear they could carry and continued their flight, leaving the whinnying horse for the wolves.

Since then, Darius had stripped his long black tunic down to a white short-sleeved top, while Mick kept the dignified, blue look of a justicar from Esselle. Together, they crested the wooded hill next to the wondrous bulwark of mountain known as Tehbirr's Spine and stopped near the beginning of a wide clearing. The sun was sinking quickly, casting its final light on the endless expanse of the Spine beside them. The two decided to stop for a short rest.

Mick looked over to his new companion and asked, "How did you know I was in the forest? Why were they looking for me?"

"If you hadn't noticed, I'll do anything to survive," Darius answered brashly. "Convincing him there was someone else in the forest was my best shot at staying alive until they found somebody or realised that I was lying."

"Lucky that you found me then."

"I just needed to make it to nighttime. I'd say you're lucky you found me," Darius told him with a wink.

Mick chuckled. "How *do* you escape every time?"

"What's a man without his secrets?" Darius smirked.

"But secrets are kept safe between friends," Mick tried convincing him.

"So we're friends now?" Darius asked, feigning surprise. "I thought you were the guy who locked me up right before I came out to the woods."

"And right after you killed someone to let me go, I forgave you. Murder doesn't bother you?"

"I don't *like* murder. I'm an opportunist. I do what I have to to survive."

Mick recalled how his father had claimed to be an opportunist of a sort. He had killed before and Mick wouldn't consider his father a murderer, why should Darius be different... because he didn't know him better?

The tall dark-haired man unslung the pack from his shoulder, placed the bag on the ground, and started rifling through the horse's gear. He found some food in the brown pack and tossed Mick a piece of dried meat.

"Thanks!" Mick said, catching it in the air.

The two chewed together in silence. Mick looked around his surroundings, hoping to recognize some sort of land marker or spot a nearby road. Darius leaned against a tree and enjoyed his food with carefree leisure, occasionally stealing a glance at his companion.

"So, did you steal Rali's artifact from the vault?" Mick finally asked.

Darius looked at him hard in the eye, ripped another bite from his meat, and looked away without answering.

They listened to the sounds of the forest as they ate.

"No fires tonight," Mick told him, breaking the silence. "We shouldn't risk it, they're sure to have sent someone after us."

"For a justicar, you have no problem thinking like a criminal," Darius remarked.

"That's why I kept catching you."

Darius smirked at that. "No one would ever catch me if I didn't want them to. I let you have me."

"That's the stupidest thing I've ever heard."

Darius smiled at Mick's response like it was a compliment. "Fine, I'll show you. I doubt that both of us will get out of this forest alive anyway."

"Show me what?" Mick asked as he watched Darius move from his tree back to where the pack lay. He unclipped a coil of rope and approached Mick.

"Take this," Darius instructed, handing Mick the coil. "And bind my hands as best you can."

The sandy-haired man swung the rope around his companion's wrists and wrapped them quickly, tying them together with expert skill. Darius yawned theatrically. "Are you finished?" he asked.

Mick smiled as he pulled tightly on the collection of knots he'd created around the man's wrists.

"Ow!" Darius complained.

Holding his hands out before him, as if begging, Darius took a step toward Mick. The justicar couldn't surmise what happened next. Darius pulled his arms apart; the rope binding them together melted through phantasmal wrists and fell to the ground as his hands flapped out, free of their bonds. Then, swinging them up and clamping them together like a crab closing its pincer, he delivered a disorienting slap to Mick's ears.

To Mick the world popped, and he saw imaginary lanternbugs float through his vision.

"What the hell!" he shouted, before rushing toward Darius. He was about to grab the thief's collar and drag him to the ground but when he reached for the man standing there, he fell through Darius as if he were a mere projection and landed hard on the earth.

Darius turned around with a smile on his face. "I thought you were a quick learner. Are you going to calm down?" he asked with nonchalant charisma.

Mick returned to the bound rope and inspected it once more before shaking his head. "I don't get it, are you Gifted?"

The man chuckled. "Touched is what I was told."

"Told by whom?"

"The man who sent me to the forest, he comes to visit from time to time. Last time I saw him was the night I escaped the dungeon," Darius answered. He went on to tell the story of an unnamed man who had called Darius Trickster. After hearing his description, Mick believed it was the same man who had found him at his camp, Drifter. He found it strange that Darius had chosen to refer to the man as Reader, as that was what Mick had accused the him of being; a reader of the Tree of Life.

Darius' encounter was much different than Mick's to hear him tell it. The man came to him in the Essellian cell, claiming to have a commission for him after he escaped. He emphasized the need for the return of the Prophecy Tablet – Mick had learned this second tablet was Rali's hidden treasure, a replica of the one King Hectore had, he wanted to assume. Reader apparently sent him straight toward the Damonai camp where he was captured shortly after. Mick asked why he didn't just sustain his Gift until he was free.

"It doesn't work like that," Darius explained. "It's more like holding your breath. I can do it for a little while, but not long enough to escape a group of scouts and doing it too much makes me dizzy."

A cooling breeze whistled through the clearing, causing a gap in the fluttering autumn leaves to reveal itself to Mick's curiosity. He rose and walked toward the branches beckoning him into the forest, pushing aside the thin wall of foliage before him, he entered. There was no path where he walked, only deeper wilderness. He could hear birds calling out for mates and chirping overhead as smaller magpies and robins flew from branch to branch. To his right, he spotted a pair of squirrels chasing one another around the root of a tree then quickly up it to lose themselves among the abundance of branches. Emerging from the forest into a small clearing, he noticed something naturally cut into the rock of Tehbirr's Spine.

It looked like something he'd only seen in oil paintings, having never ventured far enough south before: a Freefolk Chieftain. The man's long, stony face bore a hat made of tall standing feathers. By his solemn chin, Mick saw his destination. Nestled into the rock, close to what looked like sixty feet up, was a visible landing from where he could comfortably scout the area.

Darius came following through the forest. "So, what's the plan?"

Mick continued to study a path up the rock wall. "This is Tehbirr's Spine, so the way I see it, we either climb to a vantage where we should be able to find out where we are. Or we walk straight west until we find something."

Darius thought about it a moment. "It would help if we knew where we were going. I think we should climb."

Mick's need for information made him inclined to agree. He didn't enjoy the prospect of walking aimlessly through the forest, especially while being pursued. "Alright, we need to make it to the chin up there," he told Darius, pointing up with the hand poking out of his muddy blue sleeve.

He approached the mountain and climbed up until all fours were off the ground. Repeating this action again and again until he felt his first jolt of discomfort. Mick leaned out as much as he'd dare and looked down at the twenty feet he'd travelled then looked up at the climb ahead of him in its entirety. A man would be insane to scale to the top, he thought. He looked back at Darius, who was still standing some fifteen feet back on the ground. "Are you coming?"

"I don't see why both of us need to risk our lives climbing. You're doing a good job. Tell me what you see."

"This was your idea!" Mick tried to argue.

"No, it was yours. I just agreed with you."

"You know what I mean," Mick called down, frustrated.

Darius just smiled up at him devilishly, and Mick shook his head in equal parts frustration and disappointment. Cursing his new companion under his breath before he continued gave him renewed ambition. He kept climbing until he was almost on par with the treetops when he found them; his landmark, spearing straight out from the mountain's edge in a direct line, the aqueducts. Mick cursed himself, if he'd have walked another ten minutes in the forest, he would have seen the large stone waterway without the risk of falling from a great height.

Satisfied with his discovery and the height to which he'd climbed, Mick settled to start his descent. He began back down the opposite way he'd climbed, moving his hands first and his feet only after he was anchored.

The clinking of steel on steel and the thunderous rumble of hooves pounding the earth rose up with the wind. But through the density of the treetops and the rustle of their leaves, the sound from below was quieted until it was too late for Mick to shout a warning down to Darius. He risked a glance below for evidence of the dark-haired thief, but he had vanished.

Ten black riders strolled into the clearing and stopped in a circle at the base of the mountain, while two men shared a long conversation.

Mick was just out of ear shot but wondered what they discussed at such length. The burn in his arms began to spread and he felt his weight grow. Finally, one rider shouted an order to search the area. The men spread out like an outstretched hand in two-man teams.

Mick needed to move before his muscles cramped, so he made his way back down slowly to allow time for the men to clear. Moments later, he was thirty feet from the ground when his footing slipped, and he fell.

Crashing to the ground heel first, he heard a loud snap and let out a cry. Pain raced from his shin and Mick struggled to hush his moans of agony. He looked down and saw his leg had snapped and was poking against the fabric, a blanket of red blood growing around it. He was about to let out another wail when a hand clamped over his mouth. Before he knew it, he was being dragged back toward the Spine, passing into darkness as they moved under the rock.

"Shhh," a sound advised, though the hand was still covering his mouth. It was Darius.

Together, they laid low in the dark as Darius craned his neck to peep behind him through a small triangular crack in the wall. He watched the riders return and stroll through with conviction that they'd heard the sounds further away.

After a minute of silence, Darius removed his hand and helped Mick up. "Come on, I found a gold mine."

Mick hobbled through the blackness, bumping into the wall before him until he found the way. The pain in his leg was constant and intense, but the shock was already making it seem like it was not a part of him. After a few turns, they came into a room large enough to echo their voices. Darius dropped Mick to the ground haphazardly and his companion cursed him, warning him his leg was broken.

The thief sparked a flame to a wick and for a few seconds the faint orb around him was all Mick could see. He found a torch anchored in the wall and lit it. Soon the room was glowing with orange-yellow light and Mick could see what Darius had meant by "gold mine." There wasn't actual gold, but this must have been a forgotten supply mine from the Damonai HolyWar. Baulim, Mick's father, had told him that the GodKing Tumbero had insisted on creating such places. Inside were all the essential provisions for an entire battalion of soldiers. Subsequently, Pientero Jessonarioko did the same during Hectore's Rebellion.

Mick didn't care about the preserved food or anything else on the walls, his pain was all-consuming. He only wanted to fix his shin. He rolled up his pant leg, exposing the white bone that had broken at a gross obtuse angle.

He looked at Darius who was frozen with a disgusted look on his face. His eyes were indecisive as to whether they should be looking at Mick's face or the bone sticking out of his shin.

"That's disgusting!" Darius blurted with a snicker.

Mick dropped his head to the ground and gathered himself before he sat back up. "Come here, you have to help me reset it."

Darius shook his head. "No, no way. I'm not a medic."

Mick attempted to sound stern through his pain, "Come here and help me or I'll die."

"Then you can die," Darius told him. "I've already saved your life twice."

Mick wanted to throw a spear at him but he didn't have one handy, he picked up a small rock instead. "Where did you get two times from?"

"When we escaped the camp," the thief said, jumping clear of the rock, "and just now."

"Just now doesn't count. You didn't save me, you saved yourself." Mick argued as best he could between the waves of agony. "It only counts if you come help me now. What are you afraid of? A little blood?"

Darius shook his head again. "That's not a little. I'm not doing it."

Mick took a few breaths to calm himself. "Darius, please. My leg needs to be put back in place."

He stood there, looking unconvinced for another few seconds. Eventually, Darius came over and knelt down by the wounded man. "Okay, what do you need me to do?"

Mick gave him instructions; push it back in.

Darius placed his hands on the justicar's leg below the bone and grimaced his empathetic pain. He was about to push with all his force when Mick shouted. "WAIT!"

"What?!" Darius asked frantically, afraid he had already hurt him.

"Nothing, never mind" Mick said at first. "I just wish I had some of this salve. I thought it might be here, but I don't care anymore."

"What salve?"

"There's a paste my father told me about, that The Poet of Battle used to make for the king and his rebellion. A medicine that could numb pain, stop bleeding, it even accelerated the healing process."

Darius stood up, eager to remove himself from his current situation. "Well that's what you need right now, and maybe it is here, there's all kinds of stuff on these shelves, what does it look like?"

"I don't think you'll find it. Come back here."

"Just give me a chance to look around," Darius told him, trying to maintain distance.

Mick sighed in his defeat. "They kept it in jars marked with red crosses."

"You mean like this?" Darius asked, plucking a jar from a shelf and showing it to Mick.

His eyes opened wide. "That's it! Bring it here."

Darius brought the salve to Mick and he spread the thick paste generously around the exposed wound. Almost immediately, Mick felt relief, like a comfortable numbness wrapped around him.

"It's too bad we couldn't find a pantuur," Darius said.

Mick started laughing in his delirium.

"What?"

"You're daft," Mick told him. "I can't believe you evaded me for a year. All a pantuur would do right now is enjoy a nice meal."

"What?" Darius repeated, in equal parts confusion and indignation. "You haven't heard of men riding pantuurs?"

"No, men don't ride pantuurs." Mick shook his head. "Alright Darius," he said, laying his head down and closing his eyes, enjoying his euphoric numbness, "it's time."

The thief dropped to his knees and took up Mick's broken leg again. He looked at his companion, who seemed preternaturally calm. Darius took a deep breath in, pulled Mick's ankle outward, and forced all his weight down until something snapped.

Chapter 19

Of all the weapons he'd trained with, it was the mountain's longbow to which Arlahn had the most difficulty adjusting. He was going through the series of archery drills that Pientero had set out for the Brotherhood, shooting at two stuffed dummies some eighty yards in the distance – the Prince had learned it was his brother, Raphael, that had invented their movable-target pulley system. One dummy was mostly hidden behind a wall and the other was "on patrol" in empty ground. Arlahn launched an arrow high into the air and quickly fired a second straight at the open target. His second arrow hammered into the hip of the exposed dummy before his first came falling down right beside the hidden one.

"You missed," Balanor told him as he was walking by.

Arlahn ignored the comment and continued with his practice. He shot through a series of twelve targets placed out at varying distances, hitting ten. He was learning how to be better, how to be a Brother.

The next exercise introduced Arlahn to firing a bow while riding on horseback. This was where the bulkiness of the mountain longbow was a major hindrance to the Prince; he struggled to hit as many targets while riding. He looked around and watched two other archers ride and fail as poorly as he had. Arlahn was about to discredit the bow from horseback until he caught a glimpse of Pientero.

The king-in-the-mountain was dressed in his usual dark attire, his long hair, held in a clip behind his neck, bouncing with the horse's stride. He rode around in long, wide circles, firing arrows over each shoulder, using either hand to draw the bow, peppering arrows into targets left, right, and centre.

When Pientero looked back at the Prince, Arlahn knew the king-in-the-mountain was teaching him something. Repetition leads to second nature. The man's pedagogy was everlasting, his expertise in such matters undeniable. Never, Arlahn knew now, had there ever been a more accomplished fighter that wasn't Gifted.

The Prince watched as Pientero reigned in his horse on the edge of the training ground. Then, Arlahn walked over to a partitioned section of the archery compound where Brothers could attempt a specific test, only once a week. He noticed it was a scenario that was designed for failure, and Jassyka had confirmed as much. The object, she claimed, was to see how quickly your mind works under pressure and how accurate your instincts are. Here, archers were given bundles of four arrows before they took part. Four arrows for five targets.

The scenario was a prisoner being held hostage at knife point. The other four enemies were randomly set up and moved by virtue of the pulley system once the trial began.

"You want a crack at the test, Baby?" PJ asked, approaching the small, fenced in ground. Pientero always witnessed this test.

"Once a week." Arlahn told him.

He stepped up with his bundle of arrows in hand. Pientero told Arlahn to nod when he wanted to start and he would drop the black cloth hiding the practice dummies. The prince gave a nod and drew his first arrow back.

The black curtain fell to the earth.

Almost immediately, Arlahn released his first arrow, seeing it land soundly into the captor's head. Then the other four dummies began converging on the "prisoner." Arlahn quickly ripped another arrow to the string and drew it back. His mind turned off for a moment and he fired arrow after arrow, without paying any attention to what he was really doing. Soon he was out of arrows, and when he looked up, four of the five dummies had shafts coming from their faces. He was utterly shocked at what he'd accomplished, almost automatically.

"That must be a perfect score!" Arlahn called over to the king-in-the-mountain.

"It can't be perfect," Pientero told him. "You left one alive."

"That's impossible," Arlahn argued. "You only get four arrows."

"So?"

"So, there's five targets. How are you supposed to do that?" The prince assumed the test was more for decision making, he didn't realize its impossibility was based on somehow hitting all five targets.

"It's been done before."

"There's no way anyone—" Arlahn started in protest.

"You mean your father never told you?" Pientero interrupted. "That's how he saved your mother, Baby, the night we took Pellence."

Arlahn was at once bemused and amazed. Again, an untold deed of his father's had baffled him beyond comprehension. "How...?"

"I've set this up to try and find that out," Pientero explained. "By the time I found your father, all five men were on the ground and he was holding Annabel—your mother."

Arlahn stood there, contemplating for the moment when Jassyka found him and approved the Prince's performance. As they walked away, Arlahn told her about his dream in the forest. She remained quiet and seemed somewhat emotionally detached to the details, though she paid close attention to what he was telling her.

She contemplated for a moment and was about to reply when Pientero's voice boomed out the orders to begin training.

Arlahn and Jassyka moved over to the workout section of the yard.

"You shouldn't think too much of your dream," Jass told him as she hauled a rock up into her arms, "sometimes they're not meant to make sense."

Arlahn dropped a boulder into position, "What makes you say that?"

Placing her rock beside his in the pile, she turned with him. "Every few nights, I have this dream. In it, I see the wolf that led me here. I follow him into the compound, like I always did in my dreams before. Except this time, when I bend over to pet him, he snapped a bite out of my hand."

Arlahn was unsure about how to direct the conversation and chose the lame comfort, "It was just a dream, who knows what it means," though he said it in an apologetic voice.

They were rolling a huge boulder together toward one of the perimeter towers when Balanor and Balanus approached.

"Look at the two babies, trying to roll the rock," Balanus taunted.

"Shut up!" Jassyka snapped. "Go back to playing with your little sticks."

Arlahn laughed at that.

"You got something to say, Babyboy?" Balanor retorted.

"No, she's got it all taken care of herself," the Prince replied with a smile. "Why don't you grab a weapon and we'll settle this."

Arlahn's smile died then as he became stone-faced. Doing his best to keep his voice from breaking he promised, "I'll finish you after I finish this."

Balanor claimed to look forward to it and then set off with his brother to train elsewhere, while Arlahn resumed his work with Jassyka.

They had finished rolling another boulder into place, and Arlahn looked around for Balanor but couldn't find the dark-haired Brother. He no longer wanted to simply strengthen his muscles, now he wanted to fight.

"I don't know where Balanor went, but I just want to hit something now."

"Why don't you and I duel then? You can try to hit me." She told him with a challenging look.

"No..." He protested. "I wanna really go at it right now."

Jassyka simply guffawed, claiming, "Now you've made me wet myself."

Normally, the Prince would have found humour in that, but he was still too focused on Balanor. The man just had to push him one more time...

Jassyka walked over and rolled the weapon die. It drew a flail for her and she plucked it from the practice weapons. Arlahn rolled a spear for himself. He picked it up, scanning the grounds one more time for Balanor, but didn't see him.

Arlahn started practicing with Jassyka, reluctantly at first, but soon her effort required his focus as he staved off her attacks one after the other. Using his spear to keep her at bay, he was thrusting low when he heard Balanor's voice come from beside him. "Why didn't you come find me, Baby?"

In the split second Arlahn stopped and turned to Balanor, Jassyka slapped the spear out of his hand with a foot and almost crushed his shoulder with her flail. Recovering quickly, Arlahn threw himself into her, slamming his shoulder into her chest and knocking the flail out of her hands.

Most women would have been thrown from their feet when Arlahn collided into them, but Jassyka was mountain-trained and somehow absorbed the contact into a backward leap. Her anger flared and although she lost her weapon, she refused to give an inch. Jassyka quickly landed successive blows on the prince before climbing on top of his shoulder, pummelling his head with her sharp elbows.

Arlahn braced himself against the blows with one hand while trying to get Jassyka to stop with the other. He remembered part of Kael's lesson was to remain calm, but when he heard Balanor's heavy laughter hooting through the blows, he gave in to his fury. Finally, he stepped forward and heaved Jassyka off of him, roaring "JASS, STOP!"

Impossibly, she took to the air like a ragdoll, flying until she thundered into the ground and skidded through dusty earth into a nearby turret. The blow dislodged loose rubble over her head, and for a split second, a fist-sized rock teetered on the edge. The world stopped; everyone had seemingly paused to watch and saw Jassyka slam into the turret. Then, the rock fell with a solid thud against her head in the silence of the camp.

Balanor came storming up to Arlahn. "What the hell's wrong with you?"

The Prince, who was standing there in disbelief at what he'd done, didn't even feel Balanor shove him.

He only knew that he'd been displaced. He looked up at Balanor with cold hatred in his eyes. The Brother had to push him one more time...

Without being able to explain it, Arlahn gave Balanor a heavy forward boot. Again, as if suddenly he was channeling the strength of Kael's *kjut'tsir*, he sent Balanor sprawling through the air backward twelve feet to land on his back and roll over face first.

Pientero was there then, demanding to know what had happened, but Arlahn didn't answer him. He didn't even hear the king-in-the-mountain. He could only walk over, scoop up Jassyka in his arms, and beg for help.

*****

There were few things that the king was afraid of. But if anything could bring Hectore to a state of horror, it was abduction. He had memories too vivid to ignore, his hunger eating him away from within, strength fading from his muscles. Then there was the torture, for hours and hours, days and days, years and years... Hectore may only wear one white scar on his face from battle, but his upper torso and back were an orchestra of punishment from his imprisonment. He was horrified at the news of his sons' capture.

Hectore heard something move in the forest behind him. He turned for inspection when his *sciong* tingled his ears and identified the faint scrapes of metal on wood and leather.

Behind him, the soldier he had been talking to had drawn a foot of steel to bear down on the defenceless king before he grew aware. Hectore began to react, reaching for the man.

A black arrow shaft flew past the king's shoulder and landed in the soldier's eye socket. His movement became limp and the sword slid back into its scabbard as he stared into the darkness past Hectore with his remaining eye.

Men started drawing their swords clear, backing away to form a defensive line. Horses began whinnying and clapping their shoes to the earth in protest.

More Pellencian soldiers emerged, riding through the dark forest. Raphael's golden hair shone in the moonlight and was the first thing Hectore noticed about his sons, then the archer's bow. Kael rode next to him, storming into the clearing, hefting Hectore's claymore, Justice, single-handed.

Another black shaft pierced a second soldier's chainmail between the ribs, into his lung, and he fell over, grabbing the arrow.

Kael charged past Hectore, bellowing a huge war cry. His horse was just as fierce, snarling through its effort. Raphael came riding by the other side of him, with another arrow nocked and drawn to his mouth.

The seven remaining soldiers stood their formation, swords raised, but the two princes plowed through them on their horses and three men were trampled, two others falling dead from wounds. Only two survived, leaping clear. One, a very burly man, threw himself at Kael's horse and brought all three down to the ground, the horse shuffling up first and running off quickly.

Kael rolled onto his back and blocked a downward hack from an axe. Even from his compromised position, his *kjut'tsir* threw the man back several paces, allowing Kael to regain his feet. The man parried a thrust with the head of his axe and quickly snapped the butt into Kael's face.

That was when Hectore saw something for the first time in his long, experienced life. If he had ever seen anything of the like, it would have remained with him for the rest of his days, just as this would.

Kael stepped back and swung his blade to meet the axe. His *kjut'tsir* carried the sword through the thick axe head, shattering it to pieces, and leaving a block of metal on the haft. Using the same momentum, Kael swung a vicious left hook behind the sword, connecting with the man's lower jaw. It looked as though Kael's fist passed through his face, sheering the skin clean off and leaving only a row of top teeth and a long, dangling pink tongue. The man's eyes went dull and he dropped where he stood.

At the sound of the thud, one of the frightened horses broke free from its branch and galloped off into the forest. The three men paused and looked around them. The last soldier lay on the ground with two arrows in him; all the dead men were wearing Pellencian armour. Hectore asked, "Who were they?"

Kael pointed to the soldier with two arrows in his chest. "We could have asked him."

"And I wouldn't have put a second arrow in him," Raphael retorted, slinging his bow over his shoulder, "but you…" He stopped for a second to look his brother square in the eye, "… that was disgusting."

"Enough!" Hectore commanded as he looked around. He was confused. He went back to his fallen log and sat down. For a moment, all three men were heaving breaths, struggling to get their words out.

"I don't know who they were. Kael spotted the fire through the trees," Raphael answered his father's earlier question as he dismounted. "We started getting closer when I noticed Brandigit's horse was tethered up, but you wouldn't be sitting across a fire from Bran, you'd be beside him. I knew something was wrong when he wasn't here. Mother sent him out earlier with a man that came into the city."

"Who was this man?" the king asked.

"Someone from Silver Streams, he said," Kael told him as he sat down. His voice grew bitter, "I think he killed Brandigit, the bastard. That's how they ended up here."

"You think they killed Bran?" Hectore asked, unsure he wanted to believe it.

Kael saddened. "He loved that horse. He didn't even let Bregan ride it, his own son. I don't know who the hell these men are, but I'd bet that's how they got the armour and tunics."

Raphael continued his story from there, taking a seat opposite his brother. "We circled around and found a scout, then heard you say something about finding us. We came right after that."

Hectore nodded in thought. "And why were you boys out here?"

Raphael answered, "Mother sent us out to look for you."

"Why would she do that? I haven't been gone that long."

"It's been almost a full moon," Kael said. "After Ma collapsed, she was really worried about you."

"Your mother collapsed?" Hectore asked with a worried expression.

"She's fine now. She kept thinking something bad had happened," Raphael said, easing his father's tension. "How are you? What the hell's going on? What's been delaying your return?"

"Well, I died," the King answered as if it happened every other day, "but I'm feeling much better now."

"You died?" Kael asked, lurching forward in shock.

"Only for a few seconds," Hectore said, again with cool composure. "Then my friend's magic worked."

"Magic doesn't affect us," Raphael stated, despite knowing full well his father's understanding of the matter.

"This isn't your regular magicker," Hectore answered before releasing a pent-up smile. "Jole. He's an old friend that fought in the war with me for a time. He had another mission back then, so eventually we parted ways. I had never seen him again... I thought he was dead, until I found him a week ago, fighting over a score of bandits."

"That's twenty-five men," Kael said with expert military knowledge. "That's a fair bit of magic. His threa must be deep."

"It's not all magic." Then Hectore chuckled. "He carries a big black axe he calls Omega with him."

"The End All," Raphael said. "That's a great name for a weapon."

"Where's this magicker now?" Kael asked his father.

"Yeah, I wouldn't mind meeting this guy," Raphael added.

"I sent him up the mountain to the Brotherhood. He knows Pientero and Anvar from before." Turning around, Hectore looked up at the shadow of Tehbirr's Spine on the horizon, wondering if Jole remembered his instructions and how Arlahn was handling himself.

"Looks like Arlahn will make a new friend," Raphael said. "And I guess seeing you here means our little brother made it up the mountain in one piece."

"It was a tough climb, but he never gave up..." Hectore began, proceeding to tell his sons about the climb. "We should stay here for the night. I already have a camp set up. We'll leave tomorrow at first light. And speaking of friends, ours here have me questioning how far the Damonai are with their invasion."

"The Damonai are invading again?" Kael asked, taken off-guard.

"I didn't want to think so, but after my talk with PJ, my fight with Jole, and tonight, I'm sure they're here, hiding in the shadows until we close our eyes, that's their way. War is coming. I'm just not sure why."

"What's our next move?" Raphael asked his father.

"We send one of you for Halder," Hectore said.

"Halder?" Kael didn't understand. "What's the old scout going to do for us if a new Damonai army's invading?"

"Do you know why he always has a hawk with him, Kael?" Hectore asked his son.

"I just assumed he liked the bird."

"He likes the bird," Hectore started, "because he *talks* to the bird. Halder is Gifted like us. He can tap into the minds of wildlife and share his thoughts with them. That's why he's such a valuable scout. Even if he doesn't fight, his birds can provide information on the enemy's position, movement, and numbers."

"If he can do it with animals, he must be able to do it with people," Raphael calculated immediately.

"I believe he *can* use his Gift on people, but he says that people are too complicated, and he can't trust his conclusions. It's just not predictable for him. Animals don't know how to deceive the way people do."

"Why haven't you ever told us he had a Gift?" Raphael asked, understanding the true value of the scout now.

"A man has a right to his own secrets. He can choose who he tells. But right now, it's not a matter of secrecy, it's a matter of survival, we need him and that's why."

"I'll go find the scout," Kael volunteered. "But afterwards I'm going to stop at Luzy's house in Silver Streams for a short visit. Just a few days, then I'll come home."

"When the Damonai invaded us last time their numbers were in the hundreds of thousands, boys. It wasn't just soldiers but a whole continent that came over the Spine. Women and elders too. The children were few, they either protected or forced them into hiding, I guess. We'll need you in the city once we find out what's going on, Kael. When we get back, I'm going to send word out to the Wardens. I think it's time we have a meeting to discuss this as a realm."

"When we get back, Father," Raphael remembered, "I have a surprise for you."

*****

Mordo reined in his black steed outside of Drelnum's pavilion. It was late afternoon and he was tired from a long day's ride. He climbed down from the saddle and noticed that most of the men had been dispatched as per the Caliph's orders. Plumes of smoke rose from the last of the smouldering fires. The surrounding ground had been trampled from endless traffic. He noticed a man was digging a pit for a wrapped-up corpse that lay beside it, tugging his black bearskin cloak about him to fend off the breeze. Scanning the camp, Mordo wordlessly caught a pair of men glancing at him, exchanging whispers, and his gaze caused them to look away. Finally, he spotted one of the Deaders in the far distance.

Patriclus. Mordo made eye contact with the brown-haired man and waved. The far-off Deader burst into a puff of black smoke that swirled about a single point before dissipating to the wind. The next second that smoky vortex appeared right in front of Mordo but from it, Patriclus emerged. He had an aquiline nose with shaggy hair.

The two deaders exchanged a nod of greeting before entering the marquee. The room was packed for imminent mobilization and boasted little more than a well-lit table and some chairs. Surrounding the table were generals of the second battalion of the Damonai army. At the sight of Mordo, Drelnum ordered his meeting finished and the rest of the men out, sending one man for the "other one." It was time for a convening of Deaders.

Not all of the Caliph's deadly fingers were in attendance, however, she had split her council along with the Damonai army, and Evris had dispatched those under his control shortly after Mordo's visit.

DeathShadow didn't have favourites, but Drelnum's bunch were those he "preferred." His feelings about each Deader reflected his view of their Power. There was Drelnum himself with his unbreakable skin – he intrigued Mordo the most. Once, Mordo had asked Hennah if the deader could feel the pain through it, and she'd confessed to him that Drelnum's skin was incredibly thick, like an elephant's hide. There were other deaders with skills of their own, but Mordo believed the rest were outmatched.

Patriclus could do his "dimensional displacement" trick, as Hennah referred to it. Ensavan had unmatched precision with any kind of projectile, and Tracker harnessed a mastery of human senses. They had become heroes of a sort, these Powered Damonai, though none had grown their kill toll or myth as great as DeathShadow.

He and Patriclus waited for the room to clear. Ensavan was already seated and remained, getting up only to reach for a jug of wine to refill his cup. As they waited for the last of their kind, Patriclus promptly took a seat next to Ensavan, whose dark skin blended with his clothes. Mordo remained standing for the time being.

"Who's digging the grave?" he asked Drelnum.

The bald, bearded leader sat and looked at him from across the room, his thick frame exaggerating his Power.

"Hammel's brother was on watch two nights ago when a couple of men escaped. I was waiting for you to decide what to do with them."

"Who were they?" Mordo found himself saying.

"A pair of thieves. They said their names were Darius and Mick."

"And one was a Justicar?" Mordo interrupted.

That took Drelnum by surprise.

"I met them both in Esselle recently," Mordo answered Drelnum's unasked question. "They would have been worth having a conversation with. One had the ability to steal the Prophecy Tablet. I'd like to know how he did it. At least you killed the fool responsible for letting them go."

"They did in their escape," the leader confessed.

Tracker walked in then, stopping beside Mordo to glance at his company. He muttered a quick off-hand remark to himself before taking a lonely seat at the opposite end of the table.

The ensuing meeting between Mordo and the Deaders was quick and formal, ending almost as soon as time would allow it. He had orders issued for each of the men from the Caliph herself. Tracker was dispatched for retrieval, Ensavan and Patriclus were being sent away on a mission together, and Drelnum was to demobilize to a new location.

After everything had been said, Drelnum extended the offer of a meal to Mordo, who accepted it. The others left and Mordo ate quickly. Conversation was scarce, marked only by Mordo declaring his desire to kill Demonblades in combat to solidify his legend. Finishing with a belch, he nodded his appreciation toward his host before standing to make his departure.

Mordo strode from the tent and took notice of the fading light. The fool had just finished digging the grave to his right, he stabbed his spade into the earth and stood for a moment, breathing hard, then spit and wiped his brow with a forearm while the other rested on his shovel.

The man's head thumped into the bottom of the grave; his body followed shortly after. Mordo replaced his bloody sword and left the wrapped-up corpse where it lay. He didn't tolerate failure.

Chapter 20

Hectore's hand pushed the salt and pepper curls back from his eyes before re-gripping the four-inch-wide stone banister. Annabella's arm hooked around Hectore's, stealing his attention for the moment. As their eyes met, he felt his heart warm and the King kissed his queen on the lips before turning back to the scene.

"I heard you collapsed while I was away," he said as she clasped both hands over his.

"And I heard you died. But we're both still here. So life is beautiful," Annabella hummed in his ear.

At that moment life *was* beautiful. And such was Annabella's gift to Hectore. She possessed a vision of the world that made colours brighter, flavours more delicious, feelings more sensitive. Where he conveyed loss, she provided hope.

Feeling the weight of Annabella's head sink into his shoulder, Hectore remembered her previous statement. How fitting the scene in front of him was with his emotions. In the distance, incredible oranges and golds were painted across a bulwark of morning clouds. The snow-capped mountains winked diamonds here and there, the lush terrain of wooded hills and rivers swayed with the gentle breeze, the beauty and order of the Pellencian rooftops below them, artistically arranged.

Turning from the banister, Hectore walked back into the bedchamber. Sitting in a brown, padded leather chair, he pulled open the drawer of the adjacent end table. Reaching in, the King produced a small pouch and his long, curved pipe. He packed the pipe swiftly and lit it. Drawing back in his chair, his eyes gazed up at his love as she entered.

Her skin was radiant and smooth, and the curves of her midsection made a perfect hourglass shape. She still moved with cat-like grace, always in her element, hardly touched by age.

Her beautiful golden hair shone in the sun, parted in the centre so that it fell gracefully around the contours of her face. The smile on her lips and the look in her eyes were enough to melt the heart of any man.

"How come you still look so beautiful after all these years?" Hectore puzzled aloud. "I'm getting old, Anna. I feel it in my bones. Why does it feel like the weight of the entire nation is pressing on my chest?"

"Because you care more for them than you do yourself," Annabella spoke, her words carrying a hint of melancholy within them. "You have sacrificed everything for the peace in this land."

"And still war is coming."

The confidence of his statement worried Annabella slightly. The first thing Hectore had done once he returned was to check on his queen and then draft letters to his Wardens, summoning them all to Pellence.

She knew he was a phenomenal warrior. It was a part of him that she loved, but it was the same part of him that scared her more than anything else in the world. Too often, he leapt at every opportunity to get himself killed, yet somehow had always surmounted the odds and survived. Annabella was afraid that it had become a habit for the king. *He thinks himself invincible.*

Just then, a light tapping came on the door. "Come in," Hectore announced.

"Hectore, really?" Annabella teased. "You're talking about fighting a war and you can't get up to answer the door."

She moved over to open it herself. Behind the frame stood the wizened old physician, Sol. He bowed as low as his body would permit, revealing a patch of shiny scalp to the king and queen. "Your Grace, I was summoned?"

"Quite prompt, aren't you?" Annabella replied. "I just sent for you, I wasn't expecting you for another hour."

"I can return if it pleases—" he began.

"Nonsense!" the queen interrupted. "You're here now." Turning to Hectore she said, "Hec, this is Sol, the physician that saw to my recovery."

"Sol! A pleasure to meet you, I heard how you helped my Anna, and I can't express my gratitude enough. I understand you have tremendous talent," Hectore said in greeting.

"That's why I asked him here, Hec, to have a look at you. I'm worried. You've been smoking so much lately."

"Oh, I have not!" the King began to protest, but he ceased his argument when he saw the look on Annabella's face and how she glanced pointedly at the pipe in his hand.

He gave the physician, dressed in a modest, grey, rough-spun wool hood with wide sleeves, another look. "No."

Annabella knew Hectore didn't like being touched by those outside of who he considered family. Trust was hard-earned with the king. Even though this man had saved his queen's life, Hectore was still reluctant to submit to him.

"Hectore, please, for me?" Annabella asked sweetly.

After a moment's hard contemplation and a deep sigh, he gave in to her. "But don't touch me without warning, physician. I don't like being inspected."

Sol smiled and dipped his head before making eye contact with the King for the first time. "That's quite alright, Your Grace. In all my years, I haven't met a single person who does. I'm skilled in seeing defects without much… inspection. For me, it's more a matter of intuition," he explained as he stepped closer, favouring Hectore's right side to look over his figure. He had Hectore raise and lower his arms twice as the wizened man paced around him.

The king was incredibly skeptical of the man's response. "Mhm. How did you learn such skills?"

"Oh I'm afraid it's a long tale that's quite boring, lots of trade secrets and such. Not quite the same as your story. Raise them one more time please, Your Grace."

"I'm sure it is," Hectore began, lifting his arms as requested. Before lowering them, he added, "Nevertheless I wouldn't mind hearing it."

"Perhaps another time? I'm afraid I'm done here, and I have so much to take care of. My 'prentice can't be left alone too long brewing the salves and ointments. She's good, but she's still learning to detect when they're just right."

"We're done already?" Hectore asked, surprised and somewhat delighted. "What did you do?"

"I've examined your muscle structure, bone densities, and your organ functionality, Your Grace. You have a worn shoulder in your main sword arm and your lungs are working hard. Other than that though, you're quite healthy. You cracked your ribs recently, but they seem to be healing nicely."

"How can you tell all of that from a look?" Hectore didn't want to admit it, but the man was right. The king felt the pain come and go in his shoulder when he worked it too hard, and his stamina was certainly not what it once was.

"It's difficult to explain, as I said, it's more intuition and feeling. Perhaps someday I'll try to teach you, if that's alright, Your Grace?"

"Perhaps," Hectore replied, skepticism once again replacing his enthusiasm. "But if you're finished with me already, you may go."

As Sol exited the room, Hectore turned to Annabella and told her, "I think I'll go find Raphael and see this surprise of his."

*****

Kael's black steed reared up on two legs and he dug his feet into the stirrups until it reined back down safely. Asking the horse what the matter was, he patted its neck.

They had stopped beside an old, wooden fence. Weather-beaten and rotting, most of the boards had begun to sag or were feathered at their ends. Kael looked at the small thatched hut and the skinny plume of smoke streaming from its chimney, finding the man's hawk making wide circles high in the sky. It dove down, banking right before the ground, and disappeared behind the hut.

He tried to urge the animal through the wooden gate but it refused to move, despite his best attempts. Kael wanted to recruit the old scout back into his father's services quickly so he could head for Luzy's. Eventually, he dismounted, took up the reins, and dragged the horse unwillingly past the perimeter. As they approached the hut, he walked around a small lumber shed and almost jumped when he saw a massive medak bear lying on the ground, enjoying a nap in the shade.

The mare in Kael's hands started to whinny and stamp its feet, waking the beast in its fear. The medak's eyes opened and it backed away hurriedly, standing up to its full height – a daunting four feet taller than the Prince – and bearing huge teeth. Kael stared at the animal's enormous paws that hid razor-sharp talons.

Halder came out of his hut then, hawk on his shoulder. "It's alright, Kihbah," he said to the bear. "He means you no harm."

Halder and the medak exchanged a look for a few seconds before the bear lowered himself down once more and calmly rolled back into a giant black ball. Halder quickly glanced at the worrying horse and it too calmed in Kael's hands.

"I was wondering when I'd see one of you boys," he said to the Prince. "My birds have seen lots of activity near here. And some of my old friends have stopped coming around."

Kael excused exchanging pleasantries with the old scout and went straight to business. "There have been bandits hunting out the area. My father thinks they're Damonai."

"That would make sense, but I guess I was just hoping it wasn't them again," the old man said.

Halder's shoulders were broad, but bonier now than they once had been, and the pockets of his eyes were deep, with weathered bags below them. In spite of this, he was still healthy and capable enough, even at his age, to survive in the wilderness alone.

"My father sent me to get you. He said that you can speak with animals."

"I can," Halder confessed, straight-faced. "That's why my bags are already packed, Prince. I knew you were coming."

He made for his hut but stopped, turning back around with a smile on his face. "By the way, it's good to see you, boy."

The Prince smiled and dipped his head. "Likewise, old man."

Kael helped the scout with his effects, loading them onto his mare. Halder came out with a homemade harness and walked around to the back of his hut. He returned, leading a great pantuur by a leash.

"Kael, this is Shraknah," he said, introducing the two.

Kael admired the spotted beast. He'd never seen a pantuur in real life before. Their primary habitat being on remote mountainsides made them seldom seen in the country. He looked at the sinewy muscles beneath the tight fur, saw them flexing and reacting to the giant feline's smooth movements.

Finally, it stood still and allowed Halder to attach his harness, all the while staring at Kael's black horse like it was a delicious meal. Once Halder was in place atop the pantuur, the great medak rose from its rest and looked over.

"No, Kihbah. I don't think they'd appreciate you in the city. It's safer away from the humans," Halder told the beast.

As if to argue, the animal took a step toward the old man. "No!" he repeated sternly, but then in a softer voice explained, "Shraknah's different. He is impressive to the humans, but you, my friend, will be terrifying."

The medak halted then and gave the pair of riders a sad look before it dipped its head and sauntered away.

Having witnessed the exchange firsthand, Kael believed the scout had a Gift and was saddened by the beast's devotion, the validity behind the scout's words. The bear would be slain upon entering the city, if not by someone claiming self-defence, then by someone out for a trophy.

"Is he alright?" Kael asked.

"She's starving," Halder answered. "I've been feeding her everything I can but when you're that size, it takes a lot of food."

"Will she survive out there on her own?" Kael wondered aloud.

"She has to now," the old man said gruffly before pulling his pantuur around and starting off, away from his home. Seeing the man atop a pantuur made this familiar friend seem like a stranger to Kael. The scene belonged in a painting, not in the flesh immediately to his left.

Halder opened up the conversation as they passed the old fence, demanding the Prince tell him all about the current events in his family's life. Kael mentioned his father's salvation, his mother's collapse, the new war machines he and Raph were building, how Arlahn was off training, and his new woman, Luzy. Kael told him how he planned to visit her and her parents after they got on their way.

The Prince was about to stick to the beaten path when Halder suddenly banked his pantuur left. Kael stopped his horse and made the late turn. "Where are you going?"

"To see your father, young prince," Halder said. "There's a marsh this way, cuts two days off our ride. It wouldn't make sense for an army to pass through, but two people shouldn't have much trouble. You're not afraid of getting your boots wet, are you?"

Kael simply smiled at that. "Lead the way then."

The path through the marsh occasionally sank into small pools up to his horse's ankles but was more than manageable by all means. They travelled through tall, wet grasses and wooded areas full of skinny trees, then between two rocky hills until Halder's hawk came skirting through the air down to his shoulder.

The bird hopped from shoulder to shoulder and cawed every so often. Halder watched it jump around until he looked at the Prince. "C'mon, there's something this way."

He urged his pantuur into a blistering speed. Moving its front and back legs in tandem, it bound like a rabbit in long, explosive strides through the marsh.

Kael kicked his horse into a gallop after the scout, but the oversized feline was incredibly nimble, leaping giant distances without ever slowing its speed. Within a few moments, Halder was out of sight, until Kael found him again just as he crested a hilltop. The scout looked back, calling him forward, before disappearing again over the ridge. Kael heard the pantuur let out a vicious growl.

He raced to the scout's position and as he raced over the hill, he heard a man screaming, "Hurry! Come on, they saw us on the last hill."

The Prince saw the source of the shouting down in the valley; two men were rushing from something. One had the other under his shoulder and helped him limp with urgency. The second man had one pant leg cut off below the knee and Kael could see that his shin was red with blood. Halder was racing toward the men with his scimitar drawn, and Kael took off again, galloping toward them as he pulled his own claymore clear.

"There's more there!" the injured man said, pointing out Halder and Kael with a finger.

"Fuck it! You're on your own, Mick," the taller man said, then he dropped his companion without hesitation.

"You prick, Darius!" Mick shouted up from the ground.

Darius was about to run when he realized *what* he'd run into and froze. "Oh shit!" he cried out, stunned. "He's riding a pantuur!"

Kael was getting ready for Halder to stop at the men when he noticed the beast wasn't slowing its great strides. As if he hadn't even seen them, Halder flew by.

The Prince had just arrived at the pair when he saw a group of riders top the far hill. Halder kept racing toward *them*, letting out a great cry that was drowned out by the roar of the pantuur.

Kael watched as the old scout charged head-on into the line of horsemen. His pantuur leapt, swung its powerful claws out, and killed two horses, catching one neck with a widespread paw and biting the other. The horses dragged their riders down with them. Kael saw the scimitar hack into a third horseman's shoulder, snapping the man's clavicle, before the pantuur leapt away to a safe distance.

Following behind, the Prince was quickly amongst the fray, finishing off the one man, who scrambled up from the ground. Another lay pinned beneath his horse, his neck mauled out by the beast. Kael exchanged blows with another horseman, but the weight and strength behind his claymore and *kjut'tsir* were too much, and the man lost his weapon. The Prince came back with a decapitating backhand.

From behind him, he heard another bone-chilling roar from Halder's pantuur. Kael turned and noticed that the two men who were running had started to cheer as the Prince and scout began to win their melee.

Utilizing the length of his claymore, he stabbed another horseman high in the chest. A sword buried itself his shoulder then, and Kael grunted through the pain. Turning to his attacker with crazed eyes, he leapt off his saddle, dragging the horse and rider down to the ground with him. Kael forgot his sword and scrambled quickly over to the downed man. Taking up his head and chin between two hands, the Prince let out a furious grunt and twisted. There was a loud snap like a dead branch falling in a quiet forest and he dropped the body.

Kael looked up and saw the last few riders fleeing. Halder reined his pantuur next to him. "Should I go after them?"

The Prince's arm burned; the cut had bitten deeper than he'd thought. He pressed his hand to it and saw his fingers were instantly red. Kael cursed, looking behind for the other two men, but they had disappeared.

"Find the two that were running away!" he ordered.

Halder rolled his tongue back and let out a great whistle. He looked up and found his hawk in the air overhead then set about on his pantuur, sniffing out tracks. With the aid of the wildlife, Halder routed the men out of their hiding spot within a minute.

He had backed them up into the hollowed tree with his scimitar as Kael approached, holding his shoulder. "Who are you and what are you doing here?"

"First I think we should say 'thank you,'" Darius said. "Do you need something for your cut? We have this salve."

He reached into a pocket and Halder edged his blade closer. Darius noticed the incoming threat and stopped, raising his free hand to submit. "It's just a jar," he said, before slowly pulling a container from his pocket.

The Prince recognized the red cross Pientero used for his salves and grabbed the man by the collar. He pushed him back into the tree, barking. "Where did you get that?!"

"Relax!" Mick said. "We found it."

Kael looked at the injured man but kept his grip on Darius' shirt. "Where?"

"In a cave," Mick said. "That used to belong to Hectore's Brotherhood."

At that, Kael alleviated his tension on the man. "How do you know that?"

"My father told me about such places, he fought with the HighKing Hectore."

"Sure he did," the old scout retorted. "What was his name lad, your old man?"

"Baulim Deddick," Mick said proudly, puffing out his chest and showing Kael the emblem of an Essellian justicar.

Halder guffawed. "You ain't Baulim's son. Look at you."

Mick cocked an eyebrow at that and gave the man a stern look. "And who are you?"

"Never mind that," Kael interrupted. "Why are you here, Essellian?"

Mick looked at the men, judging them to be Pellencian. "To deliver a message to the king from the Warden of the West himself."

"What's this message?" Kael demanded.

The justicar hesitated, giving him a sideways look. "Why would I tell you?"

"Are you daft, boy?" Halder almost shouted. "This here's the Prince."

Mick maintained his sideways look. "And I'm just supposed to trust that?"

"You're supposed to know who I am," Kael announced, returning the man's look with an icy glare.

Mick knew the Rais by description, but it had been a long time since he had met them in the flesh. Maybe this *was* the elder, black-haired prince from the Culture Walk all those years ago. "You'll have to forgive my suspicions. Too much has happened for me to give anyone the benefit of the doubt. I'll only tell the HighKing himself, back in Pellence."

"Who were those men, and why were they chasing you?" Kael asked.

"We don't know, they just attacked us on sight," Mick lied before Darius could reveal their secret.

Kael shook his head. "Fine fool, have it your way. You will answer to the king then." He knew these men would not cooperate with his interrogation in such an informal setting.

He snatched the jar from Darius' hand and popped the lid, inspecting the contents with a sniff. Once he'd applied a coat to his cut, he turned to Halder and asked, "Can you take these two back to my father?"

Halder nodded and climbed back onto his harness. "They'll have to walk though."

"Until my father pardons you two, you are prisoners under the guard of Halder." Kael glared at Mick. "If you really are Essellians then you'll have to forgive my suspicions. Too much has happened to give anyone the benefit of the doubt."

"Ha!" Darius cut in then with a jubilant tone. "Mick, look. I told you riding a pantuur was possible!"

Kael shook his head at the remark, knowing Halder was one of his kind, and gave Mick's leg one last look. He tossed the jar to the scout. "Put another coat on his leg tonight when you make camp. Tomorrow, when you reach Pellence, he can get it looked at properly."

Climbing into his saddle, Kael's thoughts returned to the beautiful blonde woman who awaited him. "I'll be back from Luzy's in a few days. Maybe a week"

"A week? Is she that pretty?" Halder joked.

Kael smiled and winked.

Chapter 21

Anvar and Pientero were some of the best healers Arlahn had ever seen at work. They were professional, their cooperation spoken telepathically, it seemed, as they were constantly moving about one another, helping each other as they quickly cleaned and patched the wound in Jassyka's skull.

"Come on, Arlahn," Pientero told him once they were done, leading him from the cabin. "I have something I want to show you."

For four days, Arlahn walked through the mountain with Pientero. They were on a journey that the king-in-the-mountain referred to as a Walkabout. It was a welcome distraction for the Prince, and Pientero kept him well-occupied.

They had brought nothing with them, save for a coil of rope, a bow, and one arrow that Pientero carried with him. Arlahn was permitted to carry his dagger. The king-In-The-Mountain accepted that the Prince carried it everywhere, safely tucked in its sheath at the small of his back.

As they foraged for their food, Pientero would test the Prince about all he'd learned so far in the Brotherhood, teaching him further with a few parables whenever he saw fit. They slept in homemade shelters that the Prince would build. On the third day, Pientero had brought down a partridge just off the path and they dined on their first real sustenance.

Together, they made their way through the maze of footpaths and came out near a wooded valley. They descended into the tall pines until the earth gave way and they found themselves emerging out of the other end, slowly making their way up to the highest peak visible on Tehbirr's Spine.

As they reached the rocky summit, Pientero gave Arlahn an oral exam, of sorts; asking him to explain how he would go about defending his city. Every time Arlahn gave his answer, Pientero would describe a pessimistic outcome from the result. Having scouts captured and supplies raided, Arlahn was forced to adapt his plans and think beyond his soldiers as units in a game of Battleground. Eventually, it came down to depending on his brothers and their Gifts. Everything always came back to the Gifted for Arlahn lately, it seemed. And although he felt like he'd experienced Raphael's *mniman* and Kael's *kjut'tsir* and maybe even glimpsed Jassyka's dreams, he was still wanting. Incomplete, like he had been broken into pieces and a few were still missing. He had never controlled any of this power. It had simply reacted for him out of its own reflexive volition.

"Did I get everything right?" Arlahn asked, turning back to the king-in-the-mountain.

"There is no 'right' in war," Pientero answered. "It's like 'winning.' After the fact, some people might say one side 'won' the fight. But anyone who actually fought would tell you... There is no winning in battle, you can only survive it."

Arlahn thought about that for a second. "How do you know so much about these things?"

Pientero's expression grew dark, furrowing his brows until his eyes were hidden in shadow. "I don't talk about my past."

Arlahn waited a moment, before replying sympathetically, "We don't have to then, I was just curious. I thought maybe that was why you brought me here."

The summit where they sat was barren except for a thick pole staked into the ground with rope tied around it, innumerable times until it looked like one long, grey snake covering the wood from top to bottom. There was a fresh line anchored near the top of the post. It was impossibly taut and strung to the other side of the valley.

Pientero stood up then and as he walked over to the stake, he explained, "I brought you here for a distraction. It was time. I hope you remember the way back into camp; you'll be walking it alone. If you can make it back, you'll be one of us."

"Don't I get the bow?" Arlahn asked as he approached the pole.

"You have twine, build your own."

PJ slung his bow over a shoulder, took up a length of leather that had been laid out beside the post and threw it over the rope. He grabbed the two ends that hung down and lifted his legs, tucking his knees to his chest. Pientero began to slide down the rope with a speed and a holler that belied his age. Arlahn chuckled. PJ's feet began kicking out almost rhythmically in front of him until he was just over halfway down. Then, all of a sudden, he pulled his knees tight to his chest, as if bracing himself against something. That's when Arlahn heard the whistle and caught the flash passing before his face. An arrow. It flew up and split the taut rope with expert precision. The line gave way and began falling, transforming Pientero's ride into a giant pendulum.

Arlahn laughed when he saw the king-in-the-mountain swing into a wall of pine that caught his momentum. As Pientero slid to the ground unharmed, the Prince noticed the black-haired Brother that had shot the arrow standing close by.

Back on the ground, Pientero looked up at Arlahn as Balanor approached.

"You think Babyboy's ready for this test?" he asked.

"I guess we'll find out," Pientero replied.

*****

Arlahn's Walkabout would finish when he found his way back to camp. If he still hadn't returned after a fortnight, the king-in-the-mountain would send out a search party. Normally, he wouldn't bother, but Arlahn was a prince and out of respect for Hectore, he would deliver his body to him.

If it came to that.

PJ walked with Balanor, listening to the information he'd received from a scouting party. They had come across an aged woman in the forest, lurking around the foot of the Spine, spying on the king and a large man in a cave.

The scouts had managed to leave without discovery; Balanor claimed Gringoll was the one who apprehended her and brought her to an isolated shack in the mountain with a bag over her head.

Pientero insisted on going there right away and walked through the maze of footpaths without mistake. He found the small log-house amongst the trees and approached purposefully.

Touching the door latch, it instantly sizzled, burning Pientero's hand. He ripped his fingers away and blew at them.

Magic.

His temper darkened and he booted in the door.

*****

Serah-Jayne didn't realize what had happened until she regained consciousness. By then, it was too late. She could feel the rope binding her ankles and wrists. The effects of her Gift were powerful, but only while she was awake. If Serah had come to when the man had been binding her, she could have tapped into the dance of chances and woven the possibility of knotting himself to the chair in her place.

With a thick, black bag over her head that stunk of water-musk, she could only see using her *amrak*. The world underwent an extreme makeover whenever she tapped into the vibrating waves of her surroundings; she felt the world more than saw it. Sensing she was in a heavily wooded area, a tingle began in Serah-Jayne's throat and she swallowed. With extreme focus, she found the waves emanating from a circular handle just ten feet in front of her and pulled her concentration to the rays of the sun's heat, directing them toward the metal.

It wasn't long before she heard someone gasp then growl on the other side of the door. However, she hadn't expected the loud bang as the man kicked it in, and Serah-Jayne jumped a touch and gasped at the power she felt before her. He was a titan in spirit form, fierce and immovable. Her defiance flared then as she lurched forward in her seat, but she also felt a slight panic. Whenever Serah was infuriated or threatened, she lost control of her *amrak*. No longer the director of her actions, she became a passenger inside her own body. This was worse than anything for her; losing control.

"Release me, please," she begged.

"No."

Anger was swirling inside, the sensation stoking within her now. Sensing it, Serah-Jayne panicked again, which inevitably handed control to her Gift.

The giant's presence began to shrink, or perhaps her own spiritual-self grew. Soon, she was looming over the small, fragile thing before her.

The blackness fell away, and the king-in-the-mountain stood there suddenly. With dark, hard eyes he looked her down, then up again.

Now, Serah-Jayne could almost see herself from an otherworldly perspective. She took deep, calm breaths, staring at the man with fierce, unblinking eyes. The green in them took on a pearlescent, unearthly glow.

That's when her *amrak* surged, whipping up gales from small breezes that blew out a window and slammed the door shut, exploding the frame into splinters. Serah-Jayne squeezed the air around the torches in each corner until they guttered out, her anger filling the room with a daunting, preternatural darkness. It was as if her Curse had deadened the very daylight around them.

She sensed disapproval in the man and grew the strength behind the gales until a tornado raged inside the cabin. Through it all, with a voice like thunder resonating around the room, Serah-Jayne boomed,

"I WILL BRING DOOM TO YOU AND ALL WHO FEEL SAFE HERE! SHADOWS WILL FALL UPON YOU IN THE DARKNESS! YOUR HOUSES WILL BURN! YOUR WATERS WILL FREEZE! THIS MOUNTAIN WILL BE YOUR TOMB! I WILL STRIKE LIFE FROM THIS LAND AND ALL WHO OPPOSE ME SHALL TREMBLE AT THE SIGHT OF MY POWER! I HAVE BROUGHT RUIN TO THIS WORLD AND WILL BURY KINGS IN THE NAME OF MY GOD!"

After she said the word "God," there was a small explosion of air around her, putting out the tornado in an instant. The green glow in her eyes faded, and Serah-Jayne stared blankly ahead for a moment, before looking at the king-in-the-mountain. She blinked for the first time. Her breathing shuddered into a small shiver and she sank her head down.

Right before Pientero's eyes, the blonde on her head began crawling backward through strands of hair, leaving them a dark brown. It receded and settled into a single prominent lock, hidden behind her ear.

He looked at the woman again through different eyes and lowered himself closer to inspect her face. Slowly, Pientero raised his hands and began lightly pinching and tugging at her skin, gently smoothing out the wrinkles until she looked youthful. Finally, he recognized her. "It's you..."

He took a step back, and for the first time, Serah-Jayne could sense intimidation inside the man.

"I remember you..." he started, "... from Cebel, all those years ago. You were there in the beginning, with the Fallen Angel."

Suddenly Serah-Jayne remembered him as the defeated chieftain that had been crucified after the start of the Damonai invasion. The man Diyo had pulled down and saved.

Pientero thought for a long moment, contemplating her very existence before him.

"I've been watching you and the king for years," she confessed. "I kept you safe throughout your rebellion."

"What do you mean?" As far as he could remember, this was only the second encounter he'd had with the woman whose hair changed colours.

"I control chance."

The king-in-the-mountain scoffed at that.

"Think, Master Jessonarioko... How many times have you or the king defied death? You think Hectore truly danced through those arrows?"

Without any further explanation, Pientero knew of what she spoke. It had happened outside Melonia... Hectore had challenged the Damonai's champion to single combat for the field. They'd sent forth a troll... But even after Hectore impossibly dropped the monster alone, the Damonai attacked, launching a volley of a thousand arrows at the king. With supreme confidence, Hectore simply stared at the enemy until the last possible second. Then he began moving toward them, past the arrows raining down all around him. Occasionally, he would raise his sword and deflect the ones that were inescapable, but after fifteen seconds of arrows pelting down, not a single shaft found its mark.

"What about the final assault on the palace? Where do you think that storm came from? It was a beautiful day until you needed the darkness."

"How could this be? Why have you stayed hidden if you have such power?"

Serah-Jayne dipped her head. "Sometimes *chance* controls me. You saw it in the settlement and a glimpse of it now..." she paused in thought, "...Strange that it quelled so quickly this time."

Pientero stood like a statue, a pensive expression on his face. "I wish I could release you, young lady, but I don't think it would be wise to risk it. I'm sorry. My men will be around to feed you."

When she began pleading, he turned to leave, ignoring her with some difficulty as he left the cabin that was hidden in the woods.

Chapter 22

Arlahn watched the two men disappear into the trees and began gathering his thoughts, strategizing his journey back to the camp. He remembered making two rights and a left down the footpaths but that was about it until he got to the valley.

With Pientero around, he had found himself too busy answering questions or listening to parables to allow distraction. But now that Arlahn was alone, his thoughts returned to the wounded Jassyka back in their cabin. He hoped for her recovery.

Finally, deciding not to waste any more precious daylight, Arlahn began his journey back down the mountain, through the same way he'd come hours before.

Darkness was starting to win its nightly battle with the sky when Arlahn reached the wooded valley's edge. He decided to push on, hoping to come across his previous camp rather than make a new one. Once he was beneath the foliage of the forest, the darkness around him grew until it was almost palpable and strange sounds came from the shadows. Everything suddenly went quiet and Arlahn's heart sank in his chest. Then he heard it; the long howl.

Just one.

He doubled his efforts and came across a pair of simple lean-tos he'd built with Anvar. Deciding to set up a fire right away, Arlahn began to collect firewood for the night and had a small bundle in hand when he heard another howl close-by. It was abruptly cut off with a high-pitched yelp and Arlahn recognized the vicious growls and snapping of a fight. Another howl echoed around him and more growling added to the sounds in the dark.

Arlahn decided to investigate.

Venturing through the darkness, the sound of the scuffle amplified as he came closer. The Prince moved the bundle to his free hand and began fingering the hilt of his dagger.

There was another high-pitched yelp following a deep growl, and Arlahn came around a thick maple to see the pack of wolves beginning to scatter, some crying or whinnying as they hobbled away on battered legs.

He could see the back of what they were scattering from and squinted with utter disbelief at what he was looking at. At first, Arlahn couldn't decipher what kind of beast this was. Hunched over on two legs, it was feeding on a fallen wolf, devouring it by the handful. The claws at the end of its fingers were sharp enough to rip into the wolf's flesh. Four other wolves lay dead around it. At that moment, the monster sensed Arlahn's presence behind and slowly stopped its feast.

Then it rose.

It was huge, almost seven feet tall, with long matted hair that hung halfway down it's back. The creature's arms were so big they stretched the extent of skin, and its entire body was covered in slick, black scales, as if a basilisk had been dunked in oil. Slowly, it turned around and something tingled inside of Arlahn upon seeing its face. The scales pointed in different directions, contouring the monster's face with sharp cheeks and a wide jawline. On its forehead, smaller scales ran from its hairline down to its eye socket, where a sunken pocket housed a dim red glow, like a dirty ruby at the bottom of a hole.

Its face grew furious all of a sudden as it attempted a ferocious scream. Opening its maw, the monster's lips seemed to double in width, encompassing the entirety of its face and revealing a hundred razor-sharp, pointed fangs. But the sound coming from the terrifying monster was hardly more than a whisper.

In the darkness of the forest, faced with such an unnatural creature, the hushed sound was even more petrifying. Hidden within the ferocious whisper, Arlahn almost thought he heard it cry, "YYYOOOOOOUUUUUUUUUU!"

Drawing his dagger, the Prince stood ready to strike. The monster rushed toward him, lowered on all fours, almost like a giant gorilla but with the speed of a pantuur, pouncing in graceful strides.

Right before it reached Arlahn, it rose up and leapt toward him with outstretched arms, preparing to bear down.

The Prince planted his back leg and pounded his dagger toward the monster. As the pearly white blade pierced into the black scales on the creature's chest, it burst into hot white steam, like a giant gaseous bubble popping.

The steam drifted past Arlahn in the direction of the monster's momentum and he turned to step away from it. His eyes scanned the darkness feverishly, sure it couldn't be over so soon, but he couldn't find anything.

Arlahn looked back at the mutilated wolf, its body torn up and half-eaten. Its cheeks were frozen in a snarl with its tongue still hanging out of its mouth. The rest of its face was scarred and matted with blood.

Confused and scared, the Prince hurried to gather his bundle of branches and return to his lean-to. He started a fire immediately and stayed awake for as long as he could, rocking next to his fire, clutching the dagger, and scanning the forest around him constantly.

When the morning light came, Arlahn jumped up violently, realizing that he'd fallen asleep. His fire had gone out and there was an overwhelming amount of wolf tracks all around him, including a set that had seemingly walked right up to his head.

The second lonely day of his Walkabout saw him scavenging more than travelling. At first, Arlahn racked his brain over the reality of the terrifying encounter with the monster, one that was certainly never mentioned in any of Elder Rufus' lectures about the strange or ancient creatures that once roamed Tehbirr. So, he returned to where the wolves had lain dead some hours ago, but there was only a mound of decayed bones, as if they had been there for months. Looking around the site, he noticed a prominent circle of dead grass where the monster had been crouching and even more wolf tracks than there'd been by his lean-to. Arlahn decided that, even if this monster was gone, the wolves obviously weren't. Without any protection but his dagger, he took Pientero's advice and fashioned a bow. Crude and makeshift was a generous description, but it worked, albeit with a very limited range. Ammunition was next; he set out to make a few arrows with the straightest branches he could find. Arlahn bit a small length of rope off of the coil he'd brought with him and frayed the strands apart. He had also kept some of the partridge feathers at Pientero's mention to "never waste anything" during their meal. He tied them into fletching with the strands and by the time he was done he had five arrows that flew straight-ish.

Tonight, he would be better prepared. Arlahn began walking through the pines of the valley in the early afternoon and was almost out of the woods when darkness halted him for the day.

When Arlahn laid his head down for rest that night, he slept against the base of a tree with his bow and arrows in one hand and his dagger in the other, hugged tightly to his chest.

He had just begun to lose consciousness when he heard it.

"AAAAOOOOooooooooo."

It came from his right, some distance off.

Still tormented from memories of the night before, Arlahn prepared himself to jump up. But when the first howl died, another called out, this time behind him to his left. Another came from somewhere directly in front of him. And then another, and another. Until a symphony of wolves howling, in an almost taunting manner, filled the air all around him. Either the creatures had begun howling louder and louder or they were creeping closer and closer.

Arlahn's heart started to race. Never before had he felt so prepared to feel so helpless. He had a bow and arrows sure, but he heard more than eight distinct wolf voices calling into the air. After last night, he had no idea what to expect.

The voices ringing out became so loud it was excruciating to the point of insanity. But when they all suddenly stopped, the long, haunted silence that followed was somehow worse.

Gripped and yet calmly controlled by his fear, the Prince abandoned his bow and stood frozen, with his dagger clenched firmly in his fist. If they came, he'd teach them their mistake.

Suddenly, the first gleam of golden eyes showed through the darkness and he stared back at them.

The eyes came closer until a black snout revealed itself with teeth showing a silent snarl.

When their eyes met, Arlahn could tell they were looking into each other's souls. He saw into thousands of years of evolutionary instinct and felt the ancient, wary trust that existed between them. He and the wolf came to an unspoken understanding. I will leave you be, if you leave me be. There's no need to harm one another.

Arlahn lowered his dagger and crouched down, keeping his eyes fixed on those of the wolf. The beast stared back but stopped its quiet snarl. As Arlahn slowly reached behind his back and sheathed his dagger, the wolf took a few steps closer to the Prince until they were practically breathing each other's air. Swallowing, Arlahn offered the front of his hand to the animal. He let it give him a quick whiff and gently touched the wolf's head. It pulled away but Arlahn kept his hand outstretched, and the wolf maintained eye contact as it sniffed the hand once more.

"What the hell are you doing!?" a raspy voice called out from over his shoulder.

The wolf took off into the shadows as a large man came walking into sight. He was carrying a black axe over his shoulder and his eyes were glowing like one of the wolves.

"You didn't see the other twelve swarming around you?" the man asked. "You're lucky. I've never seen Kahki wolves toy with their prey before."

Arlahn was at once both shocked and confused as to how this traveller had come across him in the mountain. Had he evaded the Brotherhood somehow? He wasn't *from* the Brotherhood; Arlahn would have recognized this man if he'd been in the compound at some point during his stay. His arms were as hairy as a bear's pelt and he was as powerfully built as anyone Arlahn had ever seen, though he was not much taller than the Prince or imposing any menace. Once the man's eyes stopped glowing from the use of magic, Arlahn saw that they were two different colours.

"Who are you magicker? How did you get here?" he asked.

"I was sent here, but I couldn't remember the king's damned instructions. It's just like that hardened turd to make a maze for his entrance. Oh, and you can call me Jole," the man replied.

"King's instructions? What are you talking about, Jole?"

"The HighKing, he sent me up here to his old Brotherhood," Jole explained. "I got lost on those damned trails though, horse got eaten, been walking around for half a moon trying to find the place, even had to wrestle a bear out of her den one night. Who are you?"

"I'm Arlahn."

"The king's son?!" Jole blurted out. "Are we close to the Brotherhood then?"

"Not exactly."

The Prince told him about the current Walkabout that he was on, and although Arlahn tried to explain to Jole that he should complete it alone, the big axeman couldn't see the logic of splitting up when both men were headed to the same place.

That night they made camp and Jole flicked some wood into fire before he pulled a duck from his pack. He skewered it over the flames and sat watching it silently.

"You're familiar with Kahki wolves?" Arlahn asked eventually.

"I know all about the Wild, Prince," Jole answered. He pulled up his shirt and revealed hideous scars in thick jagged lines all over the exposed skin, pointing out a few mentionable ones.

Prince. No one had called him that in moons. "Have you been seen any big, black monsters?"

"You mean like a medak?"

"No," Arlahn answered quickly. "I mean, a real monster. With scales covering their bodies and a mouth full of a thousand teeth..." Arlahn looked away. "With almost a kind of black smoke swirling around them."

Jole made a face like he'd just smelled something rancid. "I've been almost everywhere from the Passage of the Dead to the Sunswallow Sea. I've been south to the end of Neddihw and seen the northern lights dance. The only real monsters I've ever met are human."

After that, the duck breast began to sizzle and the big man offered some to the Prince. They ate in the comforting warmth of Jole's fire.

"How did you and my father meet?"

"A long time ago, lad," Jole told him. "Right now I need to sleep though. I'll tell you in the morn if I feel like it. I don't usually talk much."

Then he tucked his axe into his arms like a lover and fell asleep. Listening to the man snoring, Arlahn stared into the fire for a second before lying down himself. He closed his eyes and slept undisturbed.

The next two days they walked together without much interaction. Arlahn perpetually questioned what had really happened with the monster that night, and it didn't help that every time he brought it up to Jole, the big man seemed uninterested. Sometime during the second day, Jole began to become more silent, so Arlahn began to voice his thoughts aloud rather than expect a conversation. As real as it had seemed at the time, he soon convinced himself that the encounter in the forest had occurred in a dream. A deeply vivid dream, like the one he had days before hurting Jassyka.

During all of this, they had somehow gotten themselves lost amongst the footpaths in the mountain. Arlahn thought he had taken a wrong turn somewhere along the way, he was about to ask Jole his opinion when he realized that the big man merely wandered everywhere with absolutely no sense of direction or urgency, as if he simply loved strolling through the forest. Each night, Jole would light a fire and Arlahn would attempt conversation, but the Prince quickly realized the big man wasn't used to social interaction.

They didn't actually speak much more until Arlahn finally recognized his surroundings. On the fourth day, they had somehow made it to the waterfall with the Yenmaraj, only they were at the bottom pool this time. Still, he generally knew his way back to the camp.

"I wonder what PJ looks like now," Jole said as they approached. "Probably just as ugly as he was when I met him."

Arlahn chuckled. "I wouldn't remind him of anything like that. What were you doing when you met?"

Jole finally opened up and told Arlahn his life story their last few hours of walking. He mentioned being a lad when his father drowned, burning a man to death upon discovering his magic, and finding Omega soon after. He recounted his life in the forest, his love for a woman – Rasha was her name – and how he had delivered her to a Cooperith town. He even told of fighting in Hectore's Rebellion for a short time and validated a few of the embellished stories Arlahn had heard, furthering his awe for his father.

"How was my father when you saw him?" Arlahn asked finally.

"While he was alive, he was fine mostly," Jole answered.

"What do you mean 'while he was alive?'" Arlahn demanded with his heart suddenly in his stomach.

"Well," Jole began, "he was dead for a few minutes, but he came back when I healed him."

"How could you heal him?" Arlahn demanded again.

"I don't know lad, I just did."

Arlahn began to worry about his family back home and decided he was done with the Brotherhood, even if they weren't done with him yet.

They hurried down to camp at a quick pace, and upon their arrival Arlahn began calling out for Pientero. But there was no one in sight. The entire compound had been deserted.

He walked through the houses calling for Tamis, Anvar, and Pientero. But no answer came. He pushed open the double doors to the main hall and was shocked to find the entire community crammed into the building.

The tables had been removed and everyone held red wax candles, burning at chest height. There was a thin carpet laid out between the candles and at the end of its length, Pientero stood waiting, with Anvar at his left.

"Come!" The king-in-the-mountain commanded, the timbre of his voice echoing through the room. He was dressed in a dark leather doublet, his hair slicked back.

Arlahn walked up to where Pientero was waiting. He noticed a hot iron burning yellow in the heat of a fire.

"Repeat these words," Pientero said. "We are the king's brother, we stand by his side, with a shield to protect all that he prides."

When Arlahn began speaking, the entire Brotherhood behind took up the words in a litany. His skin prickled when he felt the power of their voices all speaking as one.

"We are a shadow in the dark and a sword in the light. So when he calls us to arms we rise up and fight."

Again, hundreds of voices and one voice repeated the words.

"We are his right hand of justice, our coming is swift. Our deeds will outlive us and that is our gift," Pientero said first, a beacon of sound.

"We are legion."

This time it felt as though thousands of voices repeated the words with him. Ancestral voices...

"WE ARE LEGION."

"We are family."

"WE ARE FAMILY."

"We are all mortal until we're immortal," Pientero finished.

This time, when Arlahn repeated the final words he spoke them alone. Compared to the previous cacophony, his words sounded like an inward promise.

Pientero took up the hot iron and blew a few breaths on it. Removed from the coals, Arlahn could make out his family's insignia.

When his eyes turned to meet Pientero's, the king was already staring hard at him. He commanded, "Kneel!"

Arlahn bent down on his knees, and Anvar approached with a small length of wood. "Bite down on this, it'll help."

Arlahn squeezed the wood between his teeth and Anvar pulled his shoulder clear of any clothing.

Without warning, Pientero simply jabbed the iron into the back of Arlahn's shoulder and the Prince began to growl beneath his gag. His flesh sizzled and bubbled underneath the scalding iron. Burning pain bit into his skin and ripped at what lay beneath. He bit down harder until he felt like his teeth were about to break. His pinched face flushing red as his breath threw out small amounts of spittle overtop of his gag and onto his chin.

Finally, the searing agony stopped. There were still echoes of the pain left in his shoulder, but its source had finally ceased feeding it.

Arlahn fell toward Anvar at first then wiped the sweat from his brow. He forced himself from his knees without help before turning to the rest of the Brothers, *his* Brothers.

"That was quite a welcoming party," Jole announced from the doorway, turning the entire crowd back around. "I hope mine's not like that."

A voice that Arlahn knew to be Balanor's piped up from within the crowd. "Who's the new squirrel in the mountain now?"

Jole chuckled at that and looked at the face of every Brother in the vicinity of the remark. Opening his mouth to reply, he was interrupted as Pientero appeared at the front of the crowd. "I assure you, he's no squirrel. You can call him Jole."

*****

There were a few momentary stops during their enthusiastic tour of the machines that had been built in his absence. Raphael was so proud of his workers for having accomplished so much in such little time, though he secretly knew that most of the credit was owed to his twin. Hectore couldn't help but be impressed by how simple yet revolutionary some of Raphael's ideas were for improving their siege weapons and defenses.

First, the Prince brought his father to the saucer-style pads that had catapults resting on them, allowing soldiers to quickly change their target. They had bolt and hole locks to keep the revolving base from moving and a chock at the front. Hectore pieced together the function: by replacing the catapult in the exact location after it was fired, it would theoretically fire into the same spot.

Next, was the battering ram house. The enclosure was raised up on wheels and covered in a fire-retardant cloth. Inside, the massive log was suspended by ropes. Climbing in momentarily, Raphael pointed out that if the men didn't have to support the weight of what they were swinging, they could swing much harder. Hectore marvelled at the head that capped this specific ram and Raphael entertained him with Kael's story of the blacksmith as he showed his father to the top of the third city wall. The air played games of tag with their cloaks and fluttered it about their ankles. In the distance, a dark sky with shades of grey and blue, portended a storm.

In a small field between the walls below them, Raphael had ordered stuffed archery dummies to be aligned in several military formations. At the centre of all the dummies stood a crudely built shell of a siege-tower. The Prince approached one of his fully assembled drum-bows standing in position on the wall and placed a hand on it, briefly outlining its use.

"I think I'm going to call them 'rotary-bows,' they're a little different from the automatic bow I'm designing, but their function's about the same."

"I'm anxious to see it work."

Raphael ordered two men, who had been previously trained on its use, to operate the weapon, then father and son walked to the parapet's edge and leaned against the cold stone for a better view. One of the soldiers carefully loaded the arrow drum into position, while the other man took up the long, perpendicular handle of the crank. The two soldiers exchanged nods before one proclaimed, "Ready, sir."

After a deep breath, Raphael replied in a calm voice, "Fire."

The second soldier, who was behind the simple tripod, began rowing the crank in perfectly circular motions. After the first full rotation, parts of the machine clicked into position. After the second rotation, Hectore saw the resistance in the soldier's rowing change slightly as he increased his effort. He glimpsed the first arrow catch in the device's mechanism and it snapped forward with tremendous force. The king followed the arrow quickly down into its intended target, the-outermost dummy of the right formation. Before he could look back at the contraption, another arrow pounded into the target beside it. More arrows landed into targets in consecutive fashion. Once the first twenty dummies were littered with almost thirty arrows, Hectore looked back to see that the drum was only half exhausted. When he turned to the entire formation of practice dummies again, it was full of arrows.

"Watch how fast they reload!" Raphael urged.

Hectore turned once more and saw how simply the men reloaded their machine. In a few heartbeats, the first soldier reversed the rotation of his crank for one revolution before the second pulled the empty drum forward on the device and lifted it clear. He placed another fully loaded drum in the machine and pushed it back. Again, the first set of rotations brought a series of clicks, while the second brought a series of death.

"We've finished twelve already," Raphael stated proudly, "with close to thirty-five drums."

The bowmen focused on the other flanking formation this time, unloading another barrage of continuous arrows. It seemed like an arrow was landing into another target before Hectore's heart could even beat twice, until the entire column of dummies was hit. It was another half a minute before the second drum expired and the King watched with mixed feelings of pride, amazement, and dread.

"What's with the siege-tower, son?" Hectore asked, noticing that the final contingent of dummies had been set up in a perimeter around the structure's base.

"That's for my last surprise," Raphael answered with a smile. He walked over to a tarped-up tube.

"You know the black powder that flashes and smokes? The stuff assassins used to use..." he began, lifting up the cover in both hands, "... I think I've found an amazing use for it. This... is an exploder."

Raphael threw the cover away with a wide, sweeping motion. Beneath sat a contraption that looked like a long barrel of metal that had been bored out of thick walls. A convex end capped the chamber on one side with a small vent hole drilled near its top.

Hectore asked what it was, and this time Raphael only said, "Just watch."

There was a small cask beside the metal weapon and the Prince scooped out a cup of black powder and poured it down the barrel, the small rocks rattling on their descent. The Prince took up a square of white cloth and stuffed it in as well, this time using a tamper to ensure everything was packed in. Then, he picked up a ball of roped up rocks, rolled it down the tube, and returned to stand by his father behind the machine. Raphael accepted a torch from a nearby worker, making sure the ground below was clear of people.

"It's going to be too fast to see leaving the machine, so just watch the tower," Raphael advised as he double-checked his aim. Then, he lowered the torch down to the vent hole before them.

Hectore was stunned, and blown back half a step, by the sheer volume of Raphael's invention. It was as if thunder had clapped right beside them. With a massive cloud of smoke, the metal exploder jumped back, a flash of fire emerging at the end of its barrel. The king had been watching the siege-tower until it disappeared in front of him. Almost instantaneous with the cloud of smoke, the tower smashed and burst apart into thousands of pieces. Splinters of shrapnel, big and small, blew away in every direction. Just under half of the straw soldiers were hit with pieces of flying destruction, and a few of them exploded like the tower, throwing straw into the rain of debris.

The moment was eternal and instant all at once for Hectore. Through his *sciong*, he understood what the full application this invention meant, perhaps even better than Raphael. He saw men carrying around personalized versions of this exploder, wreaking havoc, turning even the most cowardly of them into a lethal threat. The thought chilled his spine.

"How many of these have you built?"

Raphael mistook his enthusiasm. "Just the one so far, but I've commissioned for three more."

"Revoke them, son."

"What?" Raphael argued. "Why?"

"Just revoke them, and destroy this one, or guard it with your best men. If the Damonai learn something like this is real…" Hectore trailed off, knowing his son understood.

Raphael recognized his father's concern. Always the Damonai. "How could they find out about this?"

"Some of them have Gifts, just like us," Hectore reminded him. "There's no telling what they could know. If you have the mind to build something like this, they could have the mind to steal it."

"I can't just destroy this one though, Father," Raphael said in a protective manner, "the men worked so hard on it."

"Then destroy your plans for it," the king urged. "Make sure it's one of its kind."

Raphael didn't say anything but nodded his head in obedient acknowledgement. He thought hard about scenarios in which he could guarantee that the power of this weapon would never fall into evil hands, but ultimately, he knew that it would be impossible.

Hectore looked his son with pride. "I know you'll do what's best."

Once Raphael's presentation had concluded, the king excused himself to return to the palace. The Prince remained behind and oversaw the clean-up of his demonstration. Afterwards, as he was wandering through the streets of Pellence on his way home, Raphael bumped into a woman. The dirty blonde-haired woman recognized him immediately and dipped her head. "I'm sorry, my prince."

Raphael excused her and continued walking. He noticed that they were headed in the same direction and once they gained onto the palace grounds, he approached her again. "Can I help you, young lady?"

The woman looked at him with beautiful blue eyes and smiled. "No, my prince, I need to find my own way. I'm the physician's apprentice. We're new here, my name's Christianne."

"Nice to meet you. Your master's a skilled healer," Raphael replied. "How did you end up working with him?"

At that, Christianne's smile darkened slightly, as if she had been reminded of an old pain. "I was traded. By my father," she said. "When he got sick, Sol healed him. But we were poor, so my pa offered me up as payment. The old man agreed a year ago and I haven't seen home since."

"You don't want to leave?" Raphael asked.

She shrugged her shoulders. "And go where, back home to a man who sold me like livestock? Like you said, Sol's skilled at what he does and there's much I can learn from him. He treats me with kindness. A physician's probably the best I can do."

"If you *could* do something else though..." Raphael trailed off intentionally, hoping she would finish for him.

Christianne shrugged her shoulders again. "I don't know, I've always liked dressing up, maybe I'd be a courtesan."

"You should probably continue honing your trade," Raphael told her as they passed through the entrance, taken slightly off-guard. He bid the girl good day and climbed the stairs toward his bedchamber.

Inside, he found Marlyonna sipping on some tisane and admiring Raphael's wall of accomplishments. She was fingering the tip of one of his trophy arrows. Once, he had hit his own arrow, burying the tip into the nock of his first shot. When Kael proclaimed it was "all the luck," Raphael set out to do it again. Eighteen times in total, he'd shot the perfect shot into another arrow, and he kept each one as a testament to his "luck."

"How was your day, my love?" Marlyonna asked as she noticed him enter and walk over to his desk in the corner.

"It went well. Father seemed impressed for the most part," he answered, going through a few of the top pages to find the blueprint for his exploder. "What have you been up to?"

She finished sipping her tisane before putting it down on the mantle next to her. "I was just thinking…" Marlyonna started before pausing to rub at the warmth in her belly, "… about the day you saved me. I knew from the first moment I saw you that you would be the best man I'd ever met."

Raphael recalled the day vividly. His *mniman* had manifested right before the battle in Corduran. He and his brother were visiting their uncle, Benson Wellcant, the Warden of the East, when they were unexpectedly invaded by hostile Pirates. Pirat was to the Damonai what Corduran was to the Sainti. Most citizens were only loyal to gold, but every now and then, a few extreme renegade ships would patrol the coast and intercept other vessels under force or, when they were desperate, launch an assault inland. After Uncle Benson had caught an arrow in his shoulder at the outset, Raphael and Kael rushed to the forefront of the action, watching men spill over the rails of their ships and splash through the waters. The brothers organized the men available to fight along the docks, forming thick walls in the front, while archers behind peppered Pirati warriors dredging through the open waters. They had repelled the first assault of the invasion before it even really started. After the sortie, much to their dismay, Uncle Benson sent his nephews home to safety. It was on their return journey that they'd found a renegade crew that had landed further up shore and was venturing along the Spine.

Marlyonna and her family were fleeing Corduran too when their carriage was discovered by Pirates. She had been ripped from the wagon along with her family and watched her father die, pleading for their lives. Dirty, unkempt men started attacking her and her mother, and she saw her mother drive the back of her head into a man before he ripped her back by the hair and slit her throat. That was when Marly gave up. She let the men push her to the earth and one fell on top of her. She waited for him to start moving but suddenly felt a warm liquid spill over her back. Marlyonna looked up and there he was, charging in on his horse with his bow already drawn back, screaming for the men to get off of her. She rolled to her side, throwing the bandit off to see that he had an arrow in his back, and watched Kael give chase to the men through the woods. Suddenly Raphael was helping her up, asking if she was hurt. She was crying tears of grief.

Right now, though, it was a tear of emotional pleasure that welled in her eye. "That's how I know you'll be the best father."

"Father?!" Raphael blurted with equal parts surprise and joy. "You mean you're…"

"With child," she finished, smiling. "There's a little Rai inside of me."

*****

After applying another coat of thick white paste over the cut, Pientero stood. "It'll have to do. Something greater than me has to pull her back now."

"I'm so sorry, PJ. I never meant to hurt her," Arlahn whimpered.

"That's why it's your actions, not what you intend, that make you who you are. Only actions exist in the real world. This was a mistake, Prince, the only forgivable action. We both know that."

"Yeah, but if I could have just stayed calm…" Arlahn trailed off as his voice broke.

"And if my aunt had a cock, she could be my uncle," Pientero interrupted with a commanding gruffness in his voice. "We don't live with ifs and coulds, Arlahn. We get with what we're given. Make the best of this."

Arlahn wanted to cry. He blinked away the blurriness in his eyes and felt a stream roll down his cheek. What had he done? Jassyka lay there in her cot with her furs covering her and he wished he could do something but didn't know what.

Abandoned, he left his cabin and walked away from the camp without direction. Only looking far enough ahead to keep him from falling, he just walked.

He wandered onto a footpath and through emptiness until finally, like a moth drawn to a light, he wound up on the ridge of cliff where he'd first really spoken to her.

Arlahn sat down on the same rock she had when she drew her sketches and looked out over the valley below.

There were tall grasses, golden and green, moving in vast waves like the top of an ocean. The sun was setting across the distant scene, basking the earth below in a golden light. He had been thinking about Pientero's words when he saw a flash of light below turn from yellow to red to blue. That gave him his answer, he wasn't quite done with the Brotherhood just yet, there was one last thing he needed to do. For his Sister.

Arlahn walked back to his cabin and gathered some jars and returned down into the valley.

As he approached the group of glittering rainbowflies, they quickly dispersed away from him, so he walked out to the middle of their field and waited until they grew accustomed to his presence.

This would be something you would do, Father, Arlahn thought, and he knew it was a good thing. The best with what he was given.

As he watched the bugs flash and change colours around him, they slowly began to calm in their flight.

Arlahn focused with extreme concentration on one particular fly. He found it fluttering around while it was still unlit, but as the fly flapped its wings, Arlahn felt as if the world around him had all but stopped. He watched the tiny electrical charge course its way into the edges of the fly's wings, illuminating them with a bright blue light.

The fly's size seemed to grow the longer he stared at it flapping through the air before him. Arlahn reached out for the bug, but his hand wasn't moving. His mind saw himself then, almost from an outer perspective, moving glacially slow. By the time he noticed that his arm actually *was* moving, its path was too far behind his target. When Arlahn realized this, his mind released its clutch on the moment and time seemed to snap back to its original pace.

He took a second to try and return to the feeling, but he couldn't will it back. It felt like a lucid dream, yet he was fully awake. Was that what his father's *sciong* felt like?

Suddenly, another fly caught Arlahn's attention and time, once again, continued at a staggeringly slow pace. Only now, understanding his precision came to him as second nature. His body *wanted* to do what his mind intended. He slowly reached out again toward the yellow flying speck and his fingers closed tightly around it, feeling its warmth pressed against the inside of his palm.

Arlahn opened a jar and trapped the fly inside. It lit up and bounced against the inside of the glass a few times before settling.

The Prince stood back up and continued to practice catching rainbowflies. Eventually, he spotted two flies at once. This time, both arms reached out at different angles and, with time slowing again, he managed to make sure that both of his hands were exactly where he wanted them to be. He began placing two flies in the jar at once.

Continuing at an unconscious pace, Arlahn snatched anything moving around him. Before he realized it, he was alone in the field once again.

Back in the cabin, Jassyka was sleeping with Balanor at her side. When Arlahn dipped into the room, the two exchanged an awkward look. Balanor was holding Jassyka's hand and released it as the Prince glanced down.

"Why are *you* here?" Arlahn asked him with gentility in his tone.

"She's lived with us for over ten years now. That's long enough to call her Sister," Balanor told him, clearing strands of hair from her eye with delicate care.

Coming to an incredible realization that put their entire hostile relationship into perspective, Arlahn stated, "You loved her."

"You wouldn't understand," Balanor answered.

"I think I do," he told him. "She's fierce but passionate. She cares more about this family than most, though you would never know it."

Balanor stood up and Arlahn swore he watched him blink away tears. "I'm going to miss her when she's gone."

Arlahn felt a pit in his stomach and dipped his head in shame. He looked up when he felt Balanor place a hand on his shoulder. "It's alright Brother, death is our unifying path."

The Prince shook his head and sniffed. He had never known Balanor to be sympathetic. The Brother, and everyone else, had stopped calling Arlahn "Baby" ever since his date with the hot iron, but hearing those kind words delivered with genuine brotherly compassion took away Arlahn's grievances in ways that moved him.

"She'll be with our ancestors in the Graceland," Balanor continued.

"Thanks Balanor, for not making this worse on me," Arlahn said through his guilt.

"This is hard for us all."

With that last bit of wisdom, Balanor walked out of the cabin, leaving the two alone. Arlahn let Jassyka sleep for a little while longer, afraid to break her peaceful rest.

Chapter 23

Mordo watched the night owl take off from his nest, swoop down, and snatch a field mouse between its talons. They were creatures of the night, hunters in the dark.

He read the note from his apprentice once more, crumpled and pocketed it. Wraith had joined up with Solin and the two were in position for the next phase of the Caliph's plan. Mordo had trained his Wraith well; Chris was better than most of the other Deaders on the council, even without a Power. He knew his apprentice was ready when he himself had been taken off-guard. Mordo had approached the bed in utter darkness, but before he could throw back the covers from the sleeping form, he felt cold metal touch his neck.

"I got you!" Wraith almost shouted in exultation. "Finally! I've been sleeping in the rafters for eight days waiting for this."

The opportunity was seized; he had succeeded. Something had stalked the DeathShadow. Yes, he thought proudly, Wraith was ready.

Mordo stepped out from behind a stack of hay bales in the corner of a stable. Keeping to the shadows, he made his way to the local tavern.

He'd arrived in Silver Streams two days prior. Upon entering the town, he'd found an old man fishing along a bank. Mordo tried to question him about the location of his deadees, but after he'd introduced himself as an uncle, the old man grew sour.

"I know the family well, they're all golden-haired. Something tells me you're not an uncle at all."

Fishermen pulled the man's body from the stream hours later. "Just too old to fight the current, I guess." He heard one of the discoverers say. The current, Mordo chuckled.

Tonight, huddled into the corner of the tavern, eavesdropping on the conversations of others, he learned that his mark still lingered in the village. After hearing an overly drunk bastard boast about the woman he was off to woo, Mordo waited for him to leave and then followed at an inconspicuous distance.

The drunkard stumbled and staggered his way through the streets, singing songs to himself. Once stopping to relieve himself and once to have a meaningfully deep conversation with a blank-faced cow.

Finally, the man's stumbling came to a halt outside of a brown house with a red door. The bottle in his hand slipped from his grasp, and his head rolled around in a half-circle as he slurred her name. "C'mere, I've got a royal cock for ya..."

Mordo had heard enough and cut the man's rambling short at the neck. He pitched the corpse into a nearby ditch and approached the home.

The Deader did a lap around it and found a quartered window glowing orange from the fire within. In his *nsuli*, he peeped through the window and saw a woman sitting in her nightgown. She was waiting patiently on her chair with a leg tucked under her, watching the fire sizzle and pop in the hearth. He stared as she walked over, bent down, and added a few logs to the dying embers. Then the woman picked up a wick and lit it for her lantern before walking into the far room. Mordo hurried around the building to see where she had gone. It was her bedroom, but she shared it with another girl. This one had golden-brown hair that covered her face in her sleep.

Two daughters. The drunk got it right. This was the place.

Mordo walked around to the front of the house and knocked twice on the red door. Before it opened, he cloaked himself behind his Power.

*****

"Kael?" Luzy asked with an elevated heart at the knock on the door. She hurried over and swung it open excitedly. But there was no one there.

Stepping out into the wind, she pushed the hair from her face and looked through the gloom but couldn't see anything in the near distance. The smile on her face withered and Luzy returned to the house.

She closed the door solemnly behind her, looking down at the ground in her lost hopes. Her eyes narrowed and she knelt, touching a bit of fresh dirt that Mordo had brought into the house with him.

The Deader pulled a curved dagger from his hip and released the clutch on his Power. His *nsuli* revealed him, already reaching for Luzy's throat.

He squeezed her windpipe between thumb and forefingers and placed his dagger tight against the skin below her chin.

"Shh," he hushed, lifting her to her feet and pushing her back against the door. "Crossing DeathShadow has its price."

Although he didn't feel attraction, he documented that this woman was pretty compared to most he saw in the streets. Underneath all of her exterior beauty, however, he knew, she was the same sack of meat as all of his other deadees. But unlike the rest of the beautiful women he'd held under his blade, her face flushed red with fury rather than dread. Luzy struggled for breath and stared hard into his eyes, until she glanced over his shoulder for a second. Mordo anticipated what was to come next and he dipped his head down, tucking it into his shoulder as he braced for the impact.

"Bastard!" growled a manly voice.

A clay pot crashed into Mordo's shielded head. He turned and smashed the butt of his dagger into the father's face, sending him whirling round.

Luzy broke free of his grip then and snatched the dagger in his hand. She squeezed the blade and tried to wrench it away, but the trained assassin ripped the weapon clear, slicing deep into her clutching fingers. Luzy gasped and grabbed at her wound.

Her father threw himself toward the Deader and brought him down. For a moment, the old lumberjack struggled to restrain the assassin's wrists.

"Luzy, get your sister and mother out of here! Now!" Then he let go of the invader's wrist to hammer a right cross into Mordo's face, bouncing his head against the ground.

DeathShadow used the blow to take up a throwing knife in his free hand. With his head ringing, he stabbed randomly and caught the man just below the ribs. The father grunted and in his moment of weakness, Mordo stabbed him once again. Throwing him to the side with a right cross of his own, the Deader rose up once more.

Luzy had run to her sister and woke her hurriedly. By the time, they ran out of the bedchamber, DeathShadow had vanished. Their father had pushed himself back up against a wall, clutching the bloody knife in his side.

"Miri stay close to your sister," his voice strained, "he just disappeared. You have to get out of here."

Their mother had been woken up by the commotion and came in. Struck still with shock and terror at the sight of her husband bleeding out, she froze.

Luzy ran over, took up her mother's hand, and tried to drag her to the exit. As they were about to pass their dying father, their mother collapsed and dropped to her knees, weeping.

Mirianne was a great beauty for her age. She already looked like a young woman but was still only fifteen, and the gravity of the situation was showing her youth. Her hands started shaking uncontrollably as she watched Luzy attempt to convince her mother to abandon their father.

"I... I can't," Mirianne whimpered as she took a step back.

"Miri, stay close..." Luzy began, looking back.

Her eyes widened, the black-haired intruder was looming behind her sister. He grabbed her by the hair, yanked her head back and cracked her with a fist, then quickly sprinkled something in her mouth. Mirianne's eyes closed and she fell into the man's arms.

Luzy got up, leaving her parents on the ground to face him.

Mordo drew his long, curved scimitar and pointed it at the girl, admiring her bravery in this final moment.

She remained silent but he could see a fire in her eyes. He had seen this same fire in other eyes. This wasn't over for her. Not yet anyway.

Luzy found the fire poker close to her feet and knelt down to pick it up, staring at the Shadow the whole time. She screamed and stepped forward, swinging her poker viciously. Mordo slapped the attack down and stepped back. Finally, he was starting to enjoy himself.

He had no problem hitting or killing a woman. He had simply refrained from doing so here out of respect for her tenacity. It was a nice change of pace. Too often the people Mordo had visited cowered, whimpering for mercy before the end. Some had offered him vast amounts of coin or prizes, women had tried to sell themselves. But, every once in a while, there was someone who had the will to fight back with every ounce of their strength, like that old Essellian general, he thought.

Keeping his blade up, Mordo deflected her incoming attacks playfully. But with Luzy's vicious assault distracting him, he barely noticed the fight rise in the mother. She had taken up two pots and swung them at the assassin.

In response, he jumped forward at Luzy, slapping away her protective poker, and punched her across the jaw. As she spun with the blow and fell into a table, Mordo dropped to one knee, ducking a pot, and buried a dagger in the father's foot to pin him to the ground. Coming up and stepping back, he spun to face the mother, sliced a pot from her swinging hand, and fed a heavy boot to her stomach. She doubled over and Mordo stepped in, savagely throwing his knee into her chest.

The mother fell to the ground, winded. Coughing and clutching at her chest, she rolled on her back, and Mordo kicked her across the face.

He swung his head, looking for Luzy, when a black fire poker came for him. He tried to roll out of the way, but the tip of the poker caught his cheek and split his skin.

Ignoring the pain, Mordo shuffled his feet and delivered a sidekick to Luzy's gut. She dropped her poker on impact and let out a great hoof. Having lost his sword, Mordo grabbed her by the collar and rushed her back, punching her in the face as hard as he could, pain fuelling his blows. Her nose broke with a crack and the force sent her sprawling backward over the table.

Touching his cheek, Mordo looked down at the blood on his fingers. His fury rose. He shouldn't be bleeding... How can a Shadow bleed?

He surveyed the room quickly, the sister and mother were both on the ground, their father still bleeding against the wall, and Luzy was laid out on the table before him. He bound her extremities to the legs of the table first. She had the most fight in her by far. Then, he quickly tied Mirianne's wrists together before returning to loom over the mother, who was looking up at him with tear-filled eyes. Reaching down, he grabbed a handful of hair and dragged her across the room to a chair. He pulled a length of cloth hanging from his belt and gagged her before binding her wrists and ankles.

Behind him, the father had pulled the dagger from his foot and was finally back up, closing in, but loss of blood had weakened him immensely and he staggered to a chair, falling on one knee.

Mordo walked over to him, grabbed the knife in his side by the handle, and pulled the man up by it. The father winced in pain but came to stand, following the killer's will as he was walked over and thrown down into another chair. "Now we're going to have a little talk," Mordo began.

The man's head sagged and rolled back and forth.

"Hey!" Mordo snapped, slapping the man back awake. "I decide when you die."

Luzy awoke then and began threatening him with promises of death if he hurt any of them further.

Mordo looked at her and cocked his head as if he didn't understand. The tilt of his skull and the dead look in his eyes filled Luzy with gut-wrenching fear. He climbed up onto the table and straddled her. Looking down at her bloodied face, the Deader reached down to wipe some of the freshest blood clear. When she began struggling, he felt her breasts press into his crotch and rub against him.

Mordo produced another curved dagger, which seemed to still her for the moment. Tracing the line of her brow, he moved the tip of the blade along the side of her face, under her chin, down to her top. He pressed the knife between skin and fabric and paused, he thought about tearing her clothes and exposing her. He had learned that this was one of the greatest humiliations for a respected woman, this exposure. Something inside of him knew this wasn't the case with her and the destruction of a person's character aroused Mordo more intimately than any woman ever had.

"You're pathetic," Luzy spat, staring into his eyes as she felt his phallus grow. "Is this what you do? Find innocent girls..."

He snatched her mouth and squeezed it. "You know nothing about me, girl."

She stared at Mordo hard and promised him through squeezed lips, "When Kael finds you, you're a dead man."

"He won't find me," the assassin said, throwing her face to the side and disappearing before her. "Not until it's too late."

He climbed off and returned to the father before releasing his *nsuli*, slapping the man twice until he regained consciousness. "I have some questions for you..."

"HELP!" Luzy tried to call, though she was unsure what type of power her voice still held.

Mordo walked over and pointed a finger into her eye. "That was stupid," he warned. "Don't do it again."

He went to the mother, who was tied in her chair, and dragged her closer. "Now, this is how this is going to work..."

The Deader explained his torturing procedure to the family while they were strapped down, helplessly. He would torture the mother if the father didn't answer, Luzy if her mother didn't answer, and both parents were tortured if Luzy stayed quiet.

"Now, I hear you were such a famed dressmaker you got the royal commission years ago," Mordo told the mother.

Without asking any questions first, he sliced along the top of one of her fingers, tracing the same line over and over, deeper and deeper. Luzy's mother slowly began to cry out louder beneath her gag. Finally, he took up her hand and poked her knuckle through the skin. That was when the scream beneath the gag doubled and the woman began sweating.

With the consequences firmly established, Mordo began by asking rudimentary questions; their names, employment, but when he asked Luzy her first question, it was about the Prince.

"Where is he? Answer the question." Growing impatient, the killer dragged her mother over to sit across from her. He pulled her head back by the hair and pressed the tip of his dagger against base of her eye. "No lying."

"You'll kill us anyway!" Luzy raged, surprisingly confident. "Why should I tell you anything?"

"Because there're lots of ways to die, girl. Trust me, it's my business," he answered, removing the blade from her mother's eye. "Let me show you."

"HELP!" Luzy called out in desperation once more.

Mordo's expression became pinched. "I warned you not to scream." He viciously broke another finger, and Luzy's mother screamed again with renewed pain.

"Is everything okay in there?" a voice asked from outside. The door opened and a neighbour stood, shocked by the disheveled house before him. Suddenly his face went blank and his head rolled forward from its shoulders. Before the body fell, DeathShadow materialized beside him with blood dripping off the end of his sword.

"Now. No more games."

First, he continued asking about the Princes. He was suspiciously interested in their health and knew they were building something. "There's one on his way here, isn't there? Too bad he isn't here now, though," Mordo said.

"He'd kill you if he was."

Mordo smiled at that. "You can't kill Death's Shadow, girl."

He asked if Luzy had heard anything about a stronghold in the mountains. She hadn't and told him as much. But the deader didn't believe her and to loosen her lips, he decided to start filleting skin from her father. First, it was his shoulder, then he sliced off an ear, and finally he cut out a section of his face. She cried and pleaded for him to stop, insisting that if she knew, she would tell him.

Luzy closed her eyes and rested her head back on the table, tears streaming down her cheeks. Finally, Mordo thought, I've broken the defiant whore.

"What have we done to deserve this?" she pleaded in a defeated cry to an empty God.

The assassin loomed over her face. "You were chosen," he answered.

There was a surreal pounding in her head. Luzy wanted to start bawling again, but all of her tears had left her. She had done so well before now, she told herself, to act like Kael, to be strong and brave. But seeing her father killed like that shattered what bit of spirit she had left.

Closing her eyes, Luzy took a deep, shuddering breath and accepted her fate. When she opened them, he was hovering over her, upside down. In a final act of defiance, she spat in his face.

A knife came up and stabbed down.

Right into the wood beside her.

"Stupid bitch," Mordo said in a calm voice, wiping his face clean. Standing once more, he looked over at the fire burning in the hearth. He walked over, rolled a log from the blaze with his scimitar and kicked it over to some naphtha. Flames were climbing the walls before Mordo had finished collecting his weapons. He picked up the unconscious Mirianne and threw her over his shoulder. Turning around in the doorway, he looked back at the girl strapped to the table. "Enjoy the warmth."

*****

Jassyka awoke to noise from outside her room, things being shuffled and dragged around. She opened her eyes just as the Prince came walking in.

"Did I wake you?" he asked her with compassionate consideration.

"No," she lied, "I've slept enough."

Jassyka made to get up but there was a heavy, dull pain pushing against her forehead and brow. Arlahn was beside her in a second, helping her lie back down, speaking soft words of strength and rest.

She felt him shudder and looked up to see tears running from his eyes. "I'm so sorry Jassyka..." he started.

"Shh, shh shh," she soothed him, placing a hand on his cheek. "It's alright. You finally found your strength in this place."

"But look at what happened," he said, taking up her hand and giving it a squeeze.

Jassyka sighed and gave him a light smile. "Truth is, I don't even feel the pain anymore, and dying's not so bad when there's no pain."

"Don't talk like that!" Arlahn scolded her. "I have something that'll help you feel better."

He guided her upright and she felt the strength wane from her petite limbs.

"What is it?" she asked, coming to stand.

"It's just in the other room. Do you think you can make it? Your hands are freezing." Arlahn put his other arm around her waist and supported her gently.

"I'll be fine," Jassyka said.

"Close your eyes. Keep them closed!" he instructed. Arlahn walked with her and drew back the curtain before them. He led her into the middle of the room and then stopped.

"Okay, open."

Jassyka gasped and her eyes lit up like a child watching fireworks for the first time. Filling every corner with tiny orbs of luminescence were lightningbugs, a million of them, it seemed. Endless streams of yellow, green, blue, pink, purple, orange, and red shone with momentary brilliance all around them. Her breath caught in her throat as she stood struck, admiring the beautiful lightshow around her. A purple stream snaked toward her, settled on her shoulder, and turned a bright red before extinguishing.

"You once told me you wished you could dance with the rainbowflies," the Prince said, holding the small of her back and walking around to the front of her. "May I dance with you?"

Jassyka's radiance shone almost as brightly as the bugs surrounding her. In that moment, she was happier than she could ever remember being. She took up his hand and stepped in closer to him.

They danced a few graceful steps until she felt her strength fade. Jassyka rested her head against his chest and their movements regressed into a subtle bob and weave between the multi-coloured lights.

"This is the most amazing thing anyone's ever done for me, Arlahn."

The Prince heard the gratitude but his eyes were closed and his body lost in the moment. It felt as though it would end if he spoke.

"Thank you," Jassyka said finally. Pulling herself away, she pressed her lips tenderly against his. She saw the tear stream down his eye, but without any words, all she could do was hug Arlahn closer, sagging her head back into his chest.

Together, they continued slow-dancing and after a minute he heard the faintest voice whisper, "I love you."

This time Arlahn replied, "I love you too."

They danced a few seconds longer between the trails of multi-coloured light before he felt her small figure fall into his, carrying a much heavier feeling along with it. He leaned over and saw peace in her soft features.

Arlahn swept Jassyka up in his arms, carried her to the cot, and laid her down softly.

She was gone.

*****

Kael had ridden hard throughout the night, hurrying to the woman that awaited him. In the predawn gloom, he arrived at the great mill of Silver Streams. He looked eastward and spotted a pillar of black smoke rising in the distance. A spectral feeling clutched his heart. Probably just the smith up early, he hoped. Kael shrugged it away and trotted his horse over one of the town's large bridges. The clapping of his horse's hooves on the wood increased when he quickened his pace in the smoke's direction.

As he drew near the source, the Prince gasped at the sight, kicking his horse toward a flaming home. He jumped from his saddle and found a man dead in the ditch, his throat slit.

Kael ran toward the burning house and barged through the door, taking in a deep breath as he crashed into the building.

The smoke was thick and it burned his eyes. He lowered himself to his belly and squinted until he could see, then Kael scanned the room. The fire was blazing all around him, hot flames licked up the walls as the inferno consumed everything in sight. On hands and knees, the Prince scurried deeper into the room and found a mother and father bound to chairs. The father was mutilated almost beyond recognition and the mother had been beaten, her fingers mangled. On the table, bound to the four legs, he found his beautiful Luzy. She too was bloodied and smoke stained her face, her gown cut open.

Ripping apart her bindings as if they were loose threads on a garment, Kael freed her within seconds. He picked her up in his arms and heard a loud crack. Turning, he saw that one of the supports had almost burned through, replacing sturdy wood with weak coal. He rushed back through the entrance in an attempt to retrieve her parents, but just as he reached her father, the beam gave way. Kael escaped as the roof collapsed in behind him, trapping her lifeless parents in the blazing building.

The Prince carried his love a safe distance and carefully laid her on the ground. He ripped off the binds on her wrists and ankles and gathered her into his arms once more. Her face was darkened from smoke and sweaty from the heat. Her nose looked like it was broken, and she was barely breathing, Kael felt for a pulse.

… … … … …. … *thump*… ….. … … … … *thump*…

After an eternity, Luzy coughed and her eyes slowly blinked open. She gave a weak smile and cupped her prince's cheek in her hand. Kael snatched it before it fell and squeezed it, holding her fingers close against his cheek. A tear fell from his eye and he kissed her loving palm.

"I'm so sorry, Luzy," Kael began, "if I would have been here…"

Luzy lifted her index finger and held it on his lips to stop him from speaking. "You have nothing to be sorry for. The man came for Miri." Racking coughs shook her entire body in his arms. "I… I was just fun for the sick bastard. DeathShadow…" She swallowed a dry throat. "He wanted…

wanted to know about you, Kael. He knew about your machines," she said before another onset of coughing took her.

"Don't speak," Kael advised softly, "you need to keep your strength."

He hugged her closer, and Luzy looked up at him. "You would have been proud of me. The whole time I was brave," she paused to cough again, "I was thinking of you."

"I love you Luzy, I'm going to save you," Kael told her, carefully brushing the hair from her face.

"You already have." He watched as she struggled to smile up at him. "Now... Save Miri..." she struggled to say between wheezing breaths.

"I'll bring her back, Luce. I promise."

Kael looked into her eyes as they glazed over and knew the worst was upon him. She still had a pulse, but she wasn't breathing.

"Stay with me!" he cried out, then his body reminded him to act.

Tilting her head back gently, he went about trying to resuscitate her.

After a minute there was still no response.

Kael refused to accept that and kept pumping her chest, occasionally delivering more air with a kiss.

But the smoke in the house had suffocated her lungs. She didn't have a chance after so long inside. There was nothing he could do to help. A tear fell on her face as Kael closed her eyes gently with his forefingers. He kissed her one last time on her thin, soft lips. "I promise I'll save Mirianne, I'll save your sister."

With cold, empty hatred in his red-rimmed eyes, Kael stared into nothing ahead of him, imagining all the ways he'd make this DeathShadow suffer. He picked up Luzy and carried her body to a soft patch of green grass where he laid her down.

By now, the sun had crested the horizon and others that had woken up stirred around in commotion, rushing to put out the burning house.

The Prince walked to the stable at the northern side of the house. Two horses had been killed while the stalls for two others were empty. He now had one mission in life. He was going to murder that killer.

First, he would return to Pellence and properly bury Luzy. Then he was going to organize a party and hunt him down.

"I'll be coming for you, DeathShadow," Kael promised aloud as he looked back from his mount at the burning home.

*****

The journey to Pellence took longer than anticipated with one man hobbling. When they arrived, they were almost turned back. The party gained entry into the city after a short, apprehensive discussion with the guard posted on the first gate. He had been somewhat reluctant to let Halder's beast in, but the old scout assumed responsibility for anything that happened.

They travelled through Pellence with awkward looks and frightened gasps, as most citizens tried to hide themselves from Halder's pantuur. Shortly after these three men entered the city's third wall, the elusive thief Darius pointed out his favourite brothel.

"I always love coming here... Get it?" he said with lifted eyebrows.

Just then, Darius saw a shapely girl walk by with a wicker basket of freshly cleaned clothes. His stare forced him to turn one hundred and eighty degrees in pursuit, as he watched her hips fluctuate with her walk.

"Where is *she* going?" he said, turning back to face Halder and Mick. He shook the scout's hand and thanked him for salvation. "Now, if you'll excuse me." With that, Darius rushed off into an alley.

"Eh! Get back here!" Halder called after him. Dragging Mick along, the scout led his pantuur sniffing down the alley. The animal followed the scent into a wall and began growling.

"I like him, but I don't" Halder admitted.

"I know what you mean," Mick answered, understanding the feeling all too well. Then a realization struck him as he thought about the thief's farewell. "Do you have your wallet?"

The scout rubbed his hand along his right hip where he always kept his coin purse tied to his belt. There was nothing there. "Never mind, I hate the sonuvabitch! Where'd he go?"

"He's gone," Mick told him. "He won't cause much trouble though, best to leave him be."

"He better not cause *any* trouble. How do you know he's gone?"

Mick lifted his shoulders, staying quiet about Darius' Gift. "I've caught him five times before. He always gets away."

The buildings along the approach to the Palace of Pellence created a sense of anticipation with their architecture, as if the last blocks of the city were formed into some grand hallway. When they reached the fourth wall, Mick took note of how there were as many guards on it as there were on others, but its shortened perimeter made their number seem doubled.

Halder called up and was recognized by the veteran guard on the gate. The order was hollered and six sentries fanned before the arch to allow them passage.

Mick had never seen the palace in person, and his eyes widened to explore the bewildering sight before him. The gardens in the front courtyard grew lush hedges in patterns that he had never seen before. Other greenery had been impossibly sculpted into animals, painted to life with blooming flowers. The building itself was watched over by gargoyle and knight statues, battling along the tops of turrets, and the colourful stained-glass windows contrasted the shades of black and white in the stone.

The place was ancient, Mick knew, but somehow its design was so timeless that it seemed brand new.

Halder exchanged courtesies with his old friend, the stable master, when he dropped off his pantuur for safe keeping.

The stable head complained but Halder simply said, "Just keep him chained in a stall by himself and you don't have to worry. Feel free to feed him some meat, he might take a liking to you."

Without waiting for a refusal, Halder led Mick away and into the palace. "Come on, you want to speak with the king? He's this way."

They entered through the main doors and Mick was again taken aback at what he saw. He couldn't fathom the detail in the sculpted murals beside him, strained to believe that such a place exists.

The scout led him up a grand staircase to a giant set of double doors. The steel-banded wood was fitted with a cast-iron decoration of the ancient Rai sigil. Halder was explaining his situation to the guards when a blond-haired man, finely dressed in a green doublet, came walking through. Noticing Halder, he turned back around.

"Halder," he said, smiling. "How are you, old man? Is Kael at Luzy's then?"

"Aye, Prince Raphael, said he might be gone for the week."

"Who's this, an Essellian?" the Prince remarked, noting the blue uniform of the justicar.

Halder explained that he and Prince Kael had found two travellers out in the wild.

"I know you're getting old, but are you really seeing double? There's only one man here!" Raphael teased sarcastically.

The old scout sourly told the Prince to bugger off then explained how the thief snuck away.

After which, Raphael led them into the throne room, where Mick's amazement was renewed. The high clerestory walls shone brightly in the daylight, and the floors he stood on were almost inconceivable, their colours breathtaking. He recognized the patterns in the swirls and clouds as far-off galaxies amongst the cosmos. Mick had seen them once in real life through the MagicEye, back in Esselle, an ancient device built so that man could look into the stars.

In the centre of it all was the HighKing. Hectore sat inside his golden, sun-shaped throne; his entire frame gilded by its surroundings, his posture indomitable. And there was something about his aura that, like the sun, at once commanded one's attention but punished glares that lingered. The king's hands rested on sunburst-like protrusions, designed to make him look divine. On the right, abstract armrest, he idly fingered a ruby.

Mick felt his insignificance standing before this man until he spoke. King Hectore's voice was welcoming, as seductive as any poet or bard Mick had ever heard.

Raphael walked before his father and bowed lightly. "Father, Halder's here at your request. His story's an interesting one."

With that, the blond-haired prince left the throne room to continue his day. Halder and Mick stepped forward when the king looked their way and nodded.

"It's good to see you, old friend," Hectore said warmly.

"You as well, my King, though I wish I was only visiting."

"Me too," the king replied before growing sour. "But there's too much at stake here."

Halder nodded in silent acknowledgement.

"Now, there's a story you want to tell me?" the King continued, turning his powerful glare toward Mick.

Mick stepped forward and prepared to speak when the HighKing recognized something. He moved in his seat and leaned forward, resting his elbows on his knees, scrutinizing Mick a moment. His gaze compelled the justicar to silence once more. "Are you a Deddick?"

Mick was surprised to be identified in such fashion. What had given him away? He had always been told he looked more like his mother. "Yes. I am, Your Grace."

"You move just like your father," the king said. "You're just smaller."

"So I've been told, my King," Mick replied. "I came here with a message from my father and Warden Rali. But so much has happened, I don't know where to start."

"From the beginning," Hectore told him.

Mick took a second to gather his thoughts. He started with the murder of the gang members and Pical. That transitioned him into the theft and sale of a Prophecy Tablet and his meeting with Warden Rali and his father. Now that he spoke directly to the HighKing, he confided the information about the Damonai's Council of Deaders that Rali had mentioned.

Hectore listened attentively and only asked questions to clarify detail. However, when Mick told Hectore about his conversation with the mysterious man he'd called Drifter and mentioned the name Harbinger, the HighKing took an exclusive interest in what Mick was telling him.

He repeated the words as he remembered them, "He said to tell you that some mountain will be found. That you have to send your sons there if it's to survive but one of them won't."

At that, Hectore thought for a moment then thanked and excused the messenger.

Meanwhile outside in the streets, Raphael had been organizing a group of soldiers to search for Darius and reiterated Mick's description of him. As he watched the team depart, he was shocked to see his brother walking toward him.

Raphael looked curiously at what his brother was carrying and grew horrified. He ran over and saw tears streaming down his brother's sweat-stained cheeks. "Kael, what happened?"

Kael looked at his twin with red-rimmed eyes and shook his head. "I was too late."

"No!" Raphael replied, tending to his distraught brother. He called for them to make way and led Kael into the palace.

Mick had been about to leave when the doors to the throne room were thrown open. The two princes stood behind it, and the blond one lead his black-haired twin into the room.

As they got closer, Mick could see that Prince Kael was carrying the corpse of a blonde woman in his arms. "I was too late," he said to his father. "I had to do my duty, and I was too late."

Hectore's face melted. He stood up and jumped down the three steps toward his son. "Kael, what happened?"

The Prince fell to his knees and laid the girl in his arms down, clearing the hair from her face to give her a kiss.

Mick didn't feel it was right to leave and stood quietly at a solemn distance.

"She was killed," he said in a defeated voice. "Because I left her..." His voice began to waver and he stopped for a short second to steady his breath.

"You never left her son, I sent you away," the HighKing said, assuming the blame to reduce his son's pain.

"I could have been there to save her."

Kael rocked beside the woman for a moment, then he stood up, let out a great cry, and stormed to a nearby pillar, slamming his fist into a marmoreal column. It crumbled beneath the blow as if it was made of sand and Mick marvelled at his strength.

"This is what I get for being a faithful son? The woman I love gets killed and her sister's taken by a killer."

"I'm sorry for your loss, son," Hectore told him. "War is coming."

"I'm sorry, brother," Raphael added. They hugged for a moment and when he pulled away, Kael had regained some of his composure.

"When you love, evil hurts that much more," Hectore said grimly. He put a hand on his son's shoulder. "We'll have a funeral for Luzy tomorrow."

"I promised I'd find her sister, Mirianne," Kael reminded himself.

"You will Kael. Who took her?"

Mick remembered hearing the name spoken once from his Damonai captor, Drelnum. He shivered now as he had back then.

"DeathShadow."

Chapter 24

Pientero stood on a dais with his hands squeezing the rail before him, the cool autumn air snapping at his cloak. He stared forward, with hard eyes furrowed, waiting. Just below him, the still figure of Jassyka was in a simple canoe made of whitewashed wood. Lying on a soft bed of rich blue suede, she was in her best satin dress trimmed with silver. Her hands held each other over her chest. The entire mountain community had gathered and stood in silent formation as they waited for the ceremony to begin. Arlahn had been the one to help Aideen with setting up the display along the riverbank, so he was naturally the first to arrive and stood right before Jassyka at the front of the growing group.

Kael's heart grew heavier as each second passed during the opening moments of the funeral. To the left, his mother hooked her arm through his, embracing it gently. He drew a long breath and looked out at his love. She was so beautiful, even now. It wasn't fair that she was taken from him in such a way. Raphael broke Kael's thoughts as his hand solemnly touched his twin's shoulder for a moment before disappearing.

Kael took one more look at his late love. Annabella and Marlyonna had dressed her exquisitely in a fine silk and covered up the bruises and cuts on her face. The pain and guilt grew until it became too much to bear. He sunk his head. Kael wanted to cry, but there was an implacable hatred petrifying his heart, not allowing the tears to surface. The result was a cold empty stare. Finally, he looked up as his father approached the lectern. He was dressed in a black tunic with a crimson sash, his humble crown resting on his head. He spread his hands before beginning to speak.

"Jassyka came to us when she was a young girl, alone and lost, innocent in her ways. We took her into our homes and she became part of our hearts. Part of my family..." Pientero paused, his knuckles squeezing until they whitened.

He projected his voice to be heard by all, but somehow it carried a softened timbre. "Her tenderness was hidden, but she cared deeply for everyone here. She was spirited and headstrong, stubborn almost." He smiled. "Many of you knew that she was special in her own way. But a lucky few of us got to know just how special she truly was."

Aideen had hooked her arm in the Prince's and she rested her head on his shoulder. He glanced at her and saw she was resisting either a joyous tear of sorrow or a sad tear of happiness as if recalling a cherished memory.

"I miss her already," she whispered softly. Balanor had appeared to Arlahn's right. He didn't say anything but shifted his weight and straightened his posture.

Kael approached the lectern and looked out at the sea of people in attendance before his speech. "Luzy possessed a purity in her that made the world beautiful. Wherever she went, she took the time to appreciate what was around her. She was a kind soul. Many of you recognized her as the kind-hearted woman down by the pools, teaching and sharing stories with you and your children. She would walk among us in the streets, humming the tune in her mind with the love in her heart. That's how she should be remembered. Not as a victim, but as a guide... to love. She treasured this kingdom like it was her family, like she was a born princess. I'd like to take this moment and think back on our relationships with our loved ones."

Arlahn dipped his head and blinked away his tears. The silence endured as he remembered all the great times they'd spent together. The days they'd gone hunting in the woods or swimming in the pool. The nights they stayed up entranced by conversation. He could still remember how she fit into his arms perfectly as they danced. A tear rolled down his cheek and he sniffled.

The large axeman, Jole, was behind Arlahn and touched his shoulder as the Prince wiped his face clean of the salty tear. "It's alright to cry, Prince. We're only human."

Pientero stepped down from his dais onto the white pebbled shore and approached the canoe. Without a word, he placed a single white rose in Jassyka's hands.

Annabella returned from the carved ebony casket to stand between her husband and son. A single, beautiful pink and white anemone lay in Luzy's hands. The queen's eyes were downcast as she took up one hand each from Hectore and Kael and squeezed them tight.

Kael hated himself in that moment. He hated his orders, his father, his whole damned kingdom. His sense of duty had been what pulled him away from her, it had always tugged them apart. But this time, he should have been there with her... Without realizing it, he voiced his thought.

"You still might not have stopped this, son," the king said. "Some things are just out of our control. You never did do anything wrong."

Kael glanced up at the king and saw his father looking back at him with a sympathetic apology in his features. The prince regretted ever thinking Hectore was to blame. He took a deep breath.

His mother released her husband's hand and wiped a tear clear before she cupped Kael's cheek and looked into his icy eyes. "I'm so sorry for you, my love," she told him.

Arlahn thanked Aideen for the kind words. She had supported him through Pientero's eulogy, providing a comforting shoulder to lean against. After the king-in-the-mountain had placed his rose in the canoe with Jassyka, Anvar had been the next to silently follow. Snaking their way through the crowd, each Brother or Sister wordlessly approached the final resting place of Jassyka Grent and left her a blooming, pure white rose.

Arlahn waited until the end, and by the time he reached her, it looked as though she was lying on a bed of roses. He took a moment to admire her once more, with his flower still in hand. He smiled at the freckles on her nose but grew sad at her closed eyes. "Be at peace, Jassyka. I hope my grandfather welcomes you into the Graceland. May your light shine brightest."

After he carefully placed the rose by her heart, Pientero, Anvar, Balanor, Tamis, and Aideen approached.

"We considered her a friend and family, just like you," Balanor told him softly.

"Will you help us carry her to the water?" Aideen asked the Prince. He was honoured.

Kael, Raphael, Hectore, Annabella, Marlyonna, and Zephoroth all carried the casket through the crowd of onlookers in perfect synchrony. The people parted for the solemn group and closed up behind, following them all the way back to the palace grounds. Kael had insisted on burying her in the royal crypts alongside their family, though she wasn't afforded the same rituals as a true Rai Queen.

The crowd stopped at the palace entrance and watched as the casket was carried to the far right where the crypts were accessed through the chapel. Winter's grasp had begun, frosting the stained-glass windows overhead and making puffs of steam out of their warming breaths. Once the pallbearers were out of sight, those gathered slowly dispersed back to their homes.

The group approached the bank. Arlahn and Pientero were the first of the carriers to step foot in the freezing current.

But the Prince didn't pay attention to the biting sensation that he felt when his skin touched the water. He waded out to his knees and took up the canoe from the others behind him, shoving it out gently into the calm stream.

Returning to the bank, Pientero accepted a bow and arrow from Balanus. There was a small fire by the water's edge and the king-in-the-mountain ignited the bolt.

This must be the way, Arlahn told himself. The Brotherhood left no traces of their existence to the outside world.

He watched Pientero steady himself and draw the bow back.

"Wait!" Arlahn called out, stopping the king-in-the-mountain. "I'll do it."

He accepted the bow and a nod from PJ then stood into position. As Arlahn drew it back, suddenly Balanor was behind him, speaking quietly, "There's a slight breeze to the east, can you feel it?"

Arlahn could, though after Balanor spoke, the impression of wind across his skin exaggerated. He took aim and held his position a few heartfelt moments.

"You can do this, Prince," Anvar whispered to himself.

Arlahn let go of the arrow and it flew through the air in a dramatically high arc, coming down at the end of the canoe, between Jassyka's toes, standing almost straight up. The roses were the first to catch. Soon, there was a fire floating down the river.

Behind him, Aideen began to sing a soft, rhythmic tune. Her words were sweet yet filled with a great despair. It was a ballad that had been created by a past Brother. The message passed on and the thought behind each word was beautiful and meaningfully chosen. But the admirable Aideen was singing with such a striking melancholy in her voice that it touched all who were listening in a more palpable sense. Couples took up their lover's hands and shared a kiss. Other people wept or sang along quietly with Aideen, joining their voices and emotions with hers.

Kael sniffled at the end of Marlyonna's song as he watched the casket slowly lower into the ground. "I know that look, son," his father told him. "Retribution can be a dark, lonely path. But I'll do whatever I can do to help you get justice."

"Isn't it the same thing here," Kael argued, still watching the casket.

"Retribution makes sure you kill this DeathShadow. Justice brings back Mirianne, no matter the cost."

Mirianne. He had almost forgotten. His sense of duty returned to him. "I promised I'd bring her back."

"I'm sure you will," Hectore replied.

The casket touched ground and the undertaker approached with two shovels, handing one to an assistant. The king and queen each picked up a handful of dirt and respectfully dropped it on the ebony wood before leaving. Kael squeezed his fistful of dirt before he let it slip out of the bottom of his fingers. He turned to leave but his feet were cemented to the ground. Something was holding him back.

The undertaker was a short, hunchback. The man smiled as politely as he could at the Prince. Approaching the mound of earth next to the hole, the undertaker plunged the spade into it, stepping on the head to drive it deeper.

Kael stopped him and took up the wooden shaft himself. He realized this was something he had to do. He owed her that much. He took up the shovelful of earth and placed it on the casket.

From out of nowhere, as if he'd been watching the entire time, Raphael came and relieved the other undertaker, taking his shovel. The two exchanged a look and Kael gave his brother a nod of approval. Raphael buried his spade and added a shovelful of his own to the hole.

For a few moments they worked in silence, all the while Raphael simultaneously dug through his mind for something to say. Finally, he opened his mouth. "I wonder how Arlahn's doing?"

Continuing his labour, Kael grimly replied, "Better than me, I hope."

*****

"Gods man, that must have hurt!" Jole roared after hearing Anvar's story of how he lost his hand. "And Raphael just cut it off?!"

"It was the only way we'd get out," Anvar told him. "That was right after you left us, could have used your magic."

Arlahn knew the Raphael from the story was his brother's namesake, an Essellian friend of his father.

He listened to them as he ate his breakfast, with Tamis and Aideen talking at his side. They were discussing their garden when Arlahn voiced a thought more to himself than anyone around him. "I think I'm ready to go home."

Everyone within the mess hall fell silent. As if his words had cut through all the ruckus and conversations that had been taking place. Eyes lingered on him for a moment, before quieter exchanges resumed. Tamis and Aideen turned to him, "You've grown so much since first coming here" his Sister told him. "Jassyka would have been proud to call you Brother."

Words that were meant to comfort stabbed an icicle into the prince's chest. He tried to smile for reassurance, but the look faded into contemplation quickly before he pushed himself up from the table. "I think I'll go pack."

Aideen recognized his anguish, she reached her hand across the table and offered it to him. The prince accepted her hand and looked her in the eye. "You'll always have a place here with us."

Returning to his cabin, he began packing his belongings for the journey home. He missed his family and felt it was finally time to go back to them.

Jole and Anvar found Arlahn outside his cabin with a travel pack over his shoulder. The one-handed man stopped, "I heard you were heading out, Prince."

"I was just about to find you."

Arlahn hugged Anvar goodbye and thanked him for everything he'd learned.

"Make sure you find the king before you leave. I'm sure he'll have something to tell you."

The Prince began walking through the white mountain town when Balanor and his twin approached. "I guess the rumor's true. You're going back home then?"

Arlahn nodded. With their mutual feelings for Jassyka surfacing in her final days, he had begun to feel as though the black-haired Brother understood him more. Respect had blossomed between them. Despite Balanor's persistent grudge against his brothers, he seemed to have reconciled with Arlahn.

"Safe travels, Brother," he added.

Balanus, who stood beside his twin, nodded, "Send your brothers our regards. We're all family here." And the two walked off together.

When Arlahn found Pientero, he was in his cabin pouring a cup of honey-mead. "You're leaving."

From his tone, Arlahn wasn't sure whether it was an order or a question until he added, "It's time." An observation.

Pientero took a sip from his cup and sat down at the table, the same way he had the first night they met. But this time, rather than suggest Arlahn sit in the corner, he offered him the seat opposite.

Arlahn accepted a proffered cup and swirled it around a bit before he took a sip.

"There's something on your mind," the king-in-the-mountain said in a tone that beckoned explanation.

"That first night, on my Walkabout, I met something in the forest."

PJ furrowed his brow and remained silent for a moment. "Tell me."

"It was something I've never seen or heard of before." The image of the monster flashed before Arlahn's eyes as he described it, visibly emitting its dark intentions. He recounted the wolf being eaten by the handful. A shiver crept up his spine when he spoke of the whispered scream before the thing rushed at him. The way it exploded into steam. All the while, PJ listened with focused scrutiny, his face as hard as granite.

After the Prince finished his story, Pientero stared at him for a second longer then downed the rest of his cup. He slammed it as gently as possible, like having to move a Battleground piece into a position which meant your defeat. He refilled his cup.

"You know what this is?" Arlahn asked but could already see that he did.

"There was a prisoner during the war. Even the Damonai thought he was a madman. He warned us there were monsters."

"And what did you do?"

"All we did was tell him we were the monsters."

"You never saw one, during the war?" Arlahn asked.

"That was the only time I remember hearing about them, but he was from as far east as you can go. And like I said, so mad even the Damonai wanted to be separated from him."

"But he was right, these things do exist!" Arlahn argued. "You fought the wrong war. It was the wrong enemy."

At that, PJ eyes grew enraged. "Fought the wrong fucking war?! The wrong enemy?! Tumbero wanted to sacrifice your father, thinking he could become some kind of God. Without fighting that war, you and your brothers wouldn't have been born. You should be grateful every day for the men and women who literally gave their lives for *you*. Your Brothers and Sisters, may their light shine brightest."

Arlahn looked away, trying to hide his shame.

PJ sighed. "We chose to fight the evil we knew, the one right in front of us. We weren't concerned about something that might happen someday."

There was a long silence between the two as they both contemplated that.

"The Damonai are coming back," PJ stated grimly.

Arlahn was too afraid to voice his thoughts, but if the Damonai were human, then they were harmless compared to the thing he'd met on his Walkabout. Maybe this time, we'll fight the right war, he thought.

"You should return home. Your family will need you. I'll have Anvar make up a pony. Do you know your way out?"

When Arlahn confirmed that he understood the treacherous mountain passes, the king-in-the-mountain graced him with a smile and a nod. "Getting lost along the paths with Jole helped you find your way through."

The Prince smiled "It's just like me to take a little longer to find my way."

"I'm glad you understand that finally, Arlahn. We all eventually learn to talk and walk and spit and shit by ourselves. We grow at our own pace, like a tree. And when we walk through the forests, we marvel more at the sheer size of great trees rather than appreciate how long it took them to grow so big. We also never think about the constant war that tree is waging, battling for moisture, sunlight, and fertile soil."

"Because it's strong roots that are most important," Arlahn concluded.

"You've grown into our hearts. And it's a hard thing to plant roots in stone. When I was about your age, I was the chieftain of a village. The Damonai came and slaughtered us..." PJ paused and took a drink. "We were farmers, lumberjacks. Didn't stand a chance. Then their GodKing walked among my people and they began murdering each other. Brothers killed one another and wives stabbed their husbands in the back while they were defending them. It was chaos, anarchy. My own children dragged me down onto a cross and pounded stakes through my hands." He thumbed his palm before snatching up his cup and taking another gulp. "After that, my best friends hauled me up in the town square where they and my family all killed themselves."

Arlahn stared at the king-in-the-mountain, speechless, understanding why he never spoke of his past.

"My roots had been torn out. My heart had become stone." As Pientero stood up, Arlahn followed, and they began to slowly make their way to the door.

"When you came here, I saw an imitation of your brothers and father. You were a reflection of the influences in your life. But when we said goodbye to Jassyka, Arlahn Rai stood in his own right. Once you stop caring about what others think, you realize it's never too late to start anything, do anything. Age is just a number. It's passion and willpower that keep us growing like the tree. You've found yourself in this place, now don't be afraid to walk your path."

*****

Darius found Mick walking through the crowded streets of Pellence alone and snuck up on him from behind. Tapping his right shoulder, the thief quickly leapt to the left and waited for him to crane his neck to see who was there. When Mick did, Darius held out a fist and walked in pace with the man. The justicar turned back, swinging his chin into Darius' knuckles and essentially punching himself in the face.

"Sonuva..." he gasped, both surprised and angered to see the thief. "Where have you been?"

"I was visiting my favourite TGIF, when some guards said they wanted to speak with me. I've been avoiding them ever since," Darius told him.

"T-G-I-F?"

"You know, tavern girl I'd fuck."

Mick nodded his head in comprehension. "I should've figured that you're not a one-woman man."

"Pfft, please," Darius said, insulted.

He led Mick round a corner and suddenly they were walking through a set of double doors. When he pushed them open, he turned to Mick and walked backwards alongside him. The room inside was full of half-dressed women, lounging on cushioned benches. Some were smoking shishas, others worked on clientele. The incense was visible floating through the air, seasoning it with the sweet smell of cinnamon.

"Why would I settle for one cow and the same set of teats..." the enigmatic thief said, raising his hands in display of the atmosphere around him, "... when I can go to the market and try a new pair every day."

He grinned widely and turned to the women, choosing a beautiful redhead with a thin piece of fabric hiding her lower half. Darius approached her, flashing his devilish grin, but she slapped him and began to refuse him angrily. When he produced Halder's stolen money pouch, however, she snatched it from his hands and lingered. They exchanged a few words before the woman smiled, took up his hand, and led him toward a backroom. As he was walking away, Darius glanced back with wide eyes and a childish expression of surprise, mouthing his intentions. Mick chuckled and shook his head.

He went to the tavern bar and ordered ale. It wasn't long before a woman approached him. She had just introduced herself as Trick when a small cohort of guards entered the room, their clinking armour and heavy boots stealing everyone's attention. Mick turned and recognized one of the men from the palace; Zeth, Prince Raphael had called him in passing. Zeth glanced around the room, scanning the faces of the patrons. He and Mick shared a look and the justicar knew he had been remembered.

Zeth walked up to Mick and removed his helmet. His black hair fell free, curling around his ears. "You're the Essellian from the palace."

Mick hesitated for a heartbeat. "I am."

"You came here with someone else. A man named Darius. Where is he?"

"What's this about?" Mick asked, suspicious that the thief had already indulged in his other pleasure.

"Our prince wishes to speak with him."

"He's in the back," the woman behind the counter said as she wiped a glass clean with her rag. "He comes in every time he's in town that one. Likes Rosy, he's with her now."

Mick followed the group into the back. The guards opened the door, but two sentries denied him access to the room. From the doorway, he stood quietly and watched.

Darius was scurrying to get his clothes back together. "What's this about now?"

"I've been looking for you…" Zeth was anxious to catch the thief. He'd been searching for the man for two days.

Darius leapt forward, using his Gift to jump through the incoming guard. Zeth was at once shocked and confused. He looked down into his chest, then turned around just in time to see Darius' fist coming for his face.

The thief landed the quick blow and instantly threw himself toward the nearest wall.

Zeth roared in anger and chased after him. Darius ran through the wall as if it was a phantasmal mirage and the guard crashed into the solid stone right behind him. Pushing himself off, he whirled to Mick in the doorway, demanding, "How did he do that? What is he, Gifted?"

Mick told him that must be the case and Zeth cursed, "What are the chances?" under his breath.

He ordered guards to check the neighbouring rooms, but the thief had escaped.

Mick left with the soldiers and watched them take to the streets and alleyways with renewed purpose and tactics. With his involvement over, he limped on his bad leg into a different, more respectable tavern and ordered another ale. He'd just taken his first sip when he heard a loud shriek from another room. A woman came rushing out. "There's a man in our latrine!" she told the owner.

Mick watched the door and sure enough, he saw Darius rush out in a similar fashion. The thief spotted Mick and dashed to the stool at his side. "That was such a better idea in my head."

The justicar began to laugh.

"It's not funny. I've seen things now, Mick... Nasty, unforgettable things..." he said with the disgust of just being shat on.

Mick was about to take a drink but stopped to smile. "That's what you get."

"What?" Darius retorted.

"You just punched a guard, Darius."

"Eh! I was taught that if you know a fight's about to start, you might as well hit first. Get a good punch in."

His companion was sipping his ale and almost spat it back into his cup before playfully asking, "And running away after? Where'd you learn that?"

"Always with the semantics."

"What were the guards after you for?" Mick questioned, wondering if he should arrest the man right there, knowing how stressful he could be to catch. But he didn't want to betray his new friendship so obviously. Maybe the Prince just wants to hear his account of their story, he wondered. "What'd you do now?"

"I haven't ever stuck around to find out. Because of you, I don't like authorities much."

An idea popped into Mick's head and he ordered a second round. This time, he bought Darius a celebratory drink and toasted. "To your newfound freedom then."

The mugs clinked together and Darius lifted his to his mouth, taking huge gulps. He looked over at Mick who was about to put down his drink and gave him a wink. He chugged and chugged until the entire ale was gone. When Darius finished, he let out a great belch and hooted. Swinging his arm up in a circle, he ordered, "Another one here!"

Mick smiled, toasting the man again once he had his drink and then took a sip. Once more, the thief drank deeply, downing half of his mug before he slammed it down with a sigh of pleasure.

They spoke for a while longer, and Mick found reason to toast this or that, and the thirsty thief happily clinked his mug each time.

Once they were beyond their drinks, Mick began asking Darius about the nature of his Gift. Darius was so drunk that he confessed he'd made a mistake, that it was foolish to drink as much as he had when he was being pursued. Alcohol weakened his ability to maintain his secret power. Mick told the thief that he was considering staying in Pellence for a little visit, with the threat of war it suddenly seemed dutiful to be alongside the Rais.

When he expressed this, Darius hiccupped and chuckled, asking, "Why would you want to do something stupid like that?"

"So when I'm old, like my father, I'll look back and be proud of what I've done."

"That's assuming you get old in the first place," Darius responded quickly before taking another drink.

Mick stood and told his companion that he'd be alright. "I think I'll get a bed here for the night."

"Okay grandpa, I'll see you tomorrow then, I'm going to find an adventure!"

*****

Hectore leaned back in his chair and took another puff from his pipe. He was contemplating all the information he'd received from the Essellian justicar, Mick. The man's story had gripped the king's attention. Never in his life had the prophetic Harbinger been wrong. If he claimed the mountain would be found, it would be. But that didn't mean the strategic land was lost. The mountain would hold; mountains were immovable, their narrow paths a maze to any foreigner walking them. The Brotherhood were unmatched in their training and tactics. Hectore thought about the second half of the messenger's statement. "One of your sons will not survive." A voice in his head denied this, he had defied both life and death before. Who's to say he couldn't defy the small prophet's words.

Kael entered the study then, dressed as if he were ready to ride out in search of his woman's killer. He had his hand on his sword's hilt as he approached his father. "I'm going to hunt down this DeathShadow."

"We will, but we have to prioritize, Kael," Hectore started. He went on to explain the importance behind Mick's message and reminded his son of the strength of the Brotherhood and the depths of the Damonai's deception. "They knew things they shouldn't have Kael. How could they find PJ after all these years? How did DeathShadow know you and Raph were building machines?"

"I don't care about any of that," Kael said finally. "Mirianne and DeathShadow are all I want."

"He's most likely part of this Council of Deaders, Kael. Normal men don't carry titles like DeathShadow..."

Before he could finish, the door opened once more, and this time his golden-haired son came in.

Raphael nodded to his father quickly then turned on Kael. "I heard you want to leave again?"

"The longer we wait the further he gets."

"Well, there's no stopping you. I can see it in your eyes. But before you go, there's one thing I want to tell you."

Kael sensed eagerness behind his brother's earnest words. "What is it?"

Raphael looked his brother in the eyes and announced, "Come back so you can be an uncle. Marly's pregnant."

Kael stood for a moment, statuesque. His sigh eventually broke the stillness and a tiny smirk touched the corner of his mouth. "That's great. When did you find out?"

"She told me after I showed father our machines. It still doesn't feel right telling you with what happened to Luzy. I just wanted you to know before we leave."

"You're not going to the Brotherhood, Raphael," Hectore cut in, standing up. "I won't let you leave with Marlyonna the way she is. You'll never understand what it means to be a true King until you hold your own baby."

The HighKing's paternal influence and sound words were convincing. Even more so when Hectore informed Raphael of the meeting he'd summoned with his Wardens and told his son he'd need to act in his stead. When Raphael asked his father where he was planning on going, he said, "With Kael."

The two black-haired warriors exchanged a look. Father and son. King and Prince. "I'll go with you to find this DeathShadow. But first we ride for Pientero."

"Why?" Kael argued.

"The Brotherhood is invaluable, son. We need them to survive," Hectore told him. "And because we don't know where DeathShadow is, but we do know the Damonai are coming for the mountain. For your brother."

Outside, Kael found Zeth standing in the centre of a busy plaza, spinning around in circles and aggressively scanning the faces of passersby. The Prince approached him and feigned sarcastic concern. "Zeth, why are you spinning around like that?"

The guard threw his hands up and shook his head. "I'm trying to find a scoundrel for your brother. But get this, he walks through walls. How in bloody hell do ye catch someone like that?"

Zeth unstopped his canteen and took a drink. "Bregan said he'd take over when I leave with you. It's a good thing too. I don't have the patience for this."

"Go prepare your things then. My father's sending birds out along the way. We're gathering a force of two hundred, a dozen or two from each garrison. We'll be riding long and hard for a few days straight, are you alright with that?"

"Of course, my prince. I'll go tell Bregan it's his turn to find the ghost."

Chapter 25

A group of fifty men rode out from Pellence, straight for the Brotherhood, only stopping every eight hours at a new garrison. Some were standalone outposts and others were skirted by villages. As per the king's orders, they quickly ate a prepared meal, traded their horses for fresh ones, and were joined by a new batch of two dozen recruits from the local area.

From time to time, when the horses were slowed to canter for a break, Hectore would hear men speaking amongst themselves about the whereabouts of the mountainous stronghold. A few claimed to have visited them, but they were quickly rebuked by some of the more veteran soldiers who remembered the Poet of Battle.

"There's no way you'd be here to tell the tale," Halder argued.

Hectore smiled at their argument, knowing his family were the only ones permitted to leave the mountain; though the Brotherhood ran deep within their blood, always a part of them.

He pushed his men hard and his horses harder. Arriving at the tall oaks garrison in the evening light, he handed off his mount to a stable-boy before accepting a drink. Others came filing in behind him, handing off their horses and then helping with further preparations.

With men all around them, Hectore, Kael, Zeth, and Halder, ate bowls of stew and discussed tactics for their journey onward.

"I've sent my bird out to scout the area. She told me that she's seen several camps, big and small. Some are mobile, others linger as if awaiting commands. We should tread lightly."

Kael volunteered to scout alongside Halder after they agreed they needed a clear, undetectable path.

Once they had finished dinner, they looked outside at the fading light and decided travelling by night was worth the risk.

After a few hours in the saddle, they grew accustomed to the darkened terrain surrounding them.

Kael and Halder remained out of sight, scouting ahead of the group. The Prince paid close attention to the scout and kept to his instructions as they passed through the forest. Shraknah, his pantuur, sniffed out a pair of men sleeping a few feet apart without a fire.

They were dressed in dark tattered clothes that reminded Kael of the bandits he'd come across months ago. Halder gave them a quick look and knew instantly. He confirmed to the Prince in a low whisper, "Damonai."

They approached surreptitiously, and one of the men awoke to the pantuur's drool dripping on his face. A moment of terror overtook him as he jerked away quickly, but the beast took it as a defensive move and snapped at the man's neck. Mauling out veins and arteries, blood soaked the man's coarse beard as the pantuur violently hitched its head back and forth.

The second man stirred awake and Kael was on him instantly. "Don't be stupid," he said.

Shraknah came toward the man, growling a low, malicious snarl, baring teeth that gleamed in the moonlight from their moisture. Its gait was smooth, keeping close to the ground as if it was ready to pounce in a moment's notice. Halder halted his beast a body-length away from the man and it ceased growling, though still showed its daunting teeth behind a twitching, wrinkled snout.

The man stayed silent and looked at the Prince with hard eyes. Shraknah inched closer. Before the pantuur could attack, Kael bound the man's wrist and wrenched up him. "We're going to have a talk."

"We should wait for Hectore," Halder advised.

"He'll catch up. Go wait for him," Kael commanded the old scout before fixing their prisoner with an estranged look.

Halder hesitated for a moment but finally obeyed and directed Shraknah away.

Once they were alone, the Damonai whispered something in his native tongue that Kael ignored. He drew out a cloth and stuffed it into the man's mouth. "I saw what your man did to my wife's parents."

Although they had never officially married, Kael knew... Her burning home flashed before his eyes. "What he did to *her*..."

He took up the prisoner's fist and stared him in the eye as he squeezed with the *kjut'tsir*, crumpling fingers and palm like his hand was a pack of dried leaves. The man began to scream a muffled sound.

"I'm not going to kill you though. Not yet."

He took the prisoner's fist and yanked it backward until it popped and knuckles touched the back of his wrist.

The man squealed again under Kael's strength and fell down to his knees. He squeezed his eyes together and dipped his head in pain. Kael released his clutch and drew the man up once more.

"I'm looking for a man named DeathShadow."

At mention of him, the Damonai looked up into the Prince's eyes and mumbled something underneath his gag.

Kael knew he had struck a chord. "You know who that is."

He pulled the cloth from the man's lips and raised his other fist, "Tell me what you know."

Quiet hooves echoed through the night as the king, Halder and Zeth rode in next to Kael and the prisoner. Hectore climbed down from his saddle and took off his leather gloves. He and Kael exchanged a look, then he glanced at the man's mangled hand.

Hectore walked up, his woolen cloak swinging gently to the rhythm of his stride and looked the Damonai in the eye. "He asked you a question."

"*Shu'jis'stu grendakah sara Moredacasana,*" the man sputtered. *Suicide looking for DeathShadow*

There was a moment of silence among the Sainti. Kael didn't know the guttural language and looked to his companions for confirmation. Halder pinched his lips together and Zeth, who was close in age with the prince, was just as confused. When Kael looked at his father though, the king was eyeing the prisoner.

"*Moredacasana ku nami i menka.*" The king's voice resonated with a power that could capture nations. "*Giu quoi... quoi're i sparrique.*"

DeathShadow is only a man. But I... I'm a demon.

"*Sparriquecoitra?*" *Demonblades?*

Hectore continued to stare coldly into the man's eyes until he understood, until he grasped this was the being who had conquered millions and dominated his way through Damonai ranks straight toward the GodKing Tumbero himself. He was something unearthly, filling all of space and all of time in that moment. Something from a childhood nightmare made real. The king knew this and used it to prey on the weakened Damonai scout.

Kael drew his father away from the prisoner for a moment to ask what they should do to him next. He wanted the man dead, along with every other Damonai that got between him and DeathShadow. But nothing was wasted on Hectore, he saw past the man's death, saw his value in life, even if it was only so that they could learn his language. Hectore had just convinced his son when they turned to face their prisoner and the Damonai sputtered, "*Bi que're as sparrique, quoi're deghata moreda.*" *If you're the demon, I'm already dead.*

Before any of them could react, the man snatched a dagger from his belt and dragged it across his own throat. Blood ran out like an overflowing bucket. For a brief a moment, he stood like that, staring at Demonblades, before he dropped, lifeless, to the ground.

"So much for keeping him alive."

*****

The first day of his journey had been spent walking out of the mountain. The footpaths Pientero had arranged were tantamount to a maze, and even though Arlahn had learned some of the avenues, he also knew there were dead-ends and traps along faulty paths. With Jole's story about getting lost fresh in his mind, the Prince kept religiously to Pientero's directions. "Twice right, twice left, twice right again and once left."

The pony he had been given was surefooted and sturdy, its endurance surprisingly strong and the Prince rode eastward toward Pellence all day.

Night rolled in early and brought with it a chill that portended the fast-approaching winter. The fading light forced Arlahn to halt. A short way off the beaten road, he found a small rocky drop that acted as a sort of retaining wall and decided it would be a good location for his camp.

Tethering his pony, he removed its cargo then went about building a small fire close enough to the rock to shield its flames from the road. Once he was content, Arlahn sat back against the wall and set his pack beside him.

He reached in and produced a carrot that he offered as a treat to his steed. The tethered animal gobbled it greedily while the Prince padded its flanks. When he sat down again, Arlahn went back into his pack and found some dried meat for himself.

He was gnawing on his food when an icy breeze blew through the makeshift camp. Arlahn drew his cloak about him tighter and looked at the fire for a moment.

It was too cold, he would need more wood. He stood up and, out of old habit, strung his ritual dagger around his waist. The ornate pearl blade sat in its sheath, nestled away behind the small of his back. It had never lost its edge, nor had Arlahn ever managed to scratch it.

In the last of the dying light, he looked behind him toward the Spine. The mountainous bulwark stretched as far as he could see in either direction. There were distant clouds hiding the Skyrim Tower and Arlahn wondered which colour shone at its top. Orange, or maybe brown. Was he in the Hunter's Moon or the Beaver's Moon? In the mountain village, he'd lost sight of the moon most nights. Time there seemed to blend each day into a blur.

Climbing the Spine seemed so long ago.

Arlahn walked into the forest and gathered firewood as he reminisced about his time there. All of the things Anvar, Aideen, and Tamis had taught him about trapping and shelters and gardening, his endless confrontations with Balanor, his condemned relationship with Jassyka. The Walkabout.

Even though he stood there alone now, just looking toward the Brotherhood filled him with a sense of familial communion. They were an entirely new family, who had taught him to become an entirely new man.

The wind died suddenly, prompting the Prince to be satisfied with his armful of wood. He was on his way back to camp when the tranquility of the forest broke.

He heard a quick squeal, a fierce growl, and then a whine that was abruptly shortened into silence.

Approaching his camp, Arlahn rounded a tree cautiously. The first thing he saw in the orange glow of the fire's light was his pony, down on the ground with wide, frightful eyes staring at him. Its neck had been torn out and blood was spattered on the ground.

Looming over the animal, stood a huge medak bear. Its black fur was thick and oily and seemed to somehow only reflect the red of the flames. It noticed Arlahn standing still, petrified by an almighty fear, and let out a low growl, bearing its chipped teeth. Taking this stance as defiance, the beast reared up to its full height. It must have been close to eleven feet tall and wider than two men standing abreast, claws and fangs bloody and razor sharp.

The anticipation in the air between them became almost palpable. Finally, the beast bellowed a vicious roar and spittle jumped from both its cheeks as they flapped under frightening force.

Before he knew it, Arlahn was already throwing the faggot in his arms toward the bear. The beast roared again, lowering itself on all fours, but the Prince swooped in a large, quick step and kicked what he could of the fire up into the bear's face.

The medak pounded one massive paw toward him and Arlahn bolted in the opposite direction.

Hearing a growl behind, he didn't take the time to look back. Instead, Arlahn ran for his life, doing his best with his limited visibility to keep from falling. He kept to wide gaps between trees to minimize the risks. A few times, his eyes adjusted themselves just in time to notice roots and rocks that would have tripped him or broken his toe.

Winded, and with his vision mostly adjusted, Arlahn heard a grunt from behind and risked a glance back.

Closing in right behind him was the beast's massive head, determined eyes staring at him above snarling teeth.

Arlahn swallowed a lump and redoubled his effort, suddenly thankful for his late-night runs with the Brotherhood. Sweat ran down his forehead and soaked his hair. The air couldn't rush into his lungs fast enough as his legs began to burn, manoeuvring through the forest's obstacles until his mouth was dry. He gradually began to slow down until he heard the medak catching up behind him once more. Arlahn peeked back and saw the beast was preparing to bear down on him so he threw himself under a felled pine and heard the old wood above him crack and strain against the bear's paw.

He rolled up onto his feet and took off again, but the medak clambered over the tree and continued its pursuit. Another shot of adrenaline surged through the Prince's muscles, dulling their pain. Pushing his legs to their capacity, pumping his arms as fast as he could, Arlahn ducked and swerved past trees until he came to a wall of cedars. Spotting a trunk split into a giant V, he veered toward it. He leapt and turned his body sideways in mid-air to slip through the gap in the foliage. Branches scraped at his face and shoulder as they rushed by, and he was almost past the brush when the medak's paw followed in a great pounding motion.

Arlahn opened his eyes to check behind and saw the paw spread out as it came for him. Ripping down, the middle claw caught his shoulder and tore a thin gash that came just short of mangling his entire right side.

He thundered into the ground and rolled as quickly as he could back onto his feet. Arlahn flexed his right arm and grabbed the wound for a second, but he heard another roar and looked back to see the bear trampling through the same gap in the trees.

The Prince turned to continue his flight but the world came crashing into him. Tripped by a root, he looked down at his feet to see the medak break through the last of the cedar wall beyond them.

The bear rumbled over to the Prince, who had begun scurrying backward on all fours. Arlahn slowly reached for the dagger at the small of his back when the beast rose again on its hind legs and let out another skin-chilling roar.

His finger touched the hilt of the dagger as something came from the blackness, thundering into the bear's side, dragging it down to the ground. The medak quickly regained itself and swung toward the Prince's saviour.

Due to the bear's girth, Arlahn couldn't see what had saved him until the two began to circle one another.

A great kahki wolf was lowered to the earth, snarling and staring up at the giant bear. The wolf's fur resembled a thick smoke floating in the night, much different from the kahkis that he'd met in the mountain. It was muscular and lithe, quick and aggressive, but still outmatched against the medak. That didn't affect the primitive state of the wolf, however; growling a low, vicious sound, it continued its confrontation.

The bear closed in and with lightning speed the kahki snapped its jaws, nicking the bear's cheek before it leapt back toward the Prince to avoid the fatal retaliation swat. The wolf played to its strength of being much more agile. It maintained a safe distance around the medak, consciously aware of the risk of death. Each time the bear got close enough, the wolf would pounce, either to safety or in for an attack, snapping at fur with powerful teeth or swatting with its own razor-sharp claws.

Thrice more, the bear came at the wolf. The first time, the kahki stood on its hind legs and batted the bear's neck and face. The second saw the wolf retreat, but on the third it bit at the medak's front leg, clamping down hard. Jaws clenched and locked and the wolf was pulled back with the bear's reaction.

The beast pressed down on the kahki and the two became entangled. Eventually, the wolf clambered onto its hind legs, mounted the bear, and bit again, at the side of its neck this time. The bear whirled and stood up, throwing its attacker off. It swooped back down, looking to slam a paw into the wolf's side, but the kahki rolled clear just in time.

Arlahn had barely had a moment to react with the commotion and intensity of the fight. But now he drew his dagger and rushed in, burying the blade a few inches before the bear threw him off with a backhand. The weight and sheer force behind the blow sent him tumbling several feet.

The medak whirled around toward the Prince for a second before the kahki had leapt back on top of it. But the bear somehow shrugged the wolf off and pounced on it. Sharp teeth bit and ripped at the wolf's neck but its thick fur protected it long enough for it to begin scratching the beast's belly with its hind legs, as if it were running on its back.

For a moment the two remained like that, exchanging blows, teeth crashing against teeth, blood soaking deeper into fur with each bite and scratch.

The Prince leapt to the kahki's salvation but the medak noticed his approach and, wary of his blade, backed off. The wolf hobbled clear and stumbled away, as the bear turned back to the Prince. Standing on all fours, blood dripping from the wounds in its flanks, it challenged him once more. Arlahn flipped the dagger in his hand and goaded the beast fiercely.

For reasons he couldn't explain, Arlahn couldn't relinquish this fight. Finally, after an eternity, that was only a few seconds in reality, the bear conceded, dropping its head, and walking off into the dark of night.

Arlahn stood there a moment, breathing heavily, trying to calm his heart that felt like drums having a parade in his chest.

Replacing his dagger, he returned to where he'd last seen the kahki. There was a small pool of blood in its place and the Prince found a trail leading into the woods. He knew some animals walked off to die alone and sensed the worst was coming.

Following the trail, he found the wounded wolf collapsed on a bed of moss, its frail breathing was ragged and intermittent.

He sat down beside the kahki and padded its neck softly. At his touch, the wolf raised its head in alarm then eased it down onto the Prince's lap. "Thank you for saving me."

Arlahn despaired at the blood staining his hand as he continued petting the wolf in long, soothing strokes. Red tainted the beautiful smoky-white fur. Finally, its breathing stopped.

"Be at peace," Arlahn said with a tone of soft finality. He dipped his head in solemn appreciation and gently placed the wolf's own heavy head on the ground.

Chapter 26

Skinny, cold fingers stretched out over his head. He felt oversized joints and blue veins bulging against skin. Behind him, Evris' gaunt frame swayed back and forth like a tree canopy in a lazy breeze. Awareness was a fickle thing with Evris' Power, if his subject was aware, he could find the desired memory at will. But when things happened in a subconscious state, more exploration was often required.

No information was lost on Evris, however. Over the years, he'd found almost any bit of intelligence could be useful. The young man before him had been an apprentice blacksmith. He'd never known his father, though his red-haired mother often spoke of his bravery. Eventually, Evris came across what he was looking for. Proof of his Power. Hidden away like a suppressed memory. Caught somewhere between dreaming and sleepwalking.

He walked through bare Pellencian streets. Nighttime songs could be heard from the nearby tavern, but all else was quiet. He entered the shop. His apron was hanging next to the door beside another. Swooping it on, he lit the furnace.

For the next few hours, he slaved over the hot furnace. Heating, pouring, pounding, quenching. He worked throughout the night, making moulds for the Prince's war machines. There was one key component missing from all his toil, however. No matter how close he got to the glowing molten, he couldn't feel its heat. This actually proved quite useful, affording him a new level of precision, allowing him to shape the metal as if it was wet sand. When he was finished, he made sure to replace all the tools back in their respective places. *Master Jonnimack hates when things aren't organized*, he told himself. Only after he was done did he realize that he didn't need to stop for food or even a break.

Outside the tent, Mordo approached the camp.

His prisoner had done little more than whine and hoof with the bounce of her horse. He had kept her bound at the wrists, and she carefully heeded his warnings against escape. After what he'd done to her family, where would she escape to?

Leading her into camp, he took notice of the looks she fetched from the soldiers. There were camp followers from their native land, but he knew his prize was exotic to them and striking at that.

Mordo climbed off his horse and handed the reins to a nearby soldier. "If anything happens to her. You die."

He made his way for the central pavilion where the Caliph stayed since she had rejoined with the Damonai forces.

As he approached, he saw the man named Tracker throw the tent flap closed and storm away toward him.

"You found the one I sent you for then?" Mordo demanded as he was about to pass.

Tracker stopped, his face was worn for a man his age, like old leather, the creases outlined by the fire's orange glow.

"I found him, yeah. He's with your Caliph and another."

"Good."

After a drawn-out moment, Tracker's brown eyes squinted. "I can't believe there's actually a heart beating in your chest. How do you sleep knowing what you do to families? My family?"

Mordo looked at him as if he'd been threatened.

"Your family's still alive, Tracker. Be grateful. I don't leave witnesses."

So long as Tracker remained compliant, the Caliph would entertain him with visits to his wife, daughter, and grandson.

"I would hunt you to the ends of the—"

"You can't hunt a shadow, Tracker," Mordo cut him off before walking away.

He pushed aside the tent flap and saw that Caliph Hennah was sitting at a table with an orb before her. Resting on an ornate stand of bone, the sphere glowered like smouldering coals, at once waning and waxing its lights.

With just the fingertips of her left hand pressed on the side of the orb, she spoke into it. "'E's wid'im now."

As if in response, the orb brightened and pulsated. Hennah held her eyes closed. "Andden?" Another answer pulsed in the light and she nodded.

Pulling her fingertips from the ball, its colours suddenly died, leaving what looked like a block of granite. The Caliph opened her eyes and acknowledged Mordo for the first time.

He questioned the nature of the conversation he'd overheard. All his life, he'd known the Caliph as the head of their order. He'd never seen or heard of anyone answering to someone different. It sounded as if she was taking orders, but who ordered the Caliph? Before Mordo could ask, she dismissed the orb and resumed the posture of a true matriarch. He didn't know why, but this eased his tension.

"Tracker hass return'd."

Mordo mentioned his encounter with him outside and nodded to another room in the pavilion. "Is he in there?"

"Wid Evris, yes."

Mordo knew the Caliph's pavilion was seasoned with magic. Ward piled atop of ward, each room was *"naturally"* soundproofed by the myriad of spells she had cast.

The Caliph stood. She still wore the simple clothes of a Sainti healer, her grey hair strewn about like a bird's nest. "'E's making shur de boy is de one."

"I thought he saw whatever memory he wanted."

"'Es Power eez like shoppin' Shadow. Most times you go to de market, you know what ya buyin'. But every now and den, you need to take ya time an' look around."

Just then, as if on queue, Evris emerged from the other room.

"He's the one, Caliph," he was saying as he entered. Finding DeathShadow in the room silenced him. He gave a curt nod. "Mordo."

"Evris." Mordo smiled, knowing what he stirred within the old leader.

"So 'e can show us de way?" Caliph Hennah asked paying no mind to their awkward encounter.

Shooting Mordo a sideways look, Evris hesitated before he answered. "There's a bit of a problem."

"Whadis it?"

Evris explained his experience under the *suuluuk*, how Billiem's Power made his memories much more difficult to intrude on than the others. That his memories of these times seemed to occur between states of consciousness.

"Dat eez because id-eez not hizz body dat eez walking, Evris, id-eez hiss sspirit."

Approaching the room, Hennah pulled aside the carpet door and looked at the prisoner. His head hung as if he slept, red curls falling to hide his face.

As he noticed the light flooding in, Billiem looked up. Hennah stood in the doorway with Evris behind her and Mordo behind him.

DeathShadow looked at the young man and couldn't believe what he saw. Two different eyes. One brown, the other green. Just like his father. Mordo boiled with rage as he remembered the boy that burned his own father. The boy with two different eyes.

"You!" he shouted.

By the time Evris and Hennah looked back for him, Mordo was hidden beneath the *nsuli*.

"Mordo, stop!" the Caliph ordered in a screech.

He reappeared with a knife at the man's throat. Billiem's eyes grew as he felt the blade bite into his skin.

"He can't die, DeathShadow," Hennah told him.

Obeying like a faithful hound, Mordo let go, leaving the red-haired man terrified.

Pacing backward, staring at him wildly all the while, Mordo retreated out of the room and Hennah let the carpet fall closed again.

"Wi need 'im for what's next," she told him as he returned to her side.

"Whenever he becomes useless, I'm going to kill him," DeathShadow promised.

"And you can. But not before."

Mordo was about to storm out of the tent when a messenger entered. "Pardon Caliph, but there's someone outside to see you. He has a message from Pellence, he says."

"Send 'im in."

Mordo veiled himself behind his *nsuli* once again, and Evris shook his head is disapproval. A pretty, brown-haired man came into the tent. He stood shyly for a moment until the messenger pushed him forward. "Go on then... He has a letter for the leader of the camp."

Hennah held out her hand to the man and he gave it to her.

"How did yew find uss?" she scolded.

The pretty man told his story. He'd worked in the palace until one night he was approached with an offer and directed toward their camp.

"What is yur name, lad?" Hennah asked, opening the sealed letter.

"My name's Tod. I was promised you could help make the Prince fall in love with me. So long as I made it here with no witnesses."

Blood burst out from young Tod's back. He gasped and looked down, red rimming his lips, as Mordo materialized with his dagger in the lad's chest. Tod stared up and saw him for the first time, terror all over his face. Before Tod had a chance to fall, Mordo pulled the blade out and slit his throat.

Evris began to move toward him. "You fool!"

Mordo looked up at the old bag and stopped him in his approach. Holding the dagger backward in his hand, he stood there, ready to disappear again, his posture screaming "Try it, fool!"

Evris paused and wilted. "He worked in the palace. Who knows what I could have learned from him?"

"You heard him, Evris. No witnesses."

*****

    Mirianne had never been as scared as she was the night her captor broke into her home and murdered her family in cold blood. She'd been petrified of the man and hadn't spoken a word to him the entire time she'd been his prisoner. All day and night she could feel his eyes on her, making sure she never even thought of escape. He was a man of few words, only ever asking questions about hunger and strength. When they rode by horseback, the evil man would hold a curved dagger firmly to her side, sometimes poking her when her horse stumbled.

    Still dressed in her white nightgown, that was stained and filthy now, Mirianne had been bound by her wrists to a tree outside of some sort of compound. Her captor had handed her to some soldier and muttered a warning. That was when the man brought her to the edge of camp, where his comrades had set up tents, and tied her to a tree. At first, the soldier looked after her diligently, but it wasn't long before the fun his friends were having had him glancing back and forth. They called him over twice, but he refused. Finally, after an hour of boredom and sobriety, he paced over and joined them.

    Mirianne looked around but couldn't recognize anything in the dark. The tent she was outside of was on the corner of the compound and she could see that most of the men were in groups, huddled around fires. They simply sat around their warming light, talking, joking, or laughing at stories about one another. There was one group she could just make out that had a pair of soldiers sparring each other within a circle of the huddled men that were cheering them on.

    To her surprise, after her sentry left for his friends, no one really paid Mirianne any attention, as if they were avoiding the tent she was by altogether. She watched and made note of the men that would have been able to keep an eye on her. Several minutes passed without a single glance from any of them. Mirianne began gnawing and biting at her bindings as she always did when she got a rare minute of solitude from her captor. Once, she'd almost been caught while supposedly relieving herself, and after that the man had watched her.

    Chewing and ripping at the rope, she made sure to consciously check on the guards every few seconds to avoid discovery.

    From around the tent, a man slowly emerged, his head tilted as if his ear were hurting. Seeing him, Mirianne's heart sank deep. She'd been caught. She stopped chewing and looked up at the man with the saddest eyes.

Mirianne didn't understand why she'd been spared from a torturous death like her family. At first, she'd simply wanted to believe that she was lucky. But after the meticulous care she'd been given during her transportation, she was beginning to realize that she was being kept for something. A pit in her stomach grew when Mirianne saw the look on his face as he came around the corner. This had been her last chance, and she just got caught.

The man eyed her a moment. His temples were spotted with silver and his brow was sharp, his deep-set eyes hiding in its shade. He looked at the girl tied to the tree. "You were just chewing, weren't you?"

Mirianne didn't know what to do, so she stayed silent.

Approaching her, he crouched down and picked up her wrists. "I knew I heard chewing. Why are you here, girl?" His voice was just louder than a whisper.

"I don't know," Mirianne told him honestly. "A man broke into my house and took me away."

"This man, what was his name?"

"I don't know," she said, racking her memory. "I've never seen him before."

"Could he disappear?"

"You know him?" Mirianne said, her previous terror doubling. "Please, please, don't tell him I was chewing..."

The man reached out and put his hand on hers. "DeathShadow," he whispered to himself before he looked back into her eyes and asked, "What's your name, girl?"

"Mirianne," she answered after a long second. "What's yours?"

"You couldn't pronounce it. Call me Tracker," he said, his expression softening.

"That monster... DeathShadow, he broke into my home and..." Her voice started to tremble as her mind replayed the image of her house on fire. Family trapped within. She wasn't sure why she was confiding in this stranger, but he was the only person who had shown her any kindness in the last week.

"I know, child," Tracker told her, moving his hand to her shoulder. "He did the same to my family."

"Kill me. Please," she whimpered then.

Tracker couldn't believe what he'd heard. "What?"

"I don't want to live if this is to be my life."

"Sometimes we all have to do things that we don't want to," Tracker told her, lifting her chin gently. "Biting a blade is what they called it in my day."

Mirianne wiped the water from her eyes and sniffled. "Have you ever bit the blade?"

"I am right now," he said softly.

Her look beckoned an explanation. He told her how DeathShadow had come from nowhere. Back then, there was another he called Wraith. They stole onto his family's land, killed his son-by-marriage, and captured the rest of his family. A wife, daughter, and infant grandson. Tracker was ready to fight to the death that day. As he reached for a nearby hatchet, DeathShadow ordered his wraith kill the baby. Without hesitation, the black figure picked the crying babe up by the ankle, as if it were livestock to be butchered. That was his breaking point. He'd been under the employment of the Damonai and their Caliph ever since. Failure to complete his missions meant torture for his family. "It's different when you know you're responsible for the fate of someone you love." That night an Oracle had found him and told him he was on his path, that following the branch would lead to salvation.

After listening to Tracker's own sorrow-filled story, Mirianne leaned over and kissed him on the forehead. "We'll get through this, Tracker. Both of us. We have to. Otherwise, there're no gods."

"What's going on over here?" a guard shouted, hearing their hushed conversation.

Tracker sank back into the shadow of the tent instantly. He signalled Mirianne to stay quiet as the man appeared, goading her on further. "Who are you talking to, girly?" he said, walking right up so that his crotch was in her face, the smell of alcohol wafting in behind him.

He gave a little look around and saw no one.

"No matter." The guard began unbuckling his belt. "I've got something for ya."

Before his trousers dropped, Tracker snuck in, snatching the man's own dagger from his belt before it fell to the ground. He tripped up the guard, covering his mouth to muffle his cries, before pulling him down to the ground and plunging the dagger directly into his heart.

Tracker's face grew furious for an instant until the man drew his last breath.

Moving around to Mirianne, who was cowering in fear, he calmed her quickly then cut her binds.

"Why would you do this for me?" she asked, her eyes bloodshot from tears.

"I couldn't just walk away..." he said sincerely before growing grim, placing the dagger in her hands, and nodding off to the forest. "You should go."

"I won't ever forget this, Tracker," Mirianne told him as she rose, rubbing her chafed wrists. "I'll pray for your family."

"Go!" He gave her a light shove and she took a step backward then turned and fled into the dark.

*****

Once the Caliph had read the message from Tod, she held an impromptu meeting with Evris and Mordo. They discussed the development of their plans, along with the new information they had received. Learning that the Wardens were gathering, Mordo urged for the Caliph to send him to Pellence. He swore to finally kill the bastard king, Demonblades, and for the first time, Hennah disgraced him. She laughed. Like he had told a joke, she laughed.

"Yew would die if yew fodd de king."

He hated how confident she was when saying it. It only fuelled his desire to fight the man. And now he was being sent away. With people. He hated people. Unreliable, stupid people.

Mordo made his way back to his tent. The past week he'd developed a sense of over-protectiveness for Mirianne, ensuring her safety for the Caliph. Out of habit, he wanted to see her. He walked around the camp, looking for the guard or the blonde-haired prisoner. Finally, he spotted the man at a nearby fire, drinking and laughing with a few others. Furious that he wasn't still watching her, Mordo stormed up and demanded, "Where's the girl?"

"She's just around the tent." The man pointed. As Mordo walked away from the fire and rounded the tent, disappointment overtook him. He found nothing but the bindings cut on the ground and a dead, fat soldier with red blood pooling out over his chest. His unbuckled belt lay around his ankles.

Mordo returned to the fire in his *nsuli*. This time, when he walked away, he and the fire were the only things that drew breath. He sent for Tracker, and a few short minutes later the tall scout arrived to examine the situation.

"This is the girl I saw you bring into camp? The blonde?" he asked as he knelt down and studied the ground. "My guess, this meathead came over here looking for a good time and she played along long enough to get her hands on his knife... then stuck him before cutting herself free."

"This is why I hate people," Mordo said, looking over at Tracker. "I've been alone with this girl for a week. And I come into this camp for a day and she's goes missing."

"Don't know what to tell you, Shadow," Tracker said, examining the scene once more. "People are unpredictable."

"Go after her, Tracker," he ordered in an icy voice, quelling the inferno within him. "Bring her back and we'll even let you hold your grandson next visit."

"I'll go get my horse," Tracker said before ducking away with a smirk on his face.

Chapter 27

"It's a sad thing," a voice drifted over, seeming to have read the Prince's thoughts.

Arlahn turned around, and for the first time since entering the clearing, he noticed an impossibly tall weeping willow tree in its centre. The overcast canvas of spiralling leaves reached out over the top of him and stretched close to a hundred and fifty feet in diameter.

Sitting at the base of the tree was a man, dressed in an earthly green tunic, dark leggings, and doeskin moccasins. He was whittling a tower out of a block of wood, seemingly oblivious to the approaching prince.

"Don't be alarmed," he said suddenly. "I'm just here to talk."

Catching Arlahn off-guard, he stopped and eyed the man.

"Valiant, what that wolf did," he started, continuing with his whittling. "You know, the kahki's only loyal to its pack. But that wolf had no pack. It was the old alpha up in the mountains until it was beaten. After that, it was outcast, a nomad with no loyalties. Yet it chose you."

His time in the mountains had given Arlahn a suspicious view of humans. Before he was too trusting, too quick to believe in the purity of a person. Now, he better understood the methodology of the world.

"You're the one from the mountain. The Firestarter's son?"

Arlahn remained hesitant to answer, instead he asked, "Who are you?"

The man stopped his whittling and sighed. "Call me what you like. I think the name Wolf suits you."

"I didn't ask what to call you, I asked who you were."

For the first time, the newcomer made eye-contact with the Prince. The man's grey eyes looked into him, his expression warning of the path he had travelled. Arlahn felt something move deep within, as if he recognized this man from somewhere already but couldn't place him.

"Don't try to get tough with me. Far greater men than you have tried and I'm right here. I'm not offending you. I just... don't remember my name."

"Then why do I feel like Origin's your name?"

"Because it is in a sense, I guess. Somewhere along Time, I stopped becoming a who and started becoming a what," he replied. "I've had countless names. Diyo, Guardian, Reader, Dreamcatcher, Oak, Oracle, Harbinger... Your brothers called me Witness and Thaumaturge."

Arlahn somehow knew this man was all of those things in his own way. And so much more. He recalled his father used the name Harbinger during their climb. Was this the same man? How could that be? He looked the same age as the young prince.

"When an immortal being is around mortal men who try to accomplish so much in their fleeting lives, he's bound to everlasting experience."

Arlahn looked at him again. "What do you mean immortal? How long have you been here?"

Origin sighed. "Eons." He took up his wood block and continued carving. "Since the birth of Tehbirr. I watched the molten cool into the earth's crust. I saw the first mountain push up from the ground, felt the first drops of rain, and helped sow the seeds of life. I've been here since the beginning of Time with Him."

The information was overwhelmingly surreal, almost questionable. Someone who had witnessed the birth of Time... could such a thing exist? Arlahn felt his time with this being was limited and knew he needed to choose his questions carefully. "Who's Him?"

"The Rahnolean," Origin answered. "The one who brought all of life here."

Arlahn sat down opposite the man, cross-legged. Origin flicked his wrist and created a fire between them from nothing. He wanted to ask about the man's magic, but something warned him their moment together was too valuable for casual conversation.

"How did you and the Rahnolean get here?"

"We fled here. Our world was dying and we made a mistake. A sacrifice to make sure our race survived. We came here so He could make everything right. There was something different with him though. He told me He couldn't make one and one equal one anymore."

Arlahn thought about that a moment. "One and one should equal two."

Origin sighed again. "I know. But He'll be back when it makes sense to Him."

"You said you made a mistake..." Arlahn started, remembering the unearthly monster from his Walkabout. "You created something?"

Origin looked the Prince in the eyes, doing his best to hide his fear.

Arlahn described the monster he'd seen on his Walkabout in the mountain.

"A Basrak," Origin whispered to himself before he looked back at the Prince. "It's here then. We're out of time."

"Then what makes you think He'll come back?"

"He needs to." Origin answered ominously. "To undo His mistake."

"And if He doesn't?"

"All life in existence will be eaten away."

"How do you know?"

"I've seen it."

The absolute confidence in his words sold absolute belief and truth. Arlahn had so many questions before him, but there was only one path that would give him the answers he sought most.

"What happened to Him? Where did He go?"

"He just... left," Origin said, leaning back against the trunk. "You or I could only hope to understand..."

"How does someone like that just leave?"

"He wrote out the Tree of Life and then hung Himself on it."

The Tree of Life? Arlahn thought, remembering the Prophecy Tablet he'd received as a birthing day gift. "So He died? Why would He hang himself?"

"He can't die. The Rahnolean's goal was always the same. Unity. Moral, spiritual, functional unity."

The Prince warmed his hands on the fire and asked him, "You say that like it's a dream, but is it your dream?"

Origin placed his wood block down beside him, looking defeated. "I don't know anymore. Once there was a time when I authored monumental actions of this world. I knew what to expect. But my past caught up with me before I could finish... I thought I had more time. Honestly, I'm not sure about anything anymore."

"What do you mean, what has you full of doubt now?"

"I never found out how His story's supposed to end."

"Then how do you know the Rahnolean will come back?"

"The Tree of Life created a bond to this world that transcends human comprehension. If he had truly died, none of this would be here." Origin felt the grass run between his fingers as he squeezed a handful. "The limbs and leaves of the Tree depict lineages and actions of the Chosen Ones throughout Time. When He wove the fate of these people, He poured his very essence into His work. His prophecy. By hanging himself in the tree, He consummated His amalgamation with Tehbirr."

"What about the Prophecy Tablet?" Arlahn again recalled his gift and the wood's elegant, dark lettering.

"They were written in His own blood."

"They? There's only one prophecy tablet."

"No. There're five." Origin continued his lesson of mythical histories. "And He'll return when the prophecy's fulfilled."

Arlahn gave the man a cock-eyed look. "The prophecy *was* fulfilled. My father—"

"Is a great man," Origin interrupted. "But he's still just a man. The prophecy speaks of a god."

"But the tablet outlines his life. He's a hero."

"A point I won't argue. But to whom is he a hero? Heroes are often a matter of perspective, Wolf. To the Sainti, he's a legendary HighKing, the saviour and liberator of his people. But do you know what they call him across the Damonai lands?" Origin leaned in for effect, firelight dancing ominous shadows over his features. "Demonblades. The devil of war." Then he leaned back. "Your father is remarkable, to his credit. Perhaps the greatest man to walk this world in an age. Blessed with a sensibility about life. But he's not the Rahnolean. All of Tehbirr will know when He has come."

"But the prophecy—"

"Is incomplete," Origin interrupted again. "There were five verses written on five pieces of the Tree."

"I've only seen one. What happened to the others?" Arlahn pressed.

"The world only remembers one, the others were lost, hidden or destroyed. I found one tablet lately and sent it to your father for safekeeping. The other was hidden from me until I felt its presence surface recently in Esselle."

"And you know these other verses, the ones on the destroyed tablets?"

"I may be the only one who does."

Arlahn asked to hear them and when Origin denied him, the Prince jumped up. "You've come to me tonight for a reason. Telling me all kinds of stories about being here, witnessing the ancient past of the world. You confessed to being unsure about what comes next. I feel like you want to ask for my help but you're refusing yourself. Why?"

"Because I can see into you, Wolf. There's a great emptiness. At first, I was curious about you, but I'm not sure you're the one to help me."

"But if the prophecy brings back the Rahnolean, and you withhold the only information about fulfilling it, are you not condemning the world and causing the very thing you're afraid of?"

Origin thought about that for an exaggerated moment. He had been here so long he didn't believe that world-born men would understand the magnitude of his affairs. Almost everyone had dismissed him as crazy as soon as he began speaking of a physical God. Up to this point, he had always given direction to the ones he met. Until a hundred years ago, he had known what the outcome of all his actions would be – that was when the branches had started to fade into charred points. Eventually, he conceded to Arlahn's logic.

"You know that each verse has its own title?"

The Prince resumed sitting and nodded.

"Then pay attention. Don't interrupt."

When Origin began speaking, all other sound seemed to drown out and his voice transformed into a soft, almost rhythmic song.

"Generation.
Spawn from darkness, I will grow from revolution,
Seeking retribution to fulfill my constitution.
Withdrawn from my partner, I will find motivation,
To fight the complacent over enslavement.
Stopping those who prey like a ruthless demon,
I'll provide the reason to incite your freedom."

Arlahn knew the prophecy from memory but the resonance in Origin's tone made him feel as if he understood the cryptic words better than he ever had. What came next was something that he had never heard before. Perhaps no one alive had. He remained silent with great anticipation.

"The Great Union.
To avoid the temptation of becoming an imitation,
Sometimes extreme action can form a mutation.
As the battle still wages pushing myself to its greatest,
Tragedy is our belief of superior races.
I'll find salvation and persevere through tribulation,
And alleviate the weights I carry of damnation."

Hearing the words sent a chill up the Prince's spine the same way they had when he had first heard the beginning. Origin stopped after the first new verse.

"What about the rest?" Arlahn asked after a long moment.

"You've just been privileged to hear something that no one else knows. Take a moment to soak it in. I like you, Wolf, but I get the feeling you've got no sense of timing."

Arlahn dipped his head disappointed.

"Here," Origin said before tossing him his wooden tower.

Catching it out of the air, the Prince gave the carving a quick inspection before he asked, "What's this for?"

No answer came.

When Arlahn looked up, the man was gone. Though his fire remained. As he stared at the flames, Arlahn heard the man's voice speaking from within them. "Sleep safe, Wolf. May your dreams bring you to happier places."

The Prince laid his head down and listened to the crackling of the fire, the soft running of water from a nearby stream. It wasn't long before he succumbed to sleep.

*****

Perception here was different. Buried deep beneath the surface, resolute in position. Rather than move physically, it seemed as if the world itself stirred, revolving around thoughts and emotions.

*****

A chilling breeze rolled over Arlahn, beckoning him to wake. He kept his eyes closed though, rolling over and drawing his cloak about him tighter, hoping to clutch at sleep for a few more minutes.

The river continued to flow in the near distance, the sound slowly growing more prominent. Memories of his favourite fountain filled his mind, the one from the courtyard. Suddenly reminded of sentiments one could only receive from family, Arlahn missed home. There was so much he had learned, he needed to inform his father, the king.

He was about to open his eyes and surrender to the morning light when something in him kept his eyes closed. Perhaps it was the warmth of his little cocoon, or maybe he just wanted to rest a while longer.

For a moment he just lay there, listening to the sound of the water. In his mind's eye, he envisioned the pristine face of the centrepiece statue back home in the palace. Slowly, the rest of the fountain came into view. Her graceful pose. He imagined the long flowing hair of the statue and the water pouring from it. On each of the three tiers, the numbers of small angels increased, spitting tiny streams in perfect arches. The water danced and rolled its way down the tiers, almost melodiously, eventually pooling into the fish-filled base. The rest of the courtyard came back to him then, and he imagined the stone paths and benches, the sculpted bushes.

Eventually, Arlahn's recollection of home became so vivid, he could have believed he was there, smelling fresh-baked bread from the kitchens, instead of sleeping on the forest floor. Holding his vision, he took a deep breath and rolled over. Home slipped through his mind like sand in a time-glass and suddenly it was gone. Disappointed, Arlahn squeezed the sleep from his eyes and opened them.

It was impossible. He was there.

Surging to his feet, confusion set in as he took in his surroundings. His breath still somewhat visible in the cool autumn air, he stared through it with amazement at the statue's face. She looked exactly as he pictured.

"Can I help you, my prince?" came a soft, unfamiliar voice from behind him.

Arlahn spun on his heel and looked the stranger up and down. He was old, almost to the point of becoming frail, wearing grey vestments with an oversized hood and wide sleeves. His silvered hair was combed over to hide his balding. "Your shoulder looks like it could use a bit of attention."

"Do I know you?" the Prince asked, somewhat suspicious. Arlahn was more familiar with those others who occupied the palace than anyone, except for his father. But he was confident he'd never seen this man before.

"We've not formally met, no. Forgive me, my prince," he said, offering a very low, respectful bow. "My name is Sol. I'm the new royal physician. I recognize you from a few portraits in the palace. Did you come in during the night?"

"I did," the Prince lied, unsure of how he would even begin to explain how he got here.

"You look tired, it must have been a hard journey. Shall I have a look at your shoulder?"

Arlahn glanced down and saw the dried blood on his sleeve. "I'll be fine. I need to speak with my family."

"Please, don't let me keep you, my prince."

He found his brother in the council room, busy laying out papers before each seat. "What's this?" Arlahn asked.

Raphael looked up through his golden locks toward his brother. "Meeting of the Wardens. Rond and Baile are already here." Then Raph grinned from ear to ear. "Welcome back, how was the mountain?"

"Terrible..." Arlahn dipped his head remembering his Sister. "I killed Jassyka." Suddenly a well of tears overflowed from his eyes and his brother was embracing him. "I didn't mean to Raph. I swear! It was an accident."

Raphael squeezed his brothers head to his shoulder, the same way he did to Kael. "It's alright brother, I know you didn't mean to." Raphael understood what this meant to his brother. Arlahn had never killed before, his soul was too gentle to deliberately harm. "One thing about the Brotherhood is they *do* believe death unites us all."

Detaching from his brother and wiping his face clean, Arlahn took a deep shuddering breath. "Thanks Raph, Balanor told me the same thing."

The room stayed still for a moment.

"When did you get back?"

"I don't know," Arlahn answered emptily. He had plucked a sheet off of one of Raphael's piles. A blueprint. "What's this?"

"I call it a rotary-bow," his brother announced proudly, after curiously dismissing Arlahn's answer.

Just then, the Warden of the North, Rodrik Rond, entered the room, courteously accompanying the queen with a hooked arm and talking the way old neighbours would.

"Is that my son?!" Annabella almost screeched.

Arlahn barely had time to whirl around before his mother had bound upon him and pulled him into an embrace. "Oh, I've missed you so much!"

Rodrik waited politely for the queen to finish her reunion before the dark-skinned Melonian offered the Prince his hand. He was handsome and in amazing health for a man his age, his grip firm beneath his overworked hand. Since the last time the Prince had seen him, he had begun to sprout silver in his curly black hair.

They spoke for a few minutes and Arlahn learned that the Warden had just arrived and was excited to "get the group together again." Excusing himself, Arlahn took his leave and let his mother speak with their guest. Unable to shake his very presence here, he wasn't interested in their casual conversation, nor did he want to raise extra attention to himself by mentioning he simply woke up here.

Walking around afterwards, he noticed a few familiar faces were missing from the palace, namely his brother and father.

He found Raph in his study, hovering over another blueprint, a quill resting between pinched fingers. His focus was so intense that he didn't notice his brother approach. He was about to write something but withdrew right before the ink-stained the papyrus.

"Where is everyone? I have something I need to tell Pa," Arlahn asked, breaking his brother's concentration.

"They left for the Brotherhood. You didn't meet them on your way back?"

"I don't know how I got back."

That caused Raphael to put down the quill in his hand. "That's the second time you've said that now. What do you mean you don't know?"

Arlahn approached his brother seriously. "You're going to think I'm crazed. But I just woke up here Raph, I swear. I was in the forest last night and I dreamt about the fountain in the courtyard. And when I opened my eyes, I was just here."

Raphael scrutinized his brother. "Are you talking about dimensional displacement?"

"Sure, whatever that is," Arlahn answered.

"It's the theory of an old Essellian. Being able to travel from one location to another in the blink of an eye. It would be an incredibly special Gift."

"Strange things have been happening to me lately, Raph..." Arlahn confided to his brother everything that had happened to him in the mountain. He explained how he'd experienced glimpses of Gifts. That he felt his brothers' *kjut'tsir* and *mniman*, their father's *sciong*, even Jassyka's dreams.

After mention of this, however, Raphael argued that there had never been anyone in history who was beyond Thrice Touched, let alone someone with five Gifts.

"I don't know how it happens, Raph. It just comes and goes on its own. All of it."

Raphael's own *mniman* was working in his mind. Arlahn could see it in his brother's look.

"Kael said he heard something about you being 'broken' right after you were born... But maybe... Hang on," he said. "I think I have a test for this."

Raphael placed his quill back in its inkwell and left Arlahn alone in the room.

Walking around his brother's desk, curiosity led him to the drawing. He took the parchment in both hands and studied the design. The picture was well-drawn, clear and precise. The basic concept had been designed like a crossbow, but the mechanisms implemented into it were much more complex. There was a list of specific materials it was to be constructed of as well: laminae of whalebone, twelve-tooth gears, tendon... A front grip had been added along its length. In the margins, there were notes about this being a reloading mechanism. Pumping back the grip would actuate a series of intricate gears, cranking back the prod until the bowstring caught the locking system that was compiled of interconnected bronze castings.

He even saw the word "safety" scribbled onto the page pointing to a locking pin.

Arlahn could also see the predicament his brother was stuck on; the user could fire one shot easily, but the intricacies associated in drawing back the prod were specific to the unit's function. In other words, he could crank back the bowstring, but replacing the arrow was impossible. There was no conceivable way to place a revolving spindle into the gear system and altering it in any way would result in a malfunction of its original purpose.

That was when something happened in his mind, something inexplicable. The picture on the parchment evolved into a three-dimensional object, floated off the papyrus into the space before him, then suddenly exploded apart. He could see every individual gear, shaft, winding, spring, and the purpose they all served in coming together to work in perfect harmony.

Then, out of nowhere, an additional piece fabricated in the midst of his imagination. A lever loop formed around the crescent-shaped trigger, along the bottom of the handle a loop of iron that would cradle the wielder's fingers. The width of the stock and handle expanded slightly to allow for a new system of shafts and gears. Cranking the lever loop would drive a rod that was connected to a crankshaft. This led into a series of gears connected to the centre of the revolving cylinder, which was now capable of holding ten arrows in the horseshoe-shaped clips, poking concentrically outward.

With the new arrangement providing an answer to the problem, the imaginary structure merged into a singular component once more then sunk back into the papyrus. One by one, as if someone were drawing it, the new components, now highlighted bright yellow in his mind's eye, continued to integrate themselves onto the blueprint.

Snatching the quill in a heartbeat, Arlahn began tracing over the yellow lines, which disappeared as they were covered with black.

"Whoa! Buddy, what are you doing?!" Raphael shouted in an attempt to stop his brother as he entered the room.

Raph touched his brother's shoulder but Arlahn quickly shoved him off, sending Raphael crashing back into the wall as effortlessly as Kael would.

He wouldn't have it. He was possessed by some force greater than him to ink out his discoveries. Arlahn continued tracing carefully, taking his time, muttering to himself in a low voice that Raph could barely make out. He was explaining what he was adding to the schematic.

As Raphael watched and listened with great consideration, he noticed something that began to startle him more and more as time passed. His brother, lost in his work, hadn't blinked in minutes. Instead, his brow stayed furrowed in concentration as his eyes scanned all around the page at a feverish rate, his quill following their movement. Occasionally, Arlahn would scratch out previous dimensions and change their size, labelling new components he'd added. When he'd finished, he placed the quill down delicately, pushed the parchment before him on the desk, and his body hiccupped, eyes closing finally for a long second.

They hurt and Arlahn squeezed them between thumb and finger to quell the headache from brewing.

"This is incredible," he heard Raphael say. The enthusiasm in his voice caused Arlahn to open his eyes.

"You did it!" Raph continued, Arlahn looked up at him. "I had thought of a separate crankshaft system to rotate the cylinder but never saw how to implement it into the design. This finger loop is genius." He pointed to the new loop. "And the way you've made it re-crank the bolt automatically means I'm not pumping between shots."

It was the strangest thing. Arlahn knew he'd drawn the additions to the blueprint but while it was happening, it was as if his consciousness was trapped in a glass bottle and he was stuck watching himself work. If he were asked right now, he would not be able to recreate the drawing, nor regurgitate his reasoning. He was thankful every note had been jotted down with all the rest in the margins. "This will work then?" he asked, almost doubtful.

Raph's eyebrows lifted high and he nodded slightly. "It's more advanced than even I could imagine. What happened to you in the Brotherhood?"

"I don't know... That's why I need to talk with Pa. Why did he go back?"

Raphael recounted everything that had been going on in Pellence. Marly's pregnancy promised good news that was short-lived. Soon after, it turned sour, beginning by recounting how their mother suddenly collapsed. How the Damonai deviously trapped Brandigit and his men. Their father's death and resurrection since leaving him in the mountain. An Essellian justicar who informed them of the Council of Deaders, Gifted Assassins. Finally, that a DeathShadow murdered Luzy and her family in their home, abducting her sister Mirianne in the process.

Arlahn was shocked to hear that so much had transpired in his absence. After a moment of contemplation, he knew he had to tell his brother.

"There's something else though, Raph. Something else coming for us, something much worse than the Damonai. Something's here, brother, on Tehbirr. Something we've never seen before, because it's not *from* Tehbirr."

"What are you talking about? The Damonai are on their way to attack the mountain. That's a threat we can do something about, something we have seen before. You want us to prepare for something we don't know exists?"

Raphael saw Arlahn's conviction in his words and conceded that they should mention it at the meeting with the Wardens. His only request was that they bring it up at the end. No one would be given the benefit of the doubt when they explained an invading, alien threat.

"What is this threat called?"

It had been the same conversation with the king-in-the-mountain, but this time Arlahn couldn't relinquish. "This is the genesis of our genocide, brother. I promise."

*****

Darius was poked awake. He saw a large soldier with a lance in hand above him. He never did find the beauty from the tavern, but his endeavours brought him to a wonderfully curvy brunette, a woman he thoroughly enjoyed until the morning light revealed her face. The thief had slipped out before she woke and passed out wherever his hangover headache had permitted him. He felt straw beneath and noticed heard the dogs in the stall move and scamper around him.

"Get up," the soldier ordered. "Prince Raphael wants to speak with you. Come with me to the palace once you've cleaned yourself up."

"Believe it or not, I haven't been here long." He told the guard, wrapping an arm around a collie. "And this bitch is a step up from the one I was next to earlier."

The soldier smirked and shook his head. "C'mon then." He yanked Darius up to stand.

Minutes later, the thief found himself entering through Pellence's fourth wall.

"The Prince is in his study. This way." The soldier led him, and Darius walked alongside his escort through the palace, admiring the detail in the reliefs beside them. He rubbed his hand along a busty woman with a vase, then a knight offering a flower. They arrived at an iron-banded door and the soldier knocked twice. After hearing a voice from within summon them, he pushed the door open and Darius contemplated one more escape.

The mere thought of summoning his secret made his stomach churn the remaining alcohol within. Rushing over to a nearby vase, Darius yanked its contents clear and hurled inside.

He heard the soldier behind him curse as he spat the last of the bile out, smirking at his small victory. Darius had never liked authority. So many men born into position believed they were better and were so determined to prove it. Those were the fools he loved to rob the most.

Feeling the soldier's fist squeeze his shoulder, he was immediately pushed into the room.

Prince Raphael, the golden prince, sat behind his desk in a chair that enlarged his frame. His golden waves hung about his shoulders, surrounding his face with a glowing aura. Another man, a brother judging by their similar features, stood beside him.

Raphael looked from his sheet of papyrus to Darius. "Is this him, Bregan?"

"It is, Your Grace."

"Excellent."

Turning to the younger man, he explained, "The other Wardens will be here soon, do you mind welcoming them with mother for me?"

"Not at all. Think about what we talked about," his brown-haired brother replied before shooting Darius a look and asking, "Are you alright here?"

"Yeah, I'll be fine. Go wait for Uncle Benson and Warden Rali." On his way out, Raphael added one more thing. "It's good to have you back, little brother."

The other prince turned at the entrance. "It's good to be home."

Home, Darius thought, what an illusion, in a single night your father lost his home. He knew the story. He had grown up in Saintos where every boy heard the story of the HighKing, Hectore Rai.

Bregan remained in uncomfortably close proximity to Darius with his spear clenched tightly in hand.

After the younger prince left the room, Raphael gave Darius a look up and down. "You're a difficult man to get ahold of."

Darius remained quiet and observed the archery trophies adorning the wall behind the Prince.

"My wife told me you walked in on her handmaiden's sister..."

There had always been something about his character, some hidden jester dancing deep within his soul, a little voice that always had something to say. Darius smirked. "That was a terrible idea."

"I'd say assaulting a guard is worse." The Prince clasped his hands together on the desk before him. "Why didn't you just go with him? You've ended up here anyway."

Darius lifted his shoulders. "In my experience, it's not always good to stick around."

"You're lucky Zeth left with my brother or else that would be sound advice."

"Who would want to be imprisoned?" the thief defended himself.

Raphael's brow furrowed and his head hitched backward in both shock and confusion. "Imprison you? No." He shook his golden hair. "I want to employ you."

Now it was Darius' turn to twitch in shock. "Employ me?"

The Prince stood up. "You have a Gift, Darius. There's no point in trying to deny it." Pacing around his desk, he stopped at the front and leaned against it. "You've already proven you're quite the thief too. Halder wants his purse back."

"You have your own thieves already…" Darius quipped. "Except you call them tax collectors."

"If you work for me," the Prince continued, crossing his arms and ignoring the thief's response, "I can promise you welcome entrance into my city and handsome compensation for your efforts."

Darius thought for a moment, handsome compensation was almost enough for him to agree.

"Finally, I'll make sure Pellence is your home."

Darius looked around, "I can live here?"

The Prince dropped his arms. "Home isn't a place Darius… Home is people."

Chapter 28

Sentries were garrisoned in pairs throughout the dark forest, the canopy overhead quelling any light given off by the moon. There were no fires to reveal their position, but men were still routinely stationed so that neighbourly contact was readily available. Some of the more diligent mountaineers carried horns with them, though, having never been discovered, others had grown complacent, making light of their duties.

A stocky mountain-man finished relieving himself on a nearby tree and returned to his partner at their post. "That wind can bugger off for all I care."

"Piss on your hand again?" the other asked, sitting on his stump.

"Well that's not the wind's fault... It's my father's." He displayed the measurement of an inch to his friend.

The sitting sentry began laughing, which caused his friend to chuckle with him. Still sitting and shaking his head, the guard noticed something in the distance at his side. It sparked his curiosity and he stood, peering through the dark foliage to try to distinguish what it was.

"What is it?" his partner asked.

Peeking around trees in the distance, he pointed his finger. "I t-t-h-hink I see something."

When no reply came from his stocky partner, the sentry turned around. He barely had time to register what he was seeing when a garotte wrapped around his neck. Taken completely off-guard, his eyes began to bulge and he clawed his neck in an attempt to free his suffocation. He elbowed his assailant and they tumbled to the ground together.

Drelnum had finished squeezing the life out of the first sentry. Dropping the wooden handles of one of Mordo's life-squeezers, he drew his tomahawk and stepped over to the pair struggling on the ground, burying his axe in the mountain-man's chest.

He gave his comrade a look before finding Mordo through the trees. They made eye contact and all was decided; they would continue on.

Drelnum was sent ahead with DeathShadow, clearing any sentries that could discover them before they were identified. Hundreds of men filling the path behind them began wordlessly moving in tandem. As they surreptitiously made their way further into the mountain, Drelnum checked the map Evris had given him.

Before they had detached from Evris' corps, Caliph Asa had ordered him to draw a map. Using a combination of the Billiem's Spiri'wu and Evris' *suuluuk*, eventually they found a trap-free path to their destination.

Approaching the last circle of sentries, the men scurried through the darkness. Recklessly, Drelnum tripped a wire he couldn't see spread across the path. A square frame soundlessly and violently swung down from above. The driving force and momentum snapped the spears against Drelnum's unbreakable skin, splintering off of him. The comrade beside him halted mid-stride. Drelnum looked over and saw two thick stakes in his chest and one in his stomach. He gave his leader a look of satisfaction and drew his last breath.

The sound of the trap, faint as it was, wrestled the attention of the sentries. Drelnum ducked next to a shrub before he saw them, but their voices drifted in, talking about how they hoped it was a moose that had tripped the wire – already fantasizing about their next meal. Peering out, the bearded leader prepared himself for when they came into view.

Just as their silhouettes emerged from the darkness, the figures stiffened.

Drelnum was just about to charge when DeathShadow appeared between the two approaching guards, arms extended to their bloody throats, as if he'd stepped out from another realm. Together, the men fell to the ground and Mordo's black-garbed frame disappeared behind the curtain hiding his existence. Despite a lifetime of training, the two Brothers had no chance against an invisible enemy.

Drelnum moved in on his position, and Mordo came out from the trees at his side, pausing before him to look toward the trap that still held the dead scout.

"It wasn't on the map, must be new," the bearded warrior insisted.

After Mordo remained silent, Drelnum moved on.

"The men know the plan?" he asked one of the officers as his train of soldiers approached.

"All of them, sir."

He looked at Mordo for confirmation before stating, "It's time."

The deader nodded his acknowledgement. Shadows don't make sounds.

Mordo and Drelnum had been dispatched together along with a brigade of Damonai soldiers. Two thousand men being led by two who could kill them all, Mordo had mused. He wished he'd been sent off on his own mission, but the Caliph stressed the importance of success here, and DeathShadow was her ingredient for success.

The sheer number of people meant their travels were much slower than Mordo was used to. So, at his behest, Drelnum split his men, a vanguard force of four hundred to blaze the trail, while the other sixteen hundred followed immediately behind them as quickly as possible.

Drelnum sent a score or soldiers in each direction from the path to finish off the remaining scouts.

"Start the countdown," he ordered.

The first file of Damonai raised their swords, waited a few seconds to gather everyone's attention and signal their intention, then cut down in synchrony.

Knowing of patrols throughout the village, DeathShadow went ahead and secured them an undetected entrance.

Ascending out of a valley, black and brown figures sprung from the tree line, pouring out through the white, square houses like poisoned water flooding river rocks.

The Damonai moved with deadly purpose, eliminating any leftover wandering outside their hut before an alarm could be raised. With everyone that was awake neutralized, Drelnum made his way deep into the enemy's camp, rendezvousing with DeathShadow.

He pulled on the iron latch of a silent hut and gently pushed his way in. The Shadow right behind him. They were standing in a small kitchen and dining room. He spotted a curtain draped over a frame in the corner and motioned to it.

They slipped through the hut and entered the second room, which contained two cots on either side. Two people slept soundly in them. Moving into position, they loomed over the sleepers. Unaware, defenceless...

Drelnum took up a small tusk horn from his belt and pressed the mouthpiece to his lips but didn't blow. They waited in complete silence, giving all his men time to take up a similar position in every hut.

He felt his heartbeat quicken as he approached the end of his countdown. The man before him stirred but didn't wake.

One ninety-eight, one ninety-nine...

Drelnum looked over at Mordo. Death's Shadow gave him a nod of approval.

He took in a deep breath and blew his horn in a single, blaring sound.

Instantly, the two Brothers stirred awake before them. The woman before Mordo didn't even have time to move before a sword was in her chest. Drelnum's victim made it up onto his elbows before he was pinned back down with a tomahawk.

All around the compound, Damonai executed men, women, and children in their sleep. Through the walls of their hut, they heard the screams and sounds of death.

The infamous Brotherhood was no more.

*****

Balanor wiped a clinging dribble of snot with the back of his hand. Posted to sentry duty, he scanned the blackness of the forest around him, unable to shake a daunting feeling that ate away at his stomach. It spawned from having forgotten his horn back in his cabin, but Balanor took solace in the fact that he'd forgotten it once or twice before and never needed it. Still, the diligence in his character was calling him home to collect it.

Sharing his duties with the newest addition to the mountain, he told the axeman, Jole, that he was returning home for a minute and he'd be back. His house was one of the closest to their path.

Balanor picked up his spear and carried it along. He was just about to turn down the intersection toward camp when something in the distance disturbed him. Stopping his approach, he waited in eerie silence, listening to the sounds drift through the woods. He heard movement, but not the one or two pairs of feet of travelling Brothers; the closer he listened, the more footfalls he counted until he couldn't anymore. Too many, he realized, but he hadn't heard any alarm. Balanor cursed himself for forgetting his horn for the first time in years.

Deciding he'd investigate further, he changed directions through the trails. He heard the feet coming from ahead of him, and, keeping low, quickened his pace. Approaching them, he heard the snap of old branches and knew one of the traps had been set off. A horrible cry filled the air. From the noises, Balanor knew that a false section of pathway had been fallen through.

"Put an arrow in him already!" a warrior ordered before his comrade shot down into the ground, silencing the cry.

Balanor began counting bodies in front of him silently.

"There's another one!" he heard one say, pointing at him. "Get 'im!"

An instinctual measure of his training dissolved any fear he might have had facing over a dozen men alone. He was mountain trained; mountain born.

About to stand his ground and challenge any who came before him, a smarter voice spoke to him in his head. Not words of flight, but a call to duty. He needed to notify his people. These men weren't alone. Balanor turned and ran.

Those closest to him gave chase through the forest, and two more fell into another punji-stick trap that they hadn't seen him leap over. This inspired him down a new trail. Intentionally allowing the fastest few of the bunch to catch up. Making his way home, Balanor glanced back and saw that three men in black were ten feet behind him. Tumbling down like he'd been tripped, he rolled through another tripwire. A square frame sprung down overhead, impaling two of the three Damonai in pursuit.

Balanor was back onto his feet and sprinting toward home. As he broke through the tree line, he saw hundreds of black-garbed warriors streaming through the village. His home was the third on his right. Before anyone noticed him, he slunk beside some barrels stacked against his neighbour's cabin, just before a stream of forty men ran past him. The last two men stopped at his door and quietly pulled the iron latch open.

Balanor checked his left and right before running across the avenue between homes. He opened the latch and saw that the men were about to enter his sleeping quarters. His twin Balanus and Tamis' sister Aideen shared a bed inside.

Raising the spear in his hand, he threw it across the room, screaming, "B, WAKE UP!"

His target looked in time to see the spear catch him in the chest, but the other intruder rushed behind the curtain.

Balanor ran over to the doorway. When he got there, his brother had grabbed the sword about to stab him and was squeezing it, blood dripping from his fingers. "Aideen, the vase!"

The brunette at his side reached beside her and swung. Glass exploded off the swordsman's head toward Balanor and he gave her a look.

Before the intruder could finish his struggle with Balanus, Balanor stepped in and stabbed the man through the base of his neck with textbook form.

Recovering, Balanor moved back into the other room and reached for his horn. His fingers just reached the smooth rind of tusk when a different horn peeled out a blaring, shrill call across the compound. Through the walls, they heard the struggles of all the Brothers and Sisters around them.

Balanus and Aideen appeared in the doorway and the twins met eyes. "We have to get King Pientero."

Aideen had picked up the sword from the dead man and cleared the hair from her eyes. Balanor saw that his brother's hands were wrapped but still bleeding. He leaned the spear his way, letting it fall toward him, and Balanus caught it in the meat between thumb and index and took up the weapon like that with both hands. Moving to the corner where he had ceremonially placed his father's short sword and round shield, Balanor pulled the blade clear and swung the shield on his left arm.

They ran out of the cabin and saw the remaining sentries rushing in from the trees, twenty or so. Warriors, dressed head to toe in black, began coming out of houses. Balanor noticed it wasn't only the men in black emerging from cabins around them. Through some miracle, some of his brethren had survived the horn blast. After taking a moment to distinguish, the two sides charged each other. That's when the war cries began.

The last fight for the Brotherhood started with only a fraction of their number. Balanor pointed with his sword, "Get them in order" he told his brother, "I'll go for the king." Then turned and raced off toward the centre of their base.

Some of the cabin doors he passed remained closed, causing him to pause. Stopping off at Anvar's house, Balanor readied himself before he pulled on the latch. When he began swinging the door open, it was pushed the rest of the way from the inside, and he was suddenly rushed up against it with a stunted forearm. A heavy hammer lifted in the air beside his head, then halted.

The hairy tutor scoffed as he recognized Balanor. "How many?"

Balanor knew what he was referring to and stayed ominously quiet.

"Come on, let's go." Anvar motioned his head toward the door.

The two encountered five warriors in the streets. But the Brothers were bred for war. Making short work of their attackers, they continued toward the king-in-the-mountain.

A man collided with him against a wall, but Balanor rolled onto the attacker with his shield. He poked the man once in the groin below his shield and finished him off with a stab above it.

Trying to reach his king, Balanor approached the hut that looked just like any other. As he arrived directly outside, the door was suddenly blasted open, exploding backward off its hinges and landing beside the warrior that had been sent through it.

Balanor looked in the door and saw his king standing behind its frame, seething with rage. Another warrior's head had been smashed in against the counter behind him. Letting out a great cry, Pientero stepped in and executed the downed man.

"KILL THEM ALL!" he shouted throughout the camp.

Balanor followed his king as they attempted to round up any survivors. They found the scout Tamis and his older brother Besath fighting outside their home.

Along the tree line, Balanus was with Aideen and a score of surviving mountain sentries, organizing a shield-wall to move back into their compound.

As the Damonai realized that some of the people emerging from huts weren't their kin, the confusion began. Soon, pandemonium broke out as they began fighting Balanus' shield-wall of sentries and scattered survivors all throughout the camp.

Anvar and PJ each had a cohort of followers with them, though their numbers were far too scarce. Damonai swarmed them from everywhere. But each mountain born was worth ten from the lower lands, Pientero had always praised them for that. Those few survivors proved that worth under the moonlight.

Balanor fought alongside his king. Eventually spotting his brother's formation through the houses.

He called out their position to Pientero and their whole unit changed direction, sweeping their way through their camp.

As they were rejoining their Brothers, Balanor took an arrow in the back of his shoulder. Archers had clambered on top of the cabins and began assaulting them from above. A handful of Brothers in the shield-wall were hit by unexpected bolts during the first barrage, and even with Pientero and his men adding their numbers, the phalanx formation shrank.

More Damonai made their way to them and soon they were overwhelmed.

Across the compound, Anvar could be heard booming curses in a fit of rage as he stormed toward the group of surviving Brothers. Pientero urged his men forward to save his old friend.

Everyone but PJ saw Anvar through new eyes. The entire time any of them had ever known him, he'd been a man solely devoted to peace and restoration. They could hardly believe the rage behind his destructive actions.

The bestial man carried a shortened battle hammer in his good hand. Punching the blockhead into a chest, he dropped to his knee and beat down heavily. The body below him began twitching with erratic convulsions. He was still about forty feet away, ferociously pounding through Damonai, taking a few cuts and an arrow to his thigh on the way.

Eventually, he struck a man that didn't fall. In fact, he barely flinched at the thunderous blow he'd taken to the ribs. The stocky, bearded Damonai stood there while Anvar lifted his hammer and pounded his face. This time, he reacted as if he'd been slapped by a hand rather than a block of steel. Again, Anvar grew furious and raised his hammer.

Then, the Damonai caught Anvar by his elbow and cleaved him in the ribs with his hatchet.

Together they held that pose for a drawn-out heartbeat. PJ cried out.

Anvar dropped to one knee then the other as his prodigal strength faded away. He coughed up blood, red dripping from his lips. Slowly, he fell to the ground.

The king-in-the-mountain broke from his formation, becoming the Howler that had haunted the Damonai's nightmares for decades. Bellowing a cry that would drown out any horn as he charged. In a blind rage, he stabbed, slashed, and hacked his way through any Damonai that got before him, snapping necks, crushing skulls. Almost a dozen brave men got between him and his friend.

The bearded warrior that had struck Anvar down stood over him, and when Pientero arrived, the king-in-the-mountain slapped the man's face with his sword. Pientero fell on his knees and pulled Anvar up onto his lap.

He tried to speak, but PJ hushed him. "Rest easy, old friend, you've done well."

Anvar lifted his bloody hand, it began shaking. "I'll go with love, Brother..."

The king-in-the-mountain took up his friend's hand and squeezed it. "Then be at peace, may your light shine brightest."

By this time, the remaining Damonai had regrouped and completely surrounded the feeble band of Brothers. Another group of forty men huddled around PJ and Anvar.

Something bit into the king's shoulder and pushed him back. Materializing from thin air, a black-haired Damonai was stabbing PJ, pinning him to the earth.

"This is the Caliph's mountain now."

The king-in-the-mountain looked up from his wound with bloodshot eyes. "Says who?"

"DeathShadow."

*****

After the chaotic night of devastation, the Damonai rounded up twenty-four surviving Brothers and Sisters, grouping them all together on the outskirt of the compound. Several of them had been wounded during the fight, their clothes variegated, blood-soaked clothes.

Mordo had contemplated killing them all after pinning the king-in-the-mountain helplessly to the ground. But for some reason, he thought of Evris and how disappointed the man had been when he'd killed the Pellencian messenger, Tod. Mordo wasn't accustomed to working with others, but he kept those who lasted through their attack alive so Evris could learn what he wanted from them.

Initially, forty-six of the Brotherhood had survived the massacre. Forty-six of the Brotherhood killed one hundred forty-three Damonai before they were eventually subdued. Even then, over half their number remained. Some Damonai took exception to their losses, the more savage of them decapitating many of the fallen Brothers and picketing their heads around camp, including a circle around the prisoners, parading their victory.

Among the surviving Brothers of the unforeseen attack were the twins: Balanor and Balanus, Aideen and her brothers, Tamis and Besath, and the king-in-the-mountain, Pientero. Bunched together in a tight circle back-to-back, their wrists were bound to their ankles. Familiar faces stared at them from skinny poles. Gringoll, Anvar, Mira, pale faces with an absence of emotion.

A tear rolled down Aideen's cheek and she dropped her head onto Balanus' shoulder. He saw she was staring up at Anvar, the gentle giant who was everyone's favourite in the mountain. Mentor and tutor for all things living. Without children of his own, he had grown to become a father for those who didn't have parents. And now he was being desecrated.

Drelnum approached the group of prisoners. The soldiers standing guard tensed to salute before he dismissed it quickly. Accompanied by the disappearing assassin, the two circled the group, surveying their captives. "How many do you think Evris will want?" Mordo asked.

"All of them."

"But if one becomes more trouble than he's worth, just kill him," DeathShadow ordered a guard he was next to.

He noticed Aideen's tear then, how she stared up at a picketed head. Mordo recognized the man from the previous night and demanded to know who had decapitated him.

"I did, sir," a guard proudly stated. "Took a while."

He crept over to the man, his eyes staring into the guard's own, even as his head bobbed back and forth at strange angles with birdlike curiosity. Stopping before him, Mordo's head settled. "And why did you take his head in the first place?"

"He was the bastard that…" the guard started.

"He deserved respect!" Mordo cut him off. "I watched him beat down nine of you while barely flinching. And with one hand! Pathetic… Now take it and put it with his body. Or I'll replace his head with yours."

With a look of insult, the guard pouted as he followed Mordo's orders.

The deader exchanged a glance with the bound leader. "I'm a killer. But even I principles."

Pientero Jessonarioko sat between Balanus and another, his left shoulder covered in blood. "Why are you here?"

"The only thing to worry about is why you're still here," Drelnum answered. He paced before the king-in-the-mountain and then lowered himself. "But we only need one of you alive to show us what we want."

"No one here's tellin' you anything," PJ promised.

"You don't need to," Drelnum said, coming to stand and challenging Pientero's everlasting stare.

Mordo witnessed their exchange and something moved within him. "Double the guard here!" he ordered. "We've had prisoners escape once already. It's not happening again."

Since the sun had dawned, a steady file of Damonai soldiers came walking into camp. The rest of the dispatched brigade. The reactions of those who arrived at the massacred compound were mixed. Some veterans paid no mind and began helping others with duties. Some men drank in their bloodlust and roared with excitement. Others walked through the camp with penitent eyes, as if put off by the violence around them.

One of the newcomers was welcomed by the guards as he approached the group of prisoners. Only speaking their guttural, native tongue, he shared a short conversation with his friend.

Eventually, the man turned to Drelnum and asked. "*Quan ebaska as bischu?*" *What about the bitches?*

Pientero's head involuntarily shook side to side and Drelnum smiled in delight, realizing he understood their language.

"*El quaneta quoi suook.*" *Do whatever you want.*

"NO!" PJ roared, trying to surge upward. A guard pressed a spear to his chest before he managed anything.

This had become tasteless to Mordo. He walked away and began rummaging through houses.

The newcomer went over to Aideen and grabbed a handful of her brown hair. The next few seconds were chaotic. Balanus, Besath, and Tamis all began writhing in their binds, attempting to save her by any means. Besath caught a spear in his thigh, and Balanus had rolled out from the group toward his love as she was dragged away.

"Nooo!!!" she cried, kicking and wrenching beneath the man's clutch.

"Nooo..." he cried into the grey sand pressed against his face.

*****

"Are we far now, Kael?" Zeth asked as they crested a hill, bringing the bulwark of Tehbirr's Spine into view.

"We'll be there by nightfall."

Hectore, Halder, Kael, and Zeth were alone, the other two hundred Sainti soldiers stationed in the valley behind them.

The king began a fit of coughing atop his horse. It became uncontrollable, racking his whole body as he grew red-faced. His eyes watered and he pounded a fist to his chest.

Kael and the others asked if he was alright and soon he stopped. Spitting to clear his mouth, Hectore took a few deeper breaths. "Don't get too old, son. It's not as fun."

Regaining his colour, he swallowed his throat clear and then pulled his pipe from his belt along with the leather pouch.

"My King, why do you keep smoking when you cough like that?" Halder asked compassionately.

"It helps me feel young."

"You're old, Hec. You should be proud of that."

Hectore smiled fondly at his friend. "There're still some things I haven't done."

"Like what, my King?" Zeth asked from beside Kael.

"There was a pair of swords," Hectore told him, "enchanted blades of mythical power. After we had taken back Esselle, the locals told stories about them. I started looking but never got the chance to find them."

"What pulled you away?" Kael asked, interested in his father's story.

"Your mother," came the answer. "That was when she was taken prisoner among the Damonai."

Kael knew the rest of the story.

"It's going to be hard... finding a man that can disappear," Zeth told Kael after a moment's silence.

Kael didn't know how he would answer that, so the king did for him.

"Mirianne is still only human. He doesn't need to find DeathShadow. Only her."

A hawk skirted through the clouds above and began its descent, spiralling in wide circles that tightened as it approached the earth, before coming to perch on the shoulder of its faithful friend. Halder exchanged conversation with it through a series of looks.

Hectore waited beside him, patiently observing the concern that befell his friend.

"I understand," the old scout told his bird. "Good job."

"What is it?" Hectore demanded.

Halder looked at Kael and Zeth before turning his sad gaze to the King. "I'm sorry, Hec."

"What? What's happened?"

Halder lowered his eyes. "The Brotherhood." Lifting his eyes again, Hectore saw the tears welling in them. "They're gone."

The king was taken off-guard, blinking a few times before he stared into the distance. Kael could tell from his father's look as he processed Halder's words that he believed them, he just couldn't believe the idea. Couldn't fathom the Brotherhood gone. "All of them?"

"There's a small group being held prisoner in the southeast corner of the camp. Not many though."

"How did this happen?" Hectore asked emptily. He and Pientero had been so careful. No one was supposed to even know they existed.

"There's something else," Halder said. He pulled off his rider's cap and scratched the white hair beneath. "Men have been showing up to the mountain all day. A train of them. Their numbers were too great for the bird to count."

Hectore's expression resolved into one of sheer determination. Without another word, he swung his horse around and descended back into the valley.

Arriving back at his men, the King dismounted. The others followed in behind him and jumped off their own horses.

"Kael, Halder!" he called. "Get everyone turned around. You're going home."

"What?!" Kael almost shouted. Quickly noticing the attention he'd gathered, he quieted himself. "What do you mean? Where are you going?"

Those who overheard spread word through the camp.

"To the mountain."

"The hell you are. You heard Halder, there're too many."

Halder nodded his agreement with Kael's opinion. "My hawk saw for herself, Hec. It's a death sentence going there."

"Oh, come on," the HighKing said, before smiling with the confidence of a man who realized he'd won a bet. "I'm sure I've been in worse positions."

Unable to relinquish, Kael pressed, "Why do you want to do this?"

The soldiers behind them began stirring, deflation written clearly through their behaviour. They realized what returning home meant; preparing for a fight without their famous Brotherhood army.

Hectore put a hand on his son's shoulder and looked him in the eye. "Kael, Pientero Jessonarioko is my brother. He might not have my blood, but it's not blood that *defines* family. It's not that I want to do this. I *need* to do this."

"So you're going to ride to your death out of loyalty?" Kael retorted, shrugging his father's hand off.

Dropping his hand, Hectore's face turned to grim stone. "I've overcome death before. The only thing that's certain in that mountain is that Brothers still alive. *Our* Brothers, Kael."

Climbing back into his saddle, he coughed twice before spitting and turning his mount back toward the mountain.

"Sometimes loyalty's all we have," the King said back to his son, tapping his horse forward.

Kael watched his father walk away with an expression that betrayed his thoughts. Turning to Halder, the man halted him with a hand before he spoke, reading his look. "I know what you're doing. And you're not going without me, boy."

Kael smiled and shook his head before stopping Zeth as he walked by. With a hand on his arm, he ordered, "You bring the men back." The Prince looked up at his father, about to disappear over the crest. "I'm going with him."

Stepping into a stirrup, he hoisted himself up onto his horse. Halder rode up beside him. "You ready?"

Kael gave Zeth one last salute before looking back at his father. "Let's go."

*****

Hectore had just lit another pipe of his Yenmaraj when he began coughing heavily again. Without an audience, he allowed the real, ungraceful sound to burst out. His mind was warning him to stop smoking, but the *sciong* was tingling his burning chest into comfort, renewing the fading strength in his arms, and providing a momentary burst of energy.

The king's vision began to blur, and his eyes strained before he blinked them hard. Since when did it take my focus to see? Hectore wondered. He meditated for a moment as his horse trotted down the path.

He was reflecting on his relationship with the king-in-the-mountain when he heard a pair of hooves behind him. Trotting up on either side, Hectore smiled to see Kael at his right, then Halder at his left. They kept riding around a wide bend, passing trees that clutched to their final leaves, hooves clapping over a fresh coat of autumn earth.

Suddenly, Zeth and three others showed up alongside Kael and Halder.

Hectore gave them a look of gratitude. He heard more hooves and peered over his shoulder to see the entire company of Sainti soldiers riding behind him. Following him into hell.

Chapter 29

"There's no way the Damonai would come back here after the way your father sent them scrambling home. Tails so far between their legs they weren't virgins anymore!" a thick Melonian said from Rodrik Rond's right, slamming his goblet on the table, sloshing mead in his emphasis.

"Nevertheless, there have been irrefutable reports of Damonai forces scattered throughout Saintos," Raphael said, reaching for calm agreement with the drunk man.

"Are you scared of a little fight?" the Melonian smiled before taking another huge gulp.

Rodrik slapped the goblet from his mouth. "Hold your tongue, fool! Did you forget where we are?!"

Say that I'm scared again and you'll see how afraid I am to draw blood, Raphael thought. His displeasure must have been evident because the burly Melonian slunk down like a frightened dog.

The Wardens of the Realm had arrived with varying sizes of retinue escorting them that was almost reflective of their realm's population and devotion to military prowess. Making use of the rarely entered War Room, they were seated around the pentagonal table Raphael's father had built after his ascension with each warden posted at a corner, offering an equal view of his counterparts. Sitting along the base of the table were ten Southern Freefolk, including three generations of Bailes and their closest friends, who had travelled for the meeting requested by their HighKing. They were naturally the last to arrive, having been the most difficult to locate; their people still moving around between pre-existing settlements. With their slanted eyes and sun-burned skin, they were the most easily identifiable race.

Across from the Bailes was the regal uncle of the Rai princes, Benson Wellcant, accompanied by a group of six of the fiercest looking men in the room. They were comprised of all races of human, their constant battle against the sea unifying and roughing them all into intrepidity.

Rodrik Rond, the Warden of the North, had the largest escort, both in stature and in number, twelve strong. Made up mostly of dark-skinned men carrying the imposing presence of the North with them.

Seated across from Rond, beside the Bailes, was the withered Warden Rali, escorted by two guards who were almost as old as him. Trust was hard-earned with the Western Warden, Raphael recalled. The justicar Mick also sat with them.

Finally, the Princes Raphael and Arlahn sat at the "head" of their table alone, representing the entirety of Pellence. With the exception of the Wardens themselves, formal weapons weren't permitted into the meeting, but nevertheless, most of those in attendance had a small dirk or knife on their belt.

"Now," Raphael addressed them, leaning forward and placing his elbows on the table. "The Damonai are here, scattered throughout Saintos. After a message from the Essellian justicar, my father believes they're looking for the Brotherhood."

"The Brotherhood's gone, my prince," Warden Rali started softly, his frailty evident.

Warden Baile interrupted and finished more forcefully, though barely. "PJ's dead. Has been for years."

"No," Arlahn spoke for the first time since they'd entered the room. The others quieted and gave the Princes a look of disbelief. "He's alive."

The table erupted in brief conversations between the Wardens, disputing the claim.

"He *is* alive," Raphael claimed with a silencing authority, "living in a tactical tract of mountain range, training his elite, isolated from the world."

"Are you telling me that PJ has been alive this whole time? Training his own fighters?" Warden Rond asked, leaning onto the table.

Raphael nodded.

Rodrik broke the silence. Chuckling at first, his giggling turned into a full-on laugh.

"What's so funny, Rodrik?" Benson Wellcant.

"If PJ is still alive, training his own army... Once the king gets back, what's there to worry about?"

"Where is your father?" Benson asked his nephews.

"On his way to the Brotherhood right now to warn them and hold the mountain."

"Hold the mountain?" Rodrik repeated. "Why hold a mountain?"

"As I said, it's a tactical tract," Raphael answered. "There are rivers that lead to aqueducts for every realm. It was designed so the Brotherhood could be dispatched quickly and effectively throughout Saintos."

"So if they don't succeed, the Damonai will have means to travel wherever they want in our lands," the former Damonai Rali stated.

"No," Raphael said, putting the turncloak at ease. "Not entirely. They would need to know which river led where."

"And if they accomplish this?" Rali insisted.

"Then we'll need to be prepared. You each have a set of blueprints in front of you. You'll notice that some of the designs are simple, the more complex ones have multiple drawings. Everything's explained in the margins."

Raphael went through each of his blueprints in detail, highlighting specific materials that would be needed and providing a schedule of operations for the most efficient building teams. "Does anyone have any questions?" he finished.

"Just one, my prince," Warden Rond asked from across the table. "Where's the food?"

"It'll be by shortly, Lord Rond. My apologies, I didn't know you were hungry."

"Don't apologize, Your Grace," he said with a devilish smile. "I'm always hungry."

*****

Stars blinked overhead as a carpet of clouds rolled in across the sky. Stuck in their tight circle, the men of the Brotherhood were helpless to stop the Damonai that had come to collect the other surviving Sisters. They raved in fury, causing their captors to mock their efforts to save one another.

Mordo entered the group and knelt before Pientero. "You have an impressive operation here. What else do you have down your paths?"

Pientero looked up at the man, hatred in his eyes. Encouraging him toward his traps, he told him, "Go for a walk and find out."

Mordo almost smiled at that. "No need," he said, coming to stand. "Caliph Asa will be here with Evris soon enough."

"Asa?" PJ contemplated. "Hennah Asa? That bitch witch from Esselle. I knew I should have killed her years ago."

The Deader backhanded him across the mouth, staring at him with a look that warned of his transgression. After a moment of silence, DeathShadow told him, "I wanted to go to Pellence. To kill your precious King. But I think you'll do fine."

PJ spat before looking back into his captor's eyes. "I'm not afraid of death. As for the king? I've known him a long time. It's gonna take more than arrogance to kill him."

This time Mordo did smile, proving his arrogance. He vanished in front of PJ and then reappeared, kneeling down at his captive's level.

"You think that little trick's gonna save you?"

Mordo's anger flashed throughout his expression, but he calmed eventually. "When we meet, he'll see me kill him."

At that, PJ guffawed. "You've got me quivering now."

The deader grabbed a handful of Pientero's hair, and the Brothers around him began stirring as Mordo produced his dagger. He ran the tip along the King-in-the-mountain's eyebrow and down his cheek. "I figured yours would be the best mind for Evris to explore, but he might be disappointed." He lowered the knife down to his throat. "How I wish your king was here to see this."

"Look!" a guard said, pointing out across the village behind Mordo.

Glancing over his shoulder, he made out a glowing light. He stood up and turned, seeing the yellow-orange flames roaring over the rooftops. Damonai scurried through the compound to help extinguish the fire. Screams and curses yelled out. Mordo thought he even heard the clang of steel.

Cursing, he ordered the guards to remain there while he started across the camp to assess the commotion.

As he watched the man leave, Balanor let out a heavy sigh, concerned for his king. But Pientero's dark eyes followed the black-garbed man down the street. Looking up at the fire past the deader, a smile grew on his face as he thought to himself, Firestarter...

"What are you smiling about?" Balanor whispered to him.

"The fool got what he wished for," PJ answered. "Hectore's here."

"What are you two talking about?" a freckle-faced guard with a horribly crooked nose interrupted.

The king-in-the-mountain looked up at him. "We're talkin' about how you broke your nose. I bet it's 'cause you're an ass sniffer."

*****

"Where the hell is Kael?" Zeth asked as he sank behind a shrub.

"Wait for the signal," Halder told him.

The HighKing had devised a plan and split his forces. Being the only two familiar with the camp, Kael and Hectore headed their infiltration into the mountain.

Slipping through the surrounding forest with preposterous stealth, the Prince brought a hundred and eighty men around to the northwest corner of the compound. They eagerly waited in watch for Kael's signal.

He snuck beside the first row of cabins, keeping to the shadows as two patrols walked past.

Hearing laughter, Kael looked into the window across the way. A silhouette of a man thrusting flickered in the bleak candlelight.

The Prince held his claymore close and rushed over the street. As the door opened in front of him, he punched his sword through the man's chest. Rushing him back into the room, he booted him off the blade and spun, poking it into the second Damonai he saw, someone trying to stand behind the table.

Kael darted through the curtain to find the man from the window rutting into a woman, who had been strapped into a compromising position. He stabbed the sweaty soldier through the back and the woman gasped before Kael covered her mouth.

Her eyes rolled toward the Prince and he knew from her features that she was from the mountain originally. Her brown hair was matted and strewn, her head puffy from silencing blows. Kael cut her free and she regained herself, booting the man on the ground twice before she bent down and pulled the dagger from his belt.

Rushing back to the door, Kael waited with his sword raised for a few seconds in case someone outside had heard the scuffle. During those few seconds, his racing heart calmed.

No one came.

The Prince grabbed a thick candle from the counter and returned to the main room. Before, rushing through in the heat of the moment, he hadn't noticed the drawings. Covering an entire interior wall were hundreds of them, their edges overlapping, the oldest ones beginning to fade.

Holding his candle aloft, Kael studied them a moment, lost in their details. Seeing the Palace of Pellence drawn on one reminded him of his purpose and he tipped the flame closer, watching as the first few drawings caught fire.

Then he grabbed a bottle of mead, stuffed a cloth in its top, and lit it aflame. The Sister did the same to two other bottles she'd found in a cupboard. Charging out of the house, Kael threw the bottle into the window of the adjacent cabin and took one of the Sister's two remaining firebombs. Pointing to one house with his sword, he catapulted the other bottle into the neighbouring cabin. The Sister threw hers at the one he'd pointed to and they rushed back to the tree line.

They were in the southwest corner of the compound and began scurrying north along the edge of town. Passing by familiar faces standing piked in a row, Kael tried not to look in fear of recognizing them.

Behind them, he could hear the commotion starting, men rushed about calling out, "FIRE!" in alarm.

Seeing the light cast around him, he knew the cabins were ablaze and that his men would be waiting for him just out of sight. They arrived at the tree line and Kael began waving his sword. Bushes and shrubs before him rustled until men began emerging.

Turning back to face the camp, he took up his sword with both hands. His formation of men came out beside him. Kael's part of the plan was almost complete. Creating an inferno in the one corner of camp, he would attack those tending to it from behind.

Beginning as a trot, Kael, the Sister, and his men soon began to jog. He spotted a Damonai with his back to him and charged, bellowing out a great battle cry that turned the warrior around just in time for the Prince to plow through him. Following soldiers, trampled the man to silence as Kael rushed on, moving to the next Damonai that heard his cry. He stepped forward with a wide-angled chop that sliced the man open from shoulder to hip, then came up to stab another in the side, the blade sliding effortlessly through the Damonai's ribs to pierce his lungs. Pulling out the claymore, Kael hefted it toward a man to his left that leapt back just in time. Recovering quickly, he advanced on the Prince and lunged low with a vicious thrust. Kael deflected the stab, swinging in reverse, and spun with the momentum to bring his blade up to shoulder height, steel slicing through skin and bone cleanly. The man fell, decapitated.

All the men behind him began shouting and roaring as they collided into the unsuspecting Damonai soldiers like wind through fallen leaves. The ones who were concerned about the fire were the first to fall. Once their presence had been noticed, however, the Damonai began gathering arms and forming a resistance.

Cries of adrenaline and agony alike filled the valley air, accompanied by the clashing of steel as men hacked and stabbed.

Heading his formation alongside Halder and Zeth, Kael pushed forward, parrying away an attack and hammering a left hook straight into the man's cheek, instantly caving it in and smashing the back of his head open against a wall. Out of the corner of his eye, he spotted a man to his right about to attack Zeth and swung his blade single-handed at the warrior. The last foot of it caught the man's exposed side and stopped him long enough for Zeth to recover and finish him off. Kael jumped back and buried his claymore in a downed man.

More Damonai came rushing over to join the battle. Having woken from their slumber, armed men began pouring out of the cabins. Coming from everywhere, Sainti soldiers behind Kael broke from their formation to meet groups of warriors head-on.

The Damonai's number began to swell and surround the invading force maintaining the northern border. They pushed toward the northeastern corner of the camp, making their way to the river path.

The first of the Sainti began to fall, the Damonai shaving a number off their right flank. From behind the attacking warriors came a horrific roar. A medak bear bulled through two men and began swatting its claws, chomping with its snout. Damonai scattered as Halder gave a laugh and cheered on his old friend. Following the medak was a couple of buffaboar. Fierce beasts of incredible size with two pointed tusks that hooked out from either side of their mouths, though the male had already broken one of his. They charged into piles of Damonai, thrashing their heads forward and bucking their hind legs, clearing the men in circles.

"We need to keep moving," Kael said to Zeth between cutting men down. "Keep rolling east to meet up with my father. Take the path to the river and use the boats to escape."

He turned to Halder, "Get to the rear and close up our formation. We need to go."

The veteran scout nodded and slipped back through the Sainti force.

"FOR SAINTOS!" Kael roared out as he continued to cut a wedge into the Damonai. His ferocious battle cries gave the Sainti men renewed vigour to carry on battling fearlessly. Covered in blood, the Prince hacked and slashed like a monster as Damonai soldiers came at him and were left dead in his wake. He ducked under a jab and dragged his blade along the belly of the attacker, moving past him and lifting his leg to deliver a huge forward boot. Another warrior took Kael's foot to the chest and flew back across the avenue, crashing into a wall. From his left, he saw another man about to stab him in the side, but Zeth stepped in, deflecting the blade down and jabbing his sword in the man's chest right before the Prince.

They made their way east, Kael forcing his men out into a wedge so that their formation resembled a spear. No matter how fierce the Sainti soldiers fought, how many Damonai warriors they slew, the enemy seemed perpetual. They were simply outnumbered.

Kael booted another man, smashing him through a pile of barrels. He looked up and saw a dark-haired man appear from thin air to stab Halder's medak in the neck. The beast, that had just been roaring, was so taken off-guard that it could only grunt and tumble down beside its killer.

The man looked over at Kael, wiped the tip of his blade clear, then disappeared from the fray.

"SHADOW!" Kael cried out. Rushing out from his men, he charged toward the spot where the deader had vanished.

He saw him reappear next to a cabin forty feet away. The man in black smiled at the Prince and rolled back behind his cover.

Kael screamed again and continued fighting toward the cabin as many more black-garbed warriors kept funnelling into the battle.

Through the cabins, Kael caught a glimpse of his father fighting. Killing with true intent in his heart. It bred newfound respect in the soldier in him, one surrendered by a terrible fear. Turning his katana into a paintbrush and the world into his canvas, Hectore dragged, dotted, poked, and stroked his way through the enemy. Like a combination of natural forces coming together in a perfect storm, he consumed all in his path, leaving bodies around him like debris in the wake of a disaster.

In that moment, Kael understood all of the Damonai's anger and resentment. All their fear. Watching him, he would have believed, too, that his father was a Demon among men.

Men came at Kael from both sides and he took a cut along his shoulder. His rage fuelled him further. Unrelenting, he fought to rendezvous with his father.

Having broken away from his formation to chase after the coward assassin, Kael hadn't realized how far he'd ventured into the enemy. Behind him, Zeth and Halder pushed the men forward, trying to fight their way to him. Two more crossed his path and he hit them both with a horizontal swing, batting them well into the air and drawing more attention to his location.

Fifteen Damonai amassed around the Prince. Taking up his blade in both hands, Kael readied himself. He was prepared to die fighting for his land. For his home.

Chapter 30

They continued discussing preparations for their standing armies. From numbers, to resources, to food, Raphael made note of everything his Wardens said, about every variable he could account for.

Before the Brotherhood, Arlahn would have sat quietly during the conversation, too timid to speak his thoughts. But after his time with Pientero, he was much more engaged, questioning certain ideas that bothered him. Like his test atop the mountain, Arlahn flipped every scenario into a pessimistic outcome. Souring their affairs but raising questions that demanded attention should the worst occur. He reminded his elders that their contingencies should have contingencies. During war, there was no such thing as over-prepared. Warden Baile remarked how his views reflected Pientero's and put to rest his final skepticism about the man's existence.

Having the smallest army, and being a turncloak, when Warden Nakoli Rali spoke, he was solely concerned about the Damonai's return. Oppositely, Rond and Baile were confident about facing them, having the largest armies. Claiming the North and South would send back any intruder who dared enter without their consent, especially with Raphael's improvement to their defences. Benson Wellcant seemed more reserved than the others, mostly listening unless directly questioned.

Servers entered and began wordlessly handing out plates of food.

"Over here! I'll take that off your hands," Rond called to the maid holding three plates, one balanced on her left arm.

Licking his lips, he nearly stood up and reached out for the pile of steaming food, but the maid smiled at his enthusiasm and passed him a plate.

Rond took up his fork and knife, gazing at his food. "You princes sure know how to eat."

Arlahn was captured by the beauty of the girl serving their guests. He didn't recognize her but excused this with his recent absence. After meeting the physician, he realized there would be a few new faces, it wasn't uncommon for his father to take in the less fortunate. The woman was strikingly breathtaking, almost out of place in her simple white and blue smock. The curve of her hips could only be found in sculpture, no real women had a shape like that, at least none Arlahn had ever seen. Her tight blouse exposed her breasts, their grandeur noticeable but not overt, as she leaned out to deliver another plate. Arlahn fell victim to their call and knew he had been caught when he looked into her face and she winked. The maid's smile revealed the top row of pearly white, perfect teeth shining between supple lips; her flaring red hair framed her face with two thick, curly locks, and her chiselled cheeks and prominent brow drew him in to the centrepiece of her attraction. Her eyes. Playful, seductive, and a shade of blue that captured the clear open sky, promising flirtation and secrecy.

She left and returned with another three plates, doing her best to avoid shooting him another look and carrying out her duties. Arlahn tried his best to ignore her back and tuned into the conversation.

"If the Damonai are scattered, why don't we go out and hunt them down?" Warden Baile's son asked, slamming his knife into the table before him. The man was in his forties by the look of him, but each generation of Baile was a younger version of their lineage.

"They'd want us to come out from behind our walls," Rond answered. "Besieging a well-provisioned city can be demoralizing."

The third time the server girl entered with plates, the pair made eye-contact again. She made her way for the Prince and was halfway around the table when another maid placed a plate down before him.

The redhead's smile wilted a touch and, keeping her stare locked with the Prince's, she wrapped around the old Warden Rali to deliver her last plate. Coming away from him, Rali leaned back in his chair, his eyes looking up at her in acknowledgement, and she smiled warmly. Running her hand off his shoulder, the maid tucked it into her other and elegantly walked away.

Warden Rali shifted his eyes from the girl to Prince Raphael, who was emphasizing the importance of their preparations.

"It's sound logic to be ready to move though," Rond added. "They can't attack us all at once."

"Our castles have no walls," Baile proudly stated to the other Wardens, referring to the forests that were their Kingdom. "We can start moving north and add our strength to your lands if need be. The South is too widespread. And they remember what we did to them last time."

Benson Wellcant promised that his ships would patrol the shoreline and deny history from repeating itself.

"They wouldn't invade by sea this time," Arlahn protested his uncle, "besides who knows how many are already here."

Benson gave his nephew a challenging look but yielded to his logic. "Very well. We'll move our men inland. I don't know how they'll feel without a ship beneath them. But our mountain passes are impenetrable."

With his Warden adding so little, and perhaps inspired by the youthful princes, Mick had begun taking more initiative during the discussion. "The Essellian TrueBlades are a proud order but small. I don't know how long they could withstand a siege without help."

"And what do you think, Warden Rali?" Raphael asked.

The Warden staring back at him didn't answer, as if the question hadn't registered. His veiny blue eyes didn't move.

A few of those around the table exchanged looks of confusion.

"Warden Rali?" Arlahn asked this time.

Again, the man stared, unblinking.

Mick stood up to check on his lord when he saw it.

Matte black and thin.

"It's a knife!"

*****

Hectore poked his head out from behind a shrub as someone snuck up to him from behind. "What are we waiting for?"

It was the magicker Jole. They had found each other on the paths shortly after Hectore separated from his son. The king learned that Arlahn had left the mountainous community before the massacre and prayed that he'd avoided the Damonai on his return. He'd also struggled to understand how the magicker was free. "Without another Brother to show me the way, I got lost on those damn paths again. Couldn't find my way back to camp in time for the fight."

Naturally joining the king in his rescue attempt, Jole was still unaware of the plan. But he remembered the lengths Hectore went to in order to save his friends and required no explanation.

"That," Hectore said, looking out at a fire that was starting in the far end of camp. Dropping back down, he turned to twenty of his men and gave them a nod. Then the King drew the katana off of his back, rolled out from behind his cover surreptitiously, and began a light, silent jog.

"What are you two talking about?" he heard a Damonai guard ask as he quickened his pace, two files of men behind him.

"We're talkin' about how you broke your nose," Pientero answered from his bondage. "I bet it's 'cause you're an ass sniffer."

The adolescent ignorance of immortality that had once coursed through Hectore began to do so again as it always had when he surrendered to his Gift. It was his guilty pleasure, fighting, and he relished the exhilaration.

The guard with the crooked nose began toward PJ when another stopped him and pointed to the growing fire. "Maybe they need our help."

The crooked nose wrinkled. "You heard DeathShadow. We stay here and guard."

Hectore felt a dead branch crack under him. The volume and proximity caused the doubtful guard to turn. Stepping out with a giant thrust, Hectore plunged the sword right into the man's neck. He threw himself into the crooked-nosed warrior and shoulder-rushed him down, darting in, kneeling, and planting his katana like a flag right before the king-in-the-mountain.

Sainti soldiers peeled out in either direction and intercepted the Damonai before anyone could attack the defenceless prisoners. Drawing the short gladius from his left hip, Hectore stabbed it between PJ's legs, cutting them free. His friend gave the sword a sharp look. "I hate when you do stuff like that!" he said then hurried to free his hands.

"Kael has a force of men along the northern border. Head for the boats."

PJ had finished cutting himself free and stood up. "The boats? There's no Damonai at the boats!" He ripped the gladius out of the ground and stormed off toward the enemy, possessed. The booming authority of his voice pushed Brothers and Hectore's Sainti force forward.

In truth, the king hadn't expected any different from the man, he knew what this place meant to him. He watched as the mountain master dove toward the first warrior he saw, killing him in the first exchange with a terrible riposte.

Formerly imprisoned Brothers, now liberated, gathered weapons off the dead and joined in the battle.

"NORTH!" Hectore demanded.

PJ changed direction and began fighting his way north. The Damonai were everywhere, direction was irrelevant to the king-in-the-mountain. Only one of the Sainti soldiers had been slain during the first attack and so nineteen soldiers and twenty-two Brothers followed him.

Surging their way through camp, the first group they came upon was too occupied with the fire to realize their prisoners had escaped.

Other armed Damonai came from cabins and rushed toward the northern ridge where Kael and his men were fighting.

Eventually, the anarchy grew to controlled chaos as the Damonai realized what was happening around them. A fire in one end of camp, a battle along another, and now their prisoners had been set free and were taking back their home. Slowly, they began to organize themselves.

Pientero stole a broken spear from one of his victims and wielded it in his free hand. It twirled and swung, thrusting high and low into men all around him. Balanor had been among the first to rush in behind his king. Balanus, not far behind, engaged a man armed with a hatchet and they exchanged blows before the Brother emerged victorious, landing a counter-riposte in the man's chest. Jole cleaved and pounded with his axe, throwing incandescent balls of flame and streams of purple lightning between cuts. Behind them, Besath rescued his brother Tamis and the duo finished off each other's man.

The rest of the allied force clashed with the black-garbed warriors, hacking and slashing relentlessly. The Damonai had abandoned the fire, and although there was another force attacking exactly opposite of the rescue team, they maintained a surplus of numbers and divided their attention accordingly as more warriors joined the battle.

Advancing their way north, like an oar through water, Sainti and Brothers repelled their attackers with remorseless vengeance.

Jole pushed alongside PJ and Balanor. Together, they were devastating. Fighting at the head of the rescue team, the three cleaved through the tip of the wedge, sending away Damonai hordes.

PJ jumped back from a vicious slice that would have disembowelled him and poked forward at his attacker. Stabbing low, he caught the man's calf, slicing the flesh open. As he came up, Pientero quickly twirled the spear into the man's head, propelling him down. He finished him off swiftly and returned to his position alongside the axeman.

Up ahead, they could see Hectore alone, fighting like a god that had descended from the skies and assumed his being. No Damonai warrior lasted more than a short exchange with him. He danced and cut his way through the warriors, leaving a trail of bodies behind him.

PJ was determined to reach his brother and pushed on with the group of Sainti soldiers, his men following loyally at his side. They had trained together all their lives and now fought valiantly alongside the king-in-the-mountain at the head of the force.

Balanus remained near the rear, closer to Tamis, protecting him as best he could against the Damonai horde.

A warrior made it through and came at him, grazing his right shoulder with the reverse slice of his riposte. The warrior hacked downward at Tamis' other shoulder, but the young Brother blocked the attack and feebly fought to hold the blade in place. Tamis could feel his strength beginning to fail him against the seasoned Damonai but before his last bit of hold gave way,

Balanus plunged his newly acquired scimitar into the man's belly. He jerked, and Tamis threw back the warrior's sword, burying his two nine-inch daggers in the man's chest.

Balanus looked back and saw three more warriors in black descend on him after watching their comrade fall.

Pushing Tamis behind him, he tried to fend off all three men simultaneously. But Tamis returned to his Brother's aid and jumped in, blocking a low thrust. He slashed one man's ribs with a reverse cut before he jumped back. Bare-chested like his brother Besath, Tamis may have been younger, but his agility was awesome. Still, much of the strength in his wounded arm had faded and he weakly clutched his weapon. Another warrior joined, outnumbering the Brothers four to two.

Balanus chose his counter attacks wisely, always keeping a defensive mindset in such close quarters. He blocked a thrust from his left side attacker and recovered in time to stop a cut that would have taken him in the neck from his right attacker, stabbing the man in the gut.

Tamis fought out of pure desperation and flailed his knives about almost sporadically. One of the warrior's blades caught him in his weakened right shoulder with the tip just protruding from his back. He let out a cry and fell back, dropping a knife. That was when Besath carelessly jumped between the attackers and defended his wounded brother.

Turning back two attacks as they came at him at once, one warrior managed to scrape his blade across Besath's ribs during their last exchange. Blood began to slowly dribble down his bare side. As he looked down and saw it, adrenaline replaced his pain and renewed his vigour. Three warriors advanced on Besath and Balanus, and this time it was the Brothers who caught one of the attackers in the back, just next to his shoulder blade, and threw him to the ground behind them. Tamis scurried over the ground and buried his knife into the warrior.

The remaining Damonai retreated to a safe distance as Besath stood tall, every muscle in his upper body flexing, his breathing heavy. Another warrior came at Balanus from his side and the Brother lunged to meet him.

Then, from out of nowhere, an arrow flew past the two Damonai warriors and took Besath high in the chest. His shoulder jerked back from the impact as the pain bit into him. Looking down, he saw a white arrow jutting from below his clavicle. Besath drew his gaze back up, past the warriors, and in the distance he could see a tall archer with a longbow, getting ready to nock another arrow.

With his focus off of them, two warriors came at the Brother and he was reduced to leaping backward and flailing his scimitar to keep them away. But one advanced on Besath, launching a thrust that he barely managed to deflect. Coming back with a reverse slash, Besath parried the attack, throwing the blade upward and stepping forward to stab the warrior between the ribs.

Just as the Damonai fell with his hand dragging down Besath's body, another arrow caught him just above his left hip. He dropped down on one knee and looked up at the archer. But the last warrior came between them; a malicious looking man storming toward him with a single-headed axe in his hand, licking his lips as he stepped in to split Besath's head in two.

The axeman began his almighty wind-up, when Balanor came crashing into the man. Abandoning his attempt to reach Hectore, he'd looked back and saw that Balanus, Besath, and Tamis were in trouble and charged back to help.

Balanor carried a large, round Damonai buckler and used it more as an offensive weapon than a defensive tool. He blocked an overhand axe and cracked the warrior in the jaw with the wooden edge of the shield. The man staggered back and Balanor drove his sword into the Damonai's chest.

Recovering quickly, he prepared himself for the archer that he'd seen strike Besath, but the coward had run off, slipping away into another place in the battle.

Balanor moved back to Besath, where Tamis had laid him down and was cradled over his chest sobbing, squeezing his hand.

Balanor knelt down and took up Besath's other hand. He had fought bravely, valiantly.

"You have to get Aideen," Besath struggled to tell Balanor through blood trickling from his lips. "Promise me."

"I promise."

Then Balanor felt the strength of his Brother's grip slip away and his eyes glossed over.

"Come on," he said, taking Tamis by the arm. He practically dragged him back into formation.

Meanwhile, along the northern edge of the battlefield, Halder, the old scout, was immersed right in the thick of the battle alongside the main force of Sainti soldiers, fighting bravely behind their prince. His two buffaboar thrashed and charged into bodies at his side.

Archers had climbed the cabins and were about to let loose when an entire flock of birds overwhelmed them from above. Dropping from the clouds, they pecked and clawed at faces as they flew by. The creatures coordinated their attacks, continuing to divert attention and waste the Damonai's ammunition. Occasionally they'd all target the same archer, swarming him with flapping wings until he dropped.

The medak went down and Halder fought alongside his prince to reach him. Arriving at the beast, a bald, bearded Damonai bearing a tomahawk came toward him.

The buffaboar on Halder's right charged past to meet his attack, but the bald warrior impossibly absorbed the buffaboar's rushing tusk. He took a step back to stop its momentum and together they crashed up against a cabin. Raising his tomahawk, the warrior cleaved once into the animal's brown hide. The buffaboar writhed in its pain and spun around, repeatedly beating the bald man against the cabin with its hooves.

Again, he cleaved viciously in its side, and this time, the buffaboar cried out and retreated. Halder screamed and came at the man. He stabbed his sword against the man's belly but, as if made of wood, it only pushed the Damonai back against the wall.

The tomahawk raised and fell into his shoulder.

Tossing Halder to the side, the bald warrior retreated before the other buffaboar arrived.

The second animal was heavily weakened already and after gathering its wounded partner, approached their master.

Halder pushed himself back against a cabin and sat there as the beasts nestled his face softly with their tusks. He opened his eyes.

"It's time for you to go." He patted one on its shoulder. "Thank you, friends."

The buffaboars limped off into the darkness of the forest, and Halder tilted his head back against the cabin to look up at the stars. Slowly, their shining dimmed until all was black.

*****

"Assassins!" Raphael roared, standing up and pulling a short sword from its scabbard hidden underneath the table, that was placed for such emergencies.

The rest of the table jumped up in a frenzy, brandishing the weapons of their native land. Arlahn unsheathed his pearly white dagger from the small of his back and began surveying the room. Eight guards had been posted within the War Room and they drew their swords.

One of them had a look in his eye that disturbed Raphael. "GUARD!" he commanded. "STAND DOWN!"

The Sainti Wardens noticed how quickly the guard discarded the Prince's order. Rodrik raised his thick, wickedly curved scimitar.

The guard approached two more steps, but a Kalendare acting as a server snuck up behind him and snapped his neck.

Seven remaining Pellencian guards began attacking the poorly armed Wardens of Saintos, and though outnumbered, they managed to take down six before they were overcome.

Everything had erupted so quickly that neither of the Princes had much time to think. Rounding the front of the table toward the door, they gathered the survivors. Three actual servers had cowered in the corner from the violence that occurred before them.

"Uncle Benson, stay here and keep them safe," Arlahn ordered, pointing quickly to the servers.

"You need to get mother. I'm going for Marly," Raphael told his brother before he opened the door.

"Where is she?" Arlahn asked, referring to his mother.

"Somewhere in the palace."

Stepping out into the hall, they found their entire house had erupted from within. Innocent servants screamed and ran through the violence, trying to find salvation. Dozens of skirmishes were being fought between Pellencian dressed guards and servant dressed Kalendare.

"Rond, grab your men! Marly's upstairs."

Raphael and Rodrik were met at the top of the stairs by a group of guards. They quickly overtook them, but a Melonian soldier went over the railing with a guard and died on impact.

Arlahn took Warden Baile and his men with him to join the fray of the main floor, fighting to clear the foyer. As they dispatched the last guard and regrouped, Arlahn thought which direction to clear next.

In the southwest corner of the foyer, a body crashed through the double doors of the library and tumbled before them. Standing in the doorway, the attacker looking at Arlahn's group gave them a cynical grin. "After this, the people will envy Patriclus more than DeathShadow."

A puff of dense black smoke swirled where he once stood. At the sight of him vanishing, those behind Arlahn silenced. The black smoke reappeared, swirling about a single point behind the Prince and Patriclus emerged from it. Arlahn's training guided him, he swung behind and caught the assassin off-guard, forcing him to duck and puff away.

Re-emerging in front of the Prince this time, Patriclus was already attacking. With almost immeasurable reaction time, Arlahn leaned back to the point of falling, deflecting the incoming thrust over him. Accepting his loss of balance, he dropped flat on his back and booted out the assassin's foot from under him.

Patriclus dropped to a knee and the Kalendare at Arlahn's side-stepped in to finish him.

Another balloon of smoke popped, and the sword carried through weightless vapours. Patriclus appeared again, behind the same Kalendare that attacked him, and poked a hole in his neck with a flash of his arm. He moved to do the same thing again to the middle-generation Baile on Arlahn's other side, but the Southerner reacted just in time, the blade slicing his ear rather than neck.

Retreating from the Baile's retaliation in another puff of smoke, Patriclus came up behind Arlahn, grabbing the Prince by the collar and ripping him back down to the ground. Rather than fall on his back, Arlahn rolled into a backward somersault, kneeing the Gifted assassin in the face.

Patriclus began to fall back toward the troop of Kalendare and Southerners when he turned to smoke once more. Arlahn lowered himself as he spun, surveying the room. The smoke materialized at the top of the stair and Patriclus fell from it. He stood up, dusted himself, gave the group below him a look that promised return, then fled.

Raphael, Rodrik, and his men fought through the upstairs of the palace. The Prince was growing more concerned with the number of guards that fought them as they neared his bedchamber.

He heard his mother scream from the end of the hall and raced ahead of his escort. Charging into his room, he found his mother and his fiancé backed into a corner. Four guards laid dead beside them, arrows in their chests. Queen Annabella clutched a knife with both hands, trying to keep two more away from her pregnant daughter, and Marlyonna had taken up Raphael's bow off the wall but the quiver hanging from her waist was empty.

Hearing the door smash open caused the guards to turn. One man faced the Prince, while the other licked his lips, relishing in the distraught queen and her harmless threats.

Raphael knew that without both men's attention on him, his time was limited. He stepped in to meet his attacker and parried his slash. Wanting to get closer to the table the guard was near, Raphael came at him with a riposte and picked up a bowl-shaped vase off the table, spinning past the guard attacking him with a powerful high cut. With a backhand, Raphael hammered the bowl into the back of the second guard's head, and the unsuspecting man fell forward. The Prince turned back to the first guard, took up his shoulder by a pressure point near the base of the neck, and punched his short sword through the man's belly.

Turning to finish the fallen guard, Raphael was utterly shocked by what he saw. Kneeling over the top of the guard, his mother, the queen, pounded her knife into his chest over and over. Nine times until she knew he was dead. Red painted across her knuckles.

When she stopped, Annabella noticed her trembling hands and let the knife roll clear. Mortified by her actions, she scurried backward into Marlyonna in the corner.

His entire life, Raphael had never met anyone with the same purity in their heart as his mother. A woman of everlasting, unconditional affection. She had certainly witnessed death, he knew, she had even prevented death as a medic. But she had never delivered it.

Marlyonna clutched Annabella in her arms, their blonde hair seemingly entangled. "He was coming for my baby."

That seemed to snap the queen out of it. "We have to hide you somewhere safe."

"The tunnel through the palace," Raphael told his mother "There's an entrance in the throne room."

Marly retrieved three arrows on their way out. As they snuck out into the hall, a group of guards discovered them from either side. Raphael charged a group of three one way, while Marly turned and took aim at a lonely soldier at the other end.

She fired at him, but he ducked out of the way just in time. Starting his approach, he began weaving back and forth down the hall. Marly fired her second arrow, but, throwing himself against a table, the guard dodged it. The distance between them began to shrink and he started sprinting for her.

"Raph!" she called out as she pulled her final arrow from her quiver.

Her prince fought ferociously to finish off his final two opponents to get back to her but downed them too late. Behind him, the soldier was about to close on Marly.

She fumbled the nock into place and pulled the bow back as quickly as she could, but the soldier before her was too close to bother aiming, so she raised her bow and let the string roll off her fingers. The man saw her nock the arrow and began lowering himself to duck and stab, but she had fired much quicker than he anticipated, and he caught the shot high in his forehead. With his momentum carrying him forward, the guard tumbled face first before Marly, fletchings tickling her toes.

Raphael's firm grasp whirled her around and pulled her through the palace, the queen holding her other hand.

Arlahn met them alone outside the throne room. "I found the real guards, their food was poisoned."

He followed his family inside where the brown-haired Patriclus stood with his backs to them, admiring the golden orb before him.

The man turned at the sound of the door and saw Prince Arlahn. His face twitched. "You again."

He went up in a puff of black smoke and appeared beside the Prince. Taking a stab at Arlahn, the Prince deflected it into a grazing blow along his side, but before he could retaliate, the deader was gone.

"Get to the throne!" Annabella ordered them, racing off for the organ in the corner of the room. Kneeling on the bench, she rhythmically played nine quick notes of an ancient, long-forgotten song. The result was incredible. The floor of the throne room began shifting. Nebulae and galaxies rotated on their axis, and the seven planets erratically spread through the floor began orbiting around the sun-shaped centre. Gears and shafts could faintly be heard beneath the floor.

The ground Raphael, Marlyonna, and Arlahn stood on began spinning to their left.

"Keep her between us!" Raphael told his brother and they sandwiched his wife-to-be, going back-to-back. The black smoke appeared before Raph this time and he safely parried the deader's attack in time.

Patriclus puffed back and forth between the Princes, making it seem as if there were four soldiers relentlessly attacking them. During their defence, Arlahn recognized the danger surrounding this man's Gift. The fact he'd survived their earlier encounter was next to a miracle. Even with his mountain training, understanding that he now battled for life and death, Arlahn would have been filled with doubt, had it not been for Raph... His brother's presence beside him inspired his confidence, knowing he was alongside someone so proven and accomplished in battle.

Somehow, they managed their way into the room.

The orbital sections of floor had settled when all of the planets aligned before the throne, and the steps before the throne began falling into the ground, creating the first three steps of a descending staircase. As the pedestal of the throne began to raise, Marlyonna dashed below it before it opened any more than she needed.

Seeing Marly slip to safety, Anna turned and hammered her hand on the low end of the organ. The pedestal slab dropped back into place and the stairs lifted up, sealing her away. The floor began shifting back.

Through all of the smoke, Raphael's *mniman* detected a pattern to his attacker's movements. One time, he anticipated where the deader would appear and stabbed his sword low into the air. A thigh appeared at the end of his blade and the deader grunted.

Punching Raph in the face, Patriclus vanished immediately.

He materialized before the queen, snatching her throat and forcing her backward. She fell onto the organ bench, her elbows crashing into keys.

"NO!" her sons shouted across the room as they started rushing to her.

As Annabella's face turned red, she looked at her sons. "I love you."

Patriclus pushed his knife between her breasts and the pain squeezed her face.

The deader vanished away before the Princes could reach them. He fell into the door on the other side of the room and touched his hand to his leg. Seeing his palm painted red, Patriclus looked back at the Princes and stumbled out of the door.

Arlahn dashed to the bench and took his mother in his arms, hugging her. He cleaned the hair around her face and cried that her graceful features remained still. She was gone.

"Arlahn," Raph's voice sounded from behind him, muffled as if on the other side of thick glass.

"Arlahn!" he repeated, this time his voice breaking through.

The young prince looked up with tear-filled eyes. "What do we do now?"

"The Wardens are still out there," Raphael reminded his brother. "We have to stop this."

Coming back into the foyer, the Princes found that another fresh batch of skirmishes had broken out.

Some of the guards stationed outside had heard the queen's scream from Raphael's room. They'd gathered a small troop and stormed into the palace. Seeing guards fighting with the Kalendare and their visitors gave them a moment's pause before they joined the fray and the confusion grew. Guards fought guards, guards fought Kalendare.

From what the Princes could tell, it looked as if the Pellencian forces were prevailing. But Raphael spotted a dark-skinned archer, somehow perched in the chandelier, picking off targets with deadly precision. Yanking a spear from a decorative coat-of-arms off the wall, he crow-hopped and hurled his spear across the room.

The archer noticed Raphael and fell clear of the spear, jerking the chandelier forcefully on one side and snapping the support taut. The spear's tip clanged off the chain holding the framework and the whole thing came crashing down. Losing most of the black arrows out of his quiver, the archer landed on a guard and rolled to his feet. He kicked open the door to the War Room and staggered inside.

Arlahn and his brother were already racing down the stairs after him. They heard their uncle goading him from inside, while Rodrik Rond and Caldin Baile's men finished off the surviving intruders with the Pellencian backup.

Entering the room, the dark-skinned archer stood at one end of the pentagonal table. Their uncle and four of his remaining men protected a score of innocents tucked into the corner at the other end.

The youngest Baile followed the Princes and tossed the quivering old physician, Sol, on the ground. "I found this one writing a message about what had happened."

The grey-haired physician dropped his charade of helplessness and looked at the archer. "For the Damonai, Ensavan!"

"For the Damonai, Sollin," the archer replied.

Before those around him could close in, the dark-skinned archer grabbed a pile of blueprints off the table before him and stuffed them into his breast pocket. His black doublet clinked with the knives in its lining as Ensavan turned and jumped at the window along the wall, crashing through the painted glass.

Raphael ran to the window and watched him run off.

Arlahn grabbed the wrinkled physician by the collar, pulling him up. "It was you that poisoned the guards!"

"You're lucky the cooks must have changed pots for *your* meal," Sollin told him.

"When my father gets back—" Arlahn started.

"Your father's already dead," the physician cut him off. His weathered features crinkling, he whispered, "I poisoned the herbs he smokes."

Arlahn heard the delight in his voice and something snapped inside Arlahn. Letting out a great cry, he raised his fist and buried his dagger into the fragile physician's chest. Thinking of his father, he yanked his blade clear and planted it back into chest bone. "Wait!" The physician cried out between stabs. Rushing the man backward, Arlahn pounded his blade into Sollin's chest once more before he let go and the body slid down the wall.

In the moment, fuelled by rage, Arlahn had thought only of the people the physician had killed. After he replaced his dagger and turned away from the first person he'd intentionally murdered, Raphael voiced a thought, "He had an apprentice. Christianne was her name."

Arlahn hadn't met her since his return. With his thoughts momentarily clear, he had a realization. Rali wasn't poisoned. The look on the serving girl's face when she smiled at him wasn't coyness, or shyness, or even flirtatious. It was accomplished.

"The server..." Arlahn said emptily, looking up at the innocent faces behind Benson. Even from across the room, the blue of her eyes called out to him. "Uncle, behind you!"

*****

The red-haired server swooped in faster than he could register. Booting the back of Benson's knee, she dropped him down and pulled a pin out of her hair, stabbing it into his side as she rolled over his back.

One of Benson's entourage reached out and caught her by her red hair. A wig peeled off her head, revealing hidden black hair that shone like onyx.

Just then, Patriclus appeared before the man holding the wig and stabbed him. "Wraith get out of here!" he shouted, before vanishing one last time.

The black-haired assassin rolled underneath a cut and sprung up next to the wall. With inhuman balance, she somehow ran *along* the wall three steps, catapulting off before the broken window toward one of Rond's burly men. She tucked her legs in and when she collided into the large man, she pushed off, simultaneously drop-kicking the man backward and propelling herself out where Ensavan escaped.

Without a moment's hesitation, Arlahn gave chase, running and leaping sideways through the rest of the glass, crashing into a roll, and popping back onto his feet.

Spotting her white blouse in the darkness, he followed her toward the ramparts. She ran like a gazelle through the open field, hardly ever breaking stride, even to leap and boot a guard in the back before dashing up the rampart stairs three at a time. The Prince didn't stop to check the man, chasing her up the stairs instead. He saw her change direction and leap over the wall.

Arlahn reached the top, bolting for the same crenellation, and leapt blindly over the wall at full-speed.

Swinging his arms as if trying to run through the air, he realized he was going to miss the landing. The Prince tucked in his knees but his shin cracked into the eaves of the roof and broken red clay fell to the ground three stories below him. Propelling himself forward, Arlahn rolled over his shoulder and began sliding down the roof until his feet dug in. His knees buckled and his left leg felt like shattering, but somehow he gained traction, propping himself up. She was already on the next roof. Glancing back and seeing his tenacity, she shook her head and doubled her efforts.

Pushing through the pulsating pain, Arlahn pursued her atop the city. Hopping over the houses of people who slept, their feet pattered along the clay tile. As they passed their second wall, after their initial burst of adrenaline fuelled energy, the Prince began to catch up to her. His lungs were deep, his muscles numbed into automation. Fighting every day through the pain he had endured in the mountain made a throbbing leg feel minor.

Closing the gap, he landed right behind the dark-haired woman on the same roof. They raced toward the apex. Just reaching the summit, Arlahn reached and grabbed the back of her shirt.

Feeling him tug, Christianne threw herself down and the pair began sliding down the two-story roof, her feet first, him headfirst.

Arlahn let go of her and tried to catch something to spin himself around or stop him altogether. As the edge of the roof appeared, he watched her crouch and launch herself off at the last second. Meanwhile, there was nothing to stop him, and he slipped headfirst over the edge.

Crashing into a merchant's awning, the cloth gave way beneath Arlahn and saved him from a broken neck. His whole body bounced on the striped fabric. Seams pulled from the sun-beaten canopy and he fell through onto an empty display table.

Swallowing a heavy lump in his throat, the Prince groaned as he rolled off the stand. But, thinking of what his father would do, he staggered on. Escape wasn't an option, he was catching her tonight. Keeping his eyes up, Arlahn limped as quickly as he could through the city. As he made his way to the tavern's outdoor stables, he caught a glimpse of her, walking calmly across the street toward the same tavern as him. He almost discredited the woman due to her lack of haste until he caught a view of her face and saw her eyes.

Tired now, they had both been thinking the same thing, horses are faster. When Christianne saw him, she sprinted toward the first horse stabled outside the building.

Hobbling his way to another horse, Arlahn climbed on and kicked his mount around and into a gallop. The sound of horse hooves clopping through the streets filled the night air, echoing into an endless chorus. Arlahn could hardly believe how naturally the girl rode a horse. Commanding her steed as well as he, she maintained a safe distance through the narrow city streets. They raced through the apartment district and past the bridge over the river before the gate of the city's second wall. Breaking through, the cluster of the city disappeared, and they flew past torches in open fields. With their horses in full gallop, Arlahn began inching closer to her with every stride. The sound of pounding dirt filled his ears, his vision tunnelling until she was all he saw.

"CLOSE THE GATE!" he hollered.

Tucking her head low, Christianne urged her horse forward in a sudden burst of speed. The heavy city gates were slowly being closed but the mount pushed on in full force straight for the middle of them with reckless abandon. Racing forward, Arlahn pushed to cover the twenty-foot gap between them.

Christianne gathered a sense of rhythm to the horse's pounding gait and let go of the reins, placing her hands by her crotch. She quickly pushed herself up to crouch in the saddle, hanging on to the pummel for balance, and rode atop the horse as they neared the gate.

Eight men pulled either door with all their might, thick, reinforced doors creeping together with groans of exertion.

Christianne slapped her horse's rear and aimed right for the middle. The horse thundered on until it realized the gate had closed too much for the beast to fit through, bracing out its front legs into a fearful stop. She used the momentum of the horse's rump to propel herself forward toward the doors. Launching through the air, she cartwheeled between the gate that was barely a foot open.

"OPEN THE GATE!" Arlahn shouted, ordering the men, who stood amazed, back into action.

Arriving before he could ride through, the Prince eagerly stamped his horse while the men began pushing the doors back open.

When there was enough room for him to squeeze through, Arlahn kicked his horse into an explosive gallop. Passing under the wall, he felt something tear into his shoulder but ignored it, pushing through to chase the girl who was sprinting toward the wooded hills. Snapping his reins once more, Arlahn's shoulder seared with fire. Finally looking back, he saw a thick black arrow with white feather fletchings sticking out of him.

Turning back, the Prince saw that his horse had begun to close on the girl quickly. His vision blurred and he tried to blink it clear. Seeing her figure coming up beside him, Arlahn reached for her and the world turned black.

The horse raced passed Christianne with the Prince hanging over its neck, riding unconsciously.

Arlahn came to with a startle, as if waking from a horrible nightmare. His horse, which had slowed to a canter now, grew scared at the sudden movement and reared. It took the Prince unexpectedly, and he was bucked off and thrown back. Coming down on his shoulder, his head slammed into a smooth boulder on the ground. He saw the horse taking off into the forest and made a feeble attempt to call it back before his arm fell and his eyes slowly closed again.

*****

Raphael watched his brother leap through the window. The sheer determination in Arlahn was different. Clearly, he was not the same man as he had been before his time on the mountain. Raphael was about to follow him when a flash of black smoke appeared. Patriclus emerged and took a swing at him.

Bregan and a Freefolk jumped in to save the prince, and Patriclus began popping up around the room sporadically, wounding or killing almost everyone he appeared near. Alone, he caused pandemonium.

Raphael watched as six of his men died unexpected deaths. He ordered the rest of them against the wall, and they obeyed, rushing to the closest walls and pressing their backs against them.

The Prince refused to move, poised near the table in the centre of the room, he waited for the inevitable attack. Like Arlahn, his training in the mountain had refined his reaction to a point of near madness. Having been Gifted himself, he knew the assassin wouldn't be able to sustain his power much more; his *mniman* had charted the algorithm of Patriclus' movements. Soon, the assassin chose only to disappear when Raphael launched attacks of his own.

During their next exchange, the Prince deflected a high cut then feigned a thrust forward. Anticipating the assassin evaporating, he flipped the blade in his hand and drove it backward toward empty air until the newest batch of black smoke appeared.

Patriclus emerged right before the tip of the blade passed into his belly. His eyes grew, and he looked down at the sword sticking his gut.

"You killed my mother," the Prince reminded him.

Taking up the sword in his left hand, Raphael grabbed Patriclus by the shoulder and drove the hilt into his belly until his feet lifted from the ground. Remembering the look on his mother's face after she had been stabbed, he wanted to remove the killer's head and spike it on the town's walls. But his father had taught him these actions served no purpose except to display cruelty. Raphael didn't want to care about what others thought. But he did.

The palace was in complete disarray. In the library, books littered the grounds, their pages ripped and scattered all over the floor. The chapel's tall candle holders had been knocked over, the red glass broken into bits, and benches were rolled over. The kitchen was an utter disaster, cookware and ingredients had been thrown and cutlery was strewn about the floor. In every room, furniture was upended and damaged, but all signs of the enemy had been vanquished.

Leaving all the survivor's behind, Raphael raced over to the Great Hall where he opened the secret door behind the plaque. Grabbing a torch, he walked the passage calling out for his fiancé and found Marlyonna in a damp corner, one hand clutching his bow, the other on her belly. She squinted and raised her hand against his torchlight. "Stay away!"

"It's alright love, I'm here now." He announced, coming to kneel at her side.

He picked her up and left to rejoin the others in the War Room. Uncle Benson was trying to get up off a chair but a serving boy insisted he stayed down.

"Get out of my way, lad. My nephews need me."

"So you best keep your strength."

Raphael showed up at his side then and helped his uncle back down. "It's over now, Uncle. Rest."

Easing back onto the table, holding his wound, Benson turned to the serving boy attending to him. "Damn Rais, they'll get ya to do anything."

"Where's Arlahn?" Raphael asked the group.

When no one mentioned the Prince's return, he grabbed his bow from Marly's hand and ran up into his bedchambers. Rushing out to his balcony, he listened intensely until he heard the faint clapping of horses racing.

He looked out and spotted a dull glimmer shining atop a roof in the distance. Remembering that the black archer wore a doublet lined with throwing knives, he realized it was Ensavan, the deader who had stolen his blueprints then retreated. The assassin was looking at the horses in the far distance then turned and saw Raph on the terrace. Raphael returned to his room and recovered Marly's last arrow.

Coming back out onto the balcony, he could just barely make out the archer aiming a shot toward the outskirts of the city. Raphael raised his own bow at a forty-five-degree angle and let loose.

His shaft flew through the air and lost itself in the blackness of the sky overhead. Ensavan was hundreds of yards away and Raphael hoped the wind didn't change.

Just then, the archer released his arrow, turned, and fired his last shot toward Raphael.

The Prince watched a second, knowing his arrow would arrive first. A spark shone in mid-air somewhere between them, and Raph realized their shots collided. Ensavan had shot Raphael's arrow out of the air, in the dark.

He saw the man face him, imagined that he smiled, then the archer climbed out of sight.

Chapter 31

The king broke off from his men and comforted himself among the enemy. Pressing forward his attack, each exchange tuned him further to the rhythm of his *sciong*. Hectore surrendered his physical actions to his mental power until they were forged into one. Once he conceded this, the world around him began to drown out until he became a single flame in the darkness. A beacon of indomitability. Efficiency was a deep-rooted quality in the king, and it transformed his battle into a graceful fluidity. Through his eyes, it was the army from thirty years ago against him now. For all this time, he had quietly relived moments like this in his mind, and because they were memories, he never lost.

Blocking and attacking in perfect synchronization, he killed Damonai warriors like they were insects, without remorse. And when two or three came at him together, they fell just as quickly.

Hectore came at three enemies, who hastily gathered their arms for the fight. When he was three steps away, he kicked up a cloud of dust. Soaring forward on an incline angle, he stabbed the first warrior so forcefully that he followed him to the ground. Coming up to see the expected halberd thrusting toward him, the King ducked underneath, let go of his katana, and took up the haft in both hands as it sailed over top of him. He redirected the blade of the halberd, pushing it forward into the third Damonai warrior. The man was coming in for his attack but ceased his advance as the blade bit through his belly like an axe eating into wood. Hectore snatched the third man's sword by the man's wrist and stabbed it into the second man's chest.

He recovered his original katana in time for two more Damonai to come at him. One had found a buckler for his sword; the other just carried a blade. They descended on Hectore in synchrony. He blocked an overhand cut from his left and a stab from his right, instantly recovering to parry another stab from his left and cut from his right. The king held fast as his attackers pushed forward, luring them into prime position. Through his *sciong*, two invisible boundaries were depicted in his mind when he fought: an orbit of safety for his foes, and the sphere in which he orchestrated all movement.

In their next exchange, the *sciong* saw the required movements that afforded Hectore his opportunity. He pushed away back-to-back overhand cuts from his left and right, booted the right man's shield, pushing him further out, and brought his blade over to the left man's shoulder. Spinning, he dragged it down across the man's jugular with a spray of blood. Hectore took up the hilt of his katana with both fists, dropped the blade's tip just low enough to sneak under the right man's buckler, and forced it up underneath his jaw, until it exploded out of the top of his head and the man's expression went terribly blank. Pivoting on his foot, the King yanked his sword free, spinning two hundred and seventy degrees, to tear his blade through another Damonai's chest.

That was when Hectore was bulled over unexpectedly from behind. He lost his weapon and began stumbling off balance. Anyone else would have been pitched to the ground, but the *sciong* was too powerful. It adjusted his body weight for him and carried him through the motions required to regain equilibrium. The result of such power took him through a sort of one-handed spinning cartwheel, and he almost stumbled into the back of another Damonai warrior when again his *sciong* took over. In his mind's eye, Hectore saw his attacker pursuing him from behind and knew a thrust was following before any evidence was shown. He grabbed the unaware Damonai before him by the shoulders and spun him around as the man behind came forward with a vicious stab. His blade punched through the belly of his Damonai comrade and kept coming toward the king in search for his guts, Hectore arced his body to avoid the sharp end just in time. Grabbing hold of the blade in his right hand for better leverage, he spun the man in his arms as viciously as he could. His goal accomplished when the hilt finally pried from the attacker's grip and the man lurched forward half a step. As the dead Damonai in Hectore's arms came half-circle, the King dropped the blade in his right hand and took up the hilt in his left. He lunged forward and grabbed the surviving Damonai by his shoulder. Together, he pushed the blade further through the one enemy and pulled the other enemy into him, punching the sharpened tip into an exposed chest.

The king dropped both bodies impaled on the sword and moved toward his katana lying next to a corpse. But another live Damonai appeared in his path. One of his Sainti brethren fell back into him then and Hectore caught him. The soldier had lost his weapon in the fray and had an arrow punched through his cheek. He saw that the man was dead already, so he ripped out the arrow before he let the corpse down.

Anything can be a weapon, Hectore reminded himself.

He reversed his grip on the arrow as the new Damonai adversary goaded him forward. Racing his hand up the nock end, Hectore stole the fletchings from the arrow. The Damonai readied himself for the king's approach and when he neared the *sciong* saw the twitch that was the precursor to a horizontal cut. The king tossed the three feathers into the man's face. It blinded him momentarily and dislodged his foreseen slice enough for Hectore to roll safely underneath it. Coming up out of the roll, he drove the arrow deep into the back of the man's knee. Hectore snatched up his katana quickly and returned to the Damonai, who was now on all fours in pain, clutching at the arrow sticking out beside his patella. The king tore him up ruthlessly then reversed the blade in his hand, and in one quick motion, brought it down above the man's clavicle, slicing down through arteries and veins, a lung, and his kidney.

A friend of this Damonai warrior saw Hectore brutally kill him and screamed his charge toward the king, as if the man's cries would frighten a prophesied hero into submission. If anything, Hectore was glad this one was announcing his attempt. In an extraordinarily calm fashion, the King waited with his left hand still on his sword hilt as he dragged a spear on the ground closer with his right foot. When the charging Damonai entered the boundary where the king authored all movement, Hectore hawked a snot-filled ball into his face, causing him to reflexively raise his free hand in defence. He didn't see Hectore flip the spear with his toe, sending it between the man's legs and stumbling him forward. When he began falling, the king directed the Damonai toward the blade in his left hand, and Hectore perfectly timed pulling out his katana so that his stroke would open the screamer's esophagus and begin his eternal silence.

Seeing two more come at him, the King booted away an incoming slash, grabbed the attacker, and spun him into the second Damonai who was coming down with a hack of his axe. Stabbing the axeman behind, he pitched both bodies to the earth.

As he moved back into the thick of battle he saw a dark-haired man slit open a Sainti throat from behind. The Damonai looked up at Hectore with malice and vehemence in his eyes. He was dressed all in black and clutched a scimitar in his hand. No introduction was required, Hectore simply knew this was the one they called DeathShadow...

*****

Mordo stood with a stare of sadistic, over-joyous pride. When he'd received the message from Wraith, he had thought the King was hosting a meeting back in Pellence. But as if he'd been rewarded by Death himself for all of his toil, Mordo was delivered this. The HighKing. Demonblades.

Hectore stepped passed the two Damonai he'd thrown to the ground, switched sword hands, and held them out at his side. As if at once both accepting an old friend and goading the Shadow forward, his katana clutched firmly in his right hand.

Mordo stepped over the body before him. "How I've wished for this day."

He stepped in and feigned an overhand, coming forward with a thrust. Hectore rolled his wrist, blocked it, and booted the deader backward. Mordo rolled through the grey sand, settling as if he'd just landed from a fall.

"Suicidal thoughts aren't healthy," Hectore told him.

Mordo's deep-rooted sense of pride kept him from vanishing yet. Like he was back with the Essellian general, Mordo needed to test himself against one of the greatest. No. *The* greatest.

Rushing back at Hectore, he thrust again, this time anticipating the block and spinning around with an elbow. The king bobbed his head out of the way and smashed the butt of his hilt into Mordo's face. His jaw snapped back but he recovered quickly, stepping into another exchange. The deader screamed and launched a terrifying series of attacks, but each blow was parried or avoided with a minimum of movement on the part of the king. At the end of the last exchange, Hectore booted the side of Mordo's knee, buckling him backward. He came back with a thrust. Hectore blocked it, grabbed Mordo by the nape of his neck and threw him away.

"I THOUGHT YOU WANTED TO BE LEGEND!" he scolded, goading the deader forward once more. "COME ON!"

Mordo began to doubt his abilities, perhaps Hennah had been right. Perhaps a Demon could kill a Shadow, who wrote such rules?

Unknowingly, he kept entering Hectore's dictatorship of movement. Each time he did so, he either ended up frantically retreating to safety or wounded, with the king goading him further, berating him about Mirianne's abduction or demanding her return. Realizing that the King was humiliating him rather than just defeating him, Mordo grew enraged.

"That's it," he told himself after being backhanded across the face. It was time.

Coming back at the king, Mordo stepped toward him and vanished behind his *nsuli*. With a thrust, the king sprang to his left and rolled his wrist before him. Somehow Mordo's invisible sword clanged away from the king. Locking blades near the hilt, Hectore stepped in and delivered an uppercut elbow into the deader's chin. His teeth snapped together, and he was instantly dizzy.

It was too late.

Even invisible, he had already become a puppet to Hectore's *sciong*.

"That's more like it!" Hectore said, taking up his katana with his right hand for the first time in the fight. He darted forward, thrusting where Mordo stood.

The deader needed both his hands to deflect the strength of the king. Rolling his wrist upward, he dragged his scimitar down the katana toward the king's shoulder. But Hectore side-stepped, directing the attack to his side, and pushed his blade past Mordo's sword. The deader jumped and together, their weapons perpetually kissing, they went back and forth attempting to exchange blows. Hectore orchestrated Mordo by the length of his katana, never allowing it to leave the deader's scimitar.

To the outside world, it looked as if Hectore was practising alone in the middle of a battle. Carefully stepping in and out of attacks, deliberately controlling his weapon with focused precision.

Lunging into a thrust that pushed both their blades into the air, Hectore and Mordo stood locked for a split second. Then the King stomped on Mordo's invisible foot and snapped an elbow into his face. The deader's clutch on his *nsuli* broke. Reappearing to the world, his head jerked as he fell back a step.

Hectore expertly rolled his wrist down and around to dislodge the scimitar, flicking the blade in the air between them. He spun, caught the scimitar at the blade's end, and swung it around, hilt first.

Mordo fell onto his back and the weapon carried through into a Damonai who was just about to intervene in their duel.

Distracted for a moment, Hectore looked up to see the Deader get up and scamper away. He disappeared and reappeared like a rainbowfly in the dark, retreating ever further from the HighKing.

The *sciong* revealed a man in his periphery, closing in for an attack. Hectore darted forward and spun, retrieving the scimitar from the dead warrior before him. He deflected the attack with his katana and as he came round, buried the scimitar in his new foe's neck. Reversing his grip, he pulled the blade clear.

More Damonai surrounded him and continued to attack until they became witness. Witness to controlled chaos, devastating destruction, and remorseless retaliation. The Damonai believed they'd find sanctuary in numbers, but they also believed Hectore was a Demon. And whenever these beliefs collided, only one proved true. Holding the swords one forward, one reversed, he both defended and attacked without being touched by his opposition. Soon, there was a causeway of dead Damonai littering the ground.

During a fight with two more enemies, the *sciong* tingled again, urging him to duck an attack rather than side-step it. An arrow whizzed right over his chest, finishing off the man before him. He turned to his right and spotted Kael.

The Prince was fighting ferociously toward his father, hacking into two men and propelling them well over their comrades behind. He too had broken from his formation. Subconsciously, Hectore counted fifteen men forming a circle around his son before he found the archer that had shot at him, slinking behind a few of his comrades in the middle of the field.

Rushing toward the man, Hectore barely stopped to drop those unlucky few who got between them.

The first warrior that came at him fell to the earth with wounds on his side and back. The second stumbled to the ground trying to stuff his entrails back into his belly, while the third caught the king's stolen scimitar with the base of his neck.

Hectore saw that the archer had another arrow nocked now. Stabbing the fourth man with both blades, he spun his body round in time to catch it.

He continued closing the gap between him and the archer. With five steps left, he sensed another Damonai coming in from his right. He hopped and heaved steep, angled blade in his left hand with all his strength. The sword hadn't even had the chance to rotate before it almost immediately lodged itself into the warrior's forehead, knocking him back to the ground. Hectore saw the archer fumbling with another arrow and lunged toward him, making up the distance in three great strides.

The man had just nocked the arrow and was ready to draw back when Hectore leapt toward him. Plunging his katana soundly into the man's ribs, his left hand gripped the bow and arrow where they met, by the rest. He stepped past the archer, hauling the bow clear and spinning around to stand behind where the man's quiver hung from his back. Pushing the dead archer down on his knees, the King positioned him upright the katana still in his side.

Hectore quickly drew back the bow and fired upon one of the men circling his son, taking him in the back of the head.

Snatching a handful of arrows from the quiver before him, the King started shooting his bow with deadly precision. Dropping body after body, he'd taken out seven of the men around Kael before they really knew who was attacking them.

He was a champion swordsman by necessity. Leading a war was more inspiring when you're right in the thick of it. But it was the bow that he had first grown to admire, and his skill was unmatched. He began nocking two arrows at once and dropping bodies twice as fast.

Shooting until he'd exhausted the quiver, Hectore had dispersed the men around Kael enough for Zeth and the others to make it to him in time. He recovered his katana and rejoined with his son.

The growing number of Damonai had become apparent. With both Sainti forces meeting in the northeastern corner of the camp, more warriors organized themselves. Being led by Drelnum, they closed about their enemy.

"Get everyone to the boats!" the King shouted through the chaos.

"Aideen!" Balanus cried as he spotted her with Kael's force.

"Balanus!" She rushed to his side.

"My brother's got Tamis with him in the rear."

"Where's Besath?" Aideen asked, concerned for her older brother.

Balanus shook his head and hugged her, just as Kael rushed by and bumped into them, claymore in hand. "Come on, to the river."

Less than fifty Brothers and Sainti soldiers combined had fallen during their blitz attack. Kael and Hectore ushered men down the path, and Balanus and Aideen volunteered to lead the party to the riverbank. Carrying Tamis between them, they hurried the group as quickly as they could.

Most of the Brotherhood had made it into the path leading to the boats and the group left in the city had shrunk small enough that the Damonai began to circle about them to close in.

Pientero refused that notion outside the entrance to the river. He'd fought his way to the king but was too stubborn to abandon his home.

The king-in-the-mountain fought on as fatigue slowly set in. He slapped a shield away from its defender and stabbed him quickly in the heart. His sword clashed high with another warrior's and he brought up his knee to catch the man low in the groin. Blind with rage, he threw away the man's sword and hacked down at his neck at a vicious angle. Blood spurted from the wound and the man fell dead.

Drelnum charged Pientero and the mountain master stabbed him in the gut. But the warrior took the impact with a step backward then continued at Pientero.

As Pientero battled through the exchange, he would have cut Drelnum twice on his shoulder and cleaved his skull, but the Powered deader fought with complete disregard to personal well-being. Constantly moving forward, Pientero fought off every attack as best he could, until finally, the bald deader caught Pientero's blade between his ribcage and arm and brought the tomahawk down on his head. The king-in-the-mountain gasped and his body froze before slumping down to his knees.

Blood spat out of his mouth and dripped from his lips. He stabbed Hectore's gladius into the ground and balanced himself on it a second before falling back.

"No!" the king screamed, seeing his friend fall from the treeline as he ushered people down the path.

He ran out toward Pientero, and Kael and Jole followed him back into the compound.

Seeing Pientero Jessonarioko fall, Jole stopped and cried out. A powerful emotion moved through his spirit. His eyes rolled back under fluttering lids and he felt the warmth starting to grow within his palms. Slamming the butt of Omega down, a giant wall of flames leapt up through the Damonai. Drelnum and a handful of others were trapped on the one side, while a dozen men retreated back ablaze into the rest of their number.

Hectore arrived at Pientero but saw there was no life left in him. Taking up the gladius that Pientero had stabbed into the ground, he charged toward Drelnum, while Kael and Jole engaged the remaining warriors.

Drelnum, who was hardly worried at first, immediately went on the offensive. But the king broke into a mad frenzy, slapping away Drelnum's blade. He smacked one of his swords against his temple and booted him in the chest, staggering the bald man back.

He came at Hectore to attack, but the king parried it away, striking his right blade against Drelnum's wrist and then bringing it up across his face, his left blade quick to follow. Drelnum staggered back and squinted his eyes, shaking his head to stop the growing headache.

The king pushed on against the unbreakable deader. As if instructing a class, he pounded repeated blow after blow into Drelnum's head, at all kinds of angles as he worked his way around him. One of the Damonai came to Drelnum's aid, and Hectore didn't even seem to slow his barrage as he felled the warrior beside them. Eventually, after being constantly batted in his head, Drelnum dropped his hatchet to raise his hands in protection.

Hectore kept hammering blade after blade into the man. Never cutting his flesh – rattling the brain in his skull was the king's intention. He kicked his heel into the side of the man's knee, and Drelnum buckled down to the ground. Hectore began one final onslaught, finishing with a vicious beat down with both swords and all his strength.

Drelnum's eyes rolled back and he fell, face first.

Too much sand moved... his *sciong* tingled. Then he felt it. Normally, the King would have been able to react in time, to avoid or deflect the blade-tip against his side. But this time, his *sciong* was exhausted. As if it had been the only thing sustaining his body during the battle, Hectore finally succumbed to something that had been killing him from within. He felt the dagger bite into him.

Before Hectore, the face of Mordo Lobo materialized. He stood there with a dagger plunged into the king's side, the blade piercing his lung.

Hectore dropped his swords and fell against Mordo. Catching his shoulders, he stared DeathShadow in the eye and promised him. "My son's gonna leave you face down in the dirt."

Kael, who saw the whole thing from a short distance away, screamed out and raced to his father as Mordo disappeared, letting the HighKing fall free to the ground with the dagger still in his ribs. The Damonai watching through the heat of the flames cheered ferociously when they saw Demonblades fall. No one noticed Kael dashing in.

Taking up his claymore in both hands, the Prince saw Drelnum beginning to rise, and he lashed out with a ferocious cleave, batting the deader with all of his strength. Drelnum took the claymore high in the chest; as if shot from Raphael's exploder, he was thrown into the air over the crowd and crashed into one of the mountain homes, which collapsed on top of him.

"SHADOW!" Kael screamed out, spinning in a circle, blade outstretched.

"Time to go," Jole said, appearing beside the Prince. "Grab the king." He went to offer help, but Kael pushed his arm away.

"I'll carry him myself," the Prince insisted. Heaving his father up into his arms, he looked around and saw the fire wall fading, the Damonai were moving in.

"We have to go," Balanor said, calling the last two from the edge of the path. "Hurry up!"

Balanor held back and killed the first warrior that had gotten too close. "Keep going," he told Kael, who looked behind.

The Prince ran with his father in his arms and Jole beside him, lumbering as quickly as he could. Arriving at the riverbank, he saw that the other survivors had already begun setting off in the white canoes. They had drifted any that were left out to the current but one remained behind for them.

Kneeling at the canoe, Kael laid his father inside and looked back for Balanor. Jole pushed the boat to the waterline and then returned to the Prince.

"Go! Go!" they heard from the darkness of the path.

Balanor appeared, bolting toward them. A pack of Damonai were close behind him.

"I'll get him," Jole announced, stepping forward.

Again, his eyes fluttered and this time he stabbed Omega into the air.

Just as Balanor broke onto the pebbled beach, a giant shockwave rippled behind him, sending the chasing men sprawling as if caught in a tornado.

Jole fell back and Kael caught him. He groaned and touched a palm to his forehead.

Racing to the canoe, Kael dragged the giant magicker inside and shoved it into the water before Balanor jumped in at the stern. They began paddling and saw arrows flying blindly overhead. Archers were firing randomly in their direction from the trees. By the time Jole's magical shockwave had waned and the pursuing force gained the beach, they had escaped.

Once they were clear, Kael turned back to Jole. "You somehow healed him once before, can you do it again?"

The magicker touched his palm to his forehead, drew a deep breath and nodded. "I'll give it a go."

Jole touched the king and instantly his head began shaking in a seizure. Cheeks flapping, eyes rolling back, teeth clattering against each other. He fell back motionless in the canoe, and Balanor expertly balanced against the movement.

Kael cursed.

They continued paddling down the river for a minute when Hectore woke in a stir. Disoriented, he leapt up and nearly flipped the canoe.

Kael brought in his oar and calmed his father. "Why don't you just lay back?"

"No!" The HighKing insisted on sitting up at first. When Jole had transferred his magic into the king, Hectore's Gift drew one last ounce of strength from it. He no longer felt the agony of pain but soothing warmth replaced it, yet he was still inexplicably weary. The king looked around and his vision began to blur, but he still recognized the sounds of the river and the smell of the fresh mountain air. "On second thought," Hectore said, leaning back and laying his head on his son's lap. "There doesn't seem to be any problem with it."

"Of course not, Father," Kael told him. Then he saw Hectore's eyes close once more.

"Hey!" He took up his father's head. "Stay with me!"

Hectore's eyes opened again and he looked up at his son, smiling a beatific grin. "You know, when you were first born, I was absolutely terrified. I barely had a childhood, let alone a father. I'm so proud of you, son."

"We'll be back home before you know it. Just hang on, okay."

Hectore raised his arm and cupped his son's face in his hand. Kael felt a tear roll down his cheek and he nuzzled further into his father's touch, holding the hand there with his own.

"Tell your mother..." He smacked his lips together, trying to wet them. "... I'll be waiting for her..."

Kael was at a complete loss for words. He still didn't truly believe what was happening. His father couldn't die. He was the thing of Legend. The man who knew everything, could *do* everything.

"You can't die dad," he argued feebly, crying into the hand he squeezed.

But Hectore never responded, never woke from his rest.

"I love you, dad."

Chapter 32

Christianne sat down on a large boulder that was jutting from the ground, gasping for air. Wiping the hair from her face, she checked behind her, and after a moment she was confident that she had shaken anyone that might have pursued her.

Reflecting on the night, she contemplated what to do next. Gaining entry into the city had been both a blessing and a curse. Sollin's theatrical rescue of the queen had granted them access directly into the palace, but the guards were ever watchful, forcing them to move forward more cautiously with their plan. She had carefully worked the servant Tod over the course of their stay, exploiting his affection for the departed prince.

Once they'd heard about the meeting of Wardens, Sollin changed their tactic and advanced their schedule. Having seen the Essellian Warden arrive earlier in the week, he refused to shut up about the old turncloak.

Sollin gave her the black knife and instructed her to kill him first. Christianne tried to tell him how she had caught the attention of the Prince, but he was blinded by his revenge and wanted to hear nothing of it. They had been ordered to assassinate the royal family and he wanted the Wardens as well.

She had been posing as a blonde while she acted as the physician's apprentice. But after they had let in Patriclus and Ensavan with their men, she'd switched to a red-haired wig and put on serving girl's clothing. Regardless of her orders, she would follow them. Putting the knife under the plate in her hand, she had walked back into the room, hoping the Prince wouldn't be watching. He was. She distracted him by leaning extra-low, watching his eyes shift from the warden to her exposed breasts. Christianne had barely been able to help herself from smiling at her success.

She had been trained under the greatest deader of them all. DeathShadow. To him, there was no such thing as failure. At best, he tolerated her leaving things unfinished for the time being. Twelve years, she had been his apprentice, mastering the lethal art of deception. He'd found her the night she escaped Master Grent's house with his rebellious daughter Jassyka. In their escape, they came across a trio of dangerous men. She had thrown herself at them and began fighting out her anger, but being so young, it wasn't long before she was subdued. DeathShadow appeared from nowhere and slew the men before they saw him. Kneeling down by her afterwards, he sensed she was like him in a way. Broken. He'd taught her to use those jagged pieces as sharp weapons. He'd also taught her to always have a sharp weapon with her. Taking off her belt, Christianne slipped a knife out of a cut in the leather and gripped it tightly in her fist.

If the Prince hadn't noticed her in the group and put it together that she killed Rali, she could still be in position to carry out her mission.

Remembering that the Prince had one of Ensavan's arrows sticking out of his shoulder as he rode by her, Christianne suddenly wondered if him slumping into the beast's neck was due to loss of consciousness.

"I have to find him," she told herself aloud. She couldn't return to the palace, but she could hunt him outside its walls.

Standing up, Christianne took off in the direction of the horse. Looking through the forest for the better part of an hour, she finally spotted the figure of a man lying on the ground. As she approached, she saw the arrow still poking out of his shoulder.

She wondered if he was dead already, but her training forced her to ensure that death was final.

The moment was tense. The air actually seemed to grow thicker around her, as if trying to suffocate her actions.

Slowly, Christianne moved over the Prince on the ground. Kneeling down beside him, she examined the arrow in his shoulder. It cut through the muscle and was lodged in his shoulder. She remembered his shin cracking on the roof as well. But when she rolled him over, she saw he was still alive. Admiring his resilience and determination, Christianne smiled at him and patted the wavy hair on his head.

With the dagger firmly in her fist, she pressed it up to his skin. The Prince had a serene look of peace about him, the softness in his features telling her that he would rescue an insect from harm or forgive her actions.

For the first time in her career, Christianne paused. Regret already ate away at her stomach and she questioned what it was that hesitated her action. Usually, she could almost see the judgment and contempt people held for others by the depth of certain wrinkles in their faces. But this face was different.

Suddenly, she remembered him.

From the market, all those years ago. Before her apprenticeship, before her innocence was stolen, before she was enslaved, before everything. She remembered looking into his eyes that day and something deep resonated within her, the same way it did now as she stared into his face.

That life was gone though, she couldn't fail Mordo.

A tear swelled in Christianne's eye and her words involuntarily slipped out, "I'm sorry."

The tear rolled down her cheek and she took a deep breath to steady her hand. She looked up to the sky, prayed to Death to give her the strength. "Please... Help me!"

"HO!" came a voice down the path.

Christianne froze, quickly placing the dagger in her boot.

"What's going on here?" the voice said again.

A floodgate of suppressed tears opened and began flowing over her face, but she couldn't place whether they were born of joy, frustration, or relief?

Up ahead, a middle-aged man sitting on a carriage came into view and mushed his horses to the side of the ditch where the couple lay.

He climbed down and Christianne began sobbing. "He's been shot! Help! Please!" she cried out deceivingly.

The man lit a lantern and approached. She saw he was stocky with sunburned skin and piercings that covered his face, with two small chains hanging between them.

He saw the arrow in the Prince's back and the man's eyes grew. "Help me get him up," he said quickly.

Clearing out a spot on the back of his carriage, he directed Christianne to carefully lift his legs and carry him over.

After they'd put the Prince down, the newcomer picked up his lantern and inspected the wound. "How did this happen?"

"We were working in the palace," she started. She knew word of the attack was unstoppable and worked that to her advantage. "A fight broke out..." she paused to feign disbelief. "He saved me."

The man held the arrow still in one fist and snapped it shorter.

"Hold him down," he instructed.

Christianne watched him push the arrow through the wound out of the front of the Prince's chest.

"Why didn't you take him to a physician?" he argued, searching through a pack on his seat and removing some sewing thread. "What are you doing out here in the woods?"

"It was the palace's physician that started the fight. I didn't know who to trust," Christianne said. She'd learned that the greatest lies were simply masked truths. The more truths she could incorporate into her story, the more convincing it would sound.

"Is he alive?" she asked the newcomer, playing dumb as she searched for a moment to make a move on him.

"He's lucky the arrow didn't seem to hit anything vital. I think he's going to be alright," he told her as he started sewing the holes closed.

"What's your name, lass?"

She was about to lie when the Prince on the carriage jerked awake. His eyes shot open and he lurched forward to sit up. Staring right at her, he almost shouted her name.

"Christianne!"

She looked into his eyes and swallowed hard. She wanted to make her move, swoop in and kill them both, but she hesitated. Instead, something within her moved.

"Whoa, whoa." The man jumped in to settle him down. "Easy."

The Prince lowered back down and looked around, confused at his surroundings. Christianne tensed, preparing to reach for the dagger in her boot.

"Do you remember what happened to you. Who are you?"

Christianne stepped in to hear the response.

The Prince blinked hard then stared forward in thought, slowly his gaze moved to Christianne. His eyes lingered on her as he racked his brain. She felt uneasy with him staring like this and calculated who she should kill first. Finally, his eyes drifted from her back toward the man.

"I can't remember..."

Come walk another Lonely Path, in *Exodus*

Glossary of Characters

The Royal Family:

Hectore Rai: HighKing of the Realm of Saintos. Father to Kael, Raphael, and Arlahn, husband to Annabella. Black-haired and handsome, he is revered throughout the world as its greatest hero.

Annabella Rai: HighQueen of the Realm of Saintos. Mother to Kael, Raphael, and Arlahn, wife to Hectore. Loving and passionate, generous and warm.

Kael Rai: Older fraternal twin to Raphael. Gifted with giant-like strength. Paramour to Luzy. Motivated and inspired to constantly challenge himself physically.

Raphael Rai: Younger fraternal twin to Kael. Engaged to Marlyonna. A genius tactician and accomplished archer, recently turning his skills toward invention.

Arlahn Rai: The youngest of the Rai children. Innocent and compassionate, dismayed at growing up in his brothers' shadows.

Marlyonna: Engaged to Prince Raphael. Beautiful and blonde-haired. Having suffered in her past, she has lived with the Rai family since the time of their meeting.

Luzy: Kael's paramour, another blonde-haired beauty who is known for her radiant smile and comprehensive knowledge.

Pellence:

Located in the heart of the Sainti realm. Home to the famous Palace where the Royal Family resides.

Halder: Former Knight Commander of Pellence, and one of Hectore's oldest friends. Chose to retire outside of the city.

Jofus Rufus: The Royal Tutor and perhaps the most knowledgeable man in all of Saintos.

Zeth: Master-at-arms and old friend of Hectore's.

Zephoroth: Zeth's son, trained soldier, and friend to the Princes.

Brandigit: Chief-Kalendare, head of the secret service charged to protect the Royal Family.

Bregan: Brandigit's son, Pellencian scout and Kael's friend.

Wender: An old travelling merchant.

Jersay: Shop owner in the upper precincts of Pellence.

Stevano Grent: Mischievous noble, father to Jassyka.

Johnnimack: Blacksmith who is employed by the Princes to smith parts for Raphael's inventions.

Billiem: Johnnimack's apprentice, a young teenager who recently lost his mother.

Sol: Royal physician and extremely talented in his trade.

Christianne: Sol's apprentice, a beautiful young woman.

Esselle:
A scholarly society with deep cultural roots, famed for its vast libraries and great discoveries.

Nakoli Rali: Warden of the West. Former Damonai captain, switched allegiances when Hectore re-captured the city.

Mick Dedic: Youngest justicar in Esselian history. Sent to deliver a message to the HighKing.

Baulim Dedic: Mick's father and Rali's advisor. A hero from Hectore's Rebellion and the HighKing's friend.

Hennah Asa: A very talented magicker who gave birth to Arlahn Rai.

Darius: A Gifted thief. Scoundrel. Rogue. A man who only looks out for himself and his survival.

Pical: A merchant.

Corduran:
A commercial hub, west of Pellence, located between the coast of the Sprit Sea and Tehbirr's Spine.

Benson Wellcant: Handsome younger brother to HighQueen Annabella and Warden of the East.

Melonia:
A vast battle-hardened nation, north of Pellence. Proud people who are fiercely loyal to the Royal Family.

Pietrun Rond: Warden of the North and veteran of Hectore's Rebellion.

Pietrey Rond: Pietrun's son, friend to the young princes, despite being a few years their elder.

Neddihwen Mountains and Cooperith Forests:
A vast wild, home to the ceremonious and spiritual Freefolk of the South.

Caldin Baile: Warden of the South, he and his son both fought alongside Hectore during his rebellion.

The Brotherhood:
Heroic company from Hectore's Rebellion, famed to the point of legend. Residing in a settlement hidden from the world.

Pientero Jessonarioko: The Poet of Battle, Hectore's best friend and leader of the famous company. Now known as the King-in-the-Mountain.

Jassyka Grent: Gifted roommate of Arlahn during his stay with the Brotherhood. She ran away from home and found Pientero when her dreams led her to him.

Anvar: The one-handed tutor for all things in the Brotherhood outside of battle.

Balanor: A well-respected Brother, one of their most prominent members.

Balanus: Balanor's identical twin, much like his brother. Involved romantically with Aideen.

Tamis: A young scout for the Brotherhood who is Arlahn's first friend in the hostile mountain camp.

Aideen: Tamis' older sister and paramour to Balanus. Kind and admired among the Brotherhood.

Besath: Tamis and Aideen's eldest brother, adopted a fatherly role for his younger siblings.

Gringoll: Hostile Brother, who says very little.

Other Notable Characters:

Diyo: A mysterious figure who claims to be the embodiment of Magic itself and have witnessed the birth of Time. Concerned with the monumental actions of the world and believer of a god-like being, the Rahnolean.

Jole: Talented magicker, who had travelled with Hectore for some time in the past. Currently living isolated in Tehbirr's wilderness.

Serah-Jayne: Believes the power of her Gift to be a curse, she helps Diyo with his personal mission out of her love and devotion to him.

The Damonai:
A continent of people who believe that a GodKing will rise from prophecy to lead them into the Graceland.

Mordo Lobo: DeathShadow. The first and most accomplished Deader in Hennah's council. Psychopath who doesn't understand the motives of other humans.

Wraith: Mordo's apprentice, a figure that always conceals their appearance from top to bottom but is highly skilled and capable.

Evris: A veteran from the Damonai's HolyWar when they first conquered Saintos. A powerful general who can replay the histories of objects and people in his mind with a mere touch

Drelnum: Powered with unbreakable skin, he quickly rose to authority within the Council of Deaders, earning him control of his own forces and the respect of DeathShadow himself.

Patriclus: Member of the Council of Deaders, powered with dimensional displacement (teleportation).

Ensavan: Member of the Council of Deaders, powered with perfect accuracy.

Tracker: Reluctant member of the Council, blessed with a mastery of his senses.

Togut: Damonai scout, who becomes the leader of his own party.

Gordun: Togut's best friend and a proficient fighter.

Palor: Member of Togut's scouting party.

438

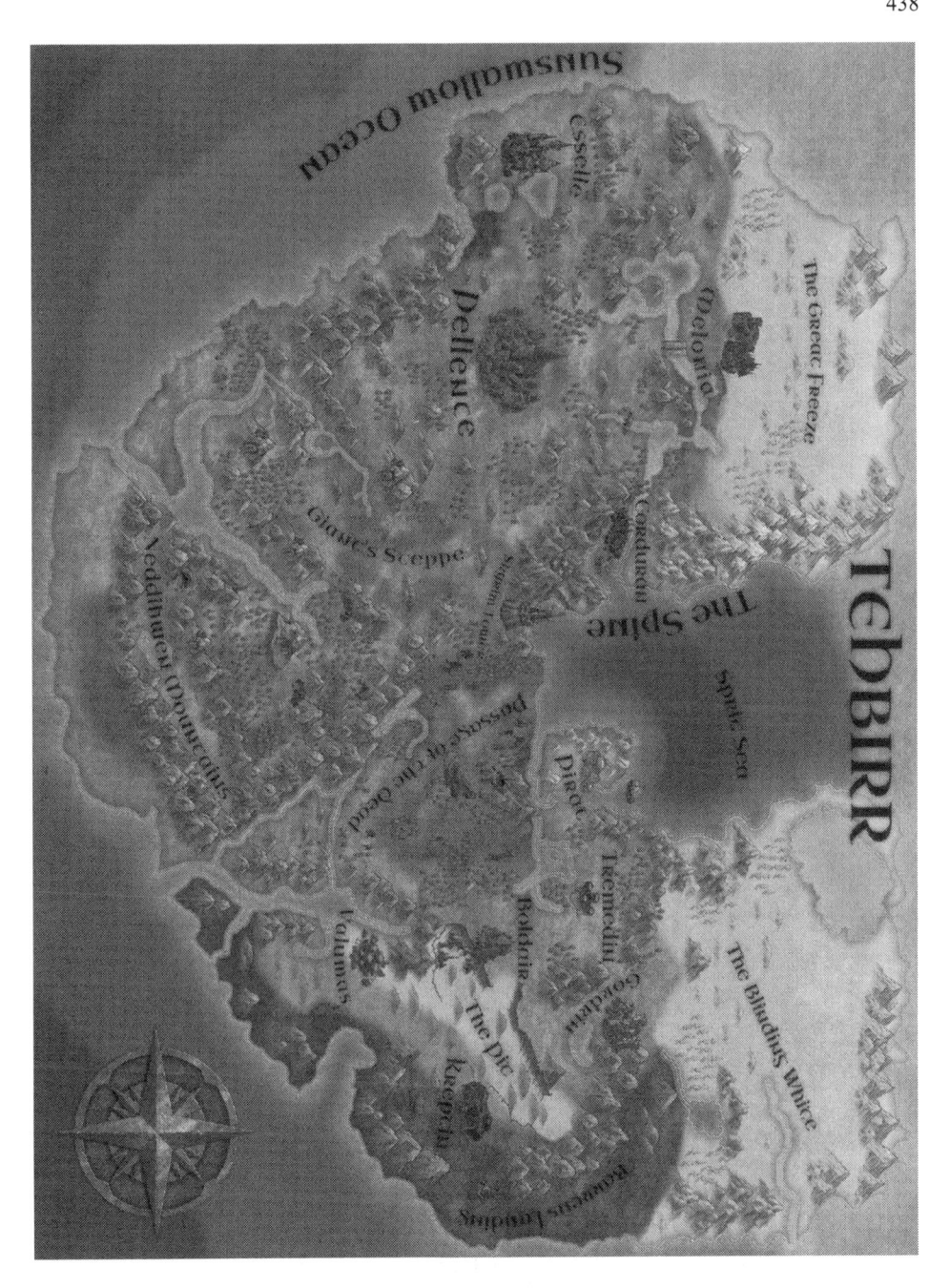

Printed in Great Britain
by Amazon